PUSHKIN PRESS

The Trilogy of Two

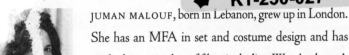

JUMAN MALOUF, born in Lebanon, grew up in London. She has an MFA in set and costume design and has worked on a number of films including Wes Anderson's *Moonrise Kingdom* and *The Grand Budapest Hotel*. *The Trilogy of Two* is her first novel.

"The wo l [Malouf] creates, through her appealing prose and her positively addictiv lustrations, feels weird and true, vivid as a dream but way more entertain g"

Michael Chabon, Pulitzer Prize-winning author of *The Amazing Adventures of Kavalier & Clay*

"Fans of evile's *Un Lun Dun* will enjoy debut author Malouf's intricate worlds, each teen ig with its own customs and creatures, as well as her equally intricate pencil ill rations, which highlight the characters' eccentricities... themes of sisterhoo nd believing in oneself will entrance readers"

Publishers Weekly

"A new Y. iovel that shuffles the teen-dystopia deck with some Narnia-style fantasy... J an Malouf sets quite a few plates spinning in *The Trilogy of Two*, her first nov She keeps it all whirling with aplomb and no broken crockery – a bit of a circus performer herself. Plus, her line drawings are exquisite"

Vanity Fair

"YA fiction's new spellbinder... The book's eccentric characters and the worlds-within-worlds they inhabit are richly illustrated... [Malouf's] prose is lyrical and evo

The Daily Beast

THE TRILOGY OF TWO

Written and illustrated by

JUMAN MALOUF

PUSHKIN PRESS

Pushkin Press
71–75 Shelton Street
London WC2H 9JQ

Published by arrangement with G.P. Putnam's Sons,
an imprint of Penguin Young Readers Group, a Division of Penguin Random House LLC

The Trilogy of Two was first published By G.P. Putnam's Sons in New York, 2015
First published by Pushkin Press in 2018

1 3 5 7 9 8 6 4 2

ISBN 13: 978-1-782692-04-1

Offset by Tetragon, London
Printed in Great Britain by the CPI Group, UK

www.pushkinpress.com

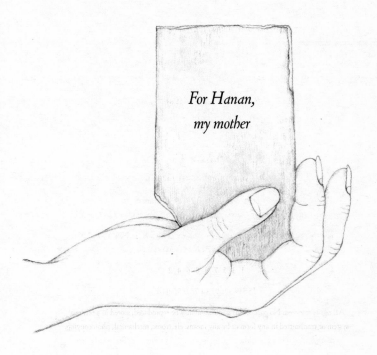

For Hanan,
my mother

Rain City

IT WAS A BLACK NIGHT, AND THUNDER GROWLED OVER the peaks and pillars of Rain City. It had not stopped raining in years. Countless drops scored pits and holes all across the purple brick facades of the Million-Mile-High buildings. Pale-faced people in hooded raincoats pedaled carriages along a network of steel tracks.

Down at the bottom of the city, makeshift houses sat on bricks stacked like stilts above the flooded streets. The sound of shoes clipping against the wet cobblestones woke a beggarman, and he scrambled out of his tent. He crouched, the ends of his tattered jacket dipping into the water, and held out his hand.

"Something for the needy?" he croaked. A pair of perfect black-and-white patent leather pumps came to a stop in front of him.

"Good evening, my humble gentleman," a voice replied. "Would you be so kind as to point us in the direction of the School for the Gifted?"

The beggarman looked up to see a tall figure in a black suit, a coat slung over his shoulders, and a brimmed hat tilted over one eye. A white Persian cat slunk around his feet, arched its back, and hissed.

"It's the next street over, m'lord. Bishop's Row—but for a coin I could show you to Mistress Quickly's." The beggarman wiped the rain from his brow with the back of his sleeve. "Real women with perfumed faces—"

"Perhaps another time," the man said, taking a snort from a diamond-encrusted snuffbox. "Tonight, the voices of youth beckon me."

He flipped a large metal coin into the air, and before the beggarman could catch it, the tall figure was briskly on his way, something sweeping behind him like a long, rippling cape. The beggarman fumbled in his jacket for a pair of cracked glasses and pressed them to his eyes. The cape looked to be a creature with a hundred heads: wet cats—dozens of them—spitting and snarling, clambered after the mysterious man as he turned the corner onto Bishop's Row.

Book
One

The Outskirts

A MILE FROM THE CITY, TWO SMALL FIGURES CROUCHED atop a massive pile of assorted junk. Their hazel eyes darted as they rummaged feverishly among rusty cans, old toys, crushed boxes, crumpled cartons, and broken bits of who-knows-what. A soft rain drizzled. Sirens blared in the distance. Humming lamps shone on the figures: identical twins with the same shoulder-length brown hair; the same long, lanky limbs; and the same ill-fitting red raincoats. Their names were Charlotte and Sonja, and the only way to tell them apart was the mole above Charlotte's right cheek.

"We'd better go," Sonja said impatiently. "It's getting late."

"Just a minute longer," begged Charlotte. She picked up a miniature plastic arm and shoved it into a bag strapped over her shoulder. What she really wanted was a very simple thing: a piece of wood. But a spare piece of wood was an extremely rare thing in the Outskirts—or anywhere else for that matter.

"I don't want to run into any Enforcers this time," insisted Sonja.

Charlotte shrugged. "They never catch us."

"One day they will, and we'll be thrown into some juvenile prison filled with Scrummagers and other troublemakers."

"Will you relax?" Sometimes Charlotte wondered how they could be sisters at all. Sonja had no guts.

A flashlight's beam raked across the hills of trash. Charlotte froze.

"An Enforcer," whispered Sonja.

A figure in a black slicker and rain goggles appeared on the wet asphalt below. He wore an armband with a lightning bolt emblazoned across it.

"I see you, Scrummagers!" he yelled. "This is city property!"

"Come on!" cried Sonja, grabbing Charlotte's arm.

Charlotte did not budge. Something else had caught her eye. From a mass of smashed tiles and scrap metal, she snatched up a broken but solid oak table leg. She held up the piece of lumber, beaming. "Bingo!"

Sonja pulled Charlotte with a firm jerk. They slid to the ground, ran between the piles of junk, and slipped through a narrow gap in the fence. The Enforcer blew three short, sharp whistles and charged after them out of the yard.

The twins flew down the empty street past more junkyards and trash heaps. Rain City loomed in the distance. Many years before the girls were born, as the populations of the world's cities grew to unprecedented sizes, an edict had been passed, and all the cities' borders were walled and gated. The surrounding towns and villages were bulldozed to use as dumping grounds for the cities' ever-growing waste, and now millions of homeless people, known as Outskirters, lived in the garbage, strictly patrolled and controlled by armies of Enforcers.

This was the world Charlotte and Sonja had been born into.

As the girls ran, another Enforcer emerged from the shadows and took off after them. Charlotte's heart raced. She struggled for breath. Charlotte only pretended not to be scared of Enforcers. She had seen them do terrible things. Maybe she had finally pushed too hard and gone too far. She had coaxed her sister into sneaking into forbidden junkyards closest to the city, off-limits and extra-risky.

"This way!" yelled Sonja.

Charlotte hurried after her sister, but as they rounded the corner, she saw a band of scruffy boys in smashed bowlers and tattered suits.

"Lookie, dookie!" announced a boy with a rat on his shoulder. "Lil' ducklin's!"

"Those is them circus freaks!" yelled another, squinting in the rain.

The Scrummagers began to slowly circle the twins, swaying and sniggering.

Charlotte turned to Sonja and smiled. She knew they would certainly escape now.

A handful of Enforcers came clambering around the corner. One of the Scrummagers shouted, "Coppers!" and the gang scattered in every direction, the Enforcers chasing after them.

The twins dashed away and hid under an overturned incinerator. They waited, trembling, as the goggled men with clunky batons chased the ragged boys. A minute later, the street was quiet. Sonja peered through metal slats. "All clear," she whispered.

Charlotte crawled out after her sister. "I'm sorry," she muttered.

"You nearly got us caught—again!"

"But we weren't, were we? And look what I found." Charlotte held up the table leg. "It was worth it, wasn't it?"

Sonja tried not to smile. "If it wasn't for those Scrummagers, we'd be locked in the back of a van right now on our way to prison."

"I hope they got away."

"I hope they didn't."

Charlotte never could understand why Sonja hated Scrummagers so much. They were orphans, just like them. Before she could respond, an air horn blasted. Ten o'clock. They were late again.

Chapter Two

Identical Twins

THE TWINS HURRIED THROUGH THE GATES OF A neglected cemetery. Half a dozen small booths had been assembled outside a large circus tent pitched among the crumbling gravestones. Posters advertised Dunk a Clown, Ride a Striped Pony, Kiss a Bearded Woman. Strings of colored lights crisscrossed overhead. A hand-painted sign read: PERSHING CRUM'S TRAVELING CIRCUS. Sonja sighed with relief. They were home.

Sonja and her sister had grown up in the circus, rumbling among the Outskirts in a long caravan, settling in one place after another, all of their lives.

A roar of laughter erupted from the big tent. Charlotte and Sonja ran across the yard and slipped through a pair of curtains into the changing room.

A broad-shouldered, soft-bodied woman with dyed-red hair and squinting green eyes blocked their way, arms crossed. She wore a sequined bikini and a rhinestone crown in her hair. Her oiled and tattooed skin shone even brighter than her sequins and stones.

"You're late," she said, frowning. On her shoulder sat a small honey-brown monkey munching on a stick of cotton candy. "Monkey and I were worried."

She was Tatty Tatters, their adoptive mother, the Tattooed Lady of the circus. Every inch of skin from the top of her neck to the ends of her painted toenails was illustrated in full color: forests, mountains, lakes, deserts, islands, caverns, meadows—and animals and creatures of every size and shape. The script across her chest read *The Seven Edens*.

"Sorry, Tatty," Sonja said, out of breath. "It was Charlotte's fault."

Charlotte rolled her eyes as the twins each hugged Tatty tightly, breathing in her familiar vanilla scent. Sonja's beating heart calmed and slowed.

"I hope you didn't go into forbidden junkyards again." Tatty studied the girls as she helped them out of their wet jackets.

"Of course not," Charlotte lied. She wriggled out of her dress and tights.

"How's the audience tonight?" Sonja asked, changing the subject. She pulled two matching blue crushed-velvet tuxedos from the costume rack.

"A little jumpy," said Tatty, "so be careful out there. We don't want anything to happen again."

"Nothing's happened in weeks," insisted Charlotte. She snapped on a red bow tie. "Uncle Tell said it was probably just a coincidence, anyway."

At first, they had thought it was a ghost: curtains blew open, empty seats moved, candles ignited. But soon, the other circus performers noticed that the strange occurrences happened only when the twins were onstage.

Applause erupted. Sonja watched as three clowns stumbled into the dressing room—Balthazar, Toulouse, and Vincent. Balthazar, with a black smile painted on his face from ear to ear, growled, "You're up!"

The ringmaster lurched in next. Pershing was seven feet tall but more like nine in his stovepipe hat. He wore a plastic flower pinned to his morning coat. "Ah, the last act is finally here." He looked at the twins. "No funny business tonight, okay?"

"Of course not, Pershing," Charlotte said boldly.

Sonja silently picked up a small black case. She did not feel as confident as her sister. In the past three months, even though the incidents were few and far between, they had grown worse: hats, umbrellas, and bags of popcorn had been catapulted into the air; lights had burst and showered the ring with glass; a thread-worn carpet had carried the Miniature Woman from backstage and flown her over the audience. After these incidents, the circus members no longer trusted the twins.

"Monkey and I will be waiting for you," Tatty said, leading them to the curtain. She kissed them each on top of the head before they stepped out.

The girls walked hand in hand to center stage and stopped next to a piano on wheels.

Bright lights shone in their eyes. Sonja could smell the buttered popcorn as she looked out at a sea of doubtful faces. Scattered applause and chitchat faded away.

"Brings back the clowns!" cried a Scrummager with muddy knees.

Sonja cleared her throat. "Ladies and gentlemen! My sister and

I were born on All Hallows Eve. We started playing music before we could walk. Allow us to entertain you!"

All her life, Sonja had dreamed of becoming a famous musician. Her idol was the great woodwind player Kanazi Kooks. She had read all about him: he was born in the Outskirts, grew up an orphan, and was discovered at age fifteen by a scout from the Schools for the Gifted, already a fully formed musical genius (and a bit of a heartthrob).

She flung open the case and pulled out a flute almost as long as her arm. Its metallic surface glinted in the light. She pressed it to her lips, tilted her head, and blew into the mouthpiece. A sharp note sounded.

Charlotte took her place at the piano and lifted the lid. She began to play. Her dark chords joined the melody of Sonja's flute.

The audience grew quiet. The dirty-kneed Scrummager sat down. Charlotte and Sonja's music was like nothing they had ever heard before. Even the twins themselves were lost in the bewitching tune. Their eyes were pressed shut and their heads bobbed slightly.

Charlotte's fingers pounded the piano keys. Sonja's bounced up and down rapidly along the length of the flute.

A rickety post shook, creaking, and the circus tent billowed from a sudden gust of wind. People in the back row turned to look behind them. People on the aisles looked to the sides. A boy up front squinted quizzically as his spiky hair danced on top of his head.

Then a swirling mist began to gather in the air at the top of the ring, and the audience watched in disbelief as the mist turned into a cloud, and from the cloud came rain. Umbrellas opened, and puzzled faces huddled beneath, murmuring. All at once, every seat in the tent slowly rose into the air. The audience was floating, shakily, ten inches off the ground. A woman screamed. A young girl started to cry. The Scrummager laughed hysterically.

The twins, oblivious, played on.

"Stop!" cried a voice.

Tatty was already in the middle of the stage, panicked, between the twins. Monkey leapt onto Sonja's back and gripped her hair like a rope in two little fists. Sonja dropped her flute. It made a twang as it hit the ground. Charlotte brought her hands slamming down onto the black and white keys in a final thundering chord. She looked up, anticipating the applause.

What the two girls saw, instead, was a roomful of chairs and people floating in space for a last, terrified instant—then falling to the floor all at once with a banging, cluttering, clacketing crash. The circus tent exploded into commotion as people screamed and scrabbled toward the exit.

Sonja watched in terrified silence. Her head pounded. She felt hot all over. This was the worst incident yet.

The cloud disappeared.

The abandoned arena was littered with popcorn and rows of upturned chairs. Charlotte wiped the wet hair from her forehead. "Pershing's going to throw a fit."

A low voice answered, "You're right about that."

The ringmaster stood behind them with his arms crossed, glowering. "I'm canceling your act."

Sonja picked up the flute and pressed it to her chest. Tears sprang to her eyes. Performing was everything to her. She could not live without it.

Charlotte pleaded, "It won't happen again!"

"That's what you said before, and this was ten times worse." Pershing took off his top hat and shook it. Droplets flew from the brim. "People like it when we scare them a little—but not when they run screaming in fear for their lives. I don't know what's happening to the two of you, and I wish I did, but whatever it is, it's bad for business."

Sonja ran to him and grabbed his jacket. "Please, Pershing. It's not our fault!"

The ringmaster shook his head. "There's nothing I can do."

Balthazar took a gulp from his bottle and smeared away his smile. He hiccupped. "I always knew they were witches." The other two clowns nodded.

"It's not true," muttered Charlotte.

Pershing snatched the bottle out of the clown's hand. "Clean up this mess, you clowns."

The twins changed out of their wet tuxedos in the dressing room. Monkey scrambled under the makeup table, searching for crumbs.

"They're ruined, aren't they?" said Sonja, holding up her costume. It was black from the rain. She wondered if it mattered anyhow. They were fired. At this rate, she would never become famous like Kanazi Kooks.

"They'll be fine." Tatty hung the child-sized suits, dripping, on a costume rack crammed with sequined leotards, striped overalls, and a gold lamé cape. She put her arms around the girls' shoulders. "We'd better go tell the old man what happened."

Monkey scampered after them, his bulging little cheeks stuffed with popcorn.

CHAPTER THREE

Mr. Fortune Teller

AT THE EDGE OF THE CIRCUS CAMP, BESIDE A WITHERED tree, was a lonely caravan with a mosaic facade of mother-of-pearl and stained-glass windowpanes. Smoke puffed out of a small chimney and filled the air with the scent of burning herbs. A lantern hung on the door, illuminating a crooked sign that read MR. FORTUNE TELLER SEES YOUR FUTURE.

Charlotte hurried ahead of Sonja and Tatty to a horse with his head buried in a bucket of grain. "Hello, Rhubarb," she whispered.

The horse looked up and shook his zebra-striped head, then huffed and whinnied. His short, stiff white-and-black mane stuck up on end like the bristles of a brush. He blinked two large, melancholy eyes.

Mr. Fortune Teller had found Rhubarb in an abandoned zoo, and Charlotte had always been

14

particularly attached to him. Like Rhubarb, Charlotte and Sonja did not know where they came from. And the way things were going, they would probably end up exhibited in a zoo just like Rhubarb had been. She brushed the flecks of grain from the horse's cheeks. "It looks like freckles," she said, smiling.

Just then the door swung open and a middle-aged woman burst out. A customer. Tear-stained tissues fell from her hands. "Don't believe a word that old man says!" she yelled, pushing past Tatty and the twins and disappearing into the night.

"I guess she didn't get the fortune she was hoping for," sighed Tatty.

They stepped inside. Leaves and twigs crackled in a small stove. Bookcases lined the worn velvet walls. Charlotte saw Mr. Fortune Teller crouched over a small brass case with a glass top. When he looked up, candlelight flickered in his white eyes. His fading irises had nearly disappeared. Charlotte knew his sight was getting worse, and that one day soon, he would be blind.

"It happened again," Tatty reported. "This time worse."

"I lifted the whole audience off the ground," moaned Sonja.

"I made it rain cats and dogs." Charlotte stared at her shoes. She searched for the words. They were simple but strange: "*Inside* the tent!"

The old man chuckled. "You gave them a performance they'll never forget."

Mr. Fortune Teller was not much taller than the twins. He had a large, hooked nose and frizzy salt-and-pepper hair. He wore a checked wool suit and a matching bow tie. A hunk of tortoiseshell dangled from a foxtail chain around his neck. He was the wisest person the twins had ever met. He had taught them how to read and write and understand the world—as it was now, and as it had been before the cities had taken over.

The old man gestured for them to approach. "Come have a look."

Monkey scaled the bookcases, scouring for hidden treats, as Tatty and the twins peered through the glass into the case. A colony of green caterpillars spun fluffy white cocoons—tiny oval clouds of silk. A single, smaller one whirled a completely different kind of thread: it sparkled bright gold. Its cocoon looked like a Turkish slipper.

Charlotte gasped. "How does she do that, Uncle Tell?"

"I injected her with a drop of your blood," explained Mr. Fortune Teller. "I wanted to see if it was true."

"If what was true?" asked Sonja.

"That you have magic in you."

"You said it was a coincidence," blurted Charlotte. They were already strange enough. They lived in a circus and had extraordinary musical talent. Other children were scared of them. This would only make it worse.

"When magic is released from the body, it appears gold." The old man pointed at the cocoon. "There's no doubt about it. You have magic in your blood."

Charlotte remembered a time when they were very young, seeing a traveling magician make a pigeon disappear. Afterward, the girls had asked the old man if magic really existed. Mr. Fortune Teller explained that it was rare, but that there *were* people with true magic in them. Where did it come from? The old man did not know, but added that one thing was certain: magic always came hand in hand with Talent.

Sonja shook her head. "It can't be true."

"Let's review the facts." Mr. Fortune Teller sank into a tired leather armchair. "A year ago, it began. Little incidents here and there when you played. Everyone thought it was Helmut the Contortionist's ghost." He chuckled. "In the past three months, it's happened four times, each incident bigger than the last. It sounds like tonight's was the biggest." His hands searched and fumbled across the desktop and settled onto a tin pipe. He stuffed it with wild sage and lit it with one of the candles. "Your magic is only growing stronger. It's no coincidence."

"What are we going to do?" moaned Charlotte. "Pershing's banned us from the show!"

"The others won't come near us," Sonja said unhappily. "They'll probably have us committed to some hospital to do experiments on our brains."

"Come, Sonja. Sit down," said Tatty, leading her to a divan. "You, too, Charlotte."

"In time, you'll learn how to control it," Mr. Fortune Teller said, taking a slow, gentle puff on his pipe. "Like every fledging." He leaned back into his armchair. A mist of scented smoke veiled his face. "At first, it falls to the ground or crashes into a tree, but eventually, it flies. It has no choice."

Charlotte paused for a moment, thinking. "Does it have something to do with our parents?"

The old man put down his pipe and wiped his mustache with a handkerchief. "Possibly."

Sonja stared at Mr. Fortune Teller blankly. "It does, or it doesn't."

The old man exchanged a silent look with Tatty. He shook his head. "I don't know for sure. In the old texts, some say it's inherited, others say it's exposure. Whatever the case, you've got it. A lot of it. More than I've ever seen."

Charlotte's heart sank. Any dreams of one day having a normal life were rapidly slipping through her fingers. All she ever wanted was to make friends her own age, maybe even have a boyfriend. "Why is this happening?" she grumbled. "It's not fair!"

"In a few years, I'll be blind. Is that fair?" Mr. Fortune Teller shrugged. "Maybe not, but it's helped me develop something else. An inner sight." He walked over to the divan. Tatty and the girls stood up, and the old man placed a creased, sun-spotted hand on each of the girls' shoulders. "One day, I promise, something good will come from these gifts. For now, you must practice every day. Don't let the music take over. Learn to stay in control."

Monkey began to snore. He was sprawled across a high shelf, fast asleep. An empty bottle of sweet wine lay beside him.

"That little rascal," muttered Tatty, taking off her shoes. She stood on the divan and picked up the sleeping monkey and cradled him. She turned to the old man. "Sorry, Hieronymus."

The old man chuckled. "Better him than me." He walked them to the door and looked out at the faint blinking lights in the distance. "Rain City," he mused. "The place of my youth. I remember when the buildings were only two stories tall and people used to walk in the streets." He shook his head. "Nothing ever stays the same."

They said their goodbyes to Mr. Fortune Teller and left him alone.

The old man listened for a moment as the footsteps trailed off across the camp. He hurried to his desk and pulled open a drawer. He unlocked a small jewelry box and took out a purple stone. He placed it delicately onto a little antique wooden stand. He rubbed the tortoiseshell pendant hanging from his neck, burnishing it, then pressed the face of it flat against the stone.

The stone lit up like a purple lightbulb and began to quietly pulse.

Chapter Four

Tabitha Tatters

Charlotte and Sonja leaned out their caravan window side by side. The circus members were all in for the night. The clowns next door sang a melancholy Gypsy song. At a porch table, Pershing played chess against a woman the size of a table lamp. Silvery moonlight gleamed down through the clouds. Sonja waved to an old lady wearing a purple turban in the caravan opposite them. A pale boa constrictor was draped across the woman's shoulders. She sneered at them and looked away.

Sonja sighed and yanked shut the two dish towels that served as curtains.

She remembered when the circus members used to fight over whose caravan would be parked closest to theirs. Most of them had never had children, and they loved being around the twins. They sang them songs, told them stories, and made them toys. As the girls grew older, and their musical abilities developed, the circus members grew more and more suspicious of them. Now they argued over whose caravan would be parked farthest away. Sonja felt rejected by the only friends she had ever had.

She looked around their tiny home. Thirty marionettes fashioned out of bits of wooden junk dangled from the caravan's arched ceiling. They were creatures and animals from Tatty's tattoos. Books, clothes, and old newspapers were piled over the floor, and stacks of musical compositions and flutes of various shapes and sizes lay scattered all around. Hanging against the peeling, flowered wallpaper were a cuckoo clock, a snapshot of Tatty and the twins, and a red accordion.

Sonja slumped alongside her sister at a table in front of the junk they had gathered, including the broken table leg. A book of sketches was propped open by two tin cans. There was a drawing of a man with wings and horns.

Sonja looked up at Tatty. "Are you scared of us like the others?"

"Don't be ridiculous," Tatty said, laughing. She plopped snoring Monkey into an open drawer.

Charlotte fiddled with the torso of an unfinished marionette. "I didn't see Bea tonight. Where was she?"

"On a date." Tatty cleared plates of half-eaten pancakes and carried them to a makeshift kitchen at the back of the caravan.

Of all the circus members, Bea had hurt Sonja the most. She had lived with them when she first joined the circus. They had loved her like an older sister. But she had changed, just like the others. Sonja looked from the drawing to the broken table leg to Charlotte. "I'll do the horns," she said matter-of-factly. "You can do the wings."

"I found the wood," Charlotte said stubbornly. "I'll do the horns."

Tatty stood over them. She wiped her hands on her robe. "Making a Tiffin?"

Sonja nodded sulkily. "We'll have plenty of time, now that we're banned."

"Remember what Uncle Tell said. Once you learn how to control it, you can perform again."

Charlotte sighed. "We haven't missed a performance since we were three."

"Except when you had the measles," reminded Tatty. She slipped off her robe and tipped a bottle of vinegar onto a handkerchief. She rubbed the smelly white liquid across her oily chest, where animals within a dense wood were inked. "What do other children your age do?"

Charlotte shrugged. "How would we know? They don't speak to us. Except Scrummagers."

"Anyway," said Sonja, "we don't want to do what other children do. We want to do something great like Kanazi Kooks." She took out a newspaper clipping from her jacket pocket. There was a photograph of a man with spiky hair and large, black-framed round glasses holding a flute. "He performs all over the world. In the biggest big-city auditoriums. He was born in the—"

"Outskirts," interrupted Charlotte. "We know. We know. We know all about Kanazi Kooks, thank you. Well, you can count me out. I don't want to go to some gifted school. And I definitely don't want to be a city girl."

Sonja crumpled the newspaper clipping. "They wouldn't let the likes of us in anyhow."

"Stop feeling sorry for yourself, Sonja, and help me," ordered Tatty. Sonja reluctantly stood up and rubbed Tatty's greasy shoulders with the vinegar-soaked handkerchief. She studied the tattooed images of sloping sand dunes, temples carved out of rock, and women hovering above the ground.

"Sometimes I think I should have sent you to live with Aunt Alexandria and Uncle Arthur," said Tatty. "Maybe your lives would have been a little more normal."

"Normal?" grunted Charlotte. "Are you kidding? They're both crazy."

"Alexandria's a chain smoker and always smells like black gin," Sonja said with a frown. "She'd make a terrible role model."

"I wish you were nicer to her."

"Nicer to her!" blurted Charlotte. "She's not nice to *us*. She can't even remember which one of us is which."

"Remind me not to get on the wrong side of the two of you." Tatty stood up and slipped a nightgown over her colorful skin, like drawing a shade over a bright landscape. "Come on, girls. Time for bed."

The twins changed into mismatched pajamas and wriggled under the covers. Tatty climbed into bed next to them. She pulled the string above her head, and the light went out.

"Tatty?"

"Yes, Charlotte."

"You're sure you don't think we're freaks?"

"I'm sure."

"Tatty?"

"Yes, Sonja?"

"You think we really have magic in us?"

"I can't say."

"Can't or won't?"

"Go to sleep."

"First, the story," said Sonja.

"You know all about that. You don't need me to tell that story again. Besides, you girls are old enough, you can just tell it yourself."

"No, Sonja's right," said Charlotte. "Tell it just to remind us."

Tatty groaned. "Okay, but then sleep."

"Agreed," they said in unison.

Sonja held Charlotte's hand under the covers. It was a habit they had formed as young children.

Tatty cleared her throat and began. "I was getting ready for bed one night when I heard a knock at my door—"

"It was your first week at the circus," Charlotte interrupted. "You were scared to live alone in a caravan."

Sonja chimed in, "You peeked outside, but nobody was there."

Tatty nodded and continued: "Just as I was about to close the door, I heard a gurgling, gargling sound, and I looked down at the ground—and there you two were. Wrapped in one woolen shawl and stuffed into a milk pail. There was a note pinned to the shawl with your names and your birthday written on it, and a heart-shaped locket with a strand of brown hair curled inside it."

Sonja opened the locket that lay on her chest. Inside, underneath the cloudy, scratched glass, was the curled lock of brown hair. The twins had a rule: they were not allowed to open the locket outside under any circumstances. They were scared of losing the only little piece of their mother they had.

"Tomorrow's my turn to wear it," whispered Charlotte.

"I had tried to have my own children," continued Tatty, "but I never could. It was at that moment that I knew why. I was waiting for my dear girls to be delivered to me in a milk pail." Tatty's voice broke. It always did when she reached the end of the story.

Sonja pressed her toes against Tatty's. Tatty tried her best to be a good mother, and even though she did not know how to read or write, or understand why the sky was blue or why the moon changed shapes, she made them laugh, comforted them when they were sad, and loved them with all her heart.

"Thank goodness we were orphans," said Charlotte.

"We love you, Tatty," said Sonja.

"And I love you, my dearies."

Monkey grunted from the open drawer.

"And you, too, of course, Monkey."

Sonja knew that Tatty had sacrificed everything for them. She had even sold her gold fillings to get them milk when they were babies. But as much as Sonja loved Tatty, she often found herself thinking, late at night, about the mother and father who had abandoned them and where they were now.

CHAPTER FIVE

The Seven Edens

A WHITE SUN ROSE ABOVE THE OUTSKIRTS OF RAIN CITY.
The gray smog hung low across the wide landscape. Rain pitter-
pattered on the tin roofs of the circus caravans. Everyone was still
asleep except for Charlotte and Sonja. They sat at the table in
their pajamas, whispering and working. Charlotte had sawed the
piece of wood into smaller blocks and was chiseling
a miniature horn out of one. Sonja was carefully
sticking little feather shapes made out of costume
scraps onto cardboard wings.

"Once we've finished the Tiffin," remarked
Charlotte, "we'll have all the creatures from
Tatty's tattoo. Then we'll only need to paint
the backdrops, and voilà: we'll have our
marionette show."

Since the twins were very
young, Tatty had told
them stories about
the Seven Edens

Tatty
&
the Seven Edens

The Forlorn Forest

the Land where the Plants Reign

the Vanishing Islands

the Golden Underground

the Shifting Tales

and the characters who inhabited them. Tatty had learned the details from the tattoo artist himself all those years ago. The girls knew the legends inside and out and backward and forward. When Charlotte was bored, she would go through the seven lands and their inhabitants like a multiplication table:

"The Changelings are from the Forlorn Forest; the Albans are from the Golden Underground; the Tiffins are from the Land Where the Plants Reign; the Swifters are from the Lost Desert; the Foretellers are from the Vanishing Islands; the Bird Warblers are from the Crooked Peaks; the Pearl Catchers are from the Shifting Lakes."

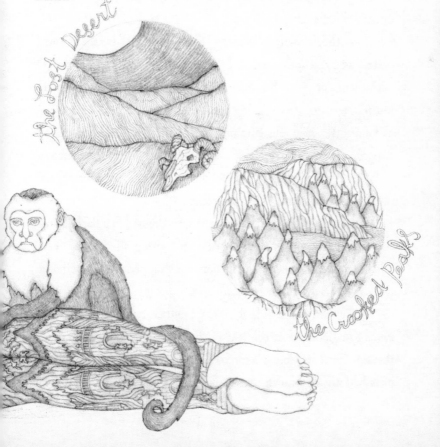

"It's my turn to wear the locket, by the way," Charlotte said to Sonja, sticking out her hand.

Sonja unfastened the thin gold chain from around her neck and dropped it reluctantly into Charlotte's palm. It was warm from being worn all night. Charlotte believed the locket gave her good luck—and hoped that one day their real mother and father would know them by the little heart-shaped pendant dangling from her neck.

There was a knock at the door. Tatty put a pillow over her head and groaned.

"I'll get it!" Charlotte called out brightly. She jumped up and opened the door.

It was the Miniature Woman. She was out of breath. "You'd better hide. There's a team of Enforcers looking for you. Pershing's with them right now. Some Outskirters complained about your act last night."

Charlotte's face fell. She peered out the window between the hanging dish towels. Pershing stood at the entrance of the cemetery with three Enforcers. He was shuffling through a stack of papers, pretending to search for his circus license.

Tatty leapt out of bed and got the girls dressed in a flash. Sonja threw a weathered tin pennywhistle on a string around her neck. Charlotte snatched up her accordion and strapped it onto her back, then grabbed a handful of marionettes.

"Don't worry, I'll hide the rest!" said Tatty. She pulled the twins to a bookcase at the rear of the caravan and fumbled along the side until she found a latch. The bookcase swung open. The girls had always known there was a door behind it, but they had never had to use it. "Go to the family tombs and stay there until I signal you." Tatty shoved Monkey into Charlotte's hands as she hustled them out. "Take him. You never know what they'll do."

The girls jumped out of the caravan and ran to the end of the cemetery, hopping over sunken gravestones. Charlotte looked back over her shoulder and prayed Tatty would be all right. The Enforcers hated Outskirters—especially travelers like them. They had orders to keep the Outskirts quiet, and they obeyed them with great brutality.

The twins reached what looked like a cluster of little houses, the family tombs of the old village. Sonja kicked open a door under the words carved in Latin: REQUIESCAT IN PACE. A blast of stale air whooshed out with a swarm of dizzy gnats. Charlotte pulled the door shut behind them, and they huddled in a corner on the dusty stone floor. Monkey, still asleep, curled into a ball on Sonja's lap.

Charlotte looked around. The walls were inscribed with names of the dead: Augustus von Stralen, Magbeth von Stralen, Brigadier von Stralen. Spiderwebs hung like hair from sculpted busts. Light trickled through a dirty stained-glass window and dappled the girls in gloomy color. It was dead quiet except for the sound of Monkey's breathing.

Charlotte shuddered. "This place gives me the creeps."

"Me, too," whispered Sonja.

They waited ten minutes in silence.

"I can't stand the suspense," said Charlotte, jumping to her feet. She climbed up onto a little altar and peeked out through the stained-glass window. In the distance, she saw the clowns: Balthazar clanging a pair of cymbals while being chased by an Enforcer,

Vincent throwing empty food cans from the roof of their caravan, Toulouse making faces from inside as two Enforcers kicked at the locked door.

Charlotte sighed. "They're still there." She sat cross-legged on the floor, feeling guilty. It was their fault the Enforcers had come. Now everyone was going to hate them even more. "I can't sit here doing nothing. It'll drive me crazy." She looped the straps of her accordion over her shoulders and pumped the bellows very gently. Her fingers wandered the keys. "If we play softly, they won't hear us."

Sonja hesitated, then blew gingerly into her pennywhistle. Her cheeks puffed in and out. A squeaky, pretty little song piped out of the crooked metal instrument.

They played together as quietly as they possibly could.

"Anything happening?" Charlotte asked. "Any magic?"

Sonja looked around. "Nothing so far."

After a few songs, Charlotte relaxed. Maybe Uncle Tell *was* wrong. Maybe they were back to normal. That is all she wanted to be: normal.

"Don't get too excited," said Sonja. She dropped the pennywhistle from her mouth. "It might be a fluke." She picked up one of the marionettes. A wooden stag dangled from six strings. She tilted the control up and down and left to right. The animal's hooves clip-clopped across the marble floor. Its head cocked to one side.

Charlotte started to sing in a whisper as she played:

> *Hear me, hear me!*
> *From a world of make-believe.*
> *Hear me, hear me!*

I sing of seven lands hidd'n from eyes to see.
Within an ancient forest,
Stalks a Changeling among the trees.
First a man, then a beast, either shape he'd like to be.
With two lives to be liv'd he growls, "You'll never conquer me!"

Sonja picked up another marionette: a man wearing a fur cape and a necklace of antlers. She swung his pink plastic arms and bent his metal knees. Monkey, finally waking, stumbled to his feet and danced alongside the two marionettes.

Charlotte laughed and continued to sing:

Underwater from lake to lake
A Pearl Catcher swims,
Her long hair flowing, paddling her limbs—

"Hold it," Sonja interrupted. She looked at the small pile of marionettes. "We didn't bring her. Do the Swifters instead." She held up three small puppets, fierce women with wild red hair and lightning bolts in their hands. Monkey covered his face. Charlotte went on darkly:

Across a sandy desert,
Float the Swifters, one, two, three.
Fiery-eyed, these spirits rise in an ancient breeze,
Bringing thunder, rain, and lightning,
Not caring whom they please.

Something hit the window.

The girls looked up, startled. Charlotte stopped playing, Sonja dropped the puppets, and Monkey hid behind the girls.

They sat perfectly still, dead silent, hearts racing.

The tomb door creaked open.

Three boys stood in the doorway, grinning.

"Yous ducklin's gots us in trouble."

It was the Scrummagers from the night before.

Sonja grimaced. "How were we supposed to know you'd be there?"

"Somes of us gots taken by coppers," lisped the boy with the rat on his shoulder. His clothes were full of holes. They could see more skin than cloth.

"We're really sorry about that," apologized Charlotte, "but like my sister said—"

"Theys hurts 'em, yous know. Beats the daylights out of 'em." The boy swung a thin club over his shoulder. A crooked nail stuck out from the end of it. "We's thinkin' ofs doin' the sames to yous, circus freaks."

A whistle blew. A booming voice exploded:

"Hold it right there, Scrummagers!"

And in a snap, the boys were gone.

The twins held their breath, waiting for the Enforcer's footsteps. None came.

Instead, they heard a soft voice call "Hello?"

Charlotte peered around the door. A boy about their age with curly brown hair sat on a gravestone. A violin lay on his lap. His clothes were worn but tidy. He smiled.

Charlotte stepped outside. She had never seen a boy with such kind, dancing eyes. She noticed a pin on his lapel: a rusty, old musical note.

"You scared us to death," growled Sonja. "We thought you were an Enforcer."

"Sorry. It's the only way to get rid of Scrummagers." He looked from sister to sister, his eyes widening. "I've never met identical twins before."

Monkey leapt out of the tomb and jumped onto Charlotte's shoulder.

"Or a monkey for that matter." He held out his hand. "I'm Jack Cross."

Charlotte stepped forward and shook his hand eagerly. "I'm Charlotte. This is Sonja. That's Monkey. I was just saying to myself I wanted to meet some kids our own age."

"I live in the Train Graveyard. Number seven seventeen. With my mother and brothers." Charlotte watched as Jack Cross nestled the violin under his chin and began to play. The strings hummed under his sliding bow. After a moment, he put down his instrument and smiled. "I'm a musician. I practice out here sometimes."

Charlotte's face flushed a little. It was a difficult tune. The boy was showing off.

"We're musicians, ourselves!" Charlotte said quickly. She could show off, too. She played a few bars from a tricky polka. Her fingers danced like crickets.

Jack Cross raised his eyebrows, surprised. "Not half bad!" He looked to Sonja. "What about you?"

"We're twins, aren't we?" Sonja reluctantly blew the first few verses of a medieval hymn.

The boy nodded, impressed. "You live here?"

"Sort of," Charlotte said, her voice faltering.

"What she's embarrassed to say," interrupted Sonja, tucking away her pennywhistle, "is that we're members of a circus."

Jack Cross' eyes lit up. "I've always wanted to join a circus. Travel the world. Meet people."

Charlotte beamed. The boy did not care that they were circus folk. He seemed to like them even more for it.

"It's not that great, traveling so much," said Sonja. "Every Outskirt looks the same."

"I imagine that's true—but I don't want to spend the rest of my life around here. I want to make something of myself."

"Me, too!" Charlotte blurted. "I want to play in a big auditorium in one of the cities."

Sonja scowled. "You said never in your life do you *ever* want to—"

Charlotte pinched Sonja hard in the arm before she could finish. Why did she always have to interfere? It was not the first time.

"Here's a tip." The boy leaned in. "There's an audition today. In the Train Graveyard. For scholarships to the Schools for the Gifted. A real chance to leave the Outskirts behind."

Just then, they heard shouting in the distance. The twins ducked behind a grave. "I think someone's trying to signal you," said Jack Cross. "A woman." They peered over the top of the stone slab. It was Tatty, waving a pair of white underwear.

Charlotte's face turned bright red. Couldn't she have used something else to wave?

Sonja grabbed the marionettes and pulled Charlotte by the arm. "We've got to go."

"Nice meeting you, Jack Cross!" Charlotte called, waving goodbye.

Jack Cross waved back. "Maybe I'll see you at the auditions!" he shouted cheerfully after them.

Charlotte turned, following Sonja across the graveyard. She felt as though she could run and sing and laugh all at the same time. "Our first friend."

"Hardly."

"We've never had a friend our own age. Don't you think it would be a good opportunity?"

"We don't need friends. We have each other."

"We don't want to be like those weird twins who live alone together for their whole lives, do we?"

Sonja shrugged. "Why not?"

Charlotte stopped in her tracks. "What's that?"

A white Persian cat stood in their path. Her frizzy tail swished from side to side. She held a crisp envelope in her pink mouth.

Sonja reached down and took it.
A name was scrawled across the
front. "It's for Bea."

"Thank you, kitty," Charlotte crooned. She bent down to pet
the cat. The creature's orange eyes flickered. Her claws sprang out,
and she swiped Charlotte's hand.

"Ow!" shrieked Charlotte, jumping back. She watched, frozen,
as the cat stared up at her with what looked like the faintest smile
on her face—then turned away with a hiss and disappeared among
the gravestones.

Chapter Six

The Bearded Lady

The twins stood in front of the pink door of a pink caravan. Sonja knocked lightly. She knew Bea hated to be disturbed during her boudoir. After a moment, a pretty young woman with thick wavy hair—and a full-grown beard set neatly into rollers—stuck her head out, yawning.

"Everyone's pretty upset about those Enforcers snooping around today. Luckily, they didn't search in here." She pointed at Monkey. "He can't come in."

Monkey stuck his tongue out, jumped to the ground, and scurried away. The twins followed Bea inside. She flopped onto her bed. Everything in the caravan was pink, including the crumpled bedsheets. "I heard you nearly brought the whole circus down last night."

Sonja frowned. "We can't help it. You'd think everyone would be a little more understanding."

Bea opened a box of chocolates on her lap. She took a minuscule bite out of one and returned it to its wrapper. "One thing I've

learned the hard way is
you can't depend on
anyone for
anything.
Especially
understanding."

Sonja stared
at Bea. She
remembered
how they used
to stay up nights,
hearing stories about Bea's life before
the circus, about how her parents had
kicked her out of the house when they
saw stubble on her chin. These days,
Bea acted as if she were too mature for
the girls. She hardly came to see them
anymore.

Bea offered Charlotte and Sonja the box
of chocolates. "Go on. Take one."

Sonja noticed that each bonbon had a
bite taken-out of it. She shrugged and
popped a half-eaten one into her mouth.
She chewed with her eyes closed. It had
been a long time since she had tasted
chocolate. She licked her fingers in
case there was any trace left.

"They're from the city," boasted Bea. "My boyfriend gave them to me."

Sonja rolled her eyes. Boyfriend this, boyfriend that. That's all Bea talked about anymore.

"He's a Richer, you know. Swimming in coins!"

"I don't like Richers," said Charlotte. "They're all money and no heart."

"What would you know?" Bea's eyes darkened. She snatched away the box. "Why are you here, anyway?"

Sonja pulled out the letter. "It was delivered by a cat."

"A cat?" Bea straightened. "A fluffy white one?"

Charlotte showed the cat scratches on the back of her hand. "She's dangerous."

Bea snatched the letter and tore it open. "He's coming tonight!" she said, reading feverishly. "To my performance." She jumped out of bed and pulled the rollers out of her beard. "I need to get ready." She ushered the twins out the door.

"But you have eight hours," said Charlotte.

"Exactly!" Bea slammed the door behind them.

Sonja shook her head. "Pathetic. All that for some creepy Richer with a cat."

"Let's give him a chance. Maybe he'll turn out to be nice."

Sonja looked at Charlotte suspiciously. It was just like her: obsessed with love stories. Sonja had to stay sharp or Charlotte would end up running away with some idiot—like that boy in the cemetery. What was his name? Oh, yeah. Jack Cross.

The other circus members' caravans were arranged in two rows of three, end-to-end. After years in the business, Pershing had figured out the perfect parking formation: the caravans were close enough to shout from one window to another, but far enough not to hear neighbors snoring. The three clowns lay sprawled on their caravan steps smoking. Their makeup was smudged, and their props and costumes were scattered across the ground, wet and trampled.

"Thank you so much for inviting those Enforcers to visit today," croaked Balthazar. He had a bleeding lip. "They were just charming."

"Oh, leave them alone," said the Fat Lady from her deck chair under an umbrella. She was a perfect square: as wide as she was tall. She sipped at a cup of hot coffee. Black drops spattered her robe. She leaned forward and whispered. "I used to have a cousin who could flip spoons just by staring at them." She winked. "Hocus-pocus doesn't scare me."

"Thanks, Gertie," said Charlotte.

The Snake Charmer stuck her head out of her caravan window. The boa slithered across her shoulders, hissing. "Alfonso's furious! He had to hide under a sink all morning because of you two!"

"I don't see how that's our fault," grumbled Sonja.

"Maybe you'll change your tune once you've seen what they've done to your caravan!"

That is when the girls noticed that the door was hanging, crooked, from one hinge. They crept up the stairs and peeked inside. Drawers were flung open; books, clothes, and shoes were strewn; the mattress was overturned. Sonja looked around, panicked. The Enforcers had never been this thorough.

"They didn't find anything," Tatty assured them. She was sitting at the table with Mr. Fortune Teller. Monkey was hovering over a plate of burned pancakes. Each time he reached for one, Tatty slapped his little hand.

"This time, they weren't trying to scare us," said the old man. "They were really looking for the two of you. They said something about your act causing unrest, and about charges they had against you for stealing from forbidden junkyards."

Sonja groaned. They *had* tracked them down the other night.

Tatty looked up at the girls, disappointed. "You promised me you'd never go to one again."

"I'm sorry, Tatty," Sonja said miserably. "We were desperate for material." She knew Tatty would not punish them. She never had the heart. Sonja's guilt felt like punishment enough. She hated hurting Tatty.

"We need to leave," insisted Tatty. Her face stiffened. "Tomorrow."

"Maybe only *we* should go," sighed Charlotte, collapsing into a chair. "Everyone's suffered enough already because of us."

"Where to?" asked Mr. Fortune Teller.

"School?" Charlotte suggested. Sonja glared at her. Was she crazy enough to want to follow that boy to school?

"School? School." The old man waved his hand. "No, that's not for you." He stood up. "We have no choice. We must move on. I'll talk to Pershing." He walked to the broken door and looked back. "Just as a precaution, don't leave the campsite today."

The old man hurried out, muttering to himself.

"Don't leave the campsite?" Sonja said hesitantly.

"That's what he said."

"But the Enforcers are always chasing someone or other," observed Charlotte. She rolled up a pancake like a cigar and ate it in three bites. "What's the big deal?"

"I'm not sure."

Sonja tore off the burned edges of a pancake and ate the chewy center. She was sick of pancakes. They ate them at every meal. She closed her eyes and pretended she was chewing a delicious, ripe banana. Sonja had almost forgotten what a banana tasted like—fruit had become nearly impossible to find as the land around the cities shrank.

"Figures we'd get up and go just when we met a friend," complained Charlotte.

"A friend?" Tatty brightened. "The boy I saw you talking with? I thought he was a Scrummager."

"Couldn't we at least say goodbye to him?" pleaded Charlotte. "It's just around the corner in the Train Graveyard. There won't be any Enforcers there."

Tatty shook her head. "I don't think that's a good idea."

"Me neither," Sonja said, swallowing. "Too dangerous."

Charlotte glared at her sister. "Sonja's only saying that because she's scared to make friends."

"Scared?" snapped Sonja. "I'm not scared."

Charlotte turned to Tatty. "You said you wanted us to meet children our age. Well, here's our chance."

"Not today, dearie." She picked up a ripped dictionary. "We've got to clear up this mess. Now, go tell the clowns we need some help with the door."

"Okay, okay," muttered Charlotte. Sonja watched her sister as she brushed her hair and tied a pink ribbon in a bow. She was up to something, thought Sonja. Charlotte pulled on her jacket and threw the accordion over her shoulder.

"What do you need that for?" Sonja asked suspiciously.

"After I see the clowns, I'm going to the tombs to practice." She turned to Tatty. "Is that still permitted in this new oppressive regime?"

"If you promise you won't leave the campsite."

"Uh-huh."

Tatty picked up the cuckoo clock from the floor. She shook it. "You've got an hour."

Charlotte gave her sister a strange look, then ran out of the caravan.

She wouldn't dare, thought Sonja. After a moment, she threw on her jacket and hurried outside.

"Hey, where are you going?" Tatty called out after her. "I need help!"

Up ahead, Sonja saw Charlotte talking to the clowns. They were still sitting on their caravan steps, but were now taking turns swigging from a bottle. Just as Sonja caught up to them, Charlotte took off again.

"I know what you're up to!" Sonja shouted.

"Mind your own business!" Charlotte yelled back.

Sonja followed her into the graveyard and past the family tombs.

Charlotte jumped over the rickety wrought-iron fence. When she reached the other side, she was about to start running when Sonja screamed, "Porcupine!"

Charlotte stopped in her tracks.

The twins had made a pact that no matter what was happening, even if they were in the middle of an argument, when they heard the word *porcupine*, they would stop what they were doing and hug.

Sonja stretched her arms over the fence. Charlotte did the same. They hugged with the metal barrier between them.

"You can't do this," said Sonja.

"Isn't it *you* who always talks about becoming famous? How many times have I heard you go on about Kanazi Kooks? You're the one who wants to leave the Outskirts and tour the cities as a world-renowned musician."

Sonja remained silent. Charlotte was right. She had always wanted those things. If she went to school like Kanazi Kooks, she just might have a shot.

"We're making it hard on everyone if we stay here," Charlotte continued. "They already resent us. We're not allowed to perform. The Enforcers are after us. If this goes on much longer, they'll start to resent Tatty. Wouldn't we be helping if we went to school and got out of her hair?"

"Perhaps," said Sonja, "but you're forgetting one big problem. The magic!"

"But when we played today, nothing happened. Anyway, Uncle Tell told us we can learn to control the magic. It can't be that hard."

"Is this because of that boy?" Sonja asked quietly.

"A little, maybe. But the more I think about our troubles, the more it seems like school is the only answer." She put her hand on her heart. "I swear that I'll never put any boy before you."

"Promise?"

"Promise."

"Okay. Let's go before I change my mind."

The drizzle stopped, and the sun peered through the clouds. People in tattered rain gear filled the streets from the various junkyards and trash heaps where they lived.

"Fresh meats straight from the city! Cured and canned!" cried a chubby man wearing a porkpie hat and a bloody apron. A pyramid of tin cans was stacked behind him. On their labels was a cartoon of a lamb, a cow, and a pig all smiling together.

Sun-blotched men sold badly bruised fruit and rotten vegetables, and big-boned women carried wooden cages on their shoulders filled with rats and mice. A wiry old man with a stack of papers under his arm shouted, "Get yer news here!"

They stopped at a gate under the words TRAIN GRAVEYARD. A poster in big block letters read:

AUDITIONS TODAY
FOR
THE SCHOOLS FOR THE GIFTED.

CHILDREN
AGES EIGHT TO THIRTEEN
APPLY WITHIN.

The twins studied the sign, anxious. If they were accepted, their lives would change forever. How would they explain it to Tatty? She would object, but she always did what was best for the girls. Sonja looked at her sister. She might lose her to Jack Cross or somebody else. Would it be worth the risk?

Perhaps, if she became the next Kanazi Kooks.

Sonja took Charlotte's hand, and they walked through the gate together.

CHAPTER SEVEN

Auditions

IN A LARGE SQUARE SURROUNDED BY ROWS OF ABANDONED train cars, a hundred young people of every shape, size, and color waited in a long line. Some carried instruments. Others clutched paintings, sculptures, and manuscripts. Parents fussed with their children's hair and clothing while the kids chatted excitedly. A platform stood in the center of the square. A young girl wearing a tutu pirouetted across it. A row of judges sat busily scribbling notes.

Charlotte felt giddy. She looked from one child to another, smiling. "I've never seen so many kids in my life!"

"Me neither," Sonja said, anxious.

A voice boomed: "Names?"

Charlotte turned to see a cross-eyed woman staring at them from behind a desk. She wore thick-rimmed glasses, and her hair was pulled back tight in a bun. "Am I seeing one person or two?" she asked.

Charlotte wrinkled her brow. "Uh—two."

"Names?"

"Maybe we should watch first," suggested Sonja.

"No watching," snapped the woman, tapping the end of her pen against the table impatiently. "You either audition, or you leave."

Charlotte could see that her sister was starting to lose her nerve. "Charlotte and Sonja Tatters," she blurted.

The woman scratched ink across a crisp white page in a thick book.

"Hold on, Charlotte," whispered Sonja. "I changed my mind. We've got to go back. Tatty's probably worried about us."

"Ages?" the woman asked without looking up.

"Twelve and a half," replied Charlotte.

The woman handed them each a name tag. "Stand in line."

Charlotte stuck hers onto her jacket. "Want yours?"

Sonja grabbed her sister's elbow. "This is a mistake."

"I thought you wanted to be somebody."

"I don't feel safe here."

"I'm nervous too, Sonja," Charlotte said softly, "but we've got to take the chance. Think what Kanazi Kooks went through to get to where he is."

"This is different. We're going to get caught. We're going to get in trouble!"

"Charlotte! Sonja!"

Jack Cross waved from the middle of a long line of children. Charlotte dove through the crowd, leaving Sonja behind.

When she stopped in front of him, she hoped her face was not as red as it felt. "You look nice—ah—I mean—I like your pin. A musical note. It's cute!"

Cute! Cute! How could she have said something so stupid? She wanted to melt into the ground and disappear forever.

Jack Cross smiled. "My father gave it to me. He played the violin, too." He pointed to a bespectacled girl with a cello case and a skinny boy holding a clarinet. "These are my friends Emily and Gustave."

Charlotte shook their hands eagerly. Sonja caught up to them, irritated. She nodded hello coolly.

"You two from the Outskirts?" asked the girl in the glasses. Her face was covered with brown freckles.

Charlotte nodded. "Uh-huh."

"They're performers in a circus," explained Jack Cross. "Good ones, too."

"My parents won't let me go to the circus," the skinny boy said glumly.

Sonja snapped, "Why? They think we'll give you the plague or something?" Charlotte pinched her. Sonja yelped, but was drowned out by the sound of a loudspeaker announcing Jack Cross to the stage.

"Wish me luck," he said cheerfully.

"Good luck! Good luck!" Charlotte yelled after him.

"Jack's really good," the girl in the glasses whispered to Charlotte.

Charlotte nodded silently. She was mesmerized. She watched Jack Cross spring across the stage from foot to foot with the violin tucked under his chin and the bow swinging up and down. The tune fluttered brightly into her ears and warmed her whole body. "I *really* want to go to this school," she murmured.

"I knew it!" Sonja burst out. "All that stuff about helping Tatty and Kanazi Kooks, that was just to get me to go along with it!"

"That's not true," insisted Charlotte. "Anyway, what's so wrong with wanting to have friends?" She realized Emily and Gustave were staring at them. She smiled feebly.

"Charlotte and Sonja Tatters," blared the loudspeaker.

"That's us!" cried Charlotte. She yanked her sister toward the platform, but Sonja would not budge.

"Please," Charlotte insisted. "I need you!"

Sonja shook her head. "No. I won't."

"Fine!" shouted Charlotte. "I'll go to school without you!"

Charlotte stepped onto the platform. Jack Cross waved to her as he descended the other side. A hundred children's faces stared up at her in anticipation. She was alone on the stage. There had been so many times she had wished she was not a twin but that she was just plain old Charlotte, not one of two. But now, there was a lump in her throat. She needed her other half.

She looked down at a long table where five female judges sat in a row. They wore stiff navy uniforms and tight hairnets. A man seated behind them wore a bright pink suit and had spiky black hair and large, black-framed glasses. He was impossible to miss. He was Kanazi Kooks. Charlotte had to catch her breath.

"What are you waiting for?" barked one of the female judges. She was short and stocky and had a long nose like a beak. Her eyebrows met in the middle of her forehead.

"She's waiting for me," announced a voice.

Sonja was standing beside her sister on the platform.

Charlotte grabbed her hand. "Do you see him?" She whispered.

"I see him." Sonja bowed to Kanazi Kooks. Kanazi Kooks nodded back to her. Sonja pulled out her pennywhistle. "Let's show him what we've got." She lowered her voice. "Remember: we're in control."

Charlotte nodded. I'm in control, she thought. She put her fingers to the keys of her accordion and took a deep breath. As the first notes pumped out, excitement surged through her. She was playing in front of Jack Cross. She looked for him in the crowd. He was smiling from ear to ear.

Sonja accompanied her with a precise yet expressive sound, and soon, a dizzy, whirling carousel of music spun out all around them. Charlotte played to Jack Cross. Sonja played to Kanazi Kooks. The more they played, the better they played.

"I'm—in—con—trol," Charlotte murmured.

But she was not.

The music had taken over. It swirled into her head, into her bones, into her blood. Sonja hopped up and down beside her with eyes shut and fingers bobbing.

A strand of lightning zigzagged down from the sky. Clouds rumbled overhead. A crack of thunder shook the ground. Hats leapt up off heads into the air and spun like tops. Drums and cymbals began banging and clanging all on their own.

The audience gasped. The judges stopped writing. Children jumped up and down, running and squealing. Kanazi Kooks remained calmly seated—with a faint smile across his lips.

Charlotte's eyes flashed open. She stumbled backward. "It's happening," she muttered. She turned to Sonja and cried, "It's happening!"

Sonja squinted one eye open and saw the chaos. Her arms fell to her sides.

There was a moment of frozen silence—and then a tin can flew past their heads. Confused, frightened faces watched them.

Charlotte saw Jack Cross in the audience. His mouth hung open. Charlotte's heart sank. She had seen that look before. He thought she was a freak.

The head judge stood up and marched toward the steps.

"Let's go!" yelled Sonja.

They leapt off the back of the stage, pressed through the crowd of bewildered children, and climbed over the crumbling brick wall.

The clouds thickened over the Outskirts, and fat drops began to fall. "Did we do that, too?" cried Charlotte. They lifted their hoods over their heads as they continued to run. People on the streets scrambled for shelter. Sonja looked back over her shoulder. No one had followed them.

After what felt like an eternity, they reached the campsite, breathless.

Pershing was standing under the painted sign. His top hat shielded his white-powdered face from the rain. Monkey sat on his shoulder rattling a cracked jug.

The soaking twins came to a stop and stood in front of him, wordless and panting.

"What's gotten into the two of you?"

Charlotte burst into tears. She would never go to school. She would never see Jack Cross. Everything was ruined because of the magic. She cursed her parents, whoever they were, for passing it down to them.

Chapter Eight

Kats von Stralen

Sonja pulled Charlotte into the dressing room. It was crammed wall to wall with costumes and set pieces and agitated performers. Lightbulbs dangled from wires overhead. Musky body odor filled the air. After what they had been through, the familiarity of everything made Sonja dizzy. Tatty stood talking to the three clowns with a nervous look on her face. It fell away when she saw the twins. She hugged them tightly. "Where did you go?"

"Call off the search party!" yelled Balthazar, slumping in front of a makeup table. The other two clowns squeezed in beside him and began to blacken their eyebrows with burned corks.

"Sorry, Tatty," mumbled Sonja. "We went to the Train Graveyard." She would not lie this time (although she might leave out a few details, like their disastrous audition and seeing Kanazi Kooks—wonderful Kanazi Kooks. If only she had gotten to see him perform!).

Tatty shook her head and sighed. "You went against my wishes again. Luckily, the old man doesn't know. Did any Enforcers see you?"

"No," Sonja said quietly.

"It's all my fault," admitted Charlotte. "I wanted to see Jack Cross. He plays the violin. He's practically a virtuoso." She suddenly stopped talking. Her lips trembled. "I'll never see him again. Ever! He's going to a school in a city, and we're—we're—we're just circus folk!"

"Careful what you say about circus folk!" chirped the Miniature Woman, who was doing the splits on the makeup table.

Tatty put her arms around Charlotte and pulled her close. Her anger had disappeared. "You'll see him again. I promise."

Sonja did not understand why Charlotte cared so much about a boy she hardly knew. Charlotte was always falling in love with someone. Jack Cross. A Scrummager named Larry. A stray dog.

Bea pulled a ruffled bodice off the rack and stepped behind a ripped screen to change costumes. "I wouldn't get too hung up on an Outskirter. They're junkyard types."

Charlotte frowned. She wiped her eyes. "He's not a type," she returned. "He's a human and a musician."

Pershing burst into the dressing room. "It's filling up out there," he said excitedly. "There's even a Richer in the audience."

Bea's face lit up. She flew out from behind the screen, bodice half-laced. "It's him!" she shrieked, pointing. Sonja looked out past the curtain into the audience. In the third row, dead center, sat a tall man in a black suit. His long legs were crossed, and a brimmed hat was tilted over one eye. He stroked a white Persian cat on his lap. The cat that had delivered the letter. Sonja stared, her eyes glued to the stranger.

"Isn't he handsome?" squealed Bea.

"Terribly," Sonja said with a shudder. There was something about the man that made her uneasy. Maybe it was his horrible cat.

"You're up, boys!" Pershing called out.

The clowns buttoned their pleated collars and snapped on their pointy hats. They ran out of the dressing room. The curtain fluttered behind them, and Monkey dashed through it with a half-eaten sandwich clenched in his mouth. He clambered onto a lumpy sofa, chewing frantically. The twins flopped onto the moth-eaten cushions beside him.

"Don't look so depressed, dearies." Tatty stepped out from behind the screen in her costume. Her skin was slathered in oil. The Seven Edens tattoos shimmered brightly. "Pershing will let you perform soon enough. Won't you, Pershing?"

Pershing looked up from a newspaper, distracted. "What's that?"

"If they ever set foot into our circus ring again," interjected the Snake Charmer, "Alfonso and I'll quit for good." The boa constrictor hissed inside its basket.

"Me, too!" squeaked the Miniature Woman, standing on her head.

"Thank you, everyone," said Sonja. "You've made your feelings extremely clear." She sank her head into her hands. Whenever she was depressed, playing in front of an audience always made her feel better. Those days were over.

The clowns burst through the curtains covered in sweat. The audience cheered behind them.

Pershing jumped to his feet. "I've got to introduce Tatty."

Sonja and Charlotte walked Tatty to the curtain. She carried a torch over her shoulder, for swallowing fire. "You don't have to wait. I'll meet you at home when I'm finished. We'll play gin rummy."

She kissed them on the tops of their heads and whispered, "Don't worry about the others. They'll come around."

Tatty ran into the circus ring waving her arms, exuberant. The audience clapped halfheartedly. The Richer whipped a pair of binoculars out of his pocket.

Pershing bumped into the twins as he strode back into the

59

dressing room. "Girls, you can't stand there. Go home. I don't want any Enforcers seeing you."

"We were just leaving," Sonja said miserably. She felt like a leper.

Outside, the rain had stopped. The sun was setting, and colored lights flickered on. The clowns were arguing and drinking as they opened their booths. The Fat Lady stood behind a cotton-candy stall, winding pink sugar onto a cone.

"I wish we could have gone to school," lamented Charlotte. "Everyone hates us here."

Sonja remembered all the frightened faces in the audience. "It'd be worse at school." Kanazi Kooks probably thought they were freaks, too. A long line waited in front of Mr. Fortune Teller's caravan. What would all their fortunes hold?

Sonja stopped walking. She faced Charlotte.

"If we found our parents, maybe we'd understand."

Charlotte clasped the locket hanging from her neck.

"Where we're from. Who we are. Why we're full of magic."

Charlotte nodded.

"The question is: how do we find them?"

Footsteps crunched behind them.

They turned to see a tall figure slinking in the dark alongside a black limousine.

He stood still and silent, watching them.

Sonja pulled her sister's hand and whispered, "Let's go!"

They hurried into a tent: "The House of Illusions."

It was a labyrinth of mirrors. A hundred reflections followed them, some with twisted heads, some with stretched-out bodies. A pair of metal-tipped shoes click-clacked across the wooden planks behind them. Suddenly, the tall figure's black reflection dazzled them from all directions. They saw grinning teeth everywhere. Charlotte screamed. Sonja yanked her out of the tent.

They raced across the campsite toward the other caravans. The lights were out, and the curtains were drawn. They heard giggling up ahead. Two people were kissing in the dark.

"Bea?" Sonja said softly.

Bea turned. "Hello, girls." She motioned them over. "This is my boyfriend I was telling you about. He's been dying to meet you. He funds the Schools for the Gifted, you know."

It was the Richer from the audience.

His face was gaunt, with deep shadows in the hollows of his cheeks. A long scar ran alongside his eye like a tear. He took off his hat and bowed his head. His black hair was slicked and stiff. "I had the pleasure of seeing you two at the auditions today. That was a tip-top performance!"

"Don't just stand there," said Bea. "Say hello."

"Hello," Charlotte mumbled.

Something brushed against Sonja's ankle. All the hairs on her body stood on end. The white cat looked up at her with fiery orange eyes.

"This is Chestnut Sabine." As the Richer introduced her, the cat snarled up at Sonja and showed off her jagged little teeth.

"We've already met," Sonja said, taking a careful step back. "Tatty's waiting for us. Nice to have met you, Mr.—"

"Von Stralen," the man said smoothly. "Kats von Stralen."

Sonja and Charlotte stumbled away.

Charlotte looked back over her shoulder. Finally, she asked, "Do you think he could get us places in school? He seemed to like our act."

"Are you nuts? I wouldn't go anywhere with that man. He's scary—and so is his cat."

"I guess so. Still."

They reached their caravan. Sonja pulled Charlotte closer and whispered, "When Tatty gets home, don't tell her about us being chased. We don't want her to worry."

"It wasn't an Enforcer."

"I know."

"Who was it, then?"

Sonja shrugged. She had an odd feeling.

Tonight, she would bolt the door.

Chapter Nine

Chestnut Sabine

THE CLOCK STRUCK MIDNIGHT, AND THE CUCKOO POPPED out of its hole and squawked. With the clowns' help, Tatty had put the caravan back in order. The nearly-completed Tiffin puppet lay on the table next to Charlotte's latest musical composition: "Ode to Jack Cross, A Talented Boy."

On one end of the bed, the twins murmured to each other in their sleep. On the other end, Tatty snored loudly with Monkey curled into a ball wheezing beside her.

The trapdoor slowly lifted.

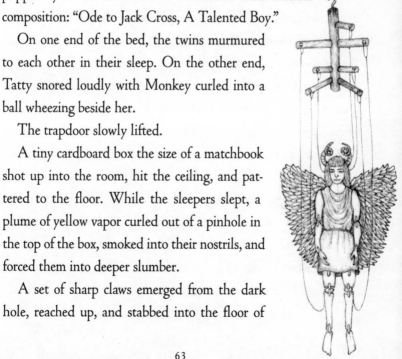

A tiny cardboard box the size of a matchbook shot up into the room, hit the ceiling, and pattered to the floor. While the sleepers slept, a plume of yellow vapor curled out of a pinhole in the top of the box, smoked into their nostrils, and forced them into deeper slumber.

A set of sharp claws emerged from the dark hole, reached up, and stabbed into the floor of the caravan. Two orange eyes peered over the edge to survey the room. All clear, thought Chestnut Sabine. She squeezed inside. She shook her white coat, spraying mud and dirt across the floor, and wiped her whiskers clean. Two small, empty glass balls dangled from her collar.

Chestnut Sabine wiped her lips with her scratchy tongue. She could still smell the salmon on her breath, and a wave of pleasure came over her as she remembered piercing the fish's eyes with her claws and slicing its cool flesh with her teeth. She climbed a stack of books pushed up against the bed and leapt onto the end where Charlotte and Sonja were sleeping. She waited a breath to see if anyone moved, then crouched over Sonja and began to lick her ear.

After a moment, Sonja's nose began to twitch. Chestnut Sabine placed her mouth on Sonja's ear and took a deep breath. Sonja gasped in her sleep. The cat sucked harder. Sonja's chest heaved up and down, her heart pounded, and finally, a glittering substance slithered out of her ear.

Chestnut Sabine caught it on her tongue, licked it into the first glass ball, and flipped the stopper shut with her snout. The gold matter danced and darted, trying to find its way out. Chestnut Sabine's eyes lit up in the glow. One more to go, she thought. She crept across to Charlotte and set to work again.

Tatty's groggy eyes opened. She clutched her head, spinning from the drug, and rolled over. She saw Chestnut Sabine hunched over Charlotte, sucking on her ear. She bolted upright, horrified.

She gasped and lunged.

Chestnut Sabine snapped her claws and scratched Tatty's face.

Tatty screamed and fell backward. Blood filled the marks slashed across her cheek.

Mr. Fortune Teller pounded on the door, shouting, "Tatty! Girls! Open up!"

Tatty fumbled for the door and opened it.

The old man flew in. He saw Chestnut Sabine take one last inhale from Charlotte's ear and slurp the glittering substance into her mouth.

Too late! thought Mr. Fortune Teller. The cat already had them.

The old man stumbled across the room as Chestnut Sabine sprang away and spat the matter into the second glass ball. He swung his cane, blasting it through the table, but the cat was too quick. She jumped between his legs and disappeared through the trapdoor. Adios, old man, thought Chestnut Sabine as she raced off into the night.

"Catch that cat! Don't let it get away!" Mr. Fortune Teller ran from the caravan.

"What's happening?" Sonja asked, rubbing her eyes and sitting up. She touched her ear. "Yuck! Monkey's been licking me again. I hate it when he sleeps with us."

"Charlotte! Wake up!" Tatty shouted as she threw on her robe and lit a candle.

Charlotte opened her eyes. "My chest hurts," she coughed.

"Let's go!" Tatty tore off the sheets and pulled the girls to their feet. "We have to help Uncle Tell!"

"Help Uncle Tell with what?" asked Sonja.

Tatty looked confused. She said simply, "Find a cat."

The twins looked at each other. They grabbed their jackets as Tatty hurried them out the door. It was cold and dark. Voices shouted from Bea's caravan. There was someone standing on the roof. Mr. Fortune Teller's lantern shone on him like a spotlight. It was Kats von Stralen with Chestnut Sabine in his arms. The balls around the cat's neck glowed brightly. She purred smugly.

"Give back the Talents, and we'll let you go!" yelled the old man.

Kats von Stralen giggled. "Let me go?" He took a snort from a diamond-encrusted snuffbox. "I'm already gone."

"You better get down here, you creep!" Tatty hollered.

Kats von Stralen's black eyes widened. A grin spread across his face. "I caught your act. Fascinating what a woman can do with fire." He flicked his gaze to the front of her robe, which was partly open. "I do admire your tattoos," he said, almost in a trance. "The Seven Edens, no doubt."

Tatty whipped her robe closed, then slammed her hands against the side of the caravan, rocking it with a violent jolt. The caravan door burst open below.

"What's all the commotion?" Bea shouted, looking up. "Kats? Are you up there?"

"Sorry, my bearded beauty, but I have to dash." Kats von Stralen pulled out a little vial from his pocket. "A little souvenir from the city." He smashed the vial on the roof, releasing billows of white smoke. It turned the air all around them into a thick, deep fog. Then they heard a thump on the ground and the sound of footsteps running away.

Mr. Fortune Teller tried to follow the sound, searching in the white cloud. If Kats von Stralen escapes, he thought, we are in deep trouble. He saw a pearly white grin through the haze. Headlights flashed. A vehicle sped away.

"I knew you'd ruin the first good thing that's ever happened to me!" Bea yelled. She glared at the old man.

"Calm down, Bea," Tatty said, climbing the caravan steps.

Bea waved her arms in front of her. "Don't come near me!"

"That man's dangerous, Beatrice," warned Mr. Fortune Teller. "He's hurt the girls."

"How could he? He was with me all night."

"With his cat."

"That's ridiculous."

"Promise me that if he tries to contact you, you'll tell me immediately."

"I'm done listening to you!" Bea's face reddened. "All of you!" She stormed into her caravan and slammed the door behind her.

Tatty led the girls back to their caravan. Mr. Fortune Teller followed, lost in thought over what to do next. We must contact Alexandria, he thought. It was the only way to find Kats von Stralen.

Charlotte broke the silence. "The cat hurt us? What did you mean?"

The old man took out his handkerchief and wiped his brow. He would have to explain everything to them. Well, maybe not everything. "This might be hard to understand," he said, stuffing the handkerchief back into his jacket pocket. Through his visions, Mr.

Fortune Teller had been studying Kats von Stralen's movements for months. But it was only days earlier that he had realized what the man was doing with all those cats.

"What happened," he began slowly, "is the cat stole your magic."

He watched the twins closely. The old man expected their bewildered looks—but what came next surprised him: they seemed happy.

"Good riddance!" exclaimed Sonja.

"That's the best news we've heard in ages," said Charlotte.

"With your magic," interrupted the old man, "went your Talents."

"Our—Talents?" repeated Sonja, confused.

"You no longer have the abilities you once did."

Now he had their attention. Ever since his sight had started to decline, Mr. Fortune Teller's other senses had heightened. Standing with the girls in the cool night air, he could hear their pounding hearts. He could smell their growing anxiety.

"You mean, our music?" Charlotte finally said.

His "yes" was so soft, he knew the girls could barely hear it.

"That's impossible!" Sonja hurried inside and grabbed her recorder off the table. She clicked it against her teeth and blew.

It screeched. It croaked. It whined like an animal—but it was not music. Her fingers tangled up as the jarring noises rang out. "What's happening?" She started to panic. She tossed the recorder aside and reached for her pennywhistle. Spit sprayed everywhere as angry notes piped in a row—but it was not a tune.

Sonja wheeled around to Charlotte. "Play something!"

Charlotte strapped her accordion over her shoulders. She stretched the bellows. The instrument groaned and wheezed. She looked down at her hands as she attempted to play. Her fingers fumbled and stumbled across the keys. It was pure cacophony. She stopped. "I can't play," she said softly. "I don't know how."

Mr. Fortune Teller shook his head sadly. He could feel their despair. It soaked into his old bones and made them ache.

"Oh, girls." Tatty hugged them close.

Sonja pulled away. She blew into her pennywhistle again. More noises screeched. She shook her head, her eyes tearing. "I'm never going to be like Kanazi Kooks." Mr. Fortune Teller put his hand on her shoulder and said, "Sit down." Sonja slumped into a chair. "All of you. Sit."

Mr. Fortune Teller positioned his chair in front of them. He took out two newspaper clippings from his jacket pocket and handed them to Charlotte. He had been collecting the articles as proof of his visions. "Please, read these out loud."

"'Cats Gone Astray,'" Charlotte started in a trembling voice. Her hands shook, rustling the paper: "'Authorities confirm hundreds of cats have run away from their owners' homes. Cats are the only legal pets allowed in the cities since the passage of the Proclamation Against the Animals. Enforcers have been urged to solve this mystery because the children of many important people will be spending their nights alone.'"

Sonja frowned. "Lost pets? What's that got to do with anything?"

"Be quiet and listen," ordered the old man. "Go on, Charlotte. Read the next one."

Charlotte held up the second clipping and cleared her throat. "'One of a chain of prominent Schools for the Gifted has temporarily closed down. The general administrator, Mistress Koch, said in a statement today that the children, quote, appeared to have lost their Talents, end quote. Auditions to re-pupil the school are already in progress.'"

Charlotte hesitated. The old man pressed her: "Finish it."

"'A peculiar footnote: witnesses report they have observed numerous cats entering and exiting the aforementioned establishment regularly during recent weeks.'"

Charlotte stopped reading. "What does this all mean?"

"Kats von Stralen is stealing children's Talents to extract the magic from them. He's found a way to detach a Talent from a child's heart before the two become one—using the *Felis catus*." The old man shook his head. "I saw him coming, and I still couldn't stop him."

Charlotte's head started spinning. "I've got to warn Jack Cross," she said. "He mustn't go to that school!" She leapt to her feet and burst out the caravan door.

"Wait!" Sonja shouted after her. "Charlotte!"

Charlotte did not stop. "I have to save him!" she yelled back as she disappeared into the night, her jacket flapping behind her.

Mr. Fortune Teller covered his face with his weathered hands. He remembered the dreadful night when the twins had been taken away from their mother. They had not stopped crying for days. Since then, he had always tried to shield them from pain. Now there was no helping it. They would have to suffer no matter what he did.

Chapter Ten

The Train Graveyard

Charlotte ran through the gate and zigzagged among the broken-down railcars. She tried to remember pieces of music she used to play, but they all blended together in a tangle of notes. The smell of frying, canned meat stank in the alleyways. Hanging wires and cables crisscrossed in a tangled mess overhead. The sound of a television blasted from one of the windows.

A pair of drunks swayed arm in arm, singing. Their eyes looked bloodshot in the dark. One yelled, "Hey, girlie! Give us a coin!"

Charlotte's heart raced as she squeezed past them. She had never been out alone at night. She quickly scanned the numbers on the cars. She stopped in front of one. A metal "717" hung from a nail on the door. It was the compartment Jack Cross had said was his home.

Charlotte hurried up the stoop and tripped over a pile of empty bottles. They clinked and clanked and rolled into the street. A dog howled. An old woman in a pink hairnet stuck her head out of the train car opposite and shouted, "Scram, Scrummagers!"

Charlotte stared at the door. What if he didn't want to see her?

What if he wouldn't believe her? She could not worry about all that now—his Talent was at stake. Charlotte took a deep breath in and knocked.

Nobody answered.

She knocked louder.

Footsteps shuffled inside.

"Who's there?" a voice shouted.

"I need to see Jack Cross!" Charlotte yelled back.

"You a Scrummager?"

"No. I'm a—I'm a friend."

The door finally opened to reveal a haggard woman holding a crying baby. Four dirty children stood behind her, rubbing their sleepy eyes.

"Do you know what time it is? You'll wake the whole neighborhood with your banging!"

"I need to see Jack Cross. It's urgent."

"Jack don't live here no more." The woman bounced the baby up and down. "He left to that school in Rain City. Got a scholarship."

"Are you sure?" pressed Charlotte.

"Of course I'm sure! He's been gone near three hours now." Mrs. Cross shook her head. "Took off and left me with these little blighters," she muttered. "Just like his father."

"It's too late," Charlotte murmured. She covered her face and sat down on the steps. "They'll do it to him, too."

Charlotte heard footsteps rapidly approaching. She looked up, bleary eyed, and saw Tatty and Sonja. "He's gone," she moaned. "He's gone."

Tatty dropped down next to her. "Uncle Tell's going to find your Talents. He'll help Jack Cross, too."

Charlotte blinked. "You really think so?"

Tatty wiped Charlotte's eyes with the hem of her robe. "I'm sure of it."

Tatty was right. If anyone could get their Talents back, thought Charlotte, Uncle Tell could.

A light flashed above them, and a man yelled from his window, "Get out of here, you circus freaks!"

The old woman in the pink hairnet now stood at her front door holding a yapping poodle. "We don't want none of that hocus-pocus!"

"You'd better be goin'," warned Mrs. Cross. "Before someone calls them Enforcers."

"I'm sorry, ma'am," apologized Tatty, helping Charlotte stand. "It seems my daughter's grown attached to your son."

The woman's face softened just a touch. "Wait." She shouted at the children to be quiet as she went back into the train car. She returned with a little package wrapped in a crumpled piece of paper. "Here." Mrs. Cross gave it to Charlotte.

The door closed firmly just as the trembling girl said, "Thank you—"

Charlotte unfolded the paper. Inside was Jack Cross' musical note pin. He had left it for her. He still wanted to be friends—even after he had seen her performance. She flattened the scrap of paper and read:

Dear Charlotte,

I'm sorry I couldn't say goodbye. Please write to the address below. Enclosed is my most prized possession after my violin in the hopes that you'll try to return it to me one day in person.

With deep respect, Jack.

Charlotte pressed the letter against her chest and let out a soft cry. If only her Talent had not been stolen. If only he was not going away to school. If only they had met before. She clipped the pin to her jacket and stuffed the letter into her pocket. She would have to act fast if she wanted to help him. She would write to him tonight.

Dark clouds thickened over the Outskirts, and fat drops began to fall. Suddenly, the rain came down hard.

"We'd better get out of here," said Tatty. She sheltered the girls under her robe and they retraced their steps to the circus.

Once they reached the caravan, Charlotte burst inside and rummaged for a scrap of paper. She wrote in a frenzy while Sonja stared blankly at the musical instruments lying on the table.

Tatty put her hand on Sonja's shoulder. "You'll feel better in the morning."

"How's that possible?" Sonja said flatly. It was the first time she had spoken in hours. Her fingers twitched restlessly.

Tatty sighed. "I don't know. But I can tell you one way to lose for sure: give up." She pulled Sonja out of the chair and led her to bed. Charlotte followed them, pressing a licked stamp onto an envelope. She might still be able to save Jack Cross, she thought. She hoped she could. She never wanted him to feel as empty as she did now, without her Talent.

Tatty pulled off their wet clothes and wrapped warm towels around them. She gave them each a clean pair of pajamas and a mug of hot water.

Monkey was still asleep. The events of the night had not disturbed him in the slightest. The twins got under the covers. The caravan jerked forward, and the convoy began to make its way onto the road.

"Where are we going?" asked Charlotte. She tucked the letter under her pillow. "I need to post this immediately."

"To visit Alexandria and Arthur." Tatty sat on the edge of the bed beside the twins.

Sonja frowned. "I don't think this is a good time to be making social calls."

"Uncle Tell believes Alexandria can help us find your Talents."

"How did our lives change so much in such a short time?" said Sonja. "I was happy the way things were."

"Sometimes change can feel unbearable." Tatty stroked her hair. "When I joined the circus, I cried every night. Everything was strange and scary—but think of it: if I had stayed where I was, I wouldn't have found you, my darlings, the light of my life."

Tatty kissed their heads.

"Anyway," she said, blowing out a candle, "it might be good to be ordinary girls for a while."

Maybe, thought Charlotte. If we find Jack Cross.

Chapter Eleven

Arthur Bloodsworth

THE CARAVAN STOPPED WITH A JOLT. THE HANGING marionettes rattled in the rafters. Sonja's eyes snapped open. Her chest ached, and her ears rang. The sun blasted through the dusty windows. She felt uneasy—and then she remembered what had happened. Sonja groaned and turned over. How were they ever going to face the day?

"Finally!" a voice squawked. She looked up. A scarlet parrot was perched on the bedstead staring at them.

"It talks!" yelped Charlotte, sitting up.

Sonja rubbed her eyes. Was she still dreaming?

"Of course, it talks," snapped the bird. "What's wrong with these girls?"

Sonja frowned. Whether she was dreaming or not, she had no tolerance for impoliteness. Even from an imaginary bird.

"Tatty," Charlotte said hesitantly, "what's going on?"

"Dottie's Alexandria's bird," explained Tatty. Monkey watched from her shoulder and sucked on a piece of stale popcorn. "I was just introduced myself."

Dottie ruffled her feathers, annoyed. "All parrots can talk. Well, the smart ones anyway." She looked from one twin to the other. "They're a little small for their age. What've you been feeding them?"

"Mostly pancakes," said Tatty.

"No wonder. Well, you girls better get dressed. The old man went ahead. He wants you to follow him."

Sonja groaned. "How could this get any worse? Not only do we have to see Alexandria, but now we're taking orders from a talking bird."

Charlotte stroked Dottie's feathered head. "You're so colorful," she said dreamily.

The parrot shifted from one claw to the other uncomfortably. "If you wouldn't mind: don't pet me. It rubs me the wrong way." Dottie turned to Sonja. "As for you, you don't need to worry about seeing Alexandria. She's not here. She left Arthur again. I'm babysitting him, of course. He can't take care of himself."

Sonja slunk out of bed, slouching. She looked out the window and pressed her face against the glass. They had parked in the middle of a field of yellowy grass and withered trees. The twins had made up a name for the few, rare plots of dying land dotted here and there across the Outskirts. A Lonely Patch. Sonja imagined her insides looked exactly like this dreary landscape.

Charlotte handed Sonja the locket. "It's your day to wear it. It might bring you luck."

"I doubt it," grumbled Sonja. Nothing mattered to her without her music. To her, it was her whole identity and, somehow, the link to their past.

The bird eyed the locket as Sonja clasped it around her neck. "Come on," she chirped. "We don't have all day."

"You girls better eat before you go." Tatty set down a plate of pancakes. She had a bandage taped across her cheek where Chestnut Sabine had scratched her face.

Charlotte smothered raspberry jam onto a pancake and folded it in half.

"What about you, Sonja?" asked Tatty.

"I'm not hungry. I'm too depressed." She put on her jacket over her pajamas and stuck her bare feet into a pair of boots. What was life without music anyway? An infinity of silence? Her fingers had not stopped twitching since she had lost her Talent. They missed playing music, too.

"Aren't you at least going to change your outfit?" asked Tatty. "Look at your sister."

Charlotte was already dressed in a pink flower-printed skirt with a blue ribbon tied in her hair. She had polished her shoes until they were shiny. It was just like Charlotte to try to see the bright side of things, thought Sonja. Well, not me. "I'd rather wear pajamas," she muttered.

Charlotte stuffed the letter to Jack Cross into her pocket, and the twins followed the parrot out the door.

The other circus members were getting on with their day. The Fat Lady was hanging a dress out to dry (which any other three people could fit into at the same time), the Snake Charmer was taking Alfonso for a slither through the grass while doing her daily exercises, and Pershing was helping the clowns set up the circus ring with the Miniature Woman on his shoulders. Sonja felt a pang of jealousy. Nothing had changed for the other circus members—but everything had for her and her sister.

Dottie flew a little ahead of the girls as they walked through the field. Most of the trees had been cut down to short stumps. The few that still stood had dry, brittle bark, and their leaves were laced with little holes.

"Used to be an orchard here," remarked Dottie. Sonja kicked away rotten apples scattered along their path. "It'll all be gone soon enough." Sonja knew that what the parrot said was true. The cities were growing bigger and bigger, and eventually, there would not be any land left between them.

They reached a cluster of tents pitched on the edge of Block City's Outskirts. Families huddled, picking at dinner scraps. Loitering men smoked cigarettes. A rat nosed through the rubbish. Sonja watched Charlotte mutter a little prayer before she popped her letter to Jack Cross into the slot of a rusty mailbox.

Charlotte turned to her, eager. "Do you think it'll get there in time?"

It was Sonja's experience that a high percentage of mailed letters were never delivered at all. She had written Kanazi Kooks five letters and had never gotten a reply. She did not want to dash her sister's only hope. She took Charlotte's hand and said, "I'm almost sure of it."

Her sister grinned. "That's what I thought."

They arrived in front of the door of an old tramcar. Dottie landed on Sonja's shoulder. "Don't tell Arthur anything that's happened."

"How come?" asked Charlotte.

"He hasn't left his home in years. He'll worry."

Dottie rapped on the door with her beak. A light in the keyhole darkened. Bolts unlocked, and the door jerked open to the length of the chain. A large man wearing thick glasses peeked through the gap. It had been years since she had seen him, but Sonja recognized Arthur right away by his unkempt beard and shy smile. He peered down at the twins and pointed to Charlotte. "You must be Charlotte." She nodded happily. "And you're Sonja."

Sonja looked at him with slight surprise. Other than the circus members, nobody could tell them apart.

"Aren't you going to let us in, Arthur?" croaked Dottie.

Arthur hunched his broad shoulders and patted down his long, matted hair. He released the chain and opened the door. Bits of

food were caught in his beard. His glasses were covered with smudges. He wore a ratty old robe, and his toes poked out through holes in his socks at the tips of his sandals. "The old man's already here," he said.

Mr. Fortune Teller sat in an armchair in the middle of the cluttered room. "Hello, girls," he said. "We were just talking about you." Dottie fluttered off Sonja's shoulder and landed on the back of the armchair.

Arthur opened the refrigerator and took out two cans labeled *Fruity Fizz*. He gave them to the twins. They popped the tops and drank big gulps. It tingled in their mouths.

"Good, huh?" Arthur said.

The twins nodded and walked around, exploring. It had grown more chaotic since the last time they had visited, thought Sonja. Boards were nailed over the windows. Broken fluorescent tubes hung from the ceiling. The small greenhouses and terrariums along the walls overflowed with wiry plants. A shaggy sheep slept on a dirty sofa, a spotted pig ate from leftover cans and tins, and a hunch-backed turtle roamed freely through the tramcar. Sonja knelt down and petted the snorting pig. "Hello, Ahab," she said. Even the pig looked a little the worse for wear.

"How've you been, Arthur?" Mr. Fortune Teller asked.

"Busy, busy. I need new specimens, but I'm making progress."

Sonja's eyes drifted from a battered microscope to a blackboard crammed with tiny equations to a table of burners, beakers, and strange-colored liquids. "What kind of scientist are you?" she said, looking up. She had never thought to ask before.

"A discoverist." Arthur pushed back his glasses. "I study ancient plant species and other life forms to find clues about how the world began. Want to see something?" He led the twins over to a black machine with a slot in the center and a small screen above it. "This can date any specimen's birth. Even one that's thousands of years old."

Arthur took out a large slide from a box. It contained a leaf pressed between two plates of glass. He put it into the machine's slot. Lights flashed on and off, a bell sounded, and a number flashed across the screen.

"Two thousand nine-hundred and thirty-six," read Charlotte. "It's nearly three thousand years old!"

Arthur nodded enthusiastically.

"Can we try another?" asked Sonja.

"Of course," Arthur said, pleased. He gave them the box of slides and a black pen. "You can help me by marking the date on each one."

Mr. Fortune Teller walked over to the machine and squinted at a label printed on the side. "What does it say?" he asked the girls.

"'United Cities Laboratories,'" said Charlotte.

The old man frowned and turned to Arthur. "Where'd you get it?"

Arthur fiddled with the insides of his cardigan pockets.

"You know you're not supposed to share your findings with any-one from the cities. We've already been through all this. That's why we moved you here."

"Don't worry, old man. I didn't get it from any city. Some Scrummagers sold it to me." Arthur picked up the turtle crawling over his slipper and stroked its underside. "Why'd you come here, Hieronymus? To interrogate me?"

"In fact, we came to see Alexandria. Where is she?"

Arthur shrugged. "She took off again. Left everything. Even that." He gestured to a purple stone standing in an antique stand.

Sonja recognized it. She remembered finding an identical stone hidden in a box in a drawer in Mr. Fortune Teller's desk. They never asked him about it because he would have known they were stealing candy. "What is it?" she asked, stroking its glassy surface.

Arthur was about to reply when Mr. Fortune Teller interrupted, "Dottie, any idea where Alexandria's got to?"

"Plenty of ideas," huffed the parrot.

"What's wrong?" Arthur said, straightening his glasses.

"Nothing, nothing. I just need a word with her."

"I'll find her," said Dottie. "Anyway, it'll get me out of babysitting Arthur." She hopped to the sill. Arthur loosened a plank of wood and opened the window. "Don't do anything stupid while I'm gone," she warned before flying off. The twins watched her soar farther and farther away until she disappeared into the horizon.

Arthur rubbed his forehead anxiously and turned to Mr. Fortune Teller. "Can you get me more samples?" He paused and looked uneasily at the girls. He lowered his voice: "I'm desperate."

"I'll see what I can do." The old man got up to leave. "We'd better be going now."

"Thanks for the Fizz," Charlotte said, smiling.

Sonja looked at Arthur shyly. She felt strangely sad to leave him. Maybe it was because she knew exactly how he felt. He was looking for something he would probably never find—just like her. Sonja held his hand. "I was happy to see you."

Arthur suddenly burst into tears.

Sonja was startled. She had never seen a grown man cry.

Arthur removed his glasses and wiped his eyes. Sonja glimpsed traces of a handsome face.

"Don't cry," Charlotte said, taking his other hand. "We'll visit you again soon."

Arthur tried to smile. "You're growing up nicely," he said softly.

He led them to the door and closed it behind them without saying another word. The locks latched.

They walked back through the tents toward the circus.

"Why'd he start crying?" asked Sonja.

"He's lonely, I suppose," said Mr. Fortune Teller.

"I bet it's because Alexandria left him." Charlotte paused for a moment and asked, "Why did she?"

"He's a hermit. He's obsessed with his work. He lives in a pigsty."

Sonja frowned. The twins had known Mr. Fortune Teller's cousin, Alexandria, all their lives, even though they had only met her a dozen times—but it was always the same, every visit: trouble. Alexandria was always making somebody unhappy. "Why'd she marry him in the first place?"

"I guess she loved him."

They heard shouting up ahead. "Uncle Tell! Girls!"

Bea was running toward them in a fake fur coat and a hat with a veil. When she finally reached them, she was completely out of breath.

She sputtered, "He—contacted—me!"

"Hold on, Bea," Mr. Fortune Teller said. "Take your time."

Bea lifted off the veil and dabbed her beard with a handkerchief. "This morning I took a walk to clear my mind. The white cat ran up to me with this in her mouth." Bea handed the old man a folded letter and a small map.

"Read it," Mr. Fortune Teller ordered, giving the letter to Sonja. The smell of cologne pricked her nostrils. The letters on the page looked like arrows and darts and daggers that might leap off the page and pierce her eyes. She forced herself to focus on the words and read out loud in a shaky voice: "'My gorgeous darling, I must see you again. Meet me at six o'clock at the X on the map. Kats.'"

The old man put the letter and map into his pocket and broke into a fast stride. "You're going to meet him," he said. Bea and the girls hurried to keep up.

"I am?" Bea said in a faltering voice. "I thought you told me—"

"I'm secretly coming with you."

Sonja's heart began to pound. Her fingers twitched. Mr. Fortune Teller looked at the twins out of the corners of his eyes.

"Girls," he said as they walked briskly through the tall grass, "I'm going to get your Talents back."

It was more than just their Talents, thought Sonja. It was everything.

Chapter Twelve

The Last Performance

Charlotte stared glumly out of the open window. The sun was setting, and the world outside was dim. She traced the outline of the musical note pinned to her sweater. She wondered if Jack Cross was thinking of her, too. She wondered if he was safe and if her letter would reach him in time.

Sonja sat beside her sister looking just as glum. They wore matching blue dresses covered in moons and stars—old costumes for their act. "Uncle Tell's been gone forever," sighed Sonja. "Where is he?"

"He'll be back," said Tatty without looking up. She kept Monkey distracted with a smushed caramel while she combed his matted fur.

A giant face suddenly popped up smack in front of them outside the window. The girls jumped back.

"Thank goodness you're here!" Pershing said, out of breath. "Hurry, Tatty. The seats are filling up, and there's nobody to perform."

"The girls aren't feeling well. I can't leave them."

"Come on, Tatty," Pershing begged.

"It's no use, Pershing. I'm not coming."

"Where are Bea and Mr. Fortune Teller?"

"I don't know," Tatty lied.

"The old man's killing me. He made us leave last night after only a few performances. He's got the clowns guarding and patrolling all over camp, and now I've lost half my acts." Pershing took a handful of pills from his pocket and threw them into his mouth. "For my ulcer. Water, please."

Charlotte filled a glass for Pershing. She watched his big Adam's apple bob up and down as he gulped. She remembered riding on his shoulders as a child. She always imagined that she was on top of a moving mountain.

"Tomorrow," Pershing threatened, "we're having a meeting with the old man. I can't run a circus like this. It just won't do."

"Well, we'll see about that tomorrow, then." Tatty closed the window and drew the curtains.

They could hear music playing from the circus ring and the faint sound of an audience cheering.

Sonja flopped into a chair and picked up the finished Tiffin marionette. She lifted and lowered its wings. The little fabric feathers fluttered. "I hate this. I want to perform."

"Me, too," said Charlotte. She ran her fingers up and down the imaginary keys of an imaginary piano. They felt stiff and clumsy. In just a day, all the music Charlotte had ever learned was forgotten. Notes and rhythms were now a foreign language to her. She could no longer call herself a musician. She groaned. "I don't even know how to play when I'm *pretending* to play."

"It's hopeless," muttered Sonja, dropping her own hands from a nonexistent flute. "My fingers won't stop shaking. They're having some kind of withdrawal or something."

Charlotte looked at her accordion hanging from the wall. A layer of dust had collected on top of it. She felt as if it was an old friend she had deserted. She walked over to it and wiped off the dust with the back of her hand. She imagined all the instruments of all the children whose Talents had been stolen buried under mounds of dust—like banks of snow.

Tatty wrapped Monkey into a baby's blanket and tucked him into an open drawer. She propped up one of her legs on a chair and started painting her toenails red. Charlotte picked up the magnifying glass and studied the tattoos on Tatty's calf: a group of pale, slender figures swimming in a golden grotto. "We always have our marionette show," she said. She started to sing. (Her voice had been a little off-key ever since her Talent had been stolen.)

> *Deep, deep underground,*
> *In grottos of golden décor,*
> *Lives a white Alban among the giant boars.*
> *His eyes see in pitch-dark blackness—*
> *And his ears can hear even a mouse snore.*

A little sack fell out of the pocket of Tatty's robe onto the floor. Charlotte picked it up. "What's this?"

Tatty looked uneasy. "Give it back to me."

Charlotte shook out Mr. Fortune Teller's tortoiseshell pendant from the velvet pouch. It was warm to the touch. "I've never seen him take it off," she said, studying its brownish-gold ridges with the magnifying glass.

Tatty hesitated. "Uncle Tell won't want you playing with it. Give it back."

Charlotte ignored her. "There's writing on it." She squinted and read the tiny letters inscribed onto the shell: "'Protector of the Vanishing Islands.'" Charlotte looked up. "That's one of the Seven Edens."

"Give it back," insisted Tatty.

"Wait. I want to see." Sonja snatched the magnifying glass. After a moment, she said, "Is this some kind of joke?"

"Give it back!" Tatty dove on the girls and snatched the pendant out of their hands. The second her fingers touched the shell, something happened.

Her skin began to glow.

"Oh, no," muttered Tatty.

Sonja screamed. Charlotte stumbled backward. Right before their eyes, the tattoos sprang to life: animals leapt through ancient trees, birds soared between billowing clouds, giant flowers opened their petals.

Charlotte stared with her mouth open. The light from Tatty's skin flickered on her face and danced in her eyes. Soon, the pictures transformed. Images of other places appeared. Some Charlotte recognized. A map was taking shape.

After a moment, Tatty's knees buckled. She dropped to the floor. The pendant rolled out of her hand, the tattoos snapped back to their original shapes, and the glowing light went out.

Sonja rushed over to Tatty and knelt down beside her. She touched her forehead. "Get the brandy," she ordered Charlotte. Tatty used to prescribe Bea with a teaspoonful of brandy whenever she had one of her fainting spells. Charlotte hurried to the kitchen. Her mind was spinning with the images she had seen. She snatched an old bottle in her trembling hands. She rushed back to Tatty and clumsily tipped the ruby-colored liquid into her mouth.

Tatty's eyes flashed open. "What happened?"

"You grabbed Uncle Tell's pendant, and your tattoos—well, they exploded!" explained Sonja. Her eyes widened. "It was unbelievable!"

Charlotte helped Tatty sit up. Her skin was hot and clammy. "I never wanted you to see that without me explaining first," Tatty said.

"Is it—magic?" Charlotte said hesitantly.

"Not exactly. Not mine. It was given to me by the Great Tiffin when I was chosen to be the Key."

The Great Tiffin? The Key? Maybe Tatty had not recovered from the fall.

Before Charlotte could ask if she was okay, there was a knock at the door and a boy's voice calling, "I's gotta special package for one Tabitha Tatters! Choc-o-lates, looks like. Won'ts want to be missin' those."

Charlotte hurried to the window and peered under the curtains:

she saw a grinning, chubby, ginger-haired boy with freckles. Three other boys huddled in the shadows behind him. "Scrummagers," said Charlotte. "Strange ones. Well dressed!"

"I's a-guessin' you don'ts want 'em choc-o-lates!" yelled the boy. Boots stomped down the steps. "I'lls be a-goin' now!"

"Away from the window." Charlotte watched as Tatty picked up the tortoiseshell by its chain, careful not to touch the pendant itself, and blew out the candles. She pulled the twins under the table. "We're going to wait here until Uncle Tell comes home."

"I'm not scared of a bunch of little—" Sonja stopped mid-sentence. Something hit the roof with a loud thump.

There was a short silence, then a second thump. Then a third and a fourth and a fifth, followed by a frenzied, scuttling commotion. Monkey leapt out of a dresser drawer and bounded toward them.

"What's going on up there?" cried Charlotte.

"No reason to panic yet," Tatty said calmly.

"I disagree!" Sonja pointed up past the edge of the table. Yellow beaks began poking holes rapid-fire through the ceiling. Splinters flew. The marionettes fell.

"We's a-got you surrounded, lil' ducklin's." The boy now spoke through a loudspeaker. "Gives yerselves up, or we's be huffin' and puffin' yer house down!"

"I don't understand!" shouted Charlotte. "What do they want?"

Tatty scrambled out from under the table with Monkey clutched to her neck. She yanked aside the dish towels and looked out the window. A barrage of burning arrows flew at them through the air and walloped into the side of the caravan. The walls caught fire. Smoke began to fill the room.

"They're going to burn us alive!" Sonja screamed.

"Come on!" Tatty pulled the twins out from under the table. She fastened the silver chain around Charlotte's neck and dropped the tortoiseshell pendant under her collar. "Don't say a word about this to anyone *ever*!" She flung open the bookcase and kicked open the door. "Let's go!" They jumped out and raced through the grass. They stopped at a cluster of trees and looked back.

A massive flock of white swans was scrambling around on the roof, darting their snake-like necks into the caravan. One bashed through and went inside, banging and squawking.

Charlotte stared, dumbstruck. She had never seen a swan before. Were they always this aggressive or was this just a mean flock?

Monkey shivered and tightened his hold around Tatty's neck as they crept in the darkness from one withered tree to the next.

The swans took off and circled above, sweeping shadows across the ground. They scanned the landscape with beady black eyes. One let out a piercing cry. He had spotted them in the trees.

"They's a-gettin' away!" a Scrummager hollered, pointing.

The boy with the loudspeaker shouted, "Archers! Fire!"

Scrummagers wearing pig masks tilted up their bows and let loose their arrows. Tatty yanked the twins behind a tree stump just as the barrage showered the ground around them.

Two snarling white animals were led into view. Bristling fur stuck up along their spines, and their mouths were crammed with massive teeth. "Release 'em beasts!" roared the boy.

Sonja gulped. "What are those?" she asked in a shaky voice.

"I think—they're—hyenas," Charlotte struggled, squinting and confused.

"Sniffs 'em ducklin's out!"

A boy unhooked the animals' leashes. They bounded toward Tatty and the twins, gnashing their teeth and tittering hysterically.

"Run, run, run!" yelled Tatty, jumping up. Monkey dangled from her neck.

They sprinted between the darkened caravans, hearts racing. Charlotte tripped on her shoelace and tumbled to the ground. She looked back over her shoulder. The hyenas were closing in fast. Drool dripped down their bloodstained chins.

Tatty yanked her up. "Keep going!" she ordered. "I'll distract them!"

"No!" wailed Sonja, grabbing her arm. "Come with us!"

Tatty gave Sonja a hard shove. "Do as I say! Go find help!"

Charlotte pulled her sister, and they kept running. Charlotte's head pounded. Her vision blurred. She felt like the whole earth beneath her feet was breaking apart. She wanted to look back, but she was too scared of what she might see.

The big-top tent came into view up ahead. They slammed to a halt and stared, speechless.

It was blazing on fire.

Charlotte watched the terrified audience flood out in every direction. A boy's shouting voice echoed, "Yous beggars people! Yous plagues of the earth! We's a-gonna gets rid of you filth, ones by one!" Well-dressed Scrummagers chased people with clubs and shot burning arrows into the circus stalls. Charlotte saw the Snake Charmer walking in a daze with Alfonso in her arms.

"You have to help us!" begged Charlotte, pushing through the crowd. "Tatty's in danger!"

"He's thirsty," the Snake Charmer said distractedly. "He needs water."

She held the snake's neck in one hand and his tail in the other. He had been bitten in half.

"He's—he's dead," stammered Charlotte. She touched his leathery scales. Poor Alfonso, she thought. Charlotte remembered when he was a young snake: he had been little enough to fit in the palm of her hand.

The shuffling, shouting crowd swept the twins away. They bumped into bodies and tripped over feet. Finally, they fell stumbling onto the ground. Screams erupted all around. Charlotte looked up to see a red-eyed white hyena hurtling toward them. She covered her face just as an ax swung with a whack into the creature's head. It dropped like a stone.

Balthazar yanked a tooth from the hyena's mouth and held it up alongside another tooth. "That's two for me," he boasted, pulling up the bloody ax.

The other two clowns helped Charlotte and Sonja to their feet. "You girls all right?" asked Toulouse.

"Tatty's in trouble," Sonja said in a faltering voice, breathing heavily. "By the caravans."

The circus tent collapsed to the ground. Lightbulbs began to explode as the fire consumed them.

"Let's go find her," rasped Vincent. "I knew doomsday was coming. I just thought I'd live out a few more years before it happened."

"This ain't no doomsday," returned Toulouse. "This is trouble from the cities."

Balthazar roared, "They just can't leave us Outskirters alone!"

They ran past the stalls, now smoldering woodpiles. Circus horses galloped, skittish, through the campsite. Some cowered among the trees. Charlotte spotted a circle of Scrummagers dancing around the Fat Lady, chanting a nursery rhyme and poking at her with a stick. "This lil' piggy went to market! This lil' piggy stayed home!" Her swollen hands covered her face as she cried. Another group of Scrummagers ran past, throwing the Miniature Woman from one boy to the next. She screamed for Pershing, who leapt after them with a rake.

An arrow hit Toulouse hard in the shoulder. He cried out and fell to the ground. More arrows flew. They jabbed into the other two clowns—one in the back, the other in the leg.

"Go on, girls!" implored Balthazar. He staggered to his feet. "We're going to have to teach these city boys a lesson."

The twins ran between the burning caravans. Fires crackled everywhere.

An overturned trash barrel lay on its side with a hyena's white tail sticking out. It was tearing through a pile of scraps.

The girls slowed down and crept by silently.

Charlotte stepped on a blackened twig. It snapped. The hyena whipped its head around. It pulled back its fleshy lips. Meat stuck out between its rotting teeth.

"Go!" shrieked Sonja.

The hyena chased them to Mr. Fortune Teller's caravan. It was the only one left that was not on fire. A lamp flickered inside.

Charlotte's face brightened. It must be Tatty.

Just before they started up the steps, a black limousine with tinted windows pulled up and skidded to a stop. Headlights flooded the area.

The twins turned back. The hyena stood in their path. It cocked its head.

The car door swung open. A man stepped out.

"Kats von Stralen," gasped Charlotte.

Kats von Stralen sniffed a pinch of black powder from his snuff-box. He wiped his nose with his gloved hand. His shoes pressed pointy footprints into the ground.

"I'd love to have a long visit with you, girls, but I've got a school full of very talented children in Rain City I need to attend to."

Charlotte thought about Jack Cross. He would not get her letter in time. He was going to lose his Talent tonight.

CHAPTER THIRTEEN

A White Glove

SONJA PULLED CHARLOTTE TO HER FEET. SHE COULD not believe her sister was crying over a boy at a time like this. The circus was on fire, Tatty was missing, and they were in Kats von Stralen's clutches. He stood over them, grinning. "I'm searching for your mother," he said. "I can't seem to get her out of my mind."

Sonja glared. "We want our Talents back!" she yelled. Her fingers jerked like rusty levers.

"I see you've developed the twitch," observed Kats von Stralen. "It happens to some of the children whose Talents I steal. Interesting phenomenon." He reached into his pocket and took out a little black gadget. "Have you seen one of these before?" Sonja shook her head. "You pull on this shiny lever here, and it fires a delightful iron corkscrew that pierces your skull, makes a complete mess of your brain, then finds its way out the other side and continues on to who-knows-where. It's called a Gatsploder Special. I just acquired it."

Kats von Stralen pressed the barrel against Sonja's forehead. His eyes were two black holes, and his powerful cologne slithered into Sonja's nostrils like poison. Her lips quivered. Sweat dribbled off her nose.

"Now, the last thing I want to do is damage either one of those pretty heads of yours, but if you don't tell me where your mother is, I won't have a dickens of a lot of choice."

"We—we," stammered Sonja, "we were looking for her ourselves."

"I don't care for liars," grunted Kats von Stralen.

Sonja felt her sister grip her arm. "We're not lying!" burst out Charlotte.

Kats von Stralen moved the Gatsploder from Sonja's head to Charlotte's. "Don't force me to insist."

"I swear!" pleaded Charlotte. "We don't know where she is!"

"Please!" Sonja begged. There was a round mark where the tip of the barrel had pressed into her forehead.

In one flick, Kats von Stralen whipped the pistol away from Charlotte's head and pulled the trigger. A wretched squeal broke the silence. Sonja turned to look. The hyena lay dead in the dirt beside her.

"Why's you go and kills our beast?" whined a boy's voice.

"Just a demonstration," replied Kats von Stralen as he recocked his weapon.

A band of Scrummagers all wearing identical black shorts, sweater vests, and bow ties approached. Sonja recognized them. They were the boys who had chased them out of the caravan. They dragged Tatty behind them. There were ropes around her legs and wrists, and bruises all over her face and neck. The bandage across her cheek had been torn off. Chestnut Sabine walked beside them, swinging her frizzy tail from side to side.

"Tatty!" the twins yelled in unison.

Tatty's voice cracked: "Hello, dearies." The girls started toward her. Chestnut Sabine arched her back. Her claws popped out from the ends of her white toes.

Kats von Stralen raised his Gatsploder. "Stop right there."

"Tell those Scrummagers to let her go!" cried Sonja.

"We's ain't Scrummagers no more," snorted the boy with ginger hair and freckles. "We's been adopted."

"You have indeed, Georgie." Kats von Stralen raised an eyebrow. "I see you've located the woman in question."

"Shes was hidin' under one of 'em rollin' homes." The boy pulled Monkey out of a sack. "We's also founds this beastie fors our mother."

"Oh, Monkey," muttered Tatty.

"Not *your* mother," Kats von Stralen said carefully. "*My* mother."

"But she's adopted *us*," shouted a boy with pimples and buckteeth.

"Well, nevertheless, Dirgert, she has but one actual son." Kats von Stralen smiled oddly. "And you're looking at him." He took another snort from his snuffbox.

"Sorry to interrupt," Tatty said, and hesitated. "I think there's been some mistake. You see, I'm nobody special. Just a Tattooed Lady trying to make a few coins."

Kats von Stralen leaned down and sank his nose into Tatty's red hair. "There's something about the poor that excites me." He pulled open the top of her robe. Tatty squirmed against the knots. The twins watched tensely. "The Seven Edens. Tattooed on your skin exactly as our informant told us. Now all we need is one little Amulet, and the source of the magic will be ours."

Sonja saw Charlotte cross her arms awkwardly in front of her chest. Uncle Tell's pendant. Was that an Amulet?

"I'm not who you think I am!" Tatty protested.

Kats von Stralen hefted the pistol in his palm—then whacked Tatty across the face with it.

"No!" shrieked Sonja. Charlotte started sobbing.

"Put her in the car!" barked Kats von Stralen. The boys dragged Tatty toward the limousine. The twins leapt after her and grabbed her by the waist. Kats von Stralen pointed the weapon at Tatty. "Let's not make this any more difficult than it already is."

Sonja looked up at Tatty's face. She had never seen her cry before. It broke her heart—and it scared her.

"I'm sure this misunderstanding will soon be cleared up," Tatty said weakly. "I'll be back before you know it." Her voice faltered. "For now, my dears, you'd better let me go."

Sonja and Charlotte watched, frozen, as the boys threw Tatty through the open door of the car.

"What have we here?" said Kats von Stralen, squinting.

Two figures on horses approached through the haze.

Sonja's eyes lit up. "Help!" she cried out.

"Over here!" yelled Charlotte, waving her arms.

"Well, aren't you little adopted fellows going to do something?" remarked Kats von Stralen.

The Scrummagers notched their arrows and launched them at

the riders—but the arrows stopped short in midair and dropped clattering straight to the ground. The riders charged over the fallen arrows and slid to a stop in front of Kats von Stralen and the children.

Mr. Fortune Teller sat astride his horse, Rhubarb. The old man's hair was frizzy and wild, and his white eyes glowed in the dark. The other rider was perched on a brawny red horse, and she had heaps of long, dark brown hair twisted and piled on top of her head. Her face was a pale oval with large chestnut eyes. She wore a waxen raincoat and tall boots laced up to her knees. Sonja knew her on sight: it was Alexandria.

"Hello, Kats," Alexandria said, jumping off the horse. Dottie swooped down and landed on her shoulder. "Where's the Contessa?"

Kats von Stralen grinned to reveal his chalk-white teeth. "I couldn't say."

Tatty screamed inside the limousine. There was a loud thwack, and her voice went quiet.

"Tatty!" yelled Mr. Fortune Teller. He slid to the ground.

Kats von Stralen raised his weapon at Alexandria. "We're having a shotgun wedding. I was hoping you could give us a present. Your Amulet, please."

Alexandria shrugged. "What're you talking about?"

"Hand it over, Alex. The pearl." Kats von Stralen threw a look to Georgie. The boy yanked out a baton from his belt and brandished it as he ripped open the front of Alexandria's coat. Her neck was bare.

Alexandria gave a sharp, quick nod of her head. The baton

smacked Georgie across the face. He looked down at it sticking out of his hands, bewildered. It struck him again, this time on the other cheek. Georgie hastily dropped the baton onto the ground.

Sonja stared, wide eyed. Alexandria had never done anything like that before. Every time they had gone to visit Alexandria, she had been slouched in front of the television, chain-smoking cigarettes and yelling at Arthur.

"What—what's that?" Georgie sputtered. "Somes sort of voodoo?"

"That's one way of putting it," said Dottie. She flew off Alexandria's shoulder and circled the boys.

"Dids that birdie just jammer?" asked Dirgert.

"What birdie?" squawked Dottie, swooping down.

"I's not stayin' here no more!" Georgie yelled. He spun around and ran off. The other boys scuffled after him. They disappeared into the smoke.

"You always knew how to clear a room, Alex," Kats von Stralen said with a smirk.

Alexandria swung her arms up above her head. The Gatsploder rocketed out of Kats von Stralen's hand and into the air. At the same instant, something riveted into Alexandria's shoulder. She yelled. Blood soaked her coat. Behind Kats von Stralen, an electric car window had been slid halfway open. A white-gloved hand, covered in diamonds, held a second weapon: a smaller, slimmer, silver Gatsploder. A thread of smoke curled out from its tip.

Alexandria's eyes flashed. Her nostrils flared. She clutched her shoulder as she stormed toward the limousine.

The car's wheels rattled. The whole vehicle shook.

Kats von Stralen's face went pale. Chestnut Sabine leapt into his arms. "Adieu, children," he said, tipping his hat. He jumped into the shuddering limousine and slammed the door just as the engine revved wildly, and the car began to speed away.

Alexandria ran after it, shouting and cursing.

The hood ornament shot into the air like a rocket. The windows exploded, showering glass everywhere. But it was too late. They were gone.

The flock of swans swept across the sky and followed the limousine into the darkness. The birds' shrill screeches echoed behind them.

The twins screamed for Tatty. There were tears in their eyes. Anxious thoughts raced through Sonja's mind. Why had Kats von Stralen kidnapped her? What would he do to her? She clung to Charlotte like a drowning sailor to a sinking raft after a shipwreck.

The old man shook his head, wiping his wet eyes. "This was planned. Kats von Stralen had Bea lead me on a wild-goose chase. She doesn't realize the harm she's done."

Dottie circled the area. "I see them!" she shouted down. "They're disappearing fast!"

"Follow them!" Alexandria yelled. "Once you know where they've taken Tatty, meet us in the Land Where the Plants Reign!"

"I won't fail you!" cried Dottie, and flew off into the night.

"They may have Tatty," said Alexandria, climbing onto her horse, "but they don't have an Amulet—yet."

Mr. Fortune Teller stiffened. He grasped at his neck clumsily.

"The Turtle Back," he said, breathless. "I left it with her." He started toward the burning caravan.

"Wait! Uncle Tell!" Charlotte unclasped the silver chain and held up the tortoiseshell pendant. "Is this it?"

Mr. Fortune Teller hugged her. "Thank goodness," he muttered. "Thank goodness." He hurriedly fastened the chain around his neck and slipped it under his vest.

"Will someone tell us what on earth is going on?" blurted Sonja. "Tatty's skin went berserk, and the next thing we know she's been kidnapped!"

Alexandria stared blankly. She turned to Mr. Fortune Teller. "You never told them?"

"I was waiting for their thirteenth birthday."

"Told us what?" said Charlotte.

Mr. Fortune Teller paced back and forth in front of the twins for a minute. He finally spoke:

"It's all real."

Charlotte stared, dumbstruck.

"What are you talking about?" Sonja asked hesitantly.

"Everything. Every land. Every creature. Every tattoo on Tatty's body. The Seven Edens are real." He pointed to his horse. "Rhubarb's a Gillypur from the Vanishing Islands."

Sonja snorted. "That's ridiculous!"

"Ridiculous or not," interrupted Alexandria sharply, "it's the truth."

The old man threw Alexandria a look.

She began to bandage her arm with a piece of fabric torn from the hem of her dress.

"If they're real," said Sonja, "well, where are they?"

"Hidden," replied the old man. "And there's only one map of them. The map . . . is Tatty. She's the Key." He tapped his tortoiseshell pendant. "This is the Turtle Back. My Amulet. I'm Protector of the Vanishing Islands. Each Eden has a chosen Protector, and each Protector possesses an Amulet. If an Amulet touches the Key, the paths into the Seven Edens are revealed on her skin."

Charlotte said evenly, "The tattoos come alive."

Mr. Fortune Teller nodded. "Kats von Stralen's been stealing Talents and harvesting magic. He seems to have figured out where to find the greatest supply. The source of all magic lies in the Seven Edens. That's why he kidnapped Tatty. That's why he'll now be scouring the world for an Amulet."

In a strange, low voice, Alexandria said: "His mother, the Contessa, is the mastermind behind it all."

"Is that who shot you?" Charlotte asked. "With the white gloved hand?"

Alexandria nodded and rubbed her wounded shoulder.

Sonja's brow furrowed. She was angry. How could they have kept this a secret for all these years? She turned to Mr. Fortune Teller. "Why did you wait so long to tell us the truth?"

"We were trying to protect you," said the old man.

"A lot of good that's done!" returned Sonja. "You haven't protected anybody! From anything!"

Alexandria said calmly, "Throw your tantrum some other time. We're in a hurry."

Sonja wheeled around to face Alexandria. Her cheeks flushed with color. "Shut up! You're just another freak like us!"

"Please, Sonja." The old man put his hands on her shoulders. "I know this is a lot for you to take right now after all that's happened, but we have to keep our wits about us if we want to save Tatty." Mr. Fortune Teller kissed her damp cheek. He hoisted himself onto Rhubarb. "You two go with Alexandria. I'll send word to the other Protectors to meet us in the Land Where the Plants Reign. The Amulets will be safe there until we decide what to do."

"But Uncle Tell—" started Charlotte.

"It'll only be a couple of days." He patted her head. "I want you to do everything Alexandria says. Understood?"

"Okay," she said reluctantly. Sonja turned away, angry. How could he leave them at a time like this? Especially with Alexandria. They had been left alone with her once for a few days when they were little. She had neglected to feed them, bathe them, or put them to bed. In fact, she had hardly said two words to them. It was a disaster.

Mr. Fortune Teller nudged Rhubarb with his heel, and they cantered away.

A raspy howl cut through the smoke. A pack of red eyes peered out at them from among the smoldering caravans. A trio of straggling hyenas were creeping slowly toward them across the camp.

Alexandria held out her hand to the girls. "Hurry," she said. She swung Charlotte up behind her.

"I'm not going!" shouted Sonja.

Alexandria sighed. She reached down, yanked Sonja up by the

collar with a hard jerk, and thumped her down behind her sister. The horse reared onto its hind legs. It burst into a gallop.

They raced through the burning circus. Sonja sat hunched over behind Charlotte, crying. There was destruction all around them. She saw the clowns fighting fires. She saw Pershing tending to the injured. She wanted to yell to them. She wanted Tatty.

BOOK
TWO

Chapter Fourteen

Alexandria

THE HORSE CALLED MORITZ RODE AT A FURIOUS SPRINT alongside an enormous pipe ten feet tall that cut across the black landscape and stretched into the horizon. Charlotte clutched Alexandria around the waist, and Sonja held tightly on to Charlotte's back. The cold air stung Charlotte's cheeks and dried her tears into a cakey, white dust. She felt weak and scared, but deep down, she already knew: to save Tatty and find their Talents, she would need all her strength. It was going to be a fight.

"It's gaining on us!" she heard her sister yell.

Charlotte looked back over her shoulder. One of the hyenas was already close behind, snarling and snapping.

Moritz's nostrils flared. Sweat flew off his brow. The hyena howled hysterically. It lunged at Moritz's flanks. There was a growl and a crunch and a scream. She looked down and saw Sonja's ankle sandwiched between the hyena's massive yellow teeth. Charlotte furiously kicked at the hyena's bony head, but she could barely reach it. The animal jerked Sonja halfway off the horse.

"Help me!" shrieked Sonja, scrambling to hold on to her sister. Charlotte's fingers gripped Sonja's arms like a vise.

Alexandria pivoted in the saddle and hammered her boot against the hyena's head. The hyena dropped, tumbling and thumping, across the ground.

Moritz galloped on. Two hyenas, not far behind, stampeded over their dazed comrade.

Sonja clutched her bleeding leg. Charlotte remembered for an instant when Sonja had fallen off a tightrope and broken her arm. Tatty had cried as she packed Sonja's belongings for the hospital, kissing each item before placing it into the bag.

Moritz dug his hooves into the earth and slammed to a halt.

"What are we doing?" cried Sonja. "They're coming!"

Alexandria whisked her hands in the air, and a hatch in the pipe opened. Moritz jumped in, and the door closed behind him. They waited in silence as the hyenas thundered past them outside.

Alexandria pulled a matchbox out of her coat. She slid it open and shook out a handful of tiny cocoons. A flock of little insects with wings emerged, buzzing and hovering. Their tails glowed brightly, illuminating a long tunnel ahead. The walls were smeared with garbage, and dirty water dripped from the rusty ceiling. The smell of trash filled the air.

Charlotte pinched her nose. "Are we in a sewer?"

"I thought you'd be used to the smell, living in the Outskirts," remarked Alexandria. She jumped down. Her boots landed on the metal floor with a heavy twang. The sound reverberated. She stood over Sonja, examining her bloody ankle. "Hold on a second."

She pulled out a tooth from the wound. "Strange," she muttered.

Sonja scrunched her face in pain. "That hurts!"

Alexandria dropped the tooth into her coat pocket and took out an old tin flask. She swigged a gulp and gasped. "I hate to waste this stuff." She poured half the flask's contents over Sonja's open wound. It sizzled and bubbled. Sonja yelped. Charlotte squeezed her hand.

Alexandria yanked off Sonja's jacket, wrapped it three times around her wounded ankle, and knotted it tight. Sonja whimpered pathetically.

"Try to be gentler." Charlotte snapped at Alexandria.

Alexandria sighed deeply and climbed back onto Moritz's back. Moritz followed the lightning bugs down the tunnel. Rats scurried past his hooves as he splashed through dark puddles.

A flickering orange light appeared up ahead. Moritz shook his mane and huffed.

"Tunnel People," murmured Alexandria. "Slow down, Moritz."

At the center of a junction with another massive drainpipe, a little tribe was huddled around a fire. The men jolted to their feet with spears in their hands. The women stopped turning skewers of hairy rats. The children stared, frozen. They were sweaty and covered in dirt, and their clothes hung off their scrawny bodies. Charlotte had seen people in miserable places before, but never as miserable as this.

The people were dead silent and dead still as Moritz trotted through the camp, and they did not stir again until the intruders were a great distance away.

"Next time we cross paths with a family of starving homeless people," Alexandria said, fumbling for something in her pocket, "try not to look so shocked. It's insulting." She pulled out a half-smoked cigarette and inhaled. The tip lit up by itself.

"Smoking turns your lungs black," Charlotte retorted.

Alexandria took another puff and looked away.

Charlotte frowned. Alexandria did not say much, and what she did say, she said rudely. It was just their luck to be stuck with her.

A circle of night sky appeared at the end of the tunnel ahead of them. They caught a faint sniff of fresh air. They emerged from the pipe onto the side of a hill overgrown with nettles. It overlooked a wide, murky swamp. Bits of trash bobbed up and down on its surface.

Alexandria handed them each a snail shell from her pocket. "These are for breathing."

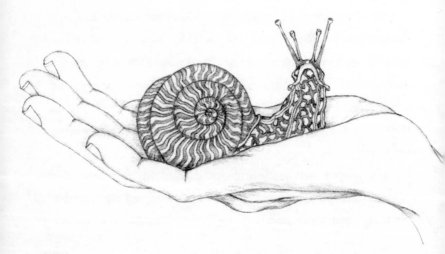

Sonja sat up anxiously. "Breathing?"

An instant later, they were descending the hill at a full gallop. Moritz gathered momentum with every step. Blood rushed through his thick veins, and the ground churned under his hooves. At the edge of the swamp, he leapt broadly, pedaling his legs in the air. Sonja screamed. Charlotte pressed her eyes shut as they crashed into the water.

Everything went silent around them. A stinging cold soaked through their clothes. Charlotte struggled for breath and remembered the shell clenched in her fist. She pressed it to her mouth. A thick slug slithered out, clamped onto her lips, and blew air down her throat. Gross, she thought. She looked to Sonja. She was sucking on her own shell.

They both looked to Alexandria. Strangely, she did not seem to need *anything* to breathe.

Moritz pulled them deeper. The lightning bugs flew alongside them, illuminating floating plastic bags, empty cans, and a headless doll. Schools of silver fish with needle-sharp teeth nibbled on the garbage. They broke it up into minuscule pieces, which smaller fish with skinny, pencil-like bodies and long snouts snorted up and flushed out through their gills in a watery mist.

Charlotte looked all around as darting bodies glittered and glowed, as metallic scales, striped and dotted, whizzed to and fro. A box-shaped fish hovered, staring curiously at her with its flat black eyes. She had never seen a living fish before.

A rumble shook the swamp. The fish scattered all at once. Out of the darkness, a powerful undertow pulled Moritz like a vacuum.

"Hold on!" gurgled Alexandria. The lightning bugs zipped back into her pocket.

The current whipped the twins off Moritz's back and sucked them into an abyss. They swung their arms and kicked their legs, but they could not fight the powerful current. A handful of fish were swept up with them, and they tumbled together deeper and deeper into the cold, dodging old shoes, broken bottles, and a bicycle wheel spinning in the fray.

Charlotte's wide eyes searched all around in the dimming light. If they drowned, maybe their mother and father would dream about them: two girls drifting, ragged, underwater like a pair of identical seaweeds.

Chapter Fifteen

Underwater

THE CURRENT DELIVERED SONJA INTO A COLD EDDY. Her jacket tourniquet had come loose. Her leg ached. She had lost sight of Charlotte a few seconds earlier. Panic set in. Where was Alexandria? Why didn't she try to save them?

Two cloudy figures appeared over her. Sonja could barely make out their blurry features, but they were reaching out to her. Whispered voices in her ears said: "We never stopped wanting you back."

Sonja's eyes widened. She reached out to the man and the woman—but her trembling fingers found, instead, the end of a dangling rope dancing in the swirling water. She gripped it, and it pulled her hard and fast. She looked back over her shoulder for the figures, but there was only a watery cloud of nothing behind her.

A moment later, shafts of light split the darkness. Sonja looked up to see Moritz's legs paddling above. The water was clear and blue. Just as she began to puzzle out the question about which direction she was going and where the bottom of the swamp might be, she burst through the surface and into the fresh air.

The shell dropped from her mouth. She gasped for air and treaded water. The sun shone on her face. There was birdsong in her ears. The smell of leaves and earth and mushrooms filled her nostrils.

They were in the middle of a lake, in broad daylight, surrounded by gigantic ancient trees. Everything was green—green moss, green leaves, green ferns. Even a green mist filled the air.

Sonja knew the place immediately. It was tattooed on Tatty's skin.

"The Forlorn Forest," muttered Charlotte, suddenly beside her. "It's more beautiful than I could have ever imagined."

> *Within an ancient forest,*
> *Stalks a Changeling among the trees.*
> *First a man, then a beast, either shape he'd like to be.*
> *With two lives to be liv'd he growls, "You'll never conquer me!"*

A voice yelled from shore. "I told you to hold on!" Alexandria stood with her hands on her hips. Her hair was unraveled. It fell past the ground and disappeared into the lake. Sonja realized the rope she was holding was actually a fifty-foot-long braid of Alexandria's hair.

Alexandria reeled it in as Charlotte helped her sister to shore, and Moritz followed. He collapsed next to them on the mossy bank. Out of the water, Alexandria's hair seemed to magically shrink. She pinned it up haphazardly and knelt down beside Sonja.

"Why are we here?" asked Charlotte. "I thought we were supposed to meet Uncle Tell in the Land Where the Plants Reign."

"We're picking up a friend along the way. We need help."

"But he'll be waiting for us. We're in the wrong place. I don't understand."

Alexandria stared at Charlotte. "Let's just assume I know what I'm doing, Sonja. At all times."

"She's Sonja. I'm Charlotte."

"I saw our parents, I think," Sonja murmured. "In the water."

"You were hallucinating," said Alexandria. "You must be sensitive to the Pathways. It happens." She examined Sonja's ankle. It was blue and swollen. "That doesn't look good."

Sonja rubbed her eyes. Her vision dimmed. Was she going blind? Maybe it was worse. What if she was dying? She grabbed Alexandria's wrist. "Am I going to die?"

"Don't be ridiculous, Charlotte."

"Once again. She's Sonja. I'm Charlotte."

"That's not important."

"Of course it is. They're our names."

"Come on, Moritz," ordered Alexandria. "There's no time to lose."

Moritz's legs wobbled as he stood up. Alexandria lifted the twins onto his back and climbed up in front of them. Sonja sat in the middle. "It's your turn to wear the locket."

Charlotte said softly, "You can wear it for another day."

Moritz strode among the giant, towering trees. Their branches and leaves shaded and dappled the underbrush. Burly roots roped the forest floor. Creaking wood echoed as the high trunks swayed in the wind.

"It sounds like the trees are whispering to one another," Sonja said. She imagined they were tiny beings traveling across Tatty's skin. The thought comforted her. "What do they look like?"

"A thousand years old. Each one's as wide as our caravan. The ground is covered in furry green moss. There are mushrooms everywhere."

A herd of antelope with brilliant blue coats and tall spiral horns burst out of the foliage. They froze when they saw the strangers, and blinked their almond-shaped eyes.

Charlotte gasped. "Blue Bucks! A dozen of them! Just like on Tatty's shoulder!"

Sonja knew the ones.

A whoosh of air fluttered through Charlotte's hair. She looked up. A flock of tiny emerald-green birds circled a tree netted with blooming vines and dipped their long, thin beaks into the centers of purple trumpet-shaped flowers. Their fast-beating wings whirred like miniature motors.

"Sweet Dippers!" Charlotte exclaimed. "They're like little flying jewels."

Sonja smiled. "The birds strung around Tatty's neck."

Charlotte nodded enthusiastically. "And over there!" She pointed to the middle distance through a gap in the trees. A pack of yellow dogs with black stripes down their backs chased one another in a clearing. "Burrup Hounds!"

Sonja could almost smell Tatty's vanilla scent as she remembered the playful animals pictured running across her chest.

Alexandria groaned. "Can't you two do this in your heads or something? I thought twins were telepathic."

"You say that every time we see you," complained Charlotte. "The answer's always the same: no, we're not telepathic!"

"Who knows? You might be someday. Want to bet on it?"

"I don't gamble."

Alexandria shrugged. "Too bad. You're missing one of the joys in life."

Moritz followed the path of a wide, winding river. Its banks were littered with plump red birds preening their small, useless wings with large, hooked beaks. He waded into the shallows of the river. The tops of the twins' shoes made stripes through the green algae. A fish with wings somersaulted out of the river and dove back in again. The water deepened, and Moritz began to kick and paddle.

Up ahead, a wooded island split the river in two. When he reached its edge, Moritz leapt up onto the shore and clip-clopped up a narrow path.

Alexandria slid to the ground and walked alongside Moritz and the twins.

The trees on the island were short and wide. Their leaves were black and shaped like little crowns. Woven sacks hung from their trunks and collected a thick amber liquid that oozed out of cracks in the bark. Insect traps were scattered all over the underbrush and buried in the crooks of branches. High up in the canopy above, they saw tree houses with bridges and ladders connecting them.

They emerged into a bright clearing and stood in the center of a ring of trees. The only sound was the current circling the island.

"Changelings of the Forlorn Forest!" Alexandria cried out. "We come to ask for your help!"

There was a spontaneous chorus of howling, growling, and barking. A large stag trotted out from the trees, followed by a black wolf with green eyes.

The stag stopped in front of Alexandria and lowered his enormous headdress of antlers. A scar marked his forehead, and a large amber pendant hung around his neck. Bears, foxes, and porcupines left their hiding places and approached behind the stag.

Alexandria grinned. "You sure know how to make an entrance, Staghart."

The stag's nostrils flared as he sniffed Alexandria's hair. He frowned. "Still smoking those city-sticks? I know it's hard to break human habits, but they'll kill you in the end." He looked at the girls with gentle brown eyes. "These must be the daughters of the Key. Smaller than I expected."

Alexandria lifted Sonja off the horse and helped her down to the leaf-strewn ground. "This one was bitten by a hyena," she said. "The wound's infected."

Sonja could only see shadows now. "It's all right," Sonja heard her sister whisper. "I'm right here."

Charlotte's voice sounded miles away. Other distant voices spoke. Sonja could not make out the words. What if Alexandria was lying? What if she really was dying? She squinted, looking for her sister. Spotlights cut through the darkness. She was back at the circus. She stood alone in the ring in front of a large audience. She looked down at her hands, but they were empty. Where was her flute? In fact, where were her fingers? They seemed to have fallen off.

Staghart turned to the black wolf standing next to him. "Get some brew and a bowl of ointment."

"Yes, sir," said the wolf, and dashed into the trees.

The stag lowered his head and studied the teeth marks that circled Sonja's ankle like a bracelet. "That's a nasty one."

Alexandria pulled out the tooth from her coat pocket. "It was stuck in her leg."

"Looks more like a dog's tooth than a hyena's."

Sonja was floating above the circus tent into a thick white sky. She stared down at the caravans below. There was Tatty and Uncle Tell and Charlotte. She tried to shout to them, but her voice was a raspy whisper. She trembled, and said to herself, Where am I going?

A black figure rose up through the mist, flying toward her. He cocked his hat and grinned. "I want you to meet Mother," he crooned. "She's a real darling."

CHAPTER SIXTEEN

Staghart and the Changelings

CHARLOTTE CROUCHED OVER HER SISTER. SONJA'S FACE WAS pale. A thin blue film lined her lips. Charlotte pressed her ear against her sister's chest. "Sonja's heart," she said, barely audible. "It's beating so slowly."

A big-boned teenaged boy knelt beside Charlotte. He looked to be about thirteen. He was wrapped in a fur cloak the same brownish-red as the hair that flopped in his face. "Don't worry, Charlotte, she'll be fine."

"Who are you?" Charlotte asked, alarmed.

The boy gave her a confused look. "I'm Moritz. You rode on my back for the last few hours." He rotated his shoulders. "I'm gonna feel it for days."

Charlotte stared in stunned silence. "You're a Changeling?" she finally asked.

"We all are," said Staghart. His snout shrank into his face. The bones shifted underneath his skin, and his fur began to recede into its follicles. Charlotte looked up as the other Changelings began to transform. Arms grew out of legs. Necks grew out of chests. Feet grew out of ankles. Ears shrank, eyes narrowed, mouths lengthened. Blood ran down newly formed fingers and mouths as nails and teeth emerged. Coats became capes over naked bodies.

The animals were transforming into humans right before their eyes.

Charlotte had learned about the Changelings. She knew they had two forms: human and animal. She knew they had two lives. She knew they ate bugs and lived in the Forlorn Forest. What she had never thought about was what it would be like to see them make the change. She felt a little sick. She stumbled.

"Are you all right?" asked Moritz.

"I don't feel well," she muttered, and then promptly fainted.

After a few minutes, Charlotte snapped open her eyes, startled. Thirty human faces stared down at her.

"See what I've been dealing with?" complained Alexandria. "Both of them out cold at once."

Staghart's antlers crossed against his chest like a breastplate, and his ragged fur hung over his old, muscular body. He had white hair and a creased olive face. "I remember when *you* first came to the Edens," he chuckled, kneeling. "You were scared of your own shadow."

"Can't stand humans," groused a teenager draped in a cape of peacock feathers.

A girl in a silky black fox coat frowned. "Me neither."

Staghart helped Charlotte sit up. She kept her eyes lowered. How had they already made enemies? They had only just arrived.

Staghart patted her shoulder. "Don't let them bother you. They're just puffing-up their chests." He turned to Sonja. "Now, let's see about your sister."

A boy with scruffy black hair and green eyes pushed through the other Changelings. He carried two wooden bowls stacked on top of each other. He handed them to Staghart and crouched on the ground beside him.

Charlotte eyed the boy. He looked a little older than the twins. He had strong features and caramel-colored skin. His eyes were striking: two smoky-green emeralds. Charlotte turned away and held on to Jack Cross' pin. She would *not* fall in love with another boy, however handsome he was.

Staghart poured an amber-colored liquid over Sonja's wound and spread a thick white paste around her ankle. Sonja twitched and blinked and swallowed. "She'll kill me," Sonja muttered. "She'll kill me." After a moment, bright yellow liquid dribbled out of the jagged tooth-holes.

"It's working," said Alexandria. She looked a little relieved.

Charlotte let out a nervous laugh and covered her face to hide her tears. If Sonja survived, Charlotte swore she would forget about making friends for at least a month.

"Is her breathing back to normal, Wolf Boy?" Staghart asked the black-haired boy.

He bent over Sonja and listened. "Seems like it."

Sonja's eyes flashed open. "What are you doing?"

The boy raised an eyebrow. "Seeing if you're alive."

"Obviously, I am!" Sonja sat up with a jolt, bumping her head into his.

"Ow!" he shouted, rubbing his temple.

Charlotte smiled. It was just like her sister to be rude to someone who had helped save her life. She kissed Sonja's cheek and whispered just like Tatty would have, "Glad you're back, dearie."

Staghart stood up and offered his arm to Alexandria. "Boys, escort our young guests to the meeting room. We'll be waiting for you." Staghart and Alexandria walked together up a staircase that spiraled around a tree. The Changelings followed, chattering and laughing.

The black-haired boy stood awkwardly beside Moritz. Charlotte grabbed his hand and shook it. "We haven't been properly introduced. I'm Charlotte. That's Sonja." She gestured to her sister still sitting on the ground.

"We've already met," Sonja replied abruptly. She looked around with a disgusted expression on her face. "What's that awful smell?"

"I think it might be us," Moritz said, laughing. "We're Changelings, you know. Can't clean the animal out of us."

"You're—real Changelings?" Sonja asked, her voice faltering.

Moritz nodded, grinning. "I'm Moritz." He lifted Sonja to her feet and pointed. "That's Wolf Boy."

"We thought you were imaginary," admitted Charlotte. "Until yesterday." Wolf Boy frowned. "Our mother, Tatty, used to tell us stories about you," she continued hesitantly. "She said Changelings

128

were stronger, faster, and more alert than both humans and animals put together. She also said Changelings have two lives." Charlotte wrinkled her nose. "Do you really have two lives?"

"Yes," replied Moritz, "but Wolf Boy and I, we've only got one left. We died in Rain City two years ago. Fell off a pedal-car track. It's kind of a badge of honor, you know. The first time you die."

"What's it like?" Charlotte asked quietly.

"I guess it's sort of like stumbling through a dimly lit labyrinth, trying to find your way out." Moritz paused. "Right, Wolf Boy?"

"Not a bad way to put it," Wolf Boy said with a grin. He then dove on top of Moritz, and they wrestled on the ground, laughing.

Sonja rolled her eyes. "Very mature," she muttered under her breath.

Alexandria yelled down from a bridge in the treetops: "Stop fooling around! Hurry up!"

Wolf Boy, Moritz, and the twins followed the last of the Changelings up the massive tree. Charlotte trailed her fingers along the damp, rough bark. Lichen and moss and fungus grew in between its woody ridges. All around her, a sea of shimmering leaves billowed in the breeze. Everything on the island was vibrant and budding and pungent. It was nothing like where she came from—a world of garbage and ugliness. Charlotte wanted to fit in, but the Changelings did not seem to like them.

They reached the top of the stairs, crossed a bridge, and entered a narrow timber house with a thatched roof. The room was packed with Changelings passing around bowls of mead. Burning incense mixed with their powerful smell. Branches crisscrossed overhead with flickering globes hanging from them.

Charlotte noticed a purple stone circled by smaller stones sticking up out of the floor among the littered leaves. They had seen the same stone at Arthur's.

"I didn't know you had a thing for humans," the girl in the fox coat said snidely as Wolf Boy and Moritz and the twins walked by. A gang of girls sitting around her snickered.

"Well, there's not much choice around here, is there, Cornelia?" Wolf Boy said, shrugging. Moritz laughed. The girl grimaced. She brushed her hair off her shoulder and looked away haughtily.

Alexandria wiped a froth of mead off her mouth. She gestured to an empty spot on the floor beside her. The twins sat down. Young Changelings entered the hall carrying wooden platters.

"Serve the guests first," ordered Staghart.

Plates were set in front of Alexandria and the girls. They were covered in slugs, snails, worms, and grasshoppers—all wriggling and crawling.

Alexandria chose the smallest caterpillar she could find and popped it into her mouth. She chewed its gooey body as fast as she could. "Delicious," she said politely.

"Go on," Staghart encouraged the twins.

They stared at the platter of insects, disgusted.

"Everyone's waiting," urged Alexandria, nudging them.

Charlotte reluctantly picked up a cricket. If she wanted to make friends, she would have to eat the poor little insect. She closed her eyes and opened her mouth. The cricket chirped. She jumped, startled. The cricket flew out of her hand and landed in her hair.

The Changelings pointed at her and whispered, laughing. Cornelia murmured "Human" under her breath.

Charlotte looked down at her lap, embarrassed.

Sonja bristled. "I won't be intimidated by a bunch of Changelings." The next thing Charlotte knew, her sister had pinched a worm between her fingers, looked Cornelia straight in the eye, and slithered it into her mouth. She chewed slowly.

The other Changelings turned to Staghart. He shrugged. "Let's eat." Hands flew into the platters. Changelings crunched shells, slurped slime, and spat out tentacles.

"I'd settle for a pancake right now," whispered Charlotte.

"Me, too," agreed Sonja, "but worm's not as bad as you'd expect."

Charlotte remembered when they were little, Tatty used to make heart-shaped pancakes. She told them they turned out that way because she cooked them with love. Charlotte caught Cornelia staring at her. She quickly wiped her eyes and looked away.

Staghart picked up a snail, held its head in his teeth, and pulled the slimy body out of its shell. "We received a message a few hours ago," he informed the room, chewing. "It concerns us all." The Changelings grew quiet. He took off his amber pendant, rubbed it against his fur cloak, and pressed it to the purple stone sticking out of the floor. As soon as they touched, a current sparked between them. It carried a voice. "Hear me, Staghart, Protector of the Forlorn Forest!"

"It's Uncle Tell!" Charlotte said, surprised. Sonja grabbed her hand.

"The Key was taken last night by humans," crackled Mr. Fortune Teller's voice. "They're after the source of the magic. We have a scout following them. All Protectors must meet in the Land

Where the Plants Reign within three days. It's most urgent that you bring your Amulet."

His voice trailed off. The connection died. Staghart put the pendant back around his neck.

Anxious murmuring spread through the room. A Changeling shouted from the back, "Will the Swifters come?"

"It's a serious enough matter," replied Staghart. "Our differences won't stop them."

"And the Albans?" asked another. "Since Tobias was killed, our messages have been ignored."

"Once we reach the Land Where the Plants Reign," said Alexandria, "we can send a scout to bring them news in person."

"I foresee a battle." Staghart traced the scar across his forehead. "I've already died once. This fight will take my life." He gestured the mark of an X across his chest.

The crowd grew restless. A few of the younger Changelings started to whimper. Alexandria shook her head. "It won't come to that. There doesn't have to be a battle."

Staghart wiped his mouth and stood up. "We'll wait until night to travel. It's safer." He put his hand on Alexandria's shoulder. "Once you've rested, we'll inform the animals about what's happened."

Wolf Boy and Moritz scooped a handful of insects each and followed Staghart out of the hall. The rest of the Changelings trailed soberly after them, leaving Alexandria and the twins alone.

Alexandria took off her coat and dress. She sat back down in her long underwear, knee-length socks, and tall boots. Charlotte could not help but stare. Alexandria's bones stuck out all over the place.

Her hands were large and heavily jointed, and her veins made blue patterns across her pale skin. She combed out her hair. It made two piles on the ground. Next Alexandria braided her hair into sections and pinned them neatly into place.

As Charlotte watched, something dawned on her. "Are you a Pearl Catcher?"

"What did you think I was? Human?"

"Is that why you didn't need a slug to breathe underwater?"

"Uh-huh." Alexandria leaned toward Charlotte. "Do me a favor, Sonja. Check and see if Staghart's gone."

Charlotte groaned. "I'm Charlotte." She stood up and stuck her head out the door. "All clear."

Alexandria pulled out a cigarette from her boot. It crackled and burned as she sucked on its end. "So how do I get this right? Which one's which?"

Charlotte pointed to the mole on her cheek. "Sonja doesn't have one."

"In fact, if you pay close attention, everything that seems the same is, actually, different," Sonja said with a hint of sarcasm.

Alexandria blew out a ring of smoke. It hovered over the twins' heads. "You seem exactly identical to me. Especially when you're whining."

Charlotte sat back down with a plop. "What happened to you? Why are you so rude?"

"I tell the truth. People learn from their mistakes, but only if you point them out."

"Maybe right now's not a good time to start teaching us

anything," suggested Sonja. "Tatty's missing, and our lives are ruined, and we're traveling in a land we thought was make-believe until a few hours ago. Be kind, if you can."

Alexandria grunted. "This *is* kind."

"The Changelings don't seem to like us, either," Charlotte said unhappily.

"Humans are hard to like."

"Why'd you marry Arthur, then?" Charlotte snapped back. "Or isn't he human, either?"

"He's human—and the rest is none of your business."

Charlotte glared at her. Alexandria was cold. She was coarse. She smelled like cigarettes. And they were stuck with her. "He seemed heartbroken when we saw him," Charlotte said with a hint of mischief. "I've never seen a man cry before."

Alexandria took another puff.

Charlotte gave Sonja a look. She nodded. "Uncle Tell said you left him because he's obsessed with his work and lives in a pigsty," Sonja remarked, playing along with her sister. "Is that true?"

"You two ask a lot of questions."

Charlotte shrugged. "Children ask questions. It's normal."

"That's probably why I stay away from them." Alexandria stubbed out her cigarette and stuffed the butt under a matt. She pulled off one of her boots and shook it until a handkerchief tumbled out. She carefully unwrapped the lace-edged cotton to reveal a large, misshapen pearl strung on a chain.

"What's that?" said Sonja.

"The Hanging Pearl. My Amulet." Alexandria clasped the chain around her neck. The pearl fell against her chest.

"You're a Protector, too?" Charlotte said in disbelief.

"Of the Shifting Lakes." Alexandria frowned. "Why do you look so surprised?"

"You don't seem the type," observed Sonja. "I mean, you've got a lot of bad habits and personal problems, don't you?"

Alexandria's cheeks flushed. "You two are incredible. How would you know what makes a good Protector? Only the Amulets can decide. *They* choose *us*."

"Who are the other Protectors?" asked Charlotte. She hoped they were a little more impressive than Alexandria.

"Are you really going to make me go through the whole list?"

"Yes!" the twins yelled in unison.

Alexandria groaned. "Okay. Okay." She scratched her nose. "Let's see. We'll go oldest to youngest. There's a hierarchy, you know. Luckily, I don't see them much, so it's no skin off my back." Her expression grew sulky. She slumped a little. "First, there's the Great Tiffin, Protector of the Land Where the Plants Reign. He's the oldest, nearly five hundred years, and the most powerful. Then come the Three Swifters, Protectors of the Lost Desert. They're pretty ancient, too, and the meanest of the bunch. After them is the Great Changeling, Staghart, whom you know, Protector of the Forlorn Forest. Next the Single Alban, Tobias. They spoke about him at the meeting. Protector of the Golden Underground, deceased."

"How'd he die?" interrupted Sonja. "Who's taking his place?"

"A boar killed him. That's to be decided."

"How's it decided, then?" Charlotte asked.

Alexandria rolled her eyes. "Really?"

"Just tell us!" Sonja said, irritated.

"There are two ways. The first is to throw the Amulet with the missing Protector into the Leading River, which borders the Land Where the Plants Reign. After a month or two, it finds its rightful owner, somehow. The second is to bring the Amulets together and do a sort of séance. The Amulets speak through the Protectors and together we find the missing Protector."

"Sounds creepy," said Charlotte.

"If you want me to continue," threatened Alexandria, "no more interruptions." The twins nodded. "We're up to the Mother of All Geese and Fowl, old Hester." Alexandria chuckled. "She looks like an antique, but she's a spring chicken compared with the rest. She's Protector of the Crooked Peaks. After her is the Foreteller, Hieronymus, of course. Uncle Tell to you. Protector of the Vanishing Islands. And finally"—she gestured to herself—"yours truly, the youngest of all. They don't let me forget it, either." Alexandria stood up and blew out the flames in the amber globes. She folded up her coat, placed it under her head, and collapsed onto her back. "That's it. No more talking. I've only got a couple of hours before I have to meet Staghart."

Charlotte and Sonja lay down on the woven mats. They were quiet for a moment until Charlotte said, "Alexandria, do you think they'll hurt Tatty? I mean Kats von Stralen and his mother."

"She'll be safe until they get hold of an Amulet."

"I hate to think of Tatty on her own."

"We're all on our own in one way or another. Now go to sleep."

"I don't know if I can," whispered Sonja. "It's so quiet here."

"You'll get used to it." Alexandria turned on her side. "That's the heartless thing about us creatures. Eventually, we adapt to anything."

The twins held each other's hands like they did every night. Charlotte stared up at the thatched ceiling. She would never adapt to their new lives, whatever Alexandria said. She would never adapt, even if it killed her.

Chapter Seventeen

The Middle of the Night

Sonja was dreaming of Tatty and labyrinths and Kats von Stralen when a voice yelled, "Rise and shine!"

She wiped her eyes. Wolf Boy stood over them with a lantern in his hand. Moritz hung back in the shadows. She turned to the empty spot where Alexandria had slept. "Where is she?"

"Waiting for us," said Wolf Boy. "You better hurry."

Moritz kept his eyes on the floor as the twins stumbled to their feet, half asleep.

Outside, it was cold and dark. Night vines exhaled a ripe scent. Charlotte and Sonja followed the Changelings across the bridge and down the tree. Candles flickered in windows. Stars peered down among branches. A Changeling mother sang to her baby.

They walked into the woods. Wolf Boy held up his lantern. The trees' shadows darkened the already dark underbrush. Little animals rustled among the leaves. An owl hooted in the distance.

Sonja kept close to the Changelings. She was not used to such dark darkness. In the Outskirts, the street lamps were always lit. "Where are we going?" she asked anxiously.

"Just a little farther now," replied Wolf Boy.

He led them under a fallen tree and through a cluster of jagged ferns. The path sloped down. At its end, they came into a primitive, moonlit graveyard. Splayed headstones stuck out of the ground. Ivy shrouds hid names and dates.

As they stepped through the gate, the air chilled. Sonja shivered. "It's freezing!"

"Shh!" cautioned Wolf Boy. "You'll wake them up!"

"Wake who?" Charlotte said hesitantly.

Both Changelings whispered, "Shh!"

It was too late.

Dozens of animals began to rise from the ground, bucking and rearing. There were deer and foxes and horses and a bear. Their bodies were entirely transparent and glowed bright yellow. Their glassy eyes bulged out of their sockets. Their quiet growls echoed and reverberated.

"Are . . . Are those ghosts?" stammered Sonja. The circus had set up in many cemeteries over the years, but the girls had never seen an actual ghost. The other circus members always claimed to have spotted one or two wandering around at night.

"Only a few humans become ghosts after they die," explained Moritz, "but all Changelings do, once they've used up both lives."

The Changeling ghosts hovered around them.

"Don't look them in the eye," warned Wolf Boy, "or they'll be released from the graveyard. Just keep walking."

Moritz sighed. "I once had that nasty old bear, Blanco Bingo, trailing after me for a month. It was terrible."

"Watch it," Wolf Boy said, holding back a laugh. "He's right behind you."

A transparent grizzly bear walked upright beside Moritz, spluttering and spitting. Moritz moaned, "Go haunt somebody else!"

The twins kept their eyes on the ground as the Changeling ghosts taunted them to look. Alongside each animal, a nebulous human form flickered alight, then disappeared again. It was the only Changeling incarnation where both forms, animal and human, could be seen at the same time.

Once the children reached the other end of the graveyard, the fading spirits watched unhappily as they disappeared down a set of worn steps.

They crossed into a stone ruin. It was roofless, and trees grew out of the crumbling walls. All the rest of the young Changelings sat cross-legged on the cracked mosaic floor. They varied in ages from twelve to fifteen. Lanterns hung from branches overhead.

"What *is* this?" Sonja burst out. "Where's Alexandria?"

"She's with Staghart," Wolf Boy said matter-of-factly. "They're meeting the animals."

Sonja's face turned bright red. "Why'd you bring us here?" she yelled, trembling.

"Calm down, Sonja," whispered Charlotte.

"To see if you're traitors or not," Cornelia replied with a smile.

"There's a good chance of it," hissed the boy with the peacock cape. "Most humans are traitors."

"Well, I'm leaving," Sonja announced, and started to go.

Wolf Boy blocked her. "No, you're not." He crossed his arms over his chest.

"What's the problem?" Charlotte said in a friendly voice. "We didn't do anything."

"The human race did," sneered Cornelia.

Moritz looked at the twins guiltily. He shuffled his feet. "Sorry. It's a tradition. We all had to go through it. Please, sit down."

"Let's just do it," muttered Charlotte.

Sonja frowned. These Changelings were worse than human children. She slumped to the ground next to Charlotte. Charlotte was always trying to please everyone. Well, not Sonja. If the others did not like her—tough luck.

Wolf Boy rubbed his hands together, then placed them flat onto the mosaic floor. The rest of the Changelings followed his example. There were little finger-sized grooves crisscrossed all over the tiles from centuries of hands rubbing its surface.

A hundred jewel-colored beetles squeezed up out of the cracks in the floor. Their iridescent backs glistened in the moonlight. They scurried between the Changelings' fingers, twirling their antennae and whispering angrily, "Release us! Release us! Release us!"

Sonja's eyes widened. "Talking beetles!"

"They're the souls of animals killed by humans long before the Proclamation." Cornelia looked darkly at the twins. "For now, they're trapped inside the bodies of beetles, but one day, they'll be set free—and their skeletons will come out of the ground and wipe out the human race." She smiled. Her black eyes flickered menacingly.

"Put your hands on the floor," Wolf Boy ordered the twins.

Sonja shook her head.

"You have to."

"Says who?"

"Says me."

Charlotte shrugged. She thrust her palms down onto the tiles. Sonja sighed and placed hers next to her sister's. The mosaic was warm and wet. If this was what it was like to have friends, Sonja thought, then she preferred not to have any. She hoped this would persuade Charlotte to feel the same way.

The beetles swarmed from the Changelings' hands onto the twins'. "The ones! The ones! The ones!" they whispered, agitated. "The ones who will release us!"

Moritz smiled. "I told you they weren't traitors."

Wolf Boy looked curiously at the twins.

"They will be strong! They will have the power against the living!" A beetle nipped underneath Sonja's nails.

"Ow!" she shrieked. A bright red droplet appeared at the tip of her finger. "I'm not doing this anymore," she huffed.

She started to pull her hands away, but Wolf Boy held them flat on the mosaic with his. The beetles covered them like two shimmery, green gloves. "Your hands will touch for many years to come!" they chanted excitedly.

Wolf Boy looked at Sonja, puzzled. Cornelia murmured, "What's that supposed to mean?"

Sonja's face burned. She tore her hands away and shook off the clinging beetles. They scattered and disappeared back into the cracks. She leapt to her feet and ran out with Charlotte chasing after her. "Wait! Sonja!"

Sonja ran into the graveyard. The moon was full and brimming with light. A mist floated among the headstones.

"Slow down!" begged Charlotte.

Sonja had to get away from that Changeling. He smelled and lied. She hated him. She wished she could go back to the Outskirts, back to the circus, back to Tatty.

Suddenly, Sonja lost her balance, tripped on a broken statue, and tumbled onto a grave. Her face planted straight into the damp earth. At the end of her nose, she saw a tiger's glowing eyes.

"Oh, no," she whispered. Charlotte jerked her back to her feet. The tiger, a Changeling ghost, leapt out of the ground, shook himself, and trotted after them. His human form flickered in and out of view, running beside him.

The twins zigzagged among the graves, dashed through the ferns, and scrambled under the fallen tree.

"I don't remember the way from here!" cried Charlotte.

"Just keep running!" Sonja shouted. She looked back over her shoulder. The translucent tiger was close behind them. His human form waved and cried, "Wait for me!"

The twins ducked under branches and hopped over roots.

They stopped short. They had reached the edge of the island.

Torches stuck out of the ground. Staghart, in his animal form, stood in the river up to his knees. A thousand glistening eyes watched him from the opposite bank. Fish stuck their silvery snouts above the water's surface. Staghart spoke in a tongue the girls did not understand. It was the language of animals.

The tiger sidled up to Sonja and purred. Sonja screamed. Staghart turned. The gathered animals across the river barked and bayed and yelped and hissed, their snarling teeth glinting in the moonlight.

"What are you doing here?" a voice asked coldly.

The twins froze, breathless.

Lightning bugs lit up Alexandria's angry face. "This is a meeting of animals. Humans aren't allowed. Let's go." She grabbed their arms and shoved them away. The Changeling ghost sauntered behind them, flicking his see-through tail.

Chapter Eighteen

On the Way

"It wasn't our fault! They told us we were meeting you!"

Charlotte sat hunched over on a tree stump watching Sonja and Alexandria argue. The translucent tiger was wrapped in a ball by her feet. Her legs felt like they were knee-deep in ice-cold water.

Alexandria pointed at him. He growled at her. "How do you explain that?"

"I tripped! It was an accident!"

Alexandria threw her hands into the air. "I don't know how Tatty puts up with you two."

"Tatty doesn't put up with us!" yelled Sonja. "She loves us!" Charlotte jumped up and put her arm around her sister. The Changeling ghost squeezed between them. "You'd make a rotten mother, Alexandria, I assure you."

Alexandria's face darkened. Her eyes narrowed.

"I hope we're not disturbing anything." Staghart strode up from the riverbank. A spotted horse without a mane walked alongside him.

Sonja wiped her eyes with the back of her sleeve. "We're sorry we intruded on your meeting. We were lost."

"Animals have a hard time accepting that some humans aren't half bad." Staghart gestured to the horse. "Atticus here had to persuade them to leave you be."

The horse stuck out his dappled neck and sniffed the twins.

"He's not a Changeling?" said Charlotte.

Staghart shook his head. Leaves fluttered off the tips of his antlers. "It's like understanding the difference between identical twins." He lowered his chin and studied the girls' faces. "Right off the bat, I can see: one has a mole, the other doesn't. But in time, a thousand particularities will reveal themselves. It's the same with a Changeling and an animal. At first, only the eyes give it away. Changelings have human eyes."

Charlotte blinked. It was true. Staghart's eyes, even when he was in animal form, were strangely human.

"Once people get to really know you," Staghart continued, "they'll find it hard to imagine they ever confused you with each other. That's how you'll feel, eventually, when you compare an animal with a Changeling, or even a Changeling to a human."

Charlotte shot Alexandria a look. "Some people will never see the difference."

"Yes, they will, my dear," said the stag, "even if they won't admit it."

A voice interrupted, breathless: "It was our fault! We took them to see the beetles! The beetles said they have the power against the living!"

146

Wolf Boy, Moritz, and the other young Changelings appeared out of the dark, now animals.

Alexandria pointed at the twins. "Power against the living? These two?"

Staghart chuckled. "They did manage to summon the dead." He turned to the Changeling ghost. "Humphrey, it's time to go home."

The tiger pressed against the twins, whimpering.

"You youngsters, escort Humphrey back. Wolf Boy and Moritz, stay with us."

Charlotte felt a little sad to see the Changeling ghost go. He was the first creature they had met in the Forlorn Forest who actually liked them.

"The shortest route to the Land Where the Plants Reign is through Rain City," said Staghart. "It will take us a day to get there. That's well before the meeting of the Protectors. You all know your orders?"

They affirmed in growls and neighs.

They were going to Rain City, thought Charlotte. She trembled excitedly. Jack Cross' school was there. She felt for the crumpled-up letter in her pocket with his address on it. Maybe she could still find him? Maybe she could still save him? Maybe his Talent had not been stolen yet?

Sonja interrupted: "I know what you're thinking. Don't!"

"What are you two standing around for?" barked Alexandria, mounting the spotted horse. "Let's go!"

Charlotte grumbled as she clumsily hoisted herself up onto Moritz. She was pretty sure she hated Alexandria.

Staghart shook his antlers and roared. He shot into the trees with Alexandria close behind him. Moritz raced alongside Wolf Boy with the twins clinging to his neck.

They crashed through the water, scrambled up the shore, and ran on. Sleeping beasts in lumps and piles raised their heads as they thundered by, and fur and feathers rustled in nests in the branches above. Up ahead, shrouded by mist, was an enormous tree as thick as a house. A large hollow was carved out of its trunk. As they drew nearer, a bright light shimmered to life inside the tree. They narrowed into single file.

"What's happening?" cried Charlotte.

"We're going in," growled Wolf Boy.

"Going in *what*?" faltered Sonja.

Staghart leapt into the hollow and disappeared. Alexandria and Wolf Boy followed him one after the other. Moritz was next. Charlotte buried her face in his mane as he flew into the dank and musty hollow. He landed with a thud and galloped on.

Everywhere around them was startlingly white. Whispers drifted in and out of Charlotte's ears. She thought she heard Pershing singing the Miniature Woman a lullaby, then the Snake Charmer crying for Alfonso, then Bea sobbing and cursing Kats von Stralen. The whispers turned into pitter-pattering droplets. She could smell burning rubber. Moritz jumped again. Charlotte found herself in midair, flying out of another tree.

They landed, skidding, in a deserted cemetery. The rain showered down in misty sheets. They were back in the Outskirts of Rain City, in the exact place where their Talents had been stolen.

Charlotte pulled her hood over her head. She pictured the

colored lights strung throughout the campsite and the glowing circus tent billowing in the wind. She looked back and imagined their caravan standing among the other caravans. She thought of Tatty and Monkey waiting inside for them.

A gang of Scrummagers was shoveling dirt over their shoulders, looking for dead people's belongings. Charlotte recognized them. They were the Scrummagers Jack Cross had scared away. She laughed as Sonja waved eagerly to them like they were old friends.

The Changelings galloped along the walls of the Train Graveyard, tracing the path the twins had taken to meet Jack Cross. Charlotte wondered if Jack Cross' mother was worried about him. She wanted to shout out, "Don't worry, Mrs. Cross! I'm going to Rain City to find him!"

They charged into a street lined with forbidden junkyards. Engines idled up ahead, and a row of headlights flashed on.

"We've got company!" warned Staghart.

Three Enforcers on rusty motorcycles blocked their path. They wore binocular-goggles and lightning-bolt armbands. One of them spoke into a receiver: "Forbidden an-imals detected!"

"You got them?" yelled Alexandria.

Staghart snorted fiercely and charged straight ahead.

As the Enforcers fumbled for their weapons, Staghart crashed through, swinging his antlers from side to side. Two Enforcers were knocked to the ground. The remaining one gunned his engine and chased after Staghart.

Alexandria, Wolf Boy, and Moritz veered off.

Thunder crackled in the sky. A towering brick wall came into view. It stretched out sideways in both directions, from one horizon to the other. Lightning struck beyond it, illuminating the tops of skyscrapers in the distance. It was Rain City.

Charlotte shuddered. All their lives, Tatty had warned them: the cities are soul snatchers. Everybody does what everybody else does. Every day is like every other day.

Finally, the girls would see a city themselves.

Beams of light swept out from the wall over a line of weary people. Their tattered clothing was soaked through, and their suitcases were balanced on their heads. They limped toward a massive steel gate. Enforcers checked their documents with stony faces. Hyenas hunched at their feet with lowered heads and growling mouths.

Alexandria turned to Wolf Boy and shouted, "Now!"

Moritz and Wolf Boy ducked off the road and scrambled behind a metal shed. Charlotte watched anxiously as Alexandria rode alone toward the city gates and galloped into the crowd.

People screamed and shouted. They fled the lines and ran for cover. Alexandria circled among them, kicking up dust and gravel.

"Lock down! Lock down!" an Enforcer boomed into a loudspeaker.

A siren sounded as the gates rolled shut. Hyenas flailed wildly at their leashes.

Alexandria skidded to a stop, then charged away in the opposite direction. The Enforcers set the hyenas loose. They ran cackling after Alexandria. The Enforcers jumped into a van and zoomed away to join the chase.

"Why aren't we going with her?" cried Charlotte.

"She's meeting us later," Wolf Boy replied calmly. "At the entrance to the pathway of the Land Where the Plants Reign."

Sonja folded her arms across her chest. "I don't trust you."

Wolf Boy shrugged. "Suit yourselves, but if you'd be so kind as to get down off Moritz's back."

The girls slid to the ground. The Changelings transformed into boys. Wolf Boy grabbed Moritz by the arm and pulled him away. "They're not coming."

"*I* am!" Charlotte said, following the Changelings. If Sonja wanted to make enemies, she could go right ahead. Not Charlotte—especially when they were delivering her closer to Jack Cross.

"Charlotte!" yelled Sonja. She waited a moment, then ran after her.

RAIN CITY was written in metal letters above a row of tall iron gates. Lightning bolts were painted across them, and warnings were plastered all over the walls: TRESPASSING PUNISHABLE BY DEATH, ILLEGAL DOCUMENTS = LIFE IMPRISONMENT, DO NOT FEED ANIMALS.

Wolf Boy quickly scrambled up a stack of crates and onto the wall. He signaled for Moritz and the twins to follow. They climbed up after him, clambered down the other side, and jumped to the ground. They ducked into a wide tunnel just as the people in line swarmed up after them.

The walls were lined with dirty white tiles. Hanging fluorescent tubes flickered on and off. Raindrops echoed. They emerged onto a high bridge. Rain City plummeted deep, deep down below them and sprang up far, far into the sky above them and spread out for breathtaking miles in every direction.

Charlotte gasped and gripped the railing. Uncle Tell had grown up in Rain City. He had known it before it exploded in size, before the pedal-car tracks were built, before it began to rain continuously (although it had always been a rainy city). He had never been back. He said it would break his heart to find it so changed.

Charlotte would tell him all about it if she ever saw him again.

CHAPTER NINETEEN

Lost in Rain City

SONJA KNEW ABOUT THE DIFFERENT CITIES. SHE HAD studied photographs of them in books and newspapers. Rain City was one of the first to become a multi-tiered city—carved into the earth, shooting up into the sky, each layer packed with streets and shops and offices. The Richers lived at the very tippy-tops of the Million-Mile-High buildings veiled in rain clouds, and the poor lived at the very bottom depths where the buildings' foundations were flooded with water every day. Sonja had read that it rained all the time because of the smoke emitted by the hundreds of factories that inhabited the city's middle layer.

Through the sheets of rain, Sonja glimpsed gargoyles plunging out of brick facades, stained-glass windows blackened by soot, and rusted metal signs swinging from the different shop windows.

An intricate system of tracks wove between the buildings like an endless roller coaster. Thousands of pedal-cars crowded the rusted rails, above and below, forming a cacophony of honking and skidding.

"I can't hear a thing," complained Sonja, covering her ears. She almost felt paralyzed among the blaring sounds, flickering lights, and constant traffic. The Outskirts seemed like a sanctuary compared with this.

"You get used to it," Moritz assured her. "Wolf Boy and I lived here before Staghart found us. We were Scrummagers."

"Scrummagers?" Charlotte said, surprised.

Moritz nodded. "It was better than rotting in an orphanage. We ran away and joined the Rain City Troop."

"I always wondered how Scrummagers became Scrummagers," Sonja murmured.

"You must know the city well, then," said Charlotte. "Any idea where the School for the Gifted is?" She pulled out the crumpled-up letter and read Jack Cross' address out loud: "Three Hundred and Thirty-Three Bishop's Row."

Moritz nodded. "The Lower Depths. That's where we're meeting Alexandria."

Sonja frowned. They were alone with untrustworthy Changelings in the middle of a strange city without proper documents, hoping to find their way into the Land Where the Plants Reign (a place they had thought was fictional until the day before), where Uncle Tell was, supposedly, meeting them to see if a speaking parrot knew where Kats von Stralen and the Contessa were hiding their kidnapped adoptive mother! How could Charlotte's ridiculous brain still be thinking about that ridiculous boy?

They walked through an enormous archway. Blank, stone faces carved into columns stared down at them as they entered an expansive, bustling station. Signs were posted on the walls with arrows pointing in every direction: PEDAL-CAR RENTAL this way, PEDAL-BUS DEPOT that way, LOST AND FOUND upstairs.

Hundreds of people waited in lines, stood at booths, and hurried by with suitcases. Enforcers checked papers at every corner.

"I tell you, my documents were right here!" A frightened woman rummaged through her pockets. "Someone must have stolen them!"

The twins stayed close to the Changelings, hidden in the crowd. They ducked behind a column and sneaked into a short corridor. At the end was a door labeled EMERGENCY EXIT. Wolf Boy pushed it open, and the rain blew in. They stepped out onto a rickety fire escape hanging from the brick facade. Sonja peered over the railing.

The stairs zigzagged five thousand feet down into the city.

"This—doesn't—look—safe!" stammered Sonja. She had been scared of heights ever since she had fallen off the tightrope years and years earlier. Her fingers twitched uncontrollably.

Wolf Boy wrapped his fur cloak tightly around his body. "Let's go."

"It's not so bad, Sonja," Charlotte said softly. "Just don't look down."

With one hand on the railing and the other in her sister's, Sonja carefully descended the wet steps. They passed rows of dripping windows and looked in at maids ironing, secretaries typing, and a bald man fixing his toupee. Sonja had always wanted to visit a city, but this was not what she had imagined. She thought it would mean freedom from Enforcers; families living in cozy apartments; culture, music, and art in every nook and cranny. She wanted to play in great concert halls like Kanazi Kooks and eat in fancy restaurants among the clouds. *That* was the city in her mind, not this tangle of chaos.

Wolf Boy pointed to a busy sidewalk bridging between two buildings. "We can get a pedal-bus down there."

The bridge was jam-packed with shops and people in hooded raincoats, goggles, and hats. A woman carrying six shopping bags knocked the twins out of the way.

"You've got to use your elbows," demonstrated Moritz, jabbing his arms out sideways, "or you'll get trampled."

Charlotte and Sonja copied him, but they could not get the hang of pushing people out of the way. Instead, for the next few minutes, they were shoved back and forth through the crowd.

A pedal-bus pulled up to the platform. A sign on its side read THE LOWER DEPTHS.

"That's our ride," signaled Wolf Boy.

The Changelings charged toward the vehicle, bumping people roughly as they went and apologizing left and right. For an instant, Sonja thought she saw Wolf Boy reach into a man's coat pocket.

"Ticketsss," drawled a conductor standing at the door of the bus. He held a torn umbrella in one hand and a hole-punch in the other.

"Here you go." Wolf Boy produced four tickets. The conductor stamped them and gestured for the children to go through.

The bus was filled with silent passengers. The walls were plastered with peeling advertisements. A monotone voice on the radio listed accidents that had taken place that day. They heard shouting outside:

"Someone took my ticket!"

"Mine, too!"

"I had two tickets in my purse!"

Wolf Boy walked down the aisle with the stamped tickets in his hand.

"Did you steal those?" accused Sonja.

"Of course," said Wolf Boy.

Sonja's face turned bright red. "City property, I understand! You can't steal from other people! How would you feel if I did that to you?"

They squeezed past a well-dressed man reading a plastic-covered newspaper. Behind him, a teenaged girl in a polka-dotted rain coat powdered her nose. Next to her, an old woman stared anxiously at the Changelings and clutched her purse. Wolf Boy grabbed Sonja by the wrist and pulled her into the back row.

"You've probably never starved or sat cold nights shivering in the rain," he hissed. "Well, Moritz and I have. We learned how to survive, and that's what we're trying to—oh, just keep your mouth shut, and do what you're told."

He let go of her and collapsed into a seat. He looked out the window with his shoulders hunched over. Sonja's eyes welled up. She stuck her fingernails into her arm so she would not cry.

The front door slammed shut, and a horn sounded. The driver released the brake. He started to pedal.

Sonja slid over to the other side as the bus descended through the city. The seats were cold and wet. She rubbed her fingers on the fogged-up glass and looked out. There was an accident below. A young woman had crashed into the back of another pedal-car and was sprawled out on the tracks.

The more time Sonja spent here, the more she hated it. Tatty used to tell them about her years in Block City working at a tattoo parlor. On her days off, she would walk to the farthest edge of the city just to catch a glimpse of a little patch of sky. She must have felt as empty as Sonja did now.

Moritz leaned over. "I know you don't approve"—he hesitated—"but I swiped these off a shopper." He handed them two brown doughnuts. "They're gravy flavored."

"Thank you," Sonja said gratefully. Her stomach rumbled. The only thing she had eaten in hours was a worm. The doughnut was dry and tasteless and smelled like old shoes, but it was food. Well, sort of.

The bus rolled past a platform lined with canned-food shops, a salon specializing in electric hairpieces, and a bank with two armed guards at the door. There was a huge billboard promoting a Kanazi Kooks concert. Sonja pressed her nose to the window. His face looked blurry through the fogged-up glass. Perhaps it was a sign not to give up. Perhaps he would help them somehow. He had once been an Outskirts kid, too, after all. And hadn't he smiled at them at the auditions?

"Look!" Charlotte pointed to another billboard. This one was of a man in military uniform with a thick mustache and a stern brow standing next to a woman with slick black hair under the words UNITE THE CITIES.

Sonja recognized her white gloves and her diamonds. "The Contessa," she muttered.

The bus stopped with a jolt. A pedal-copter hovered down in front of them, shining a light through the windows. The passengers inside murmured to each other anxiously. The twins overheard a man whisper, "Documents check."

"We'd better get out of here," said Wolf Boy. "Moritz?"

Moritz quickly examined the rear window. He jiggled the knob. A bolt slid sideways. The glass opened a few inches. He jammed his hand out the gap and started unscrewing a latch.

The pedal-copter landed. Two Enforcers stepped out onto the tracks. The bus door zipped open.

"Hurry!" begged Sonja, wringing her hands. "They're coming!"

The well-dressed man watched them over his newspaper, curious.

The window snapped open. Moritz and Wolf Boy squeezed out and motioned for the twins to follow. Sonja looked back as the Enforcers stepped on board. One of them called out to the passengers, "Identification."

The twins scrambled out the window and climbed onto the Changelings' shoulders. A pedal-car waiting behind the bus started honking frantically. A woman wearing oversized rain goggles leaned out and shrieked, "They're getting away!"

"What now?" cried Charlotte.

Traffic whizzed by from the opposite direction. A pedal-car towing a cart slammed to a stop, then swerved to pass them. Wolf Boy gave Moritz a signal, and the Changelings threw the twins into the passing cart and tumbled in after them. By the time the girls realized what was happening, they were bouncing along at full speed, squeezed between stacks of crates and bumbling boxes.

Sonja whipped her head around and glared at the Changelings. "A little warning might be nice!"

"Sonja, do you have any friends whatsoever?" returned Wolf Boy.

"That's none of your business."

"If you do, which I'm guessing you don't, I'd like to give them a medal for putting up with you."

Moritz tried to hide a laugh with his hand. Charlotte smiled against her will. Sonja's face tensed. "Is that supposed to be a witty remark?"

The pedal-car took a sharp turn. They peeked out and saw an electric gate sliding open. There was a dark, gloomy building on the other side. Black smoke billowed out of its tall chimney stacks. A bronze swan with outspread wings hung over its doors. It clutched a sign in its claws: UNITED CITIES FACTORIES.

The pedal-car drove across a concrete yard and into a large loading dock. Just as they stopped to park, the children jumped out and dashed into the dark. They opened the first door they came to and looked inside. There was a long, low vestibule lined with raincoats on hooks and shiny black boots in a row.

"What—is—this place?" stammered Charlotte.

"A factory of some sort," whispered Wolf Boy.

They heard footsteps approaching through the garage. They ducked inside, opened the next door, and slipped through it. They stopped and stared with their mouths open. They stood at the end of a vast room filled with a thousand children crouched over humming sewing machines.

Women in starched, navy-blue uniforms walked up and down aisles, shouting and slapping the workers' hands with rubber batons. All the windows were boarded up, and dim lamps hung low, emitting a greenish light. Leaky pipes dripped into plastic buckets scattered around the floor.

"Let's get out of here," Sonja said, backing away.

Just then, a brawny, blond guard with her hair pulled tightly into a bun appeared in front of them with her arms crossed against her chest. "Where do you think you're going? Break's not for another twenty minutes. Put your smocks on and get to work!"

Chapter Twenty

The Factory

Before they realized what was happening, Charlotte and Sonja were pulled in one direction, and Wolf Boy and Moritz were shoved in another. "The older boys to the chopping and dicing sector!" A baton whacked Wolf Boy in the head as he looked back at the twins. Two female guards kicked him and Moritz through a pair of swinging doors.

The blond guard dragged the girls across the room between tables of pale, sickly children in stain-spattered aprons who watched from the corners of their eyes. Some of their hands trembled like Sonja's. The guard shoved the twins into two empty seats. "If I see you wandering around again, you'll be sent to the mistress."

Sonja looked bewildered. Charlotte started to explain: "I think we're in the wrong—"

"Open your mouth again, and I'll smack the words right out of you. Got it?"

Charlotte nodded feebly and slumped back down. The guard stormed off. The other children around the table stared—except for a brown-haired boy who kept his head down.

Charlotte studied his fidgeting hands. His fingers were long and thin. His hair was thick and brown and curly. Charlotte's jaw dropped. She gasped. She gripped the edge of the table.

Was it possible?

Charlotte hurriedly wiped her face and straightened her eyebrows. She gave the musical note a quick polish. She said to Sonja, "You've worn the locket for two days in a row now, and I need some good luck. Hand it over."

Sonja stared at her sister. She reluctantly unfastened the locket and gave it to Charlotte, who quickly clasped it around her neck.

Charlotte cleared her throat.

"Jack Cross," she said.

The boy looked up. He had rings around his eyes and a furrowed brow, and his cheerful smile had disappeared, but there he was, in the flesh.

Charlotte wanted to jump out of her seat and holler for joy. In all of Rain City, she had found him. It was destiny.

Sonja shook her head. "Oh, no."

Charlotte grabbed Jack Cross' hand. "Did you get my letter? I tried to warn you! Did he steal your Talent?" She looked around and lowered her voice. "Is that why you're here?"

Jack Cross stared at her blankly.

"Don't you remember me?" asked Charlotte. She pulled at her sweater and showed him the musical note. "You left me your pin!"

Jack Cross reached for the metal object, but then dropped his hand. He turned away without a word.

Charlotte's mouth quivered. She felt as though her heart might break. Was it possible Jack Cross had forgotten her?

"Morning delivery!" a voice interrupted. A boy rolled a metal trolley to a stop.

"Don't just stand there!" barked a guard with a widow's peak. She stood at the far end of the table. "Pass them out!"

The boy cursed under his breath. He reached into his trolley and lifted out what looked to be the head of an animal. He dumped one of them onto the table in front of each child.

Charlotte stared at the grisly object through cloudy eyes. The sharp peroxide smell stung her nose.

"What—*is* it?" stammered Sonja. Her face was a little greenish.

"We're making stuffed animals for Richers," whispered a girl sitting beside her.

"Quiet down over there!" roared the guard. "Where do you think you are? A birthday party?"

Charlotte looked across the table at Jack Cross again. He sat staring into space. Something was very wrong with him. Whether he remembered her or not, she had to help him. Charlotte wiped her eyes and examined the head sitting in front of her. On closer inspection, she saw that the head was in fact a metal cage covered with white fur. It had holes for the eyes, ears, nose, and mouth.

Charlotte looked down into a metal bowl in the middle of the table. An assorted selection of eyeballs stared up at her. She screamed and leapt to her feet.

She felt a thwack across her back, and her chest slammed down against the table. "Get to work, or you'll be sent to the mistress!" Charlotte had never been hit by an adult before. It sent a shock through her body.

"Are you okay?" whispered Sonja.

Charlotte nodded feebly. Her back ached. She felt dizzy. All around them children were sticking eyeballs into sockets, hammering teeth into mouths, and sewing together hunks of fur. Before Charlotte could figure out what to do next, a bell rang.

All the children stood up at once.

The guard with the widow's peak rapped the table with her baton. "Fifteen minutes lunch break!"

Charlotte hurried to keep up with Jack Cross. Sonja hurried to keep up with Charlotte.

"I can't believe you're chasing that boy," hissed Sonja. "We don't have time for romance right now. I don't want to spend the rest of my life making stuffed animals for Richers. We have to find the Changelings and go."

They entered a long, narrow room filled with crowded tables of children greedily shoving food into their mouths.

"I don't see how we're supposed to do that," whispered Charlotte. They joined the end of a lunch line. She watched Jack Cross get his lunch and sit down. "Too many guards everywhere."

A tray was shoved into their hands. A tiny cup of processed meat and a box of beige water were slammed on top of it.

"That doesn't sound like you," Sonja snapped back.

"Well, one of them just smacked me. Sort of puts things into perspective."

"It's something else, or should I say *someone* else."

Charlotte groaned. Sonja was impossible. Jealous. Didn't she understand Jack Cross needed their help? She walked over to his table and sat down between the other children. Sonja squeezed in beside her.

"I'll trade you a cherry-flavored lip gloss for two gum balls," said a boy with a shaved head.

Before the twins could answer, a shadow crossed the boy's face. He averted his gaze. Charlotte turned to see a guard standing over them. The woman looked the table up and down, slapping her baton into her hand. Finally, she moved away, and the children started whispering again.

"I remember you two," a skinny boy said from across the table. "You caused that big ruckus at the auditions."

"That's us!" exclaimed Charlotte. She remembered him, too. "You're Gustave." She turned to a freckled girl in glasses. "You're Emily."

Jack Cross sat between his friends. He did not look up from his tray.

"You're Jack's friend," said the girl. "He was talking about you all the way from the Outskirts until we arrived."

Charlotte sighed. "He doesn't remember me now."

"He hasn't been the same since—" Emily stopped talking.

"I was awake when the cats arrived," shuddered Gustave. "There were a hundred or more. All kinds of them. Then *the man* came." He swallowed. "That's all I remember. I was so scared, I must have fainted. In the morning, I couldn't play the clarinet anymore."

"He took our Talents, too," murmured Sonja. "And he kidnapped our mother."

"We couldn't play our instruments, so they kicked us out of school." Emily pushed her glasses back up onto the bridge of her freckled nose. "They told us we'd be put to work while we waited to hear from our parents. They brought us to this factory two days ago. The children here all had the same thing happen, and none of them have heard from their parents in months." Emily's voice broke. "Even if our parents came looking for us, they wouldn't be allowed into the city." She wiped her fogged-up glasses. "Nobody cares about Outskirts children."

A quiet voice beside them said, "Soon, we'll become like the others." Charlotte looked to Jack Cross. His eyes were filled with despair. "Our hearts will break without our Talents."

"What does he mean?" asked Sonja.

"The older you get without your Talent," explained Gustave, "the more of yourself you lose. Until you're like some kind of a robot."

"We've seen teenagers like that around," said Emily. "That's what scared Jack. That's when he lost hope."

"We have to escape!" cried Charlotte, standing up.

"Shh," shushed the children across the table.

Sonja yanked her sister back down into her seat.

Gustave's eyes darted across the room like a frightened deer. When he saw no guards close by, he leaned in and whispered, "Many have tried to escape, but they were all caught and never seen again."

"Time's up, you dirty brats!"

A bell rang again, and everyone jumped up.

Charlotte unclasped the musical note and pinned it onto Jack Cross' smock. "Don't forget who you are. You're a musician. We'll find our Talents, and we'll get yours back, too."

Jack Cross looked confused. He stared down at the pin.

"Come on, Charlotte." Sonja yanked her away. "We've got to look for the Changelings."

"We'll get back your Talent!" Charlotte yelled over her shoulder. Jack Cross stood frozen in the crowd. Charlotte thought she saw a tear roll down his cheek. "I promise!"

There was a glimmer of hope in his eyes, she could see it. Jack Cross had become Charlotte's friend when nobody else would. Now she would repay him. Whatever it took, she would help Jack Cross.

CHAPTER TWENTY-ONE

White Beasts

SONJA SCANNED THE CROWD OF CHILDREN, BUT WOLF BOY and Moritz were nowhere to be found. If the Changelings were not going to look for them, they would have to look for the Changelings. Sonja hated taking risks. It was more her sister's department.

Sonja yanked Charlotte under a table as the guards herded the children out of the cafeteria, threatening them with batons. Soon, the room was empty.

"What are we doing?" said Charlotte. "We have to follow the others."

"Shh!" warned Sonja. A guard stomped across the cafeteria and unlocked a door on the opposite end of the room. The words STRICTLY FORBIDDEN were stamped into the metal. Sonja swallowed. Her fingers twitched. She was sick of this stupid tic. She dug up her courage. Before the door swung shut, Sonja dashed out and stuck the tip of her boot into the closing gap.

She gestured for her sister to hurry. Charlotte reluctantly approached. They waited for a moment, then sneaked inside. The guard's footsteps rang down the corridor.

"I want to go back," insisted Charlotte. "We need to help Jack Cross."

"The only way we can do that is by getting out of here."

"I won't leave him! He needs us!"

"Lower your voice," shushed Sonja. "You'll get us caught. Have you forgotten about Tatty? Have you forgotten about *our* Talents?"

Charlotte folded her arms across her chest. "You're jealous."

"Ha! Jack Cross doesn't even remember you."

Charlotte's eyes filled with tears. She kicked the wall. She tore away from her sister and started toward the door.

Sonja's stomach dropped. As long as she could remember, it had always made her sick when she was mean to her sister. She knew how vulnerable Charlotte was underneath it all. "Porcupine!" Sonja yelled in a flash.

Charlotte stopped dead in her tracks. Sonja ran to her, and they hugged tightly. "I promise," swore Sonja, "once we get out of here and find Tatty and our Talents, we'll help Jack Cross."

"And the others?"

"And the others."

The door swung open. The blond guard burst into the corridor with a baton drawn. "I *thought* I heard a kerfuffle!" She glowered. "It's you two again. This time you're going straight to the mistress!"

Sonja grabbed her sister's hand, and they bolted down the corridor. The guard stormed after them. Sonja's heart raced. It was like they were back in the Outskirts being chased by Enforcers. The difference was that this time, they did not know the territory.

The twins zigzagged through a labyrinth of hallways until they reached a staircase. They flew up the steps and turned a corner. Growls, squawks, and wild laughter echoed down the corridor.

Sonja looked behind them. No guard, but footsteps fast approaching. This was their chance to hide. They skidded to the end of the corridor and ducked inside a darkened room.

They waited for a moment, catching their breath.

All of a sudden, a light turned on. The twins froze. A teenager with a blank expression rolled a trolley through a pair of swinging doors toward a row of steel tables. He mechanically dumped a large white lump onto each one with a thwack.

Sonja blinked. They were dead animals, stitched together at the joints like dolls. Why would anyone want to display such gruesome creatures in their home?

A buzzer rang. Two more teenagers entered. One carried a tray of needles. They went from one motionless animal to the next, repeating the same action: the boy peeled back a patch of fur or feathers from the animal's chest, and the girl stabbed it with a needle.

Sonja watched, transfixed.

They were injecting a glittering gold substance into each animal's heart.

Sonja remembered what Uncle Tell had said: when magic was released from the body, it turned gold.

One by one, the animals began to twitch until the whole row was jerking and shaking. Suddenly, a hyena's eyes snapped open.

It was alive.

Charlotte screamed and pressed against Sonja. They trembled

together like two leaves on a branch. The teenagers looked up from what they were doing. Sonja felt a cold slap across the back of her neck. She spun around and saw the blond guard looming over them.

"Got you!" she boomed. The guard grabbed the twins and dragged them away.

Sonja looked back over her shoulder. A swan opened its rusty beak and squawked. A hyena arched its deformed back and howled. This was a factory—for monsters! Sonja remembered the swans that had attacked their caravan, and the hyena that had bitten her ankle. Something terrible was happening here, and Sonja had a bad feeling that Kats von Stralen and his mother were behind it.

Chapter Twenty-Two

Mistress Koch

"Mistress Koch? I have the girls." The blond guard spoke into an intercom next to a door at the end of a long corridor. Charlotte struggled to break free under her tight grip. She could hear Sonja muttering to herself, frightened.

A voice crackled, "Enter."

The door buzzed, and the guard pushed the twins into an office. Charlotte recognized the music on the radio: Kanazi Kooks. A short, stocky woman wearing a hairnet sat at a desk in the middle of the room with her back to them. Her fingers clicked across the keys of a typewriter. A large screen behind her was filled with numerous smaller screens televising every room in the factory. Charlotte's eyes darted from one image to the next. Thousands of children. Slaves. She knew Sonja was right: the only way to help Jack Cross and the others was from the outside. She scanned the room for an escape route. Her eyes fell on the stacks and stacks of letters piled in towers all around the floor. Charlotte squinted to read them. They were addressed to different children at the School for the Gifted.

The guard cleared her throat.

"One moment," snapped the woman. She stopped typing and spun her chair around to face the twins.

She was the head judge from the audition. Charlotte remembered her long nose and thick eyebrows that met in the middle. Her uniform was stiff, and she smelled of bitter almonds. "You're the two who made trouble at the audition," she said, narrowing her small, brown eyes.

"What audition?" Sonja hesitated and then said, "We weren't at any audition."

Mistress Koch's little eyes squinted, making them even littler. "That's a lie."

"A lie," repeated the guard. She gave each twin a shove.

Charlotte stumbled into a tall stack of letters, which toppled all over the floor. She imagined they were from the families of thousands of the factory children. None had been delivered. She thought of her letter to Jack Cross, unopened. Her jaw clenched. Her brow furrowed. She scooped up a handful.

"We know what you're doing!" she burst out. "You're keeping these children prisoners!"

Sonja stepped forward. "Please, ignore my sister," she apologized. "She's a little out of sorts."

"I'm going straight to the newspapers!" threatened Charlotte. "I'll tell them what you're making here! People will shut this factory down!"

Mistress Koch's bird-of-prey nose twitched. She glared at the girls, her eyes now only minuscule dots. "They're to be incarcerated!"

"To be incarcerated," repeated the guard. She hooked her brawny arms around the twins. Charlotte wriggled underneath her fleshy limbs like a fish. "Let go of me, you bully!"

"Hold—on—a—second," stammered Sonja. "We can explain."

A voice squawked through the intercom, "I have the boys."

"Ah, your accomplices!" exclaimed Mistress Koch, jumping to her feet. She was not much taller standing up than she was sitting down. She rummaged through a rack of canes. She pulled out the thickest one and swiped it several times in the air.

The door opened, and Wolf Boy and Moritz stumbled in. Their arms were bound with ropes. A bigger, even more powerfully built guard followed them.

"Hello, ladies," cooed Wolf Boy.

"Wolf Boy! Moritz!" cried Sonja. Charlotte cheered. They were sure to escape now.

"You've been busy, haven't you, boys?" Mistress Koch strode up to Wolf Boy and poked his cheek with the tip of the cane. "First, you damaged factory property. Second, you aided an attempted escape. Both highly punishable crimes."

"Fun, too," admitted Wolf Boy. Moritz nodded in agreement.

Mistress Koch ignored him and continued, "We're ready to be lenient, *if*—when I say *if*, I mean *if*—"

"She always means what she says," interrupted the powerfully built guard.

"*If*," Mistress Koch repeated, annoyed, "you tell us what rebellion you're associated with."

Wolf Boy thought for a moment and with a big smile said, "The rebellion against the mean, fat, ugly prison guards!"

Moritz chuckled. The powerfully built guard slapped him with her baton.

"Why'd you hit *me*?" Moritz whined. "*He* said the funny line! I just laughed."

The powerfully built guard whacked Wolf Boy, too.

Charlotte giggled.

Her sister said under her breath, "It's not funny."

Mistress Koch rolled up her sleeves, steaming. "I've dealt with boys exactly like you a thousand times. You never learn."

"Really?" said Wolf Boy.

"Really," said Mistress Koch.

"Exactly like us?" said Wolf Boy, grinning.

"Exactly like you," said Mistress Koch, grinning back.

"I find that hard to believe," grunted Wolf Boy. Black fur began to sprout across his skin. "What do you think, Moritz?"

Moritz neighed. His body twisted. Red hair grew down his back, and the ropes snapped loose. Mistress Koch's mouth dropped open as the boys became animals right before her eyes. With a kick and a shove, Wolf Boy and Moritz spun the two guards across the room, banging them into the bookcases.

Mistress Koch ran to her desk and fumbled through the drawers. Just as she pulled out a Gatsploder, Moritz butted the table with the top of his head and flipped it upside down. It landed on top of her. She reached for a black button and jammed her finger into it.

Sirens rang throughout the factory.

Down on the floor, Charlotte saw a little framed photograph of Mistress Koch and Kats von Stralen. She was certain: whatever the factory was doing, Kats von Stralen was a part of it. She stuffed the picture into her jacket pocket. It might be evidence for the newspapers.

Moritz stamped his hooves, and the twins scrambled onto his back.

"I know an escape route!" growled Wolf Boy. They raced out of the room and galloped down the corridor. They bolted through a storeroom, turned a corner, and skidded to a stop. The hallway dead-ended in a window.

"I thought you knew a way out of here," yelled Sonja.

Wolf Boy grinned. "You're looking at it."

Moritz shook his mane and flared his nostrils.

"It's our only choice, Moritz," urged Wolf Boy.

"You can't be serious!" cried Charlotte. "We'll die!"

There was a shout behind them. "Hold it right there!"

A squad of Enforcers dressed in black from head to toe piled into the corridor from two directions with steel batons drawn.

Sonja gulped. "Where did they come from?"

Wolf Boy looked from the advancing Enforcers back to the window. He took a deep breath and said, "Ready, Moritz?"

Before the girls could say another word, Moritz charged toward the window. Wolf Boy followed close behind. Charlotte and Sonja covered their faces as they crashed through glass. Shards flew everywhere. They dropped through the air—then landed with a sudden thud.

The falling rain showered their faces.

Charlotte peered down over her shoulder. They were balanced on the edge of a narrow pedal-car track. There was nothing below except more tracks crisscrossing one another in midair straight down for a mile. Her sister trembled behind her with her hands wrapped tightly around Charlotte's waist. Charlotte held on to her arms and whispered quietly:

"She was getting ready for bed one night when she heard a knock at her door—"

Sonja put her chin on Charlotte's shoulder and said in a shaky voice, "It was her first week at the circus. She was scared to live alone in a caravan."

"She peeked outside, but nobody was there. Just as she was about to close the door, she heard a gurgling, gargling sound, and she looked down at the ground—"

"And there we two were. Wrapped in one woolen shawl and stuffed into a milk pail."

Enforcers at the smashed window above pointed their weapons.

"Let's go!" exclaimed Wolf Boy.

They raced down the track. Corkscrew bullets whizzed past them, one after the other. The factory's gate burst open and a giant

178

hyena bounded onto the track after them. A few children spilled outdoors, cheering. They were quickly surrounded by guards. Charlotte thought she saw Jack Cross. She waved and yelled wildly as they disappeared around a corner.

"We have to jump," Wolf Boy said determinedly.

"Jump?" shouted Sonja. "Where?"

Wolf Boy dove into the air and landed on a lower track, scrambling not to slip. "Your turn!" he shouted up to Moritz.

"No!" Sonja begged. "Don't kill us, Moritz!"

The track shook behind them. Charlotte whipped her head around. The hyena was a breath away. "Go, go, go!" she screamed.

Moritz jumped onto the lower track. The twins shrieked as they slid sideways. A pedal-car was speeding toward them. The driver honked his horn as a woman in the backseat continued her conversation on the telephone. The hyena neared the edge of the higher track, about to dive down on top of them.

"One more!" Wolf Boy yelled to Moritz. The Changelings leapt into the air and landed on an even lower track just as the hyena jumped down from above and the pedal-car smashed into him. He was thrown back into the air and splattered on a track ten stories below.

Lights beamed down. Propellers sliced through the rain. A fleet of pedal-copters hovered above. Enforcers stuck their heads out the sides and roared into loudspeakers: "Runaway animals carrying two suspected traitors!"

The Changelings bolted down the track. It cut through a building. They ducked inside and hid in the dark as pedal-cars zoomed by, back and forth. The twins climbed down from Moritz's back, and the Changelings transformed themselves back into boys. Pedal-copters hovered into view on both sides of the tunnel.

Charlotte looked left and right. They were surrounded. There was nowhere to run. Sonja clung to her and whispered, "There was a note pinned to the shawl, and a heart-shaped locket."

Charlotte tapped the locket against her chest. It might still bring them luck. "She had tried to have her own children, but she never could. It was at that moment that she knew why. She was waiting for her dear girls to be delivered to her in a milk pail."

The Changelings were searching the walls frantically. "Has to be here somewhere," Wolf Boy said anxiously.

Moritz rubbed some dirt off a metal switch plate on the wall. A small red button blinked faintly. The word REFUSE was printed above it.

"Found it!" declared Moritz. He pressed the button. A pair of heavy steel doors zigzagged open with a screeching groan. The boys climbed into a cramped metal box. A few leftover scraps of garbage littered the floor.

The pedal-copters entered the tunnel.

"Come on!" urged Wolf Boy.

Sonja shook her head. "We're not refuse!"

Wolf Boy stuck his head out of the opening. "If you don't get in here right this minute, you will be."

Charlotte pushed Sonja inside and jumped in after her. Their bodies were squashed together like sardines. The doors slammed shut, instantly muffling the sound of the whooshing pedal-copter propellers.

It was pitch black, dead quiet, and nearly impossible to breathe.

"I think I'm going to be sick." Sonja coughed, pulling her head out of Wolf Boy's armpit.

An alarm sounded. The box jerked forward and locked into place. Gears crunched and rolled, and they began to tip over sideways.

"What—what's happening?" stammered Charlotte.

"Imagine it's a roller coaster," Moritz said cheerfully.

"I hate roller coasters!" Sonja said, starting to panic.

"Will you trust us, for once?" shouted Wolf Boy.

"Trust you? You're the one who got us into this mess!"

The box stopped flat on its side.

The bottom swung open, and they all dropped straight down. Charlotte's fingernails scratched across the metal as she fell, flailing her arms and legs, grabbing at anything. She tumbled for what seemed like a full minute. Suddenly, she landed hard next to Sonja and the Changelings in a pile of garbage in a gigantic, dark room. Bits of wet paper and rotten food rained down on them. They crawled out from plastic bags and slimy cartons.

Charlotte covered her mouth. The stench was unbearable. Sonja pulled an old toothbrush out of her hair. "How could you do this?" hissed Sonja. "Don't you know this place is festering with disease?"

"I didn't hear anyone else come up with any ideas," Wolf Boy replied, pulling a banana peel off his shoulder.

Voices echoed off the walls. Workmen in gray jumpsuits were shoveling garbage into the backs of dump trucks to take to the Outskirts. Wolf Boy motioned for everyone to follow him, and they slid down the trash pile. He waited until the whistling workmen moved on, and dashed into a short tunnel, turned down a bright hallway, and spun through a revolving door out onto a sidewalk. They were finally outside. The flooded streets were below them. They had reached the bottom of the city.

Wolf Boy and Moritz washed their faces in the rain and wiped the grime off their fur cloaks. Sonja shook out their hair and peeled noodles and slimy wrappers off their boots. Charlotte took several gulps of air and looked up. The never-ending city was whizzing and whirling for miles above them. She thought of Jack Cross caught somewhere in the middle. She pressed her eyes shut. Maybe if she concentrated hard enough, she could send him a message:

> *Dear Jack Cross,*
> *Sorry we left in such a hurry. Don't despair.*
> *We'll be back with your Talent. I promise.*
> *Best regards, Charlotte*

CHAPTER TWENTY-THREE

The Lower Depths

A DULL GRAY SMOG FILLED THE LOWER DEPTHS. RAIN peppered the standing water. Old houses from the original city were squeezed between the foundations of the Million-Mile-High buildings. Flickering lamps hung from rusted tracks above. This was the old city Uncle Tell must have known, thought Sonja.

The Changelings sloshed full speed through the flooded street.

"We're close now," Wolf Boy said over his shoulder. "Only a few blocks away. I hope Alexandria made it."

"Won't you slow down a little?" moaned Sonja. She was aching all over. She had had enough of garbage and factories—and Changelings, for that matter.

"We can't," Moritz said breathlessly. "We don't want to run into—"

"Old friends?"

A Scrummager in a striped vest stood leaning against a broken-down pedal-car ahead of them. He flipped a coin. Another

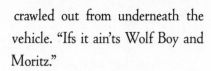

crawled out from underneath the vehicle. "Ifs it ain'ts Wolf Boy and Moritz."

Five more dirty, skinny boys appeared out of the wreckage and ruins dressed in tattered old suits and moth-bitten hats and surrounded the Changelings. Sacks were slung over their bony shoulders.

The familiar sight comforted Sonja. She never thought Scrummagers would one day warm her heart.

"Our old compadres!" Wolf Boy said heartily. "How's dodging these days?"

"Fair, fair," replied the one in the vest. "Wheres you twos been?"

Moritz shrugged. "Here and there."

"Figured yous been adopted by that Richer. Lady's been takin' alls sorts. Even tooks that grot-brain, Georgie."

"That true?" asked Wolf Boy. "What's she doing with them?"

"Dressin' 'em in fineries. Feedin' 'em real grub and stuff. Givin' 'em weapons and beasts and things. Makin' 'em real tough!"

"I's wishin' she'd adopts the likes of me!" chirped a muddy-faced little boy.

Sonja thought for a moment. The Scrummagers who had helped Kats von Stralen kidnap Tatty sounded exactly like the boys they were describing. That was why they had been so well dressed and clean and had bows and arrows and batons—the Contessa was adopting them to do her dirty work.

"Now listen, compadres," interrupted Wolf Boy. "I'm afraid

184

we're in a bit of a hurry. How about we come see you in a couple of days and have ourselves a real Rump-Fest?"

"Yous owes us coins, compadres."

Moritz chuckled. "We owe everyone coins."

An angry murmur spread among the boys. Wolf Boy gave Moritz a look. Moritz nodded. Wolf Boy grabbed Sonja while Moritz snatched up Charlotte, and they all took off running. Water splashed everywhere as the Scrummagers raced after them, cursing and yelling, lugging junk-filled sacks on their backs.

"Put me down!" insisted Sonja. She hated being close to Wolf Boy. He smelled even worse than Monkey.

"Will you be quiet?" he yelled back. "Don't you see we're in the middle of a chase?"

The rain came down harder, and the Lower Depths darkened. They ran past a row of narrow houses. Brown smoke puffed from the chimneys, and dead flowers drooped from broken pots on the windowsills. A woman dumped a bucket of dirty dishwater out her front door.

The Changelings ducked into an alleyway and hid behind a row of overflowing trash cans. The gang of Scrummagers ran rumbling by.

Wolf Boy laughed. "They fall for it every time." He let go of Sonja. She stumbled into a murky puddle.

"Try and be more careful!" she cried, pulling her drenched shoes out of the water.

Wolf Boy shrugged. He walked off ahead of them. Moritz gave Sonja an apologetic look and ran after Wolf Boy.

Sonja simmered, angry. She wished she could bite his nose or pinch his arms or kick him in the shins. She turned to complain to her sister.

Charlotte was standing in front of a detached house with boarded-up windows. There were posters of Kanazi Kooks plastered all over the walls. A sign on the door read SCHOOL FOR THE GIFTED.

Charlotte swallowed. "This is where they lost their Talents." She handed Sonja Jack Cross' crumpled-up letter. Sonja examined the address. It matched the grimy street sign: BISHOP'S ROW. The front steps were covered in muddy paw prints, and graffiti scrawled across the door in black paint read, *The King of the Kats was here*.

"Do you think about playing?" Charlotte asked quietly.

Sonja held up her twitching fingers. "All the time. My fingers don't let me forget."

"Isn't it funny?" said Charlotte. "I've always wanted to have something in common with other children, and now we do." She smiled sadly. "Jack Cross and the others. They've all lost their Talents and their parents and their homes. Just like us."

"Over here, girls!" Sonja heard Moritz yell. The Changelings were across the street at a telephone booth.

Sonja put her arm around her sister. "Remember, we're going to help them as soon as we've found Tatty and our Talents."

Charlotte nodded and leaned her head on Sonja's arm. "Thank goodness we still have each other." It was good to hear Charlotte say that. Sometimes Sonja worried her sister did not need her at all.

The twins stopped in front of a telephone booth attached to a rickety, old building. Filthy children lowered cans from the windows of the orphanages overhead, shouting for coins.

A beggarman crept out of his makeshift home. He opened his palms and croaked, "Something for the needy?"

Wolf Boy sighed. "Nothing changes around here." He stepped into the telephone booth, picked up the telephone receiver, and said, "Code word: Amadeus."

The side of the telephone booth swung open, and a small man with a pencil-thin mustache wearing a white suit and a pink bow tie appeared in the doorway. "Velcome!" he said, and ushered them inside.

They entered a dark, shabby room. Ripped oriental lanterns hung from the ceiling. Faded posters peeled off the walls. An old-fashioned song played on a scratchy record player. Sonja recognized it. Tatty had sung it to them when they were babies. Men and women reclined on dirty divans, drinking from bottles and smoking from tall, gurgling hookahs. A woman with messy hair and smudged

makeup whispered to a man wearing a bear costume, and they both burst out laughing. Sonja counted only ten teeth between them.

Moritz tripped over a snoring body

sprawled across the floor, bumped into a waiter carrying a platter of dirty plates, and sent dishes, bones, forks, knives, and gravy crashing and splattering everywhere.

"I'm awfully sorry," Moritz apologized. He bent down and started to pick up bits of broken plate.

The waiter stamped his foot down on Moritz's hand. Moritz squealed and looked up.

"You dirty Scrummager!" roared the waiter.

"We're not Scrummagers," Wolf Boy said, gritting his teeth. Sonja grabbed Wolf Boy's cloak and whispered, "I think we should go."

Wolf Boy shoved her off and spat, "Mind your own business."

The waiter rolled up his sleeves, revealing a carpet of hair on his arms. "I bet my momma's false teeth you're Scrummagers!"

"I bet *your* false teeth we're not!"

The waiter paused. "I don't have none."

"But you will." Wolf Boy leapt up and punched him in the mouth.

The waiter smiled a bloody smile. He grabbed a chair and lifted it up over the top of his head—but before he had a chance to bring it slamming down, it flew out of his hand, rocketed across the room, and banged into two reclining men in red velvet turbans. They dove for cover.

The waiter looked puzzled. He turned around.

A woman seated at the bar pulled back the hood of her coat. "I thought you might need some help." Alexandria smiled.

Sonja laughed nervously. For the first time in her life, she was happy to see her.

CHAPTER TWENTY-FOUR

The Captain and the Library

ALEXANDRIA LED THE CHILDREN AROUND THE BAR, through the back corridor, and down a narrow staircase. They entered a cellar filled with metal barrels. Charlotte looked around the candlelit room, confused. Alexandria twisted the rusty tap on a barrel. A gush of black gin poured out into her open flask. Charlotte frowned. They did not have time to indulge Alexandria's addictions. They had people to save.

"Where's Staghart?" Wolf Boy asked. "Is he meeting us here?"

"Shot in the shoulder," said Alexandria. "He's back in the Forlorn Forest. We'll send word once we know Tatty's whereabouts." Alexandria shoved the flask into her coat pocket and pulled out Staghart's Amulet. "You're in charge of the Amber Drop now."

Moritz stared wide eyed as Wolf Boy timidly took the gold-colored pendant. Moritz gulped. "You trust him with that?"

"*I* don't. *Staghart* does."

Wolf Boy put the Amber Drop around his neck. It lit up for a moment, then faded again. Moritz touched the warm, brilliant stone. "Staghart said it was more precious than his life."

"*Much* more," reiterated Alexandria. She looked at Wolf Boy. "You get the idea?"

"Yeah," Wolf Boy muttered. "I get the idea."

"What happened to you, anyway?" asked Alexandria. She grabbed a candle and walked to the middle of the room. "I've been waiting down here for ages."

"Wolf Boy got us trapped in a factory," Sonja blurted.

Charlotte rolled her eyes. Being a tattletale was one of her sister's worst qualities. Wolf Boy already hated her. This would make it worse.

Wolf Boy glared at Sonja. "Funny, I thought I was the one who got us *out* of there."

"A steel factory?" Alexandria interrupted. She started to rub the sawdust off a flagstone with her boot. "One of the Contessa's?"

"Not steel," corrected Moritz. "Animals."

Alexandria straightened. "Animals?"

"Creatures." Wolf Boy grimaced. "It was awful."

"They injected something into their hearts," Charlotte said quietly, "and suddenly they were alive."

"Alive?" Alexandria said hesitantly. She grabbed Charlotte by the shoulders. "Are you sure that's what you saw?"

Charlotte nodded, a little taken aback. She could feel Alexandria's fingers press into her skin. "Tell her, Sonja."

"It's true. They injected something gold. Sort of floating and glittering." Sonja paused. "Is it magic?"

Alexandria's bewildered expression turned into a horrified one. She let go of Charlotte. "I thought it was an old wives' tale that magic could bring the dead to life."

190

Charlotte pulled out the framed photograph she had stolen. "I took this. It's the woman who runs the factory shaking hands with Kats von Stralen. They have children working there against their will. They'll die. They need our help."

Alexandria stared at the photograph. "Only he would have found a way to make it work," she muttered to herself. "He's stealing Talents to get magic out of them. That's where all the white beasts are coming from." She paused and then raised her eyebrows. Charlotte saw a terrible thought enter her mind. In a barely audible whisper, Alexandria said, "He's building her an army."

Alexandria flung the photograph against the wall. The glass behind the frame shattered into a hundred little pieces.

Charlotte groaned. "That was evidence."

"Why an army?" said Sonja. "There's no war."

"There will be. Just like Staghart said."

Alexandria hastily kicked sawdust off a flagstone. A winged man with horns was roughly engraved into it. Charlotte recognized that it was a Tiffin. This was the Pathway into the Land Where the Plants Reign.

With a quick flick of her wrist, Alexandria swiped the stone away. Underneath it was a wooden door. She snapped her fingers. Nothing happened. She tried again, but the door remained closed. "Help me, boys," she said, kneeling down. Six hands grabbed the iron handle and pulled. The Changelings' faces turned purple. They let go, breathless. The door would not budge.

"Power stronger than mine has blocked the Pathway. The Tiffins are preparing for the worst." Alexandra thought for a moment.

"We're going to have to go another way. We still have time. The Protectors won't be there until tomorrow."

"Wait a second!" interrupted Sonja. "We have to meet Uncle Tell!"

"Are you deaf?" returned Alexandria. "The Pathway is blocked."

"We've been up and down and all over the place!" yelled Sonja.

"There's nothing we can do except go another way. Do you understand?"

Sonja glared at Alexandria, silent.

Alexandria's eyes flashed with anger. "I'm warning you. If I hear another peep from either of you, I'm leaving you behind."

Wolf Boy raised his hand. "I agree."

"Who asked you?" snapped Sonja.

"I didn't even say anything," mumbled Charlotte. She was always being blamed for Sonja's attitude. That was the price of being identical. Among other things.

Alexandria whipped the stone back into place and charged to the other end of the cellar. Her coat swept across the floor. Sawdust flew everywhere. She kicked open a short, arched door and strode out. The stink of rotting fish swept in. The Changelings followed her.

"I hate them," fumed Sonja. "All of them. Well, not Moritz."

"We don't have time for this," said Charlotte hurriedly. "I think she really will leave us here." Charlotte pulled the reluctant Sonja onto a platform overlooking a network of canals. Long, narrow motorboats surged through the water, carrying goods from one part of the city to the other. Black moths swarmed around lamps hanging from the vaulted ceilings. Cockroaches fed on a slimy film that coated the brick floor.

Uncle Tell had told them that the canals were once the tunnels of an underground train system. As the city grew upward and the rainfall grew heavier, the tunnels were deserted and the cargo boats moved in.

Charlotte felt as though it had been years since she had seen Uncle Tell, and even longer since she had seen Tatty. If only she would wake up and it would all turn out to be a dream.

Dear Jack Cross,
> *Remember when we spoke about leaving the Outskirts and our homes? Now I wish we could go back.*
>> *Best regards, Charlotte*

"Stand behind me," ordered Alexandria. She flagged down a half-empty boat.

The skipper, red faced and unshaven, slowed his motor. He wore three jackets, one on top of the other, and a blue woolen hat. A mottled dog barked as they reached the edge of the platform.

"We want to go to the old city library," Alexandria called out to him.

"Nah, we never go there." The man scratched his beard and motioned to the dog. "Barnaby don't like it."

Alexandria pulled out a coin from her pocket and dropped it into the man's hand. The man stared at the coin blankly. Alexandria dropped in two more. The man grinned. His teeth were black from gin.

"My gracious lady," he said, bowing, "please, do accept me humble apologies. I misunderstood you. It'll be me pleasure to escort you to the ole library."

Moritz helped the twins onto the boat. Rusted metal crates were stacked everywhere. Charlotte looked around, unsure where to sit.

"Make yourselves at home." The skipper took a swig out of a bottle wrapped in a paper bag. "Just don't all sit on one side. We don't want to be fallin' into this stinkin' water." He tapped a tin plug in his ear. "That's how I lost half me hearin'. Blessed filth."

The twins squeezed together between two crates. Alexandria sat a little distance away near the front of the boat. Charlotte wanted to ask her why they were going to the old city library and how it was going to bring them to the Land Where the Plants Reign, but she was too afraid to be yelled at or even worse—left behind. Barnaby sidled over to her, sniffing curiously. She scratched under his chin. He licked her hand appreciatively. His rough-cut metal dentures glinted in the light.

"What happened to his teeth?" Charlotte asked curiously.

"Sold 'em for coins," replied the skipper as he steered the boat away from the platform. "Up in 'em factories." Charlotte thought about the tooth they had found in Sonja's ankle—a dog's tooth. "Barnaby never forgave me. Even after I made 'im a new pair." He took another swig of black gin and belched. "Saved 'is life, they did. Scrummagers tried to take 'im when we was asleep, but Barnaby bit one of their hands clean off." He chuckled. "Glad I carved those jammers sharp."

The dog barked as they glided past a pair of Scrummagers standing over the edge of a platform holding a net into the water.

"Surprised he ain't taken a chunk out of you two," the man said to the Changelings. "Doesn't usually like boys. Thinks they're all Scrummagers."

"He knows we're different," said Wolf Boy, petting Barnaby. "He can smell it."

"It's unavoidable," muttered Sonja. "We all can."

Wolf Boy growled. Moritz sighed.

"What are they fishing for?" asked Charlotte, changing the subject.

"Some of our finest cuisine's in these canals: four-legged pike, one-eyed newts, paddlin' rats."

Charlotte wrinkled her nose. "Sounds delicious."

The skipper took another drink and squinted at the twins. Charlotte was used to people staring at them. She felt that it gave her the right to stare back. She studied his face: it was grizzled and ruddy with two sad blue eyes. Charlotte wondered what had happened in the skipper's life that brought him to these canals with only Barnaby as company.

"I see you two been born lucky," he said finally. "That's what the old captain used to say: two born the same, born lucky."

"I'm not sure we *are* very lucky," Sonja returned unhappily.

Charlotte wrinkled her brow and said, "Old captain?"

"Used to sail the waters with 'im before the seas dried-up. Died of a broken heart, he did. Missed 'em blessed waves too much. Now alls I got is this stinkin' boat and me ole pal Barnaby." The skipper threw his empty bottle into the canal and rummaged for a full one in a box by his feet. "Sorry times, these."

Charlotte agreed. She leaned her tired head on Sonja's shoulder. It was hours past their bedtime. Her thoughts drifted to Jack Cross. She imagined him in a little cot next to a hundred little cots of sleeping factory children. She pictured Tatty alone and scared in a cell. And Monkey? Goodness knows where. If they made it out of this mess, Charlotte promised herself, she would sleep for a hundred years.

They turned into an adjoining waterway and saw an impressive old building standing before them. Letters engraved in the stone facade spelled the words MUNICIPAL LIBRARY. Massive columns lined the entrance, and a sculpted sphinx flanked each side.

"Everyone thinks it's haunted." The skipper nervously fiddled with his cap. "That's why we stay clear away."

Charlotte had seen a photograph of Uncle Tell as a young boy standing in front of this very building. He said the library had sunk into the canals because of the rain. The same thing had happened to many of the old buildings, but nobody who mattered lived below the thousandth floor, so nobody who mattered bothered to do anything about it.

The skipper brought the boat as close as he could to the submerged steps. Alexandria dropped another coin into his sweaty palm. "Get some dinner," she urged as she stepped off the boat. The children followed her. "That stuff'll kill you. I should know."

The skipper took off his cap and bowed his head. "It already has, my gracious lady. It already has."

Barnaby stuck his snout out the side of the boat and barked. Charlotte waved goodbye. Even after the boat disappeared around the corner, she could still hear Barnaby barking.

The library door was chained shut. A sign read DO NOT ENTER.

Alexandria clapped her hands together hard. The lock broke, and the chain unraveled into the water. The doors swung open. A gust of trapped air rushed out. It smelled of moldy books and dead animals.

Alexandria peeled the skin off a handful of lightning bugs. They flew into the library and lit the room. The stacks were wrapped in spiderwebs, and desks and chairs were overturned and broken. A large chandelier still hung from the ceiling, but all its crystal tears had smashed onto the ground. They glittered among animal droppings and half-eaten books.

Little creatures skittered in every corner as they walked to the end of the room. Alexandria shoved open a brass door with her shoulder. Inside was a small octagonal chamber lined with beautifully gilded leather almanacs.

"Look at all these books!" Charlotte exclaimed. She pulled one out, blew off the dust, and carefully turned the fragile pages. It was an old dictionary with words she did not recognize, such as *jargogle* and *quockerwodger* and *slubberdegullion*.

"Where do we go from here?" Wolf Boy asked.

Charlotte put away the book and looked where Alexandria was pointing. There was a large gold seal on the floor with images of numerous small, delicate, childlike people engraved into it.

"Those are Albans," Charlotte said, approaching. "Does that mean we're going to the Golden Underground?"

Alexandria nodded. "It's the only other way to get to the Land Where the Plants Reign." She swept her hand through the air with a forceful thrust. The seal slowly slid open to reveal a hole. The lightning bugs dove down into it.

Alexandria sighed, relieved. "At least *this* Pathway's open." She buttoned her pockets and tightened her cloak. "Protect your heads with your arms. It can be quite a tumble."

Sonja peered into the hole. "I'm not going down there!"

Alexandria looked to Wolf Boy. Wolf Boy nodded. Alexandria stepped into the darkness and disappeared down the hole. Her hair unbuckled after her.

Sonja turned to Charlotte with a frightened expression. Charlotte knew she was the braver of the two when it came to heights and speeds and . . . courage. She felt especially brave now. They had to save not only Tatty, but also hundreds of factory children. She was starting to feel ashamed of Sonja. She wished her sister was not such a coward. "Don't be scared," she said soothingly. "After all, you survived the trash chute."

"That was just blind luck."

"Look, Sonja," said Moritz, side-stepping to the edge of the hole, "It's easy!" He jumped in and yelled, "Bombs away!"

"It's our turn," said Charlotte.

Sonja shook her head. "I won't."

"I'll take her," insisted Wolf Boy.

"What?" Sonja cried. "Charlotte!"

Charlotte let go of Sonja and smiled. "You'll be fine."

Wolf Boy grabbed Sonja's hand.

"Don't touch me."

"Why not?"

"Because I told you not to."

Wolf Boy stared at Sonja. "How about this?" He wrapped his arm around her waist and squeezed tight.

Sonja slapped him and wriggled. "Let me go!"

Wolf Boy laughed and ducked, but held on.

"You act like an animal."

"Well, I *am* an animal." Wolf Boy grinned.

"I hate you."

"The feeling's mutual."

Charlotte watched as they plummeted together deep down into the darkness, then dove in after them.

Dear Jack Cross,
  I travel farther away from you in body, but not in heart.
  I hope you're thinking of me. I'm thinking of you.
                    Best regards, Charlotte

Make that: Love, Charlotte

Chapter Twenty-Five

The Golden Underground

Sonja's eyes snapped open. They had tumbled out of a fireplace and lay on the floor of a large stone room. She sat up and gasped. A small boy with luminous white skin and pink eyes stood over them holding a dagger in his fist. He was barefoot, and his hair was as white as his skin.

> *Deep, deep underground,*
> *In grottos of golden décor,*
> *Lives a white Alban among the giant boars.*
> *His eyes see in pitch-dark blackness—*
> *And his ears can hear even a mouse snore.*

"Hello, Ansel," Alexandria greeted the Alban. She stood up and dusted off her coat.

The boy's mouth broadened into a smile. He had a gap between his front teeth. He put away his dagger and hugged Alexandria. The top of his head barely reached her waist.

Alexandria peeled away his little arms from around her legs. "You know I hate hugs."

The boy laughed. "I'm sorry. I can't help myself."

Sonja started to say something, when Wolf Boy interrupted her. "Let me guess. Your mother told you all about the Albans." He smiled at Ansel. "Don't let it get to your head. She told them all about the Changelings too."

Sonja's face turned bright red. If only she was a giant and could stomp on top of Wolf Boy until he was as flat as a pancake—then, maybe, she would be happy.

"Ansel, meet Charlotte and Sonja. They're the daughters of the Key. Those two clowns over there are Wolf Boy and Moritz."

The Alban shook hands with everyone enthusiastically. His hand was cold, thought Sonja. He smelled like licorice.

The lightning bugs circled the stone room. Frescoes had been chipped away from the ceiling, and tiles and panels had been pried off the walls. "What happened here?" said Alexandria, looking around. "The entrance moved?"

The boy's smile faded. His gaze flickered to the ground. "This is where my father was attacked. Edgar thought it would be safer to move the palace deeper underground."

Alexandria touched his shoulder. "Your father was a great leader. One of the best."

"Thank you," Ansel said softly.

"We've come for help. The Key's been stolen. The Protectors are meeting in the Land Where the Plants Reign. We need passage through the Golden Underground."

"I'll take you to my brother. He now wears the Golden Knot. It was our father's last wish that he'd become Protector."

Alexandria looked confused, then doubtful. "It wasn't his decision to make."

"I know. It's time someone told Edgar."

The Alban led them into a tunnel that had been stripped clean of any decoration whatsoever. Only the faintest shadows of painted faces remained. "Lucky I heard you coming," he said over his shoulder, "or you'd have been lost for days. I was tracking a boar close by to lure him away from our gates. So he doesn't get hurt." The boy paused. "Hold on a second." He dropped to his knees, pressed his ear to the ground, and listened. "I think I hear him now."

Sonja shivered. The giant boar tattooed above Tatty's calf was the scariest creature on her body.

A distant rumble echoed down the tunnel. The ground trembled.

Ansel unwound a charm from around his neck. It was a small box with holes pierced into its sides and hung on a long leather string. "You'd better hide."

"Don't worry about us," growled Wolf Boy. "We can take care of ourselves." He and Moritz began to transform into animals.

"Let's see how you feel afterward," Alexandria said, cupping the lightning bugs in her hands.

The sound of stomping hooves filled the cave. Sonja watched, transfixed, as a pair of spiraled tusks, scarred and scored like ancient weapons, emerged slowly, curling out of the darkness. A massive, hairy head followed into the half-light. The boar was three times bigger than even Sonja had imagined. He blinked once, snorted, then charged, roaring down the tunnel, dirt spraying behind him.

Sonja darted into an alcove where Alexandria and Charlotte were hiding. She peeked out. The boar smashed through the Changelings like a cyclone. They flew, spinning, in different directions. The boar skittered to a stop and swiveled. The Changelings crawled, panting and dazed, on the ground. Shock had jolted them back into their human form. The boar narrowed its already tiny eyes. It lowered its head and charged again, squealing.

"They're going to get killed!" cried Charlotte.

Alexandria shrugged. "It's their own fault."

"You don't really mean that, do you, Alexandria?" Sonja said in a panic. "I don't like them much, but even I don't want them to die!"

"Don't worry. Ansel's there to help."

"What can *he* do?" yelled Sonja. "He's practically a child."

"Don't judge a book by its cover, Charlotte. You'll see."

Sonja's face burned with indignation. How could Alexandria still not know their names? "I'm SONJA!" she thundered.

Charlotte pointed. "Look! There he is!"

Ansel stood in the boar's path, swinging his charm. Smoke ribboned out from the holes in the little box. They could smell it from fifty feet. Ansel swirled the vapors into a cloud and jumped out of the way. The boar raced through the smoke, wheezing. It staggered and stumbled backward.

Ansel sprinted to the boar, grabbed it by the tusks, and flung his pale body up onto the giant creature's back. The boar bucked weakly as the Alban gripped his coarse fur. Ansel swung the charm again, casting another puff of smoke. The boar stood motionless. His eyes glazed.

"It's safe now!" Ansel called out to the others as he hung the charm around the boar's neck.

Alexandria charged into the tunnel and helped the Changelings to their feet. "The girls were worried. They thought the two of you might be killed."

"We're fine," Wolf Boy insisted. He stood up, wobbly, and wiped the blood off his mouth.

Moritz gulped. "That thing nearly poked a hole straight through—"

"We're fine," Wolf Boy interrupted sharply.

The twins hid behind Alexandria and stared at the massive creature. He eyed them with one of his little pin-sized eyes.

Ansel put his hand in front of the boar's snout. It licked his knuckles.

"He's harmless," encouraged Ansel. "He might lick you. Not the most pleasant experience, but quite safe, I assure you."

"How did you do that?" Sonja asked, approaching the boar timidly. Charlotte followed.

"It's an Alban tradition." Ansel gestured to the charm around the creature's neck. "Inside's an ancient mixture of herbs. It binds them to us, sort of like an umbilical cord. Go on. He won't bite."

Sonja touched the boar's wiry fur. His skin was warm and trembled under her fingers. She could feel his giant heart pump. Charlotte closed her eyes and pressed her ear against his chest. "Sounds like thunder," she murmured.

"Want a ride?" asked Ansel, offering his hand. Sonja grabbed it and climbed the side of the boar like a hill. Charlotte clambered up after her. The creature's back was cushioned by a layer of fat and covered in soft downy fur. "Pretty comfortable, huh?" Ansel said with a wink.

Sonja nodded, trying not to look down.

Ansel clicked his tongue, and the boar marched. The others followed on foot down the tunnel and into the next. They arrived at a pair of doors. A lantern hung on the wall. The wick was a glowworm curled on the end of a twig.

Ansel yelled into the gap between the doors. "It's me!"

A slot slid open. An Alban's face appeared through the grate. "Who're they?"

"Honored guests."

"Look like humans."

Alexandria bent down and pressed her face against the slot. "Open this door, or I will!"

The slot slammed shut, and the doors swung open.

A company of Albans in thick leather tunics greeted them with raised spears. One swung his weapon and scattered the flock of lightning bugs. Some fluttered into Alexandria's pocket.

"Why are you pointing weapons at us?" demanded Alexandria. "I'm Protector of the Shifting Lakes."

"What about *them*?" The Alban gestured to the Changelings. "Those humans."

"Humans?" Wolf Boy grunted, knocking away a spear. "Don't you know a Changeling when you see one?"

Sonja slouched low behind Ansel. It seemed like all the creatures in the Seven Edens disliked humans.

"We've told you who we are," Alexandria said indignantly. "Now let us pass."

"A warning first. There are guards throughout the Golden Underground who will be watching you." He gestured for the other Albans to put down their spears. He turned to Ansel and pointed at the boar. "You know you can't bring that filthy creature inside. Edgar's orders."

Ansel slid down from the boar, cursing under his breath. The twins jumped down after him. He pulled off the charm and pushed the boar backward. "Sorry, my friend," he whispered, closing the door on him.

"Drawbridge!" shouted the head guard. Wheels clanked and chains creaked as a wooden drawbridge lowered. It slammed into place with a thud. Alexandria walked alongside Ansel. Her boots clipped across the wooden planks.

"That was quite a warm welcome," said Alexandria.

Ansel nodded gloomily. "A lot has changed since my father's death."

The children followed close behind. Sonja looked over the edge into a deep chasm. She remembered Tatty telling them about the Albans. They were descendants of humans and, like the boars, were trapped underground thousands of years earlier by an earthquake. Through the years they had evolved to suit the sunless, rocky environment. They could see in the dark, hear a pin drop a hundred yards away, and smell even the faintest scent. So far, all Tatty's fantastical tales were true.

Sonja ducked her head beneath a low passageway and entered a vaulted grotto. There were murals of dancing women and men in gold armor painted across the rock. There were stone bridges and staircases leading in every direction. Everything everywhere glittered and sparkled.

Sonja caught her breath. "All this gold—is it *gold*?" she asked. Tatty used to slather oil onto her skin before a performance. The golden caverns tattooed on her calves would shimmer the brightest.

Ansel looked slightly bemused. "As far as I know."

Humming voices filled the air. Milky figures in gauze tunics emerged from nooks in high walls. White flowers decorated their chalky hair, and crystals hung from their slim necks. Their pink eyes turned to watch the visitors.

Ansel led the party down a flight of stairs, across a bridge, and into a short tunnel.

They entered an even bigger grotto. Light blazed from a domed ceiling encrusted with twinkling golden rocks. Alban homes were scattered throughout: a village of thick, pointy stone spires. An Alban woman waved from one of the windows as she braided her hair. A gang of Alban children ran by, chasing a spotted shrew.

There was a lively market in full swing. Chattering Albans traded in muslin dresses; crystal necklaces; eggs, breads, and fruits; and garlands of sweet-smelling flowers. Everyone stopped what they were doing and stared at the visitors. A pair of Alban girls pointed at the Changelings and giggled. A young boy ran up to Alexandria and hid under her coat.

Sonja laughed as Alexandria herded the boy out from under her hem. It was the first time she had laughed in days. The Albans were friendly compared with the Changelings—or Alexandria, for that matter. She wanted to throw her arms around every one of them. Everything was beautiful and shimmering and clean. Even the air smelled sweet. Sonja felt as though she was in a dream, and for a few moments, she forgot her worries.

They walked through an archway into a warm, humid grotto. Three old Alban men sat on a stone bench pushing worry beads through their thumbs and forefingers while staring across the lagoon. Black water lapped against the shore. Stepping-stones dotted the surface. Lights flickered in the far distance.

"We'll find Edgar there," said Ansel, pointing to the lights. He stepped onto the first rock. "Watch out. It's slippery."

Alexandria and the children cautiously followed the Alban down the stone trail across the black lagoon. Striped eels slithered by their feet.

Sonja shuddered. "Do they bite?"

Ansel shook his head. "They sing."

"Sing?" gasped Charlotte.

The Alban's eyes twinkled. "You must hear for yourselves. Use the oxygen bubbles to breathe."

Sonja snorted. "You're never getting me in there."

An instant later, Sonja was thrown through the air. She smacked into the cold water. Wolf Boy pulled her deeper and deeper into the lagoon until they were surrounded by a throng of striped eels. He turned to her and grinned, then let go and disappeared into the swarm.

Before she could react, she was distracted by a beautiful song. Well, not exactly a song—but certainly almost music. The tune escalated and descended and trembled. Sonja's tears dissolved into the black water as soon as they left her eyes. She had not heard a note of music since the night Tatty was kidnapped. She realized how much she missed it.

Chapter Twenty-Six

Underwater Again

Charlotte dove in after her sister. The water was crisp and clear and a little salty. She sucked in an oxygen bubble as it floated by. A breath of air filled her lungs. An eel brushed her hand. Its skin felt like velvet, and its big globular eyes stuck out on either side of its head. She swam after it. The eel joined a hundred other eels as they flicked their silky tails up and down their backs. Sonja floated among the swarm, swaying back and forth. Charlotte grabbed her hand. She had not seen her sister this happy since they were last onstage. Charlotte listened, hypnotized. The eels' music was slowly bringing something in her back to life.

Dear Jack Cross,

I know why you're so sad. I feel the same. I hope we'll be able to play music together one day.

Love, Charlotte

Charlotte felt a poke in her side. She swished around. Moritz waved and paddled away. Sonja kicked the water violently. Wolf Boy was holding on to her ankles. He finally let go and swam off. Charlotte watched as Sonja shot to the surface, but instead of following her sister, she swam after the Changelings.

They were nowhere in sight. Charlotte inhaled another oxygen bubble. She saw white bodies ahead, swimming playfully in the gentle current. They were Alban girls in little smocks. Painted shells were tied around their wrists and ankles. Their white hair zigzagged behind them.

Charlotte felt the chain around her neck slip under her dress. She looked down. The locket was sinking fast into the blackness. She swam after it, paddling wildly. A pale figure whooshed under her and swiped the locket. It was a full-sized boy. He stopped in front of her. It was not Wolf Boy or Moritz.

Charlotte stared at him curiously. He had cloudy blue eyes and strong shoulders. His hair was long and blond. He returned the chain to her neck and reclasped it; then before she knew what was happening, he pulled her face to his and kissed her on the mouth. Charlotte jerked back, stunned, and kicked frantically to the surface. She wiped her eyes.

Ansel, Alexandria, and Sonja waved to her from the shore.

"Come on, Charlotte!" beckoned Moritz as he and Wolf Boy swam past her.

Charlotte emerged from the water, dripping, and walked dizzily among Alban girls lounging on the rocks. Garlands of white flowers draped over their chests, perfuming the air. An underwater boy had kissed her—her first kiss ever—and she did not even know who he was. She touched her lips. They tingled.

The palace was carved into a rock wall. Precious stones, gold tiles, and statuettes removed from the old palace crisscrossed the facade like a patchwork. Doors and curtains had been refitted for their new home.

"Hold it!" a voice shouted from above. Descending guards approached from every direction and surrounded them. The startled Alban girls fled to the corners, covering themselves.

"What's all this ruckus?" Ansel said, frowning. "They've come to speak to Edgar."

"He's swimming," barked a guard with a lantern jaw.

Wolf Boy stepped in front of him. "You Albans are beginning to annoy me."

The guard reached for a knife on his belt. "I suggest you turn around and go out the way you came in."

Alexandria grabbed his arm. "I suggest you put away your toy so you don't get hurt."

"She's right, Igor," a gentle voice said.

Everyone turned to look as the full-sized boy walked out of the water followed by a harem of Alban girls. One of them helped him into a gold-trimmed gown. The soldiers moved aside to let him through. Charlotte blushed. It was the boy who had kissed her.

"Edgar?" Alexandria hesitated. "You were only a child when I met you. I'm—"

"Alexandria. I never forget a face." The boy's wet blond hair hung lank, and a large gold nugget dangled around his neck. He kissed Alexandria's hand and looked up with a smile. "To what do I owe the unexpected pleasure of this visit?"

"The Key has been stolen," replied Alexandria, discreetly wiping her hand. "The Protectors are meeting in the Land Where the Plants Reign. This was the only open Pathway. We were going to send an emissary, anyway, as none of our messages were answered after your father died. We need you and Ansel to accompany us to the Land Where the Plants Reign." She eyed the gold pendant. "With the Golden Knot."

"The boar that murdered our father also destroyed the enchanted armor." Edgar placed a hand on Ansel's shoulder. "Ansel can't go above ground anymore."

"My skin would burn to a crisp without it," Ansel said miserably.

"I, on the other hand, would be pleased to accompany your party."

Edgar turned to the boys. "Changelings, I presume?"

Wolf Boy nodded. "I'm Wolf Boy, and this is Moritz."

"Oh, come now, aren't we brothers?" Edgar embraced them heartily. He turned to the twins. "And you?"

Charlotte mustered up her courage and stepped forward. "I'm Charlotte. That's Sonja."

"There are two of you," Edgar said, smiling. "How nice." He

reached out and touched the mole on Charlotte's cheek. "I see how to tell you apart."

Charlotte had never seen a boy so beautiful. He was even a couple years older than she was. Charlotte realized she was staring and quickly said, "You don't look like an Alban."

"I'm only half. My other half is Longwalker. Closer to humans."

"My mother told me about the Longwalkers." Charlotte knew they were human travelers who had found their way into the underground centuries after the Albans. They were more like humans than any other race in the Seven Edens. "Where do they live?"

"I'm afraid I'm the only one left."

> *Dear Jack Cross,*
> *I met someone else. I'm still going to help you get*
> *your Talent back. I hope you understand.*
> *Best regards, Charlotte*

A guard ran toward them yelling, "Two boars have broken in through the North Gate!"

The Alban girls exploded into shrieks and screams. They scrambled up the palace steps in a frenzied mob and pounded on the doors with fifty little white hands.

"There's no need to panic!" Ansel yelled after them. "Stay calm, and the boars won't harm you!"

The doors swung open and the Alban girls disappeared inside the radiant halls.

Charlotte did not understand what all the fuss was about. She had just seen Ansel tame a boar.

A small army on yellow ponies galloped in from all directions and joined the other Alban guards. They fell into formation in two rows. Edgar buckled a leather belt around his waist. A dagger hung from either side.

Ansel gripped Edgar's arm. "Call off your men! I can tame the boars!"

"We have females with us," Edgar returned coolly. "We can't take risks."

"Ansel's right," interjected Alexandria. "You, of all people, should know what happens when the boars are slaughtered. Your mother's clan paid the price."

Edgar turned to her and snapped, "You know nothing of the Longwalkers."

Rumbling footsteps shook the grotto. Two boars blasted into view, storming toward them. Alexandria yanked the twins up the palace steps. The Changelings followed. Edgar pulled out his daggers and said evenly, "On my command."

The guards raised their spears. The jeweled tips glinted in the dim light.

"Please, Edgar!" Ansel reached for a charm. "Let me tame them."

"Sorry, Ansel." Edgar turned to the guards and yelled, "Attack!"

The first row of Albans launched their spears. They whizzed through the air and jolted through the thick skins of the approaching boars. The animals squealed in pain but pressed on. Blood gushed thickly from their fur.

Sonja cried out, "Stop!"

Charlotte looked away, disgusted. She had heard a boar's beating heart, felt its warm skin, and ridden on its back. How could they kill them?

"We have to do something," said Wolf Boy, starting toward the guards.

Alexandria jerked him back. "This isn't our fight. Remember what we're here to do."

Another volley of spears sailed. The boars began to fall, one by one, crashing thunderously. The bloody poles stuck out of their backs like the spines of porcupines. Edgar marched to the writhing animals with his daggers in hand.

Ansel jumped onto his brother's back. "I won't let you do it!"

Edgar slammed Ansel onto the ground. "Don't you care that our father was murdered by these beasts?"

"It must have been a mistake—one bad egg," pleaded Ansel. "Our father loved the boars."

Edgar plunged a knife deep into the first boar's neck. It wheezed and whined. He bent over the second boar and stabbed it, too.

Sonja sobbed on Charlotte's shoulder. Charlotte looked up at Edgar. How could this beautiful boy be such a savage? There had to be a reason. There just had to be! She needed to know.

"You had no right!" Ansel sobbed. His face was drenched with tears. "You'll bring a massacre on the Albans!"

"Calm down, brother," Edgar said gently.

"You'll be the destruction of your father's people!"

Edgar's eyes turned stormy. "If you can protect the Albans better than I can, why don't you take over?" He shoved the daggers into his belt and leapt onto a pony. Charlotte's heart sank as she watched Edgar disappear down the tunnel. She wanted to call out after him. She wanted to go with him.

Ansel looked to Alexandria. He wiped away his tears. "Me and my brother. We don't see eye to eye."

Alexandria helped him to his feet. "You should meet my family."

"I know where he went," Ansel said. "I'll take you there."

An Alban guard hammered planks of wood across an enormous, boar-sized hole in the middle of a gate. He held three nails in his mouth like a tailor's pins but managed to murmur: "You just missed your brother. He was in a hurry. Didn't stop to say hello."

"Boris, can you let us through?" asked Ansel. Alexandria and the children accompanied him, each riding a yellow pony.

The guard pushed open the ruins of the gate. He shook his head. "The boars never used to bother us before. Now we can't seem to keep them out."

The pitch-black darkness smelled like dung and dirt. A wind moaned and wailed as it swept through the tunnels searching for a way out. Alexandria released the lightning bugs from her pocket. The earthy walls were teeming with worms and maggots. The Changelings each scooped a handful of dirt, sifted out the insects, and popped them into their mouths, one after the other. The bugs crackled as the Changelings chewed and spat.

"Disgusting," Sonja said under her breath.

Charlotte looked away. She was too busy thinking about Edgar to trouble herself with the Changelings.

"What's wrong with you?" Charlotte heard her sister say.

Charlotte shrugged. "I'm just thinking."

Sonja sighed. "Jack Cross."

"For your information, I was thinking about something totally different." In fact, she was a little worried about herself. What type of person fell out of love and into love just like that?

The ponies trotted in single-file through a labyrinth of tunnels until they reached a cave lit by a colony of glowworms. Charlotte was dazzled by the tiny wiggling lights. It was beautiful in the underground. It made perfect sense that Edgar came from here.

"I wouldn't eat those," warned Ansel as Moritz reached for a glowworm.

"Why? Are they poisonous?"

"Well, not exactly, but they pack quite a punch."

"Maybe I'll just try a little bite." Moritz hesitated, uncertain. Then he plucked the shortest one he could find off the wall and popped it into his mouth. Sparks crackled against his teeth. "Aargh!" he shrieked, and spat out the little electric creature.

Wolf Boy laughed as Moritz stuck out his burned tongue.

Sonja rolled her eyes and muttered, "Changelings never learn."

The cave opened up into a vast cavern twinkling with diamonds. There were patches of barren rock where the gems had been chiseled away. White bats flapped paper-thin wings and circled and swooped above them, hunting vermin.

Charlotte saw a castle in the distance surrounded by a moat of murky water. Headless statues perched on turrets, and threadbare flags hung like rags from their poles.

"The Longwalkers' castle," announced Ansel. "Jagged Rock."

They followed a stone road to the front door. The drawbridge was open, and it rattled as they rode across it. Rubbish floated in the moat below: bowls and jugs and a leather boot. Skeletons littered the courtyard in piles, huddled and cowering. A few still grasped spears in their bony hands. The wind blew through the archways. A broken door swung open and closed.

The air was heavy and oppressive, making it harder to breathe. "What happened here?" Charlotte asked.

"For centuries, the Longwalkers killed boars for sport," explained Ansel. "We warned them to stop, but they didn't listen. Finally, the boars attacked the castle. The Longwalkers were outnumbered. They killed every one except for Edgar. Perhaps because of his Alban blood."

This is where his ghosts lived, thought Charlotte. She was starting to understand. Edgar was looking for justice. With maybe a bit of revenge, too.

Edgar's pony stood in a corner munching on weeds sprouting between the broken flagstones.

Ansel jumped to the ground. "He's here somewhere."

"Let's split up and look for him," suggested Alexandria.

The twins were sent to search in the east wing. They looked in stone rooms and under staircases, peeking over their shoulders every few seconds, convinced they heard footsteps or whispering. Charlotte glimpsed a glint of light through a window in the tallest tower.

"Well, he's not here," said Sonja, poking out from under a torn tapestry. But nobody replied. Charlotte was already running across the courtyard.

She slipped into a doorway and hurried up a narrow spiral staircase. When she reached the top, she stopped to catch her breath. At the end of a long, dark hallway, she saw an open door. A thin light streamed out of it.

Charlotte ran for it and burst in. "Edgar!" she cried out.

The room was filled with piles of golden armor, hanging boar skins, and jars of teeth. A bag of diamonds lay scattered on a table. Edgar shoved something inside his shirt and turned. He looked to Charlotte with a smile. "You shouldn't be here."

"We came looking for you. The others are downstairs."

Edgar hooked his arm into Charlotte's and walked her out of the room. He locked the door behind them.

Charlotte looked back over her shoulder. "I thought you said the armor was stolen."

Edgar sighed deeply. "Since my father died, the Albans have been careless. They don't realize that the armor doesn't work. I have no choice but to lie. It's the only way to protect them."

"Is that why you killed the boars?" Charlotte asked in a small voice. "To protect them."

Edgar led Charlotte into a dim room. Thirty lit candles were clustered under a painting of a woman. She looked like Edgar.

"My mother was the queen of the Longwalkers. My father was an Alban, Tobias, Protector of the Golden Underground. He didn't care much for us. Like the other Albans, he thought the Longwalkers were an inferior race. When the boars came, the Albans did nothing. Even my father abandoned us." Edgar's voice broke. He looked up at the portrait. "I saw my mother killed by the boars."

"Ansel said it was the Longwalkers who caused the massacre. He said—"

Edgar grabbed Charlotte by the wrist. "Ansel's lying! He's against the Longwalkers just like the others. We were the only race living among the Seven Edens who weren't chosen as Protectors. They wanted to get rid of us all along. I wouldn't be surprised if they planned the massacre themselves."

"How terrible!" Charlotte exclaimed. "The Albans seem such a gentle people—"

Edgar pulled Charlotte toward him. She shivered. His blue eyes glistened. His voice grew gentle. "All that's in the past now because I've found *you*."

"Me?" faltered Charlotte.

"The girl I've been waiting for."

Charlotte laughed nervously. Nobody had ever spoken to her like that before.

He stroked her cheek. "We'll rebuild Jagged Rock together and return it to its former glory." He paused. "I'm going to kiss you again."

She felt his sweet, warm breath on her face. The instant their lips touched, something like an electric current surged through her. She wished it would never stop. She did not care about the boars or humans or Albans or the future. She did not care about anything.

"Promise not to tell the others about the armor," he whispered.

Charlotte trembled. "I promise."

"Charlotte!" Sonja was standing in front of them with her hands on her hips. "What are you doing?"

Charlotte wanted to leap into Sonja's arms and tell her everything, but she stopped short. Sonja hated anyone or anything she thought would come between them. When Larry, a reluctant Scrummager with oversized glasses, had asked Charlotte to go steady with him, Sonja told Tatty that he had spent six months in juvenile prison. Larry was banned from ever visiting the circus again. When Charlotte befriended a stray dog one summer, Sonja complained to Tatty about its fleas until it was sent away. Well, it was not going to happen with Edgar. For once in her life, Charlotte was going to keep Sonja out of her affairs.

CHAPTER TWENTY-SEVEN

The Hidden Stairway

IT WAS JUST LIKE CHARLOTTE TO FALL IN LOVE WITH somebody else so quickly. And a boar-killer too! Sonja shook her head. What about poor Jack Cross?

She followed her sister and Edgar back to the ground floor.

"I'm sorry I ran off like that," apologized Edgar as they entered a courtyard. Alexandria and the Changelings were waiting. "The boars are a touchy subject between me and my brother. We'd better tell him I'm all right, or he'll be worried." He looked around. "Where is he?"

Ansel emerged from a doorway and dove on top of Edgar. "I'm sorry, brother!"

Edgar laughed and hugged him back. "Me too, Ansel."

"We've wasted enough time," interrupted Alexandria. "Are you ready to go, Edgar?"

Edgar nodded. "We're near the Pathway to the Land Where the Plants Reign. We can walk from here."

"If there was only one suit of armor remaining," lamented Ansel, "I could come with you."

Sonja saw Charlotte dart Edgar a look. He turned away and put his arm around Ansel's shoulders. "The Albans need you."

"You're right, brother." Ansel bowed. "Send word once the Key is found."

"We will," Alexandria assured him. They all took turns shaking hands with Ansel. He climbed onto a pony, gave a final wave, and rode out of the courtyard. The rest of the herd trotted off after him.

Charlotte and Edgar held hands as they crossed back over the drawbridge. Sonja walked a few steps behind them, brooding. This was worse than Larry or the stray dog or Jack Cross. Charlotte was acting like Sonja did not exist.

They joined a stone road down a hill. It dead-ended in a wall. There was a small smooth circle chiseled into the rock. Alexandria pressed her Amulet against it. A door clicked open.

"The Longwalkers could have been saved if they had had an Amulet at the time of the massacre," Edgar said coolly. Alexandria stared blankly. He shrugged. "Too late now, I guess."

Sonja was the last to enter the rectangular chamber. The walls were sculpted out of blue quartz. She brushed her fingers along the cool indigo stone. There were spiders, dragonflies, and caterpillars frozen inside like amber. An endless, rocky staircase ascended a narrow corridor up into the distance. The others were standing at the foot of it. Sonja raised her eyebrow. "I hope we're not climbing *that*."

"That's exactly what we're doing," said Alexandria.

Wolf Boy leapt up four steps at a time as he transformed into a wolf. He looked back over his shoulder, swishing his black, bushy tail, and challenged Moritz, "Wanna race?"

Moritz, now a horse, broke past him at a gallop, and Wolf Boy howled and bolted after him. Edgar watched as they disappeared up the staircase.

"Incredible," he said, mesmerized. "I've never seen a Changeling changing."

"I have," muttered Sonja. "Too many times."

Alexandria pulled out a smashed cigarette and turned to Edgar. "Make sure they keep up with you." She placed the tip between her lips and strode up the stairs. "Maybe I can puff this in peace." A trail of smoke unspooled behind her.

Edgar extended his hands to the twins. Charlotte grabbed one hand. Sonja brushed past the other. She turned to her sister. "It's my turn to wear the locket."

Charlotte nodded cheerfully and handed it over, then walked ahead arm in arm with Edgar. Frowning, Sonja clasped the little gold heart around her neck and trudged after them.

Every hundredth step, there was a statue of a man or woman with horns and wings. Their eyes were colored marbles, and their teeth were bleached bone. Sonja was exhausted as she reached the thirtieth statue.

Tiffins, Sonja thought. The last marionette they had made was a Tiffin. Those days seemed like a lifetime ago. Sonja pictured Tatty telling them as little children about the winged creatures inked on her belly: "They can fly a thousand miles without resting, and they can live a thousand years, but only if their wings don't get damaged."

She looked up wearily. Charlotte and Edgar were still climbing at a fast pace. She sank down by the statue's feet and leaned her head against it.

Sonja had always sensed her sister's need for independence, even when they were little children. She felt like Charlotte had been waiting her whole life to escape from her. Sonja, on the other hand, could not imagine a moment without Charlotte by her side. She was Sonja's other half—and only together did they make a whole.

Out of the corner of her eye, Sonja saw something move. She peered behind the statue. A figure was huddled in a ball on the floor, trembling.

"Are you all right?" whispered Sonja.

It was a woman with a shock of red hair. A scent of vanilla wafted in the air. Sonja's heart stopped. It could only be Tatty.

Sonja gasped. She covered her mouth with her hands.

The woman jumped to her feet and bolted up the stairs.

"Tatty!" Sonja shrieked. "Where are you going?" She started to race after the woman.

Charlotte grabbed Sonja's arm. "Who're you talking to?"

Sonja pulled away, confused, but Edgar caught her. Sonja struggled to break free. "Let go! I've got to catch Tatty!"

"But there's nobody there!" yelled Charlotte.

Sonja's head drooped. Her legs gave out. Edgar lowered her to the ground.

Alexandria heard the commotion and ran back down the stairs.

"Sonja?" Charlotte hesitated. "Can you hear me?"

Sonja stared at them bleary eyed. "I saw Tatty." She looked toward the top of the stairs. "I could smell her. I almost touched her."

"Another hallucination," said Alexandria. "I told you, you're sensitive to the Pathways."

"Remember, Sonja," Charlotte said softly, "you thought you saw our parents in the swamp."

Edgar whispered something into Charlotte's ear. She giggled. He helped her to her feet. "I'll see you up there," she said distractedly, and walked on, hand in hand, with Edgar.

"Wait," Sonja pleaded. "Charlotte." New tears sprang to her eyes.

"Come on," Alexandria said impatiently. "Get up."

Sonja covered her face. "Leave me alone."

Alexandria sighed deeply. "What's wrong now?"

"Don't pretend you care. You don't care about me. You don't care about anyone!"

Alexandria swallowed and stared.

Sonja shook, crying. "You're always annoyed with me. You think I do everything wrong!" Her face was puffy and tear stained. "You know what? I don't blame you. Without my Talent, I'm a loser. A real nobody. Even my sister hates me."

"Hates you?" grunted Alexandria. "Because of that boy? That's only a stupid crush."

"She's always falling in love with someone or something, just to get away from me."

"You can't depend on each other all your lives. You have to find out who *you* are, as your *own* person."

Sonja hunched her shoulders. Her voice lowered. "I really thought I'd do something special in my life. Now I know I won't."

"One thing I've learned: you never know anything for sure. You might be surprised. You might just prove yourself yet." Alexandria kneeled down in front of Sonja and handed her a handkerchief. "In regard to me thinking you're annoying, I don't. I'm just a bitter, unhappy woman. Don't mind me."

Sonja wiped her eyes and murmured, "Okay."

Alexandria helped her to her feet.

"Alexandria."

"Uh-huh."

"Why are you being nice?"

Alexandria thought for a moment. "I'm not sure. I'll probably regret it later."

The last few steps were covered with plants and roots. Sunlight and shadows dappled them.

"You go ahead," urged Alexandria. "I need a minute before I face the Protectors."

Sonja hurried past Charlotte and Edgar, and with the last of her energy, she ran to the top. The sun glared in her eyes. She squinted. She stood in the middle of a meadow dotted with wildflowers. More meadows, gardens, and woods rolled to the horizon. They had finally made it to the Land Where the Plants Reign. This had always been Sonja's favorite Eden. As a tattoo, anyway. It was the one she knew the best because it was inked across Tatty's chest, where Sonja most liked to rest her head.

A soft breeze carried flowery scents. Butterflies spun around like a colorful tornado. The tall grass fluttered through Sonja's fingers. It was magnificent.

> *In meadows and whispering fields,*
> *Of butterflies and buzzing bees,*
> *A fertile land of flowers and trees,*
> *Where the Tiffins fly wherever they please!*

"Oh, you made it, too," interrupted a voice. She looked down. Wolf Boy and Moritz, boys again, were collapsed in the grass by her feet. Their capes were covered in swarms of butterflies.

"I hope you're not going to eat them," Sonja said, horrified.

"They're too beautiful to eat," Moritz returned dreamily. He lifted his thumb to show her a butterfly with rainbow-colored wings.

Wolf Boy sat up and pointed. "What's that?"

Not far away, a small red dot dropped from the bright blue sky. Sonja saw Alexandria run through the meadow and catch the falling, fluttering object. Sonja dashed toward her and peered over her shoulder, breathless. Dottie looked up feebly from Alexandria's hands. A dart stuck out from the side of her neck. Blood stained her feathers. She wheezed out a laugh. "The Contessa got me."

The bird's eyes rolled back in a daze. Sonja looked down at her, worried. "Will she be all right?"

The others joined them. Charlotte's eyes widened. "Is she going to die?"

Alexandria studied the little projectile. "Okay, Dottie, this might hurt." In one motion, she yanked out the dart. The parrot squeaked a wounded peep.

Alexandria doused the gurgling wound in black gin.

Dottie opened her trembling beak.

Alexandria poured the last drops into her mouth. "Stay awake, Dottie. Help is on the way." A trumpet blared in the distance. "Let's go." Alexandria gathered Dottie up in her coat.

They hurried through the meadow and down a path into a garden. A pungent mist filled the air. Tatty's tattoo had not prepared

Sonja for what she saw. Giant flowers towered over them: camellias, roses, dahlias, and peonies. Their stalks were as thick as broomsticks, and their tops were as big as umbrellas. The clashing scents made Sonja a little dizzy, and she stumbled along after the others.

A grasshopper the size of a dog leapt out from behind a bush. Sonja jumped back and screamed. Charlotte hid behind Edgar. The grasshopper wiped its glassy eyes and hopped away.

"What was—was that?" stammered Sonja.

"These are the Ancient Gardens," said Alexandria. "Everything grows bigger here. Something in the soil."

"One bug like that could feed a whole village," Moritz mused in a faraway voice.

Alexandria led them to the end of the garden where two tall creatures waited side by side. Thick, coarse horns twisted out of their temples, and velvety fur covered their long wings. They both smiled widely. Their teeth were large and square. "We delight in welcoming you."

Sonja stared at them, mesmerized. "Tiffins. Real live Tiffins." She reached out slowly to touch one of their wings. She had cut a hundred little pieces of fabric to make feathers to match theirs.

Alexandria jerked away her hand. "Sorry about that," she apologized to the smiling creatures. "We just climbed the Hidden Stairway. She's a little tired."

Alexandria herded the children into the clearing.

Nine wooden chairs were arranged in a circle. A Tiffin sat in the largest one. His eyes were closed, and his colorful wings were draped across the ground behind him. He had purple hair as stiff as straw and smooth, alabaster horns. He was the Great Tiffin.

Sonja remembered Alexandria saying he was the oldest and most powerful of the Protectors. It was funny: he looked more like forty than four hundred.

It was the same with the three women sitting beside him. They seemed about Alexandria's age, but Sonja recognized them as the Three Swifters—ancient beings. Their pale skin was sprinkled with freckles; and long, wild locks of orange hair hung down over their red, linen dresses. A sand rose dangled from each of their left ears. They stared out into the distance, silent.

Two seats away sat the Mother of All Geese and Fowl, Protector of the Crooked Peaks. Sonja knew that she was the youngest of the five seated Protectors even though she looked, by far, the oldest. She wore a patch over one eye and a feathered cloak around her hunched shoulders. She clutched the handle of a misshapen cane with her leathery hand. Crows sat perched on the back of her chair. One buried its beak into her ear and squawked.

The other seats around the circle were empty. Sonja looked around, worried.

"Excuse me," said a familiar voice. "Do you know where the Protector of the Vanishing Islands is supposed to sit?"

Sonja wheeled around to find Mr. Fortune Teller standing behind her, smiling. He looked tired. Dark shadows circled his white eyes. She rushed into his arms.

Hieronymus, Mr. Erstine Teller, Protector of the Vanishing Islands.

Nya, Cri, Tem, The Three Smellers, Protectors of the Lost Desert.

The Great Tiffin, Protector of the Land Where the Plants Reign.

Stagheart, Protector of the Fodon Forest.

Alexandria;
The Earth Bearer,
Protector of
the Shifting
Lakes.

Tobias, Deceased, The
former Protector of the
'Golden Underground.'

Hegler;
The Weather-
alterer &
former Protector
of the
Crooked Peaks.

The Protectors of
the
Seven Edens

CHAPTER TWENTY-EIGHT

The Land Where the Plants Reign

CHARLOTTE RUBBED HER FACE ON MR. FORTUNE TELLER'S scratchy wool jacket to make sure she was not dreaming. "It's you," she said softly. "It's really you."

"When has your Uncle Tell ever let you down?" The old man kissed the top of her head. "Who are your friends?"

"Wolf Boy, Moritz, and . . . Edgar." Charlotte was a little scared that Uncle Tell might not approve of Edgar. He was stricter than Tatty and never encouraged them to have friends.

Alexandria pushed through the chairs and laid Dottie in the Great Tiffin's hands. His eyes remained closed as he pressed the wrapped bundle against his bony chest.

"Alexandria, is that you?" croaked the Mother of All Geese and Fowl. Her voice was dry and scratchy. She put a large conical shell into her ear.

"Hello, Hester," Alexandria muttered, uneasy.

The old woman squinted her one good eye. "I see Dottie's got herself into a scrape again." The crows shifted from one foot to the other. They squawked and wriggled their black tongues.

234

Alexandria slumped into a chair, leaving an empty one between herself and Hester. She fidgeted with her sleeves.

Alexandria seemed out of place. Charlotte remembered her telling them that there was a hierarchy among the Protectors. Alexandria was definitely at the bottom.

The Great Tiffin's eyes popped open. They were large, round, and purple like his hair. "Protectors and their representatives, please, complete the circle." His voice was soft and musical.

Mr. Fortune Teller led Wolf Boy and Edgar to their seats, then found his place between Hester and Alexandria. Moritz and the twins dropped onto the ground in front of him. Edgar shot a smile at Charlotte. She burned with pride. He looked dignified among the circle of Protectors.

"Are you going to stare at him all day?" she heard her sister say. Charlotte blew Edgar a kiss to annoy her.

"Look," whispered Moritz. "He's doing something to the bird."

The Great Tiffin was bent over Dottie. His purple lips were pressed to her neck. His veins twitched under his thin, pale skin. His heartbeat thumped out loud. He was the most gentle-looking creature Charlotte had ever seen. Every movement he made was exact and precise. He would have been a good piano player, she thought.

After a moment, Dottie staggered onto her wrinkled gray claws. She cocked her head to one side and stretched her wings. The wound had disappeared. She looked up at the watching faces all around her. "They took Tatty to the City of Steel and Smoke. That's where I was shot."

Charlotte's heart skipped a beat at the mention of Tatty's name.

"Did you see her?" blurted Sonja. Her eyes were wide and worried.

Charlotte wrung her hands. It was the moment of truth. Please, let her be alive. Please, please, please!

Dottie nodded weakly. "I couldn't get close, but she spotted me. She knows we're coming for her."

Charlotte leapt to her feet. Tatty was alive. Sonja joined her, and they hopped up and down yelling, "She's alive! Tatty's alive!" Charlotte's eyes twinkled. Her face glowed. Their dear, dear Tatty was alive.

Sonja tugged on Mr. Fortune Teller's arm. "What do we do now? Let's go get her!"

"Hold on, girls." The old man gestured for them to sit back down. "We must listen to the others first."

The twins slumped to the ground reluctantly.

Alexandria cleared her throat. "I have something to say."

The Three Swifters finally lifted their gaze from the distance and looked all at once to Alexandria. Charlotte shuddered. Their dark eyes looked like they could turn someone into stone.

Alexandria kept her own eyes lowered as she said, "The Contessa and her son are building an army of white beasts. That's why they're looking for the source of the magic."

The Three Swifters bore their jagged, pointy teeth and spoke one after the other in sharp, quick voices:

"The Pearl Catcher should be silenced."

"She is to blame for what has happened."

"Her privilege as Protector must be revoked."

Charlotte saw Alexandria's face turn hot and red. She glared at the Swifters. Their chairs shook. "That's not true!" Alexandria yelled.

The Three Swifters' eyes flashed with rage. Their orange locks slithered in the growing breeze like serpents.

"How dare you raise your voice at us."

"You are only a mere Pearl Catcher."

"Our powers put your meager ones to shame."

Alexandria's jaw clenched. Her lips pursed. "We'll see about that."

Mr. Fortune Teller touched her arm. "Don't."

Alexandria brushed him off and snapped her fingers. The Swifters' chairs flew out from under them. The three women tumbled to the ground in a mass.

Hester hid a laugh behind her hand. The crows cawed. The Swifters looked up to the clear sky.

Gray clouds converged overhead and shrouded the sun. A bolt of lightning shot down and rumbled the earth all around them. Charlotte gasped. They could change the weather, like she had once done.

> *Across a sandy desert,*
> *Float the Swifters, one, two, three.*
> *Fiery-eyed, these spirits rise, in an ancient breeze,*
> *Bringing thunder, rain, and lightning,*
> *Not caring whom they please.*

"Enough!" roared the Great Tiffin. Dottie fluttered off his lap. He gripped the arms of his chair. The veins popped out between his bony knuckles. The Swifters shrank into their seats, muttering and cursing. Alexandria slumped, embarrassed.

Mr. Fortune Teller tapped his cane nervously. "I've had visions of this beastly army. There will be a battle. I don't see a city, though. It's a dry, barren land."

Alexandria looked up. "Staghart also had premonitions of war."

The Swifters wheeled around and stared at the twins. One launched a finger at them. Her nostrils trembled. Her voice wavered. "The daughters of the Key will defeat them," she announced. "They have the power against the living."

Mr. Fortune Teller shook his head. "Impossible. Their powers were stolen."

Hester popped the shell out from her ear and pulled up her patch. A large, shiny bird's eye bulged out between her eyelids. It moved around, jerky, in its socket, sizing up the twins. "The Hawk's Eye thinks they're too old to have lost their powers."

"They aren't yet thirteen," said the old man.

"If their magic was strong," rasped Hester, "it's in their blood already."

The Three Swifters rocked back and forth in their chairs and whispered from one to the next:

"Only the essence was stolen."

"The rest fled into hiding."

"Their powers must be found and recovered!"

Charlotte could feel the Swifters' eyes on her. A prickly breeze crept across her face and slipped into her ear. "Come! Come! Come!" it whispered.

Charlotte grabbed Sonja's arm. "Did you hear that?"

"What?" said Sonja.

The Swifters reached for the twins with their freckled arms. Their nails were long and as sharp as the tips of arrows. "The daughters of the Key must come to the Lost Desert!" they chanted in unison. "We will hunt down their powers!"

The Great Tiffin shook his head. "Out of the question. They will stay with us. We must fight our enemies together."

The Swifters rose. Their bare feet hovered off the ground. "We will take no part in your fight. We have said our piece, and not a one listened."

"If that's your wish. You must leave your Amulet behind."

The Swifters clamped their hands over their left ears. "No! We *have* never—and *will* never—take off the Roses of Sand."

Without another word, the Swifters floated from the circle. The smell of exotic spices lingered in the air after them. They disappeared among the poppies. The clouds parted, and sunlight returned.

Charlotte watched them go, confused. A little bit of her wished she could follow them.

The Great Tiffin sighed deeply. "We have no choice but to fight without the Swifters."

"Good riddance," muttered Hester.

Dottie flew back onto the Great Tiffin's lap. He stroked the soft feathers down her back with his long, slender fingers. "Before we all part, we must confer with the Amulets and find the Protector of the Golden Underground."

Edgar looked surprised. "I'm the Protector. My father named me."

"It wasn't his right," said the Great Tiffin. "There are six Amulets present. That is enough to name the true Protector. It may be you, it may be another. Do you understand?"

Edgar was silent. Finally, he nodded.

The Great Tiffin gestured to the ground in the middle of the circle. Edgar sat down cross-legged. The Protectors closed their eyes. Their Amulets began to glow. An even stronger light came from the Great Tiffin's stomach.

Wolf Boy joined in with the Protectors as they chanted a list of Alban names. They repeated the names over and over, randomly, but within a few minutes, the list had dwindled to two. "Edgar, Igor," recited the Protectors.

The Great Tiffin's lips quivered. He straightened in his chair like a bolt and blurted out a new name: "Ansel!"

The twins looked at each other. "Ansel?" Charlotte turned to Edgar, worried. His face looked as white as an Alban's.

Soon, all the Protectors were saying Ansel's name.

The light went out in the Great Tiffin's stomach. His eyelids fluttered open. "It has been decided. The Protector of the Golden Underground is an Alban named Ansel."

Edgar jumped to his feet. "Ansel should be Protector of the *boars*! That's what he cares about."

"We understand your disappointment," the Great Tiffin said softly, "but we must do as the Amulets tell us. That is the law."

Edgar shook his head. "I won't accept it. I just won't. Ansel can't even come above ground. How is that power? I would make the whole underground into one land. Bring back the Longwalkers—"

"The Longwalkers?" Mr. Fortune Teller said skeptically.

"Yes, the Longwalkers!" Edgar burst out. He pointed at the Great Tiffin. "A people he helped destroy!"

The Great Tiffin bristled. "You speak falsely, Edgar. We warned your people to stop slaughtering the boars. They did not listen. The massacre happened before we could reach the underground."

"That's not true!" Edgar shouted.

Charlotte's eyes brimmed with tears. She had witnessed how deep Edgar's wounds were back at Jagged Rock. Charlotte grabbed Mr. Fortune Teller's leg. "Do something, please."

"Edgar," the old man said, clearing his throat, "you know it isn't only the Protectors who have a role in defending the Edens. You can still play an essential part, if that's what you wish to do."

Edgar opened his mouth and began to respond, but then his eyes met Charlotte's. She smiled through her tears. Edgar's face softened. He hunched over and mumbled, "You're right, old man. I apologize. I was angry."

Mr. Fortune Teller stood up and escorted Edgar back to his seat. "No harm done, my boy."

"Once you return to the Golden Underground, Ansel must be told he is Protector," the Great Tiffin said to Edgar. "But first, you, Alexandria, and the Changelings will accompany the daughters of the Key on a rescue mission. We will meet you once we have assembled our fighters. Hester, you'll return to the Crooked Peaks and ask the Gobos for help. Hieronymus, you will do the same with the Gillypurs in the Vanishing Islands."

Charlotte had always believed Rhubarb was like them—no family or history—but as it turned out, he was from the Vanishing Islands and part of an ancient herd. The twins, on the other hand, still did not know where they came from or who their parents were. But more and more, Charlotte had a feeling that their own history also had something to do with the Seven Edens.

The old woman turned to the crows and clicked her tongue. The crows bobbed their heads, hopping and cawing, and burst into the blue sky. Dottie flew up after them and then returned, circling the Protectors.

The Great Tiffin stood up and snapped open his wings. Charlotte stared at the four large eyes looking out from the swirling patterns on the soft velvety folds. "You'll rest here for the night and leave for the City of Steel and Smoke in the morning." He turned to Alexandria. "It's where you were born, and you'll know how best to maneuver within its walls." He handed her a small bottle of clear liquid. "In case you need it." He rose into the sky, his wings beating on either side of him, and flew away.

The two Tiffins guarding the entrance of the clearing stepped forward. One bowed and said, "If you please, Protectors, your Amulets." The other held open a box lined with bits of broken Tiffin wings.

Alexandria undid her necklace. "It's going to be strange without this old thing." She reluctantly dropped the Hanging Pearl into the box. "You, too, boys." Wolf Boy and Edgar gave the Tiffin their Amulets.

Charlotte put her arm through Edgar's. "Sort of glad to get rid of it," he whispered. "Takes away some of the pressure."

"Goodbye, dear friend." Mr. Fortune Teller kissed his tortoise-shell pendant before placing it in the box.

Hester frowned and lifted her patch. She dug the Hawk's Eye out of her socket and threw it in with the others. "I'm going to have to find my old eye," she grumbled. "I hope the buzzards didn't eat it."

"What about the Great Tiffin's Amulet?" asked Sonja.

"The Tiffin's Rock is actually inside his body," explained Mr. Fortune Teller. "It can only be removed when he dies."

They followed the Tiffins through the cluster of poppies into a smaller clearing. The ground was covered with woven mats. One of the Tiffins rolled them up. There was a mud pit underneath that bubbled and spluttered and stank like rotten eggs. The Tiffins said a prayer, then dropped the box into the pit. The box sank quickly.

Charlotte looked up at the Protectors. All three were holding back tears as the box disappeared. Charlotte knew what it felt like to lose something so essential. She squeezed Edgar's hand. Maybe they would be as lucky as she had been and find something to take its place.

Chapter Twenty-Nine

Memories of Home

Sonja watched the sun set through an orange haze. Her hands twitched by her sides. She was getting used to her tic now. It kept her company. Mr. Fortune Teller called her name and she ran after the others into the Ancient Garden.

The giant flowers had closed for the night, trapping their scents inside their petals. A line of rat-sized ants emerged from between stalks of white roses. They carried massive leaves over their heads, and their lacquered black eyes swiveled. Sonja held on to Mr. Fortune Teller. She would never get used to the giant insects.

Wolf Boy turned to the old man. "Hieronymus, can we leave the girls with you?"

"Hieronymus, you say?" chuckled Mr. Fortune Teller. "Okay, go on. I'll keep an eye on them."

As the Changelings ran off, Wolf Boy cried out, "No twin-sitting tonight!"

Sonja folded her arms across her chest angrily.

"You like that Changeling, don't you, Sonja?" said Mr. Fortune Teller.

Sonja's jaw dropped. "Wolf Boy? Are you crazy?" She would never forgive him for lying to their faces in the Forlorn Forest or accidentally taking them to a monster factory or forcing them into a filthy trash chute or pulling her deep into the water with a hundred slithering eels (though their music was nice). *Like* Wolf Boy? She despised him.

Edgar cleared his throat. "I see you've got a lot of catching up to do." He kissed Charlotte on the cheek. "I'll meet you there." He took off after the Changelings.

Mr. Fortune Teller shook his head. "That Edgar worries me. He seems troubled."

"I agree," said Sonja. Finally, somebody was going to do something about Charlotte and Edgar. "He kills boars."

Charlotte put her hands on her hips and said sharply, "He's the only Longwalker left. He saw his family massacred."

"When something terrible happens to someone, it's in their hands to come out of it stronger." The old man tapped his head. "In here." He pointed to his chest where his heart was. "And here."

"Edgar will," insisted Charlotte. "I'm sure of it."

"I wonder how we'll turn out," said Sonja. "The Protectors say we still have our Talents." She glanced at Charlotte. "Well, have you seen any sign of them?"

"Maybe we're not trying hard enough. Maybe we have to practice."

Sonja thought for a moment and looked up at the old man. "What do they mean, we'll have power against the living?"

"The Great Tiffin has the power to *heal* the living. You saw how he saved Dottie." Mr. Fortune Teller paused for a moment.

He looked concerned. "Well, you see, the power *against* the living, that's more like the opposite. It's the ability to harm with only the flutter of an eyelash or a puff of a breath."

The twins looked shocked. "We don't harm *any*thing," insisted Charlotte.

"We don't even hurt bugs," said Sonja. "Well, except for that worm in the Forlorn Forest."

Mr. Fortune Teller nodded but did not say another word.

They entered a meadow of normal-sized buttercups and bluebells. Tiffins lounged in the grass, eating and drinking. Butterflies rested on their shoulders, and snails inched up their arms and legs. The air buzzed with cheerful chatter.

Beside a glistening pond was Mr. Fortune Teller's caravan.

Charlotte gasped. "It wasn't burned!"

It sat there like a memory. In a way, for a moment, Sonja felt like they were home. "Come on!" she yelled, charging ahead. Charlotte followed, pulling the old man behind her.

They ran past Hester and Alexandria and the boys kneeling in the grass watching Tiffin children race caterpillars. They stopped breathless in front of the caravan. Sonja was unsure whether to laugh or cry. It stood as it always stood, with the curtains drawn and smoke puffing out the chimney. Rhubarb rushed to greet them.

The twins wrapped their arms around his neck and pressed their faces into his striped coat. Sonja breathed in the familiar aroma of chamomile and hay. "He smells the same," she said dreamily.

"He always does," said Charlotte, nuzzling her nose into his stripes. "And to think we thought he was from some broken-down zoo. He's a Gillypur from the Vanishing Islands!"

Rhubarb snorted happily and gritted his square teeth. Sonja laughed. It felt good to be with Charlotte again without Edgar or Jack Cross on her mind.

"Follow me, girls," beckoned Mr. Fortune Teller from the caravan steps. "I've brought some of your things."

Everything inside looked the same: the peeling walls, the dripping candles, the dusty furniture. Sonja ran her fingers across the spines on the bookshelves, mouthing the familiar titles. She imagined if they walked outside again, they would be back at the circus: the Fat Lady sitting on her deck chair sunbathing in the rain; the Snake Charmer and the Miniature Woman gossiping about Bea; dearest, loveliest, kindest, gentlest Tatty mending their costumes with Monkey on her shoulder. She would look up with her little twinkling blue eyes and say, "Hello, dearies! You're home!" If only they were home, Sonja thought gloomily.

Mr. Fortune Teller sat down in front of his desk and lit his tin pipe. He pointed to the bed. The last of their possessions were scattered on the mattress. "The clowns saved what they could."

"My pennywhistle," gasped Sonja. Her fingers went into convulsions. Even her lips trembled. Sonja snatched up the little instrument, swallowed nervously, and blew into it. It wheezed, sounding scratchy.

Charlotte's accordion lay among a little pile of clothing. It had warped slightly in the fire. Charlotte flung its straps over her shoulders, jerked open the bellows, and started to play. Her fingers tripped over one another as they slipped against the keys. The instrument moaned and grumbled and shook the caravan.

Mr. Fortune Teller covered his ears as the twins played a duet, it sounded like two dogs quarreling.

After a few minutes, Sonja stopped, out of breath. "Those Protectors don't know what they're talking about." She tossed the pennywhistle back onto the bed. What did she need her Talent for, anyway? She did not care about fame or success anymore if it had anything to do with cities. Where else could she play? The circus was probably gone forever.

Sonja picked up a broken marionette. It was a Pearl Catcher. The long brown yarn hair was singed at the ends. An arm was missing.

> *Underwater from lake to lake,*
> *A Pearl Catcher swims,*
> *Her long hair flowing, paddling her limbs.*
> *Beneath the waves she, silent, slips,*
> *A secret power in her fingertips.*

"It figures: the only marionette that survived," Charlotte said, making a face, "turns out to be Alexandria."

"I hope the two of you have been kind to her," said the old man.

"Kind to *her*?" huffed Charlotte. "She's not kind to *us*! She still doesn't know which one of us is which."

"I'm not sure," Sonja said, thinking. She stared at the marionette's blackened, cracked face. "She was sort of nice to me when I had that hallucination in the Hidden Stairway." Sonja wanted to add: *Remember, Charlotte, when you ignored me and walked off with Edgar?* But she did not.

Mr. Fortune Teller tapped his pipe on the edge of a small brass case. "Come and look." The twins walked over to the case and peered into the glass. The green caterpillars they had seen back at the circus were now colorful butterflies—their wings like miniature watercolors. Among them was a completely gold one.

"Was that the caterpillar who wove the glittering cocoon?" asked Sonja, studying the luminous creature.

"The very one," replied the old man.

"She's got our blood in her," murmured Charlotte.

"And our magic," said Sonja. "That's why she's gold, right?"

Mr. Fortune Teller nodded. He opened the lid and cupped the little insect in his wrinkled hands. It fluttered out between his fingers and flitted around the twins, its sparkling wings twinkling in their eyes. There was a little part of them inside her, Sonja thought. She watched the butterfly drift to the window. She knew what it wanted. It was the basic right of every living creature. Sonja looked at the old man. "Can we set her free?"

"You can set them *all* free," said Mr. Fortune Teller. "They're from here, you know. Alexandria gives them to me from time to time so I'm reminded of the Seven Edens. It helps to see a little color when you're traveling through the Outskirts."

"Uncle Tell," Charlotte said softly. "Why did you stay with the circus? Why didn't you live in the Vanishing Islands?"

"Partly to take care of you, partly because I was looking for others like myself. Staghart found other Changelings among the humans of the cities and Outskirts. I thought I would try to do the same for the Foretellers." The old man sighed. "In all these years, I haven't found a single one. I'm afraid I might be the last of us."

Charlotte took his hand and squeezed it. "Edgar's on his own, too."

"We went to Rain City," interrupted Sonja. "You were right, Uncle Tell. You wouldn't like it there much anymore. We saw the old library, though."

The old man closed his eyes. "I remember its dusty smell and the quiet sound of turning pages." He smiled. "Also, the librarian with the pink beehive who used to shush me even when I wasn't talking." He mused for a moment. "Memories. They sometimes give you hope that the future can't be all bad."

Sonja pushed open a small stained-glass window and released the fluttering insects into the air. Their antennas twirled left and right—overwhelmed by a hundred nectars. The gold butterfly was the last out. A spray of golden dust trailed behind her.

Sonja watched the full moon rise into the dimming sky. She wondered if Tatty could see the moon where she was.

"Mr. Moon," she said. "Please, tell our Tatty—" Her voice cracked. "Please, tell our Tatty we miss her." Sonja started to cry. Charlotte quickly followed. Mr. Fortune Teller put his arms around them. He tried to say something sensible but could not find the words. A tear rolled out of his eye, down his cheek, and disappeared into his mustache. He missed Tatty, too.

"Uncle Tell," said Sonja. "Has Tatty ever visited the Seven Edens?"

The old man shook his head. "I'm afraid not."

"I hope she will one day to see how beautiful they are."

The door opened. Alexandria poked her head in. "If you don't come soon—" She saw the old man and the girls huddled together, and her voice trailed off. "I'll see you outside." She turned away awkwardly and closed the door.

Charlotte wiped her eyes. "Alexandria's probably never cried in her life."

"She's cried," said the old man, standing up. "Enough for a hundred years."

"Does it have something to do with why the Swifters hate her so much?" asked Sonja.

Mr. Fortune Teller blinked. "Don't ask me to tell you, because I won't."

Sonja looked at her sister. She raised her eyebrows. Something terrible had happened to Alexandria at some point in her life. Perhaps it was why she acted the way she did.

Charlotte pulled out a red plaid dress from the pile. "I wish something I *liked* wasn't burned."

"At least they're clean," Sonja said, shrugging. She put on an orange dress with checks all over it and a lumpy sweater hand-knit by Tatty. She caught a glimpse of the pennywhistle lying on the bed. Maybe Charlotte was right. Maybe they should practice. Sonja quickly stuffed it into her sweater pocket.

The old man wrapped his scarf around his head and turned the knob of the door. Sonja felt Charlotte take her hand. She held it firmly. Her sister had not forgotten her after all. Sonja walked outside, smiling. Being back with Mr. Fortune Teller in his caravan with memories of the circus everywhere gave Sonja a little strength. Maybe it would grow, especially with Charlotte by her side.

CHAPTER THIRTY

The Tiffins

ALEXANDRIA WAVED FROM THE OTHER END OF THE POND as Mr. Fortune Teller and the twins walked hand in hand across a wooden bridge. A Tiffin leaned over the railing, skipping stones. Another dipped her toes into the pink-blue water. Singing and laughing filled the air.

Dottie sat perched on top of a post. She opened one eye and said, "Those Changelings are foaming at the mouth. You better hurry, or there'll be nothing left."

Charlotte dropped Sonja's hand when she saw Edgar. He was sitting next to the Changelings on the grass, playing a game of jacks. He grabbed Charlotte and pulled her down next to him. "I missed you," he whispered. Streaks of silver had crept into his blue eyes, and his pale cheeks were rosy from the sun. He was more beautiful than ever, thought Charlotte. "I missed you, too," she said shyly.

A banquet of delicately prepared foods was spread out before them: bowls of violet soup, honeysuckle cake dusted with bright pollen, and sweet-stem scones oozing with rose jelly.

"Well, what are you waiting for?" Alexandria said— but before the words could leave her mouth, the Changelings were wildly attacking the platters.

Moritz slurped the jelly. "Yummy!" he gushed, licking his lips. His nose was sticky and pink.

"Mine's good, too!" Wolf Boy said with a mouthful of cake. Crumbs flew everywhere.

Sonja frowned. "Not very good table manners." She took a sip of the soup. "Really delicious." She tipped her head back, swallowing the entire bowl in one gulp. When she finished, she wiped her mouth with the back of her hand and burped.

"Now, that's ladylike," remarked Wolf Boy. Moritz laughed, half choking.

Edgar and Charlotte split a sweet-stem scone. Charlotte's face brightened when she bit into the crumbly, moist treat. It was sweet and fragrant and tingled in her mouth. She wondered if it tasted so good because she was sharing it with Edgar.

Mr. Fortune Teller sat between Alexandria and Hester on a bench. He dabbed his mustache with a handkerchief. "My chest feels cold without my Amulet. It used to warm me up on a chilly night like this."

"My Amulet used to make the faintest hum," said Alexandria,

wiping off a dollop of lemongrass custard from her mouth. "It helped me sleep at night."

"I have it worst of all," sniffed Hester. "I can hardly see without my Amulet."

"Do you know where the Amulets come from?" Mr. Fortune Teller asked the children. They shook their heads. "They're ancient relics, each from its own Eden, blessed by the beings we all descend from. These beings hid the Seven Edens after a prophecy foretold that one day the world would be covered in steel, and life on its surface would wither away." The old man's white eyes glowed in the dim light. "They believed that if these lands remained untouched, they would be strong enough to sustain the rest of the world's destruction."

"That's why the Amulets are so important." Hester munched on a rose-hip macaroon as she spoke. Crumbs sprinkled all over her feathered cloak. "They're our connection to our ancestors and their will to protect the world. Not only do they give us passage into the Seven Edens, but they also unlock many doors within them. Only the oldest Protectors know where the most ancient doors lie, including the one that leads to the source of the magic."

Sonja stopped eating. "The source of the magic?" She swallowed the half-chewed biscuit. "That's what Kats von Stralen and the Contessa are looking for."

"If it's that hard to find," said Charlotte, "then why are you so worried? They'll probably never find it."

Alexandria's face darkened. "They'll ravage the lands, and the world will lose its lifeline. It's a matter of our survival."

"There shouldn't be a Key in the first place," said Edgar.

"As long as there've been Amulets, there's been a Key," returned Hester. "We don't believe in shutting the good out, even if from time to time the bad slips in."

"There've been other Keys?" Sonja asked, surprised.

"Hundreds. They're chosen for the pureness of their heart," said Mr. Fortune Teller. "That's why the Great Tiffin picked Tatty."

A Tiffin girl with dark spiral curls appeared, carrying another platter. She offered them each a large, dried flower petal. Wolf Boy jerked on her arm and whispered something in her ear. She burst into peals of laughter.

Charlotte saw Sonja roll her eyes. Why was her sister such an old curmudgeon? She hated to see anyone young and happy and in love. It was embarrassing. If only they were not identical. She snuggled closer to Edgar.

Moritz grabbed a spotted blue petal.

"I wouldn't eat too much of that," warned the Tiffin girl.

Moritz took three big bites. "How come?"

"The Blue Fancy is quite strong. You'll feel funny inside."

Wolf Boy snatched the petal out of Moritz's hands. He took a bite and paused. "Does kind of make you light-headed."

"Can I try?" asked Edgar. Wolf Boy passed it to him. He ate some and handed it to Charlotte.

Charlotte was about to say, "No, thank you," but she changed her mind. She wanted to be the fun twin, the courageous twin, the uncomplaining twin. She took a dainty bite. "Mmm," she said, quickly taking another. "You've got to try it, Sonja," she giggled. "It makes you feel happy."

Sonja folded her arms across her chest. "I prefer to feel like myself."

"But we'd prefer if you were someone else," joked Wolf Boy. The Tiffin girl hid a laugh behind his shoulder.

Sonja glared at her. "At least *some*one finds you funny."

It was becoming more and more clear to Charlotte: other children did not like her sister. She wished Sonja would go to sleep and leave her alone with Edgar.

Hester folded up what remained of the Blue Fancy and popped it into her mouth. She looked at Charlotte. "Can you believe I was once young like you?" she mused. "Young and in love with a Changeling."

"A Changeling?" Wolf Boy asked.

Hester hiccupped. "Staghart, of course. He was busy finding Changelings to repopulate the Forlorn Forest, and I was caught up in learning the birding way. Now that I'm old, I'm full of regret." She pointed her cane at the children. "Heed this warning. Don't deny your love, whatever happens."

"We won't," Edgar said happily. "Right, Charlotte?" He leaned over and kissed her on the mouth.

Mr. Fortune Teller's face turned bright red. He poked the end of his cane into Edgar's back. "Watch it, youngster."

Charlotte sighed. Her family was so aggravating.

A young Tiffin boy with a mass of orange hair ran up to the Tiffin girl, out of breath. "We're all taking dives off the cliff," he announced. "Come along, and bring your friends!" He ran off, stopping now and again to invite more children along the way.

"You'll come?" the Tiffin girl asked the Changelings.

"Of course," said Wolf Boy. "Moritz?"

"I can't move." Moritz lay flat on his back staring up at the sky. "I'm paralyzed."

The Tiffin girl laughed. "I told you not to eat too much of the Blue Fancy."

"Charlotte and I are in," Edgar said, helping Charlotte to her feet.

Mr. Fortune Teller shook his head. "I don't think that's a good idea. It's getting late."

Charlotte had to find a way to persuade him. "Please, Uncle Tell," she begged. "Tatty would let me go." She could see the old man softening at Tatty's name. "I'll only be an hour."

"One hour," warned Mr. Fortune Teller, "then straight to bed. Sonja will accompany you."

Sonja shook her head. "I'm staying." She looked at Charlotte smugly. "That means you can't go."

Charlotte glared at her sister. She had had quite enough of Sonja for one day.

"Great!" exclaimed Wolf Boy. He rose and pulled up the Tiffin girl. "Lead the way, my lady."

The Tiffin girl ran off, laughing. "Wait for me!" Wolf Boy yelled, chasing after her.

Charlotte was not going to lose her chance. She grabbed Edgar's hand and they hurried away. She heard Sonja yell after them, "He didn't say you could go without me!" A smile erupted on Charlotte's face. Every hair on her body stood on end. It was the first time she had truly rebelled against her sister and she liked it. She was free! At least for an hour.

Chapter Thirty-One

Crackus

Sonja watched Charlotte and Edgar disappear into the dusk-lit meadow. She slumped down beside Moritz. He was sprawled across the grass, snoring. Moritz was the only one who was nice to her. Otherwise, she was surrounded by traitors like Charlotte.

"If I were younger," Hester said, eyeing Sonja with her one eye, "I'd have gone with them."

Sonja nibbled on a pink petal. "I don't want to. They're immature."

"She shouldn't be left alone with that boy," said Mr. Fortune Teller.

"Well, why didn't you stop her?" Sonja snapped back.

"Go find them, Sonja," ordered Alexandria.

Sonja blinked and said, "That's my name. I *am* Sonja." It had always been a fifty-fifty chance, but nevertheless, for the first time, Alexandria had gotten it right.

She stared at Sonja. "Well? What are you waiting for?"

Sonja groaned and stood up. "It's not fair," she muttered as she plodded off.

Tiffins were pitching silk tents and building fires. Steaming teapots rattled and filled the air with the smell of seasoned flowers. Sonja pressed her lips to the mouthpiece of the pennywhistle. She slowly and methodically moved her fingers over the little holes, trying to remember the notes. She might as well practice if she was going to spend the rest of her life alone. She saw a glimpse of red plaid fluttering up ahead. It was Charlotte. She broke into a run but knocked over a bowl. Water splashed everywhere.

"I'm terribly sorry," Sonja apologized to a wrinkled, old Tiffin. She clumsily wiped his wings with the hem of her dress.

"No worry," he said, chuckling. "No worry."

Children were gathered at the edge of the meadow. Charlotte and Edgar mingled among them. Sonja ran up to her sister, out of breath. "I've been looking for you," she said. "We should go back."

"Go back?" Charlotte laughed, munching on a piece of Blue Fancy. "We just got here. I have an hour."

Sonja frowned. "Where'd you get that? You'll make yourself sick."

Edgar pulled Charlotte toward him. "Don't worry, Sonja. I'll take care of her."

Sonja turned away. She wanted to scream. She had never felt more distant from Charlotte in her life. The Tiffins' laughter rang in her ears. Her head spun. She stumbled backward.

"Watch it," warned a voice.

It was Wolf Boy. His arm was wrapped around the Tiffin girl. He pointed.

Sonja was standing right at the edge of a sheer cliff that dropped straight down into blackness. She swallowed and stepped forward slowly.

"What're you doing here, anyway?" asked Wolf Boy.

Sonja shrugged. "It's a free world."

An excited murmur swept through the crowd. Everyone cleared back away from the cliff. One Tiffin stepped forward, alone. The others shouted encouragement. The Tiffin bowed, took three quick steps, then leapt out into the sky, somersaulted in midair, and tumbled down into the chasm. The others whistled and clapped. Another bolted forward and over the edge, spinning away like a top. More Tiffins jumped, each with his or her own stunt.

Sonja watched in awe. She wished she was not such a scaredy-cat.

"Want a turn?" the Tiffin girl asked Wolf Boy.

He nodded enthusiastically.

She hooked her arms around his waist, flapped her wings vigorously, and lifted him off the ground.

"I'm flying!" Wolf Boy sang out, rising through the air. "I'm flying!"

"I want to try!" begged Charlotte. "Someone take me!"

"Lower your voice," Sonja whispered, grabbing her arm.

"Why?" yelled Charlotte. She wriggled her arm free. "I want to fly!"

Wings flapped overhead. Suddenly, Charlotte was whipped up off the ground. She laughed ecstatically as a Tiffin boy carried her away.

Edgar followed shortly, embraced by another Tiffin. "It's incredible!" he exclaimed, treading his feet through the air.

Soon, Sonja was left on the edge of the cliff with only a wingless Tiffin. He had bony stumps where his wings should have been. After a moment, he sullenly walked away. Sonja trembled in the dark, alone. She blew into the pennywhistle. It shrieked. Without her Talent, she was a nobody. Without Tatty, she had no home. Without Charlotte, she might die of a broken heart.

Sonja dropped to her knees. Alexandria said the Seven Edens was the world's life support. Well, Charlotte was hers.

She grabbed the locket around her neck and cried out, "Come help me, Mother and Father, whoever you are!"

Sonja's hair flapped in a gust of wind. She looked up. A Tiffin boy hovered over her. "Your sister told me to get you."

Sonja scrambled to her feet. Charlotte needed her! The idea of flying over the precipice made Sonja sick, but she had to be brave for her sister's sake.

"I'm—I'm ready," she stammered.

The Tiffin flung his arms around her waist and yanked her up into the sky. Her dress blew up like a balloon. Sonja looked down at her feet dangling in midair. Her stomach leapt into her throat. They were soaring across the dark landscape at breakneck speed. Before she could find her voice to scream, the Tiffin boy brought her gently to the ground. She staggered.

"You okay?" he asked.

Sonja lifted her head. They stood in a wide patch of glowing flowers, small, gleaming buds illuminating an entire field.

"It's so beautiful," she murmured.

"Lightning struck here so many times, its energy got trapped permanently in the ground."

A voice shouted: "Let's find Crackus!" Other voices yelled and cheered and formed a boisterous crowd.

"Who's Crackus?" asked Sonja.

"A strange old Tiffin. A sort of a hermit, you might say. Traveled in the Outskirts for years with a sideshow. Made him a little… unsteady. The Great Tiffin finally brought him back, because he reads trees."

"Reads trees?"

"Hears vibrations and voices from the roots underground. There's a network, you know. It spans the entire world. Sometimes, he can even hear voices from the cities."

The young Tiffins started through the field, singing. Charlotte's head stuck out above the others. She was perched on Edgar's shoulders.

"We'd better go, before they leave without us." The Tiffin boy dashed off. Sonja hurried after them. She reached Edgar and Charlotte, out of breath.

"Did you need me, Charlotte? Are you all right?"

Charlotte looked down at her and smiled lazily. "Of course I am."

"I flew down with a Tiffin. Can you believe it? You know how I am about heights. I was scared, but I—" Sonja stopped midsentence. She could see Charlotte was not paying attention. She was twirling Edgar's hair.

They entered a thicket of trees. Blossoms twinkled among the leaves. Sparkling acorns hung from low branches. Glowing pitcher plants and snap-traps grew in clumps around their trunks, their silvery insides luring insects to their death. A red squirrel with tiny black eyes jumped from one tree to the next until it landed on the roof of a small timber hut.

A Tiffin with enormous ears and balding hair all combed to

one side was crouched on the roof twiddling his thumbs. Two sets of little purple wings stuck out of the back of a ragged suit, and a string threaded with acorns hung around his neck. "What does Crackus hear?" he said, cupping one of his giant ears. His voice creaked like a door on a rusty hinge. "What does Crackus hear?"

The squirrel scurried up his arm and rested on his shoulder. The young Tiffins giggled. "Crackus hears nine beating hearts," he announced, scrambling to the ground. His back was crooked, and one shoulder was higher than the other. The squirrel munched on an acorn dangling from his necklace. Bits of shell dusted his shoulders.

Sonja felt a sort of kinship with the Tiffin. She imagined a sideshow was similar to a circus. Everyone who comes to watch you thinks you are different, a freak. Now, back with the Tiffins, Crackus was still considered different, still considered a freak. It was the same for Sonja. She did not fit in the Outskirts, she did not fit in the Seven Edens, and she most certainly did not fit in with her sister's new life. She would probably end up by herself in an isolated shack with a squirrel on her shoulder just like Crackus.

"What does Crackus hear?" the hermit said excitedly. "A Changeling, Crackus hears."

Just at that moment, Wolf Boy burst into the thicket with the Tiffin girl.

Sonja gasped. "He's right."

"Name, Changeling?" asked Crackus.

"Wolf Boy, sir."

Crackus hobbled briskly to a tree and pressed his right ear against its trunk. "What does Crackus hear? Crackus hears Wolf Boy's name spoken by a girl." Crackus chuckled. "A Changeling. She prays he will wed her once the leaves change color."

Wolf Boy turned to the Tiffin girl, blushing. "Don't worry, I prefer girls with wings."

"Wait, wait. What does Crackus hear? Another Changeling speaks." The Tiffin stroked the bark with his fingers. His nails were bitten down to his cuticles. "He says soon Wolf Boy will replace him. He says soon Wolf Boy will make him proud."

Sonja looked at Wolf Boy. His smile had faded. She knew he was thinking of Staghart. Did the Tiffin really hear his voice?

"Crackus asks your names." The Tiffin turned an ear toward the twins. Sonja stared, startled.

Edgar lifted Charlotte off his shoulders and placed her on the ground. "Charlotte and Sonja Tatters," Charlotte said shyly.

"Ah, the daughters of the Key." The Tiffin put his ear to a higher spot on the trunk. He listened. "What does Crackus hear? Crackus hears a woman restless in her sleep. She whispers 'Charlotte' and 'Sonja' and swears she will see them again."

"It's Tatty!" Sonja exclaimed. Everyone turned to stare. "It's our mother!"

"Crackus hears another mother," the hermit continued. "A mother who gave them away. A mother who hopes they will forgive her."

Sonja stared, silent. Everything went blurry around her. The only thing she could hear was her pounding heart. Was Crackus listening to their real mother?

Edgar stepped forward, grinning. "What about me? Anyone speaking of me? I'm Edgar of the Golden Underground."

The Tiffin stooped low and pressed his ear against a knot protruding out of the tree. After a moment, he spoke: "What does Crackus hear? Crackus hears a human. Her hands jangle with jewels. Her voice scratches Crackus' ears." The Tiffin's eyes darted nervously from left to right. Sweat trickled off his brow. "Now she shouts! Oh, my. Now she screams!" His earlobes trembled at his chin. The squirrel leapt off his shoulder and disappeared up the trunk.

Sonja glanced at Edgar. He looked scared. Who had Crackus heard?

Edgar yanked the hermit away from the tree. There was a nervous murmur from the crowd.

"Edgar," Charlotte said hesitantly. "What are you doing?"

"Tell them you're a liar!" Edgar shook Crackus violently. Crackus covered his face with his hands, scared. "Tell them you're making this all up!"

Wolf Boy tackled Edgar and tore him away from Crackus. Crackus limped off, whimpering as the boys tumbled onto the grass. "No more," he sniveled. "No more." He scrambled into his hut and closed the door behind him.

Edgar squirmed out of Wolf Boy's hold and jumped to his feet. He wiped his bloody nose.

They stared at each other coldly.

"Sorry, brother. I didn't like the old man spinning stories." Edgar stuck out his hand. "Friends?"

Wolf Boy frowned but grabbed his hand. Edgar pulled him up.

"Good!" Edgar hooked arms with Charlotte. "The night awaits us!" They ran off together through the trees.

Wolf Boy nudged Sonja. "Come on."

Sonja shook her head without taking her eyes off the hermit's hut. She had to speak to Crackus.

"Don't complain later that I left you." Wolf Boy put his arm around the Tiffin girl, and they walked out of the thicket with the other children.

Sonja took a breath and walked over to the little shack. She gently knocked on the door. It creaked open, and Crackus peered out. "Is he gone?" he whispered. There was dirt in the creases of his face. His eyes were big and brown and shiny.

"Edgar? He's gone."

"Crackus doesn't like him."

"Me neither. He's taken my sister away from me. Also, he kills boars."

The hermit laughed excitedly.

"Can I ask you something, Crackus?"

"Please, please."

"Do you know who my real mother is?"

He shook his head. "Crackus only hears voices."

Sonja paused. "Did she seem nice?"

"Very nice," replied Crackus. "Also, very sad."

Sonja thought for a moment. "The voice that scared you," she said softly. "The one who spoke Edgar's name. Any idea *who* she is?"

He shook his head and shuddered, then stuck his grizzled fingers through the opening. "Sonja Tatters, *you* are nice."

"Nobody else seems to think so." Sonja held on to his hand. It trembled in hers. "I traveled the Outskirts, too, in a circus. I know what it feels like to be different."

A tear rolled down the hermit's cheek. "Crackus understands people. They don't mean to hurt you. They're just scared. More scared than you or me." He smiled sadly and quietly pressed the door shut.

Sonja ambled out of the thicket in a daze. She clicked open the locket. It went against her agreement with Charlotte to never open the locket outside, but she did not care. Her sister had abandoned her. She looked at the brown lock of hair curled under the cloudy, scratched glass. Their real mother had left a piece of herself with them all these years. She wanted them to remember her. Sonja kissed the glass and snapped the locket shut. She wished she had something of Tatty's to kiss, too. She walked through the trees. It made her feel less lonely knowing that, somewhere out there, both of her mothers were thinking of her, too.

Chapter Thirty-Two

Stargazing

THE SKY WAS BLACK, AND EVEN THE VERY FAINTEST STARS were visible. Charlotte's head rested on Edgar's chest. They lay in a meadow among the other sky-gazing couples. Charlotte had only ever seen one or two stars in the Outskirts before, and her eyes were lost in the dark depths of the cosmos.

"It's like sitting on the turrets of Jagged Rock," mused Edgar, "with all those sparkling diamonds above you." He paused. "I'll show you sometime."

Charlotte turned to look at him. "Will you really?"

"Sure. When we're married."

"Aren't we . . . a little young to get married?"

"All Longwalkers marry young. Hold on a second." Edgar jumped up and scrambled about the glittering meadow. Charlotte watched him eagerly. Her heart fluttered in her chest. She wished this night would never end. It was the first time she had been alone with a boy—or anyone, for that matter. The questioning, frightened, second-guessing voice of her sister was absent.

Edgar returned hiding something behind his back. "Guess what I've got."

Charlotte thought for a moment. "A star," she said, enchanted.

"A whole constellation!" exclaimed Edgar. He pulled out a wreath of glittering flowers and placed it on her head. He bowed deeply. "The Queen of the Longwalkers."

Charlotte's eyes brimmed with tears.

Edgar slumped on the ground, disappointed. "I thought you'd like it."

"Don't you see?" She threw her arms around him. "I like it too much!" Edgar smelled like everything good: candy and buttered popcorn, cake and ice cream, jam—even pancakes! Charlotte looked into his eyes. "I think I love you," she whispered.

"Sorry to bust in on you like this." It was Wolf Boy. He motioned to Sonja fidgeting beside him. "She forced me to come looking for you. I was in the middle of serenading a beautiful Tiffin girl."

"Hello there," Charlotte said a little stiffly. "Edgar made me a tiara. I'm going to be the Queen of the Longwalkers."

Sonja frowned. "Everyone was worried."

"About me? But I'm with Edgar."

"Exactly!" Sonja burst out.

Wolf Boy covered a laugh with his hand.

Edgar helped Charlotte up. "I hope you're not too angry, Sonja. I'm sorry I've taken up so much of your sister's time."

Sonja glared at him. "What I want to know is, who was that woman Crackus heard?"

Edgar lowered his head and said quietly, "It was my mother right before she died. He was hearing an echo from the past."

Sonja blinked, speechless.

Charlotte grimaced. "Apologize!"

Sonja glanced back and forth between Edgar and Charlotte. Finally, she looked away and muttered stubbornly, "I won't."

A shadow fluttered up ahead through the dark sky. Dottie hovered above them.

"The old man says: time's up!" she squawked. "For all of you!"

"Hold on!" Wolf Boy yelled after her. "I've got a girl waiting for me!"

"If you haven't forgotten, we've got an important day tomorrow. More important than a date!" Dottie circled over them and then flew out of the field.

Edgar put his arm around Wolf Boy's shoulder. "Don't worry. There'll be others." They walked ahead, leaving the twins alone.

"That was awful!" Charlotte erupted. "Why didn't you apologize? Don't you know I'm in love with Edgar?"

"In love?" snorted Sonja. "With that Longwalker?"

Charlotte's face grew stony. Why did Sonja have to make things so difficult?

"I don't trust him."

"Typical. The minute I like someone, you get jealous. It's been happening all our lives."

"I'm trying to protect you."

"Protect me from what? From being happy!"

"From getting hurt, Charlotte."

"The only person who's hurting me is you! Not Jack Cross. Not Edgar."

"I'm glad you mentioned Jack Cross. I thought you'd forgotten him."

"How could I forget Jack Cross? He's my friend. I promised to help him."

Sonja grunted. "You said you were in love with him first. Now you're in love with Edgar. I can't keep up with you."

Charlotte reflected for a moment. Did she love Jack Cross or did she love Edgar? She was only twelve and a half years old. How was she supposed to know? The one thing she was sure of was that her sister needed to butt out. She yanked Sonja toward her. "Edgar and I are getting married."

"That's ridiculous."

"Why?"

"Well, for starters, you're too young."

"Edgar said all Longwalkers marry young."

"You can't live underground."

"Of course, I can."

"Tatty won't let you."

"Well, Tatty's not here, is she?" All of a sudden, Charlotte felt a sharp slap across her face. She stared a hard stare at her sister. Sonja looked fierce but guilty. Her hand was frozen in the air. Without saying another word, Charlotte turned and marched away.

"Wait, Charlotte!" she heard her sister yell. "I'm sorry. PORCUPINE!"

Charlotte stopped walking. She felt an ache where Sonja had

slapped her. She touched her cheek. No. She had to teach Sonja a lesson. She ran ahead, hooked arms with Edgar, and raced up the hill. She did not look back . . . but she thought of Sonja standing alone where she had left her. Tears sprang to her eyes.

It could not be helped. It was time for Sonja to grow up.

Chapter Thirty-Three

Ladybug

Sonja ran through the dark meadow, lost. Her sight was bleary from crying. Had the bond between her and her sister been broken forever? A wingless silhouette approached. Charlotte *had* come back. The bond was unbreakable.

Sonja's heart sank. "Oh, it's you."

"They made me come find you," grumbled Wolf Boy. "By the way, you ruined my chances with that Tiffin girl. Thanks for that."

Sonja's eyes narrowed. "Why do you care so much about a girl you're never going to see again?"

Wolf Boy shrugged. "Animal instinct," he said.

"What?"

"Never mind." He paused for a moment. "How come you never laugh or smile or have any fun? You spend too much time rolling your eyes and complaining."

"I have things on my mind. If you haven't noticed, our mother was kidnapped."

Wolf Boy nodded. "My mother threw me into a stinking orphanage. Better not to sulk about it, though."

"You mask your sadness by clowning around. I read it in a magazine. One day you're going to have some kind of a breakdown. Anyway, that's what the article said."

Wolf Boy frowned. "You really are uptight, aren't you?"

"Are you kidding?" snapped Sonja. "I'm a musician! Artists are *not* uptight!"

"Some musician. You can't even play a note."

Sonja stopped in her tracks. All the strength went out of her body at once. She burst into tears and covered her face. Charlotte was the only person who truly knew her. She understood how sad she was at being abandoned. She understood how much music meant to her. She understood every dream and aspiration she ever had. They had been sole companions for twelve and a half years. Now she had nobody. Her voice grew very quiet. "I don't really know who I am anymore."

Wolf Boy stared at Sonja. He bit his lip, then gently said, "Nobody knows who they *really* are." He pulled her hands off her face. "Look at me. Sometimes a boy, sometimes a wolf. Imagine how confusing that feels."

Sonja wiped her tears away with the back of her sleeve. "What's it feel like to transform?"

"Sort of like changing expressions on your face from happy to sad." Wolf Boy thought for a moment. "I've got two versions of myself. Sometimes, I feel like being one; sometimes, I feel like being the other."

Sonja nodded. "Kind of like being a twin. The only problem is the other version of myself has abandoned me."

"They always come back in the end. You'll see." Wolf Boy hesitated. "Mind if I ask you something?"

Sonja shook her head.

"What's wrong with your fingers? They're always jiggling about."

"It started when my Talent was stolen. I think they miss playing. I guess it's sort of an expression of how I feel inside."

They walked side by side into the Ancient Gardens. In the dark, the giant flowers were big creepy shadows. A breeze whistled through their leaves. Sonja grabbed at Wolf Boy's fur cape and whispered, "What if one of those enormous ants attacks us?"

"Don't worry," he replied, laughing. "Remember, I *eat* insects."

At that precise moment, a ladybug the size of a cat buzzed out of the grass.

Sonja shrieked. The insect flew toward her, flapping frantically. Wolf Boy jerked Sonja out of the way. "It's only a ladybug!" he yelled.

The ladybug disappeared over the flower tops.

Wolf Boy's arms tightened around Sonja's waist. She looked up at him. His green eyes flashed. "You look nice when you're not talking."

"Is that a compliment?" Sonja asked, confused.

He touched the end of one of her curls. "Your hair. It's sort of pretty. You should let it grow down to your feet like Alexandria."

Sonja's face turned bright red. "That's ridiculous," she said, pulling away. She felt her heart pounding against her ribs.

"Oh, well. Forget I said anything." Wolf Boy trudged off into the meadow.

275

Sonja followed quietly behind, her mind whizzing. Maybe Wolf Boy did not completely hate her after all. She pulled out her pennywhistle and, stepping in Wolf Boy's footprints, played some broken notes.

Tiffin silhouettes moved around inside the thin cloth tents. Stars twinkled on the surface of the pond. A family of frogs slept on a lily pad. Charlotte and Edgar were already sitting with the three Protectors. They all stood up when they saw Wolf Boy and Sonja.

Sonja looked at Charlotte sheepishly. Charlotte gave her a small smile, then turned away.

"These old bones need some rest," Hester said, yawning. Mr. Fortune Teller escorted her to a nearby tent.

"By any chance did a Tiffin girl come looking for me?" Wolf Boy asked.

"She left a few minutes ago," said Alexandria. "She didn't seem too pleased." She pointed to Moritz on the ground. He was snoring heavily. "Let's move him."

Wolf Boy reluctantly grabbed Moritz's arms. "Edgar, we need your help. There's a whole horse hidden inside this body."

"Good night, your majesty." Edgar kissed Charlotte's hand. He smiled at Sonja. "I hope we'll be friends." Then he bowed and ran off to join the others.

Charlotte pressed her hand to her face. "Isn't he wonderful?"

Sonja scoffed. She could not help herself. "You're beginning to sound like Bea," she said coolly.

Charlotte wheeled around, furious. "Just because we're twins doesn't mean I have to end up an old spinster like you. Living alone, talking to yourself, eating cat food from a can!"

"I'd rather be a spinster than make a fool of myself!"

Charlotte seized Sonja by her shoulders and shook her. Sonja's cheeks flushed. Her lips curled. In a fit of rage, she bit one of Charlotte's hands. Charlotte shrieked and shoved Sonja. Sonja's eyes went black. She dove on top of Charlotte, and they fell to the ground, wrestling. They had never had a real fight before, an actual fistfight, and every little slight and hurt from all the years seemed to be coming out in their hits and kicks and slaps.

"Enough!" yelled Mr. Fortune Teller. He stood in front of them with his hands on his hips.

The twins looked up. Alexandria, Wolf Boy, and Edgar were staring at them, shocked.

"This is no time to fight. We need to focus on finding Tatty."

Charlotte looked away, embarrassed. "Sorry, Uncle Tell."

"I'm sorry too," mumbled Sonja.

"Good. It's settled."

Edgar started toward Charlotte. Mr. Fortune Teller blocked him with his cane. "You'll see her in the morning."

The twins stumbled to their feet. They were covered in scratches and bruises and marks. They limped up the steps of the caravan. Mr. Fortune Teller opened the door. The velvet curtains were drawn, and a candle flickered. A teapot sat on the desk, steaming from its spout.

"I made some wild-nettle tea to help you sleep. Here's some ointment for your wounds." He handed Sonja a little ceramic bowl, then started to chuckle. "Remind me where you two learned to throw punches like that."

Sonja shrugged. "Seeing the clowns fight."

"Well, now, you can make up like the clowns."

"We don't drink black gin," said Charlotte.

"You know what I mean."

The twins hugged awkwardly. Even though their bodies were pressed together, Sonja felt a barrier between them.

They put on their pajamas and got into bed. Mr. Fortune Teller gave them each a cup of tea. They sipped the hot, bitter drink.

"Aren't you going to sleep?" Charlotte asked the old man.

Mr. Fortune Teller shook his head. "No time, my dears. I have too much to discuss with Alexandria."

The twins set their cups aside and lay on their backs. They had not slept in two days. It felt good to be in a real bed, thought Sonja. She moved her feet around under the starchy sheets. They brushed against Charlotte's. Charlotte awkwardly pulled hers away. Sonja pretended not to notice. She looked at the old man at the end of the bed and said, "Uncle Tell?"

"Yes, Sonja."

"We met Crackus."

"Ah, the hermit."

"He heard Tatty through a tree." Sonja touched the locket. "Tatty and our real mother." She hesitated. "Who is she, Uncle Tell?"

"I wouldn't want to say."

"But you *know*?"

Mr. Fortune Teller nodded.

"You've known this whole time?"

He looked down at his fidgeting hands.

"I understand, Uncle Tell," Sonja said softly. "It wasn't your choice. Can you answer this at least? Do you think we'll ever meet her?"

The old man sighed. "I hope so. One day."

"I don't want to," interrupted Charlotte. "I just want Tatty back."

"I want Tatty back, too," said Sonja, "but aren't you curious?"

Charlotte shook her head. "One mother's enough."

Mr. Fortune Teller patted the girls' feet over the covers. "I have to go now. Alexandria will be waiting for me."

"Do you really have to leave us again?" moaned Sonja. She would be stuck with Alexandria and the Changelings—and, even worse, Edgar and Charlotte.

"If I can persuade the Gillypurs to fight, we might have a better chance against Kats von Stralen and the Contessa."

"I can't wait for the day we have no more duties or worries," sighed Charlotte.

"I'm afraid, my dear, that day may never come." The old man stood up. "Now, time to sleep." He kissed each girl on the forehead.

"Good night, Uncle Tell."

"Good night, Charlotte."

"Don't forget to say goodbye before you leave," said Sonja. She was so sleepy, it dulled her anxiety about Uncle Tell leaving. Out of habit, she went to take Charlotte's hand, but Charlotte's arms were crossed tightly across her chest. Sonja turned onto her side and closed her eyes.

BOOK
THREE

Chapter Thirty-Four

Dreaming

MOONLIGHT BEAMED INTO THE CARAVAN THROUGH THE little stained-glass window. Charlotte lay in bed, awake. Her head was spinning with anxious thoughts. She looked over at Sonja muttering in her sleep. She wished she had let her sister hold her hand. Then perhaps she would be asleep too.

A handful of pebbles pattered against the window. Maybe it was Edgar, she thought. Charlotte jumped out of bed, fumbled through the dark, and pushed open the window.

Cool air swept into the room. Edgar's pale face appeared. His hair was rumpled, and his skin was damp and blotchy. He took Charlotte's hand in his. "I couldn't sleep."

"Me neither," said Charlotte. With her free hand, she pinched her cheeks for color.

"Run away with me," Edgar said earnestly.

"What? Where? Now?"

He wrinkled his sweaty brow. "I need to leave the past behind. It might kill me."

"What about the rescue mission?"

"The others can take care of that."

Charlotte's face tensed. What about Tatty? What about Sonja? Charlotte looked back over her shoulder at the little sleeping lump in bed. As much as she wanted her freedom, she knew leaving Sonja would break her heart.

"Don't you see?" Edgar urged, squeezing her hand. "You and I, we're the future."

Charlotte turned to him with tears in her eyes and said in a whisper, "I can't. I'm sorry."

Edgar's face flushed. He threw off her hand. "I knew you wouldn't help me. It's all going to end because of you!"

"I want to help you, Edgar," Charlotte said, crying, "but she's my mother. My mother! You'd want to save yours if you could, wouldn't you?"

Edgar covered his face with his hands. He shook his head and groaned. After a moment, he looked up. His eyes were swollen and watery. In a low, trembling voice, he said, "You know, I haven't been myself since my mother and father died. Please, forgive me." He leaned into the room and kissed her cheek. "We'll start our life together another time." He gave her a sad sort of smile. "I'll see you in the morning." He turned away, and his wan figure disappeared into the night.

"Wait, Edgar!" Charlotte called after him, but he was gone. She closed the window. Tears streaked her face. Tatty always told her love had its ups and downs. Charlotte crawled back into bed, sniffling. She wiped her eyes on the sheet. She wanted to wake up

Sonja and tell her what had happened, but she knew her sister would never understand.

Her accordion was on the floor beside her. She picked it up and strapped it over her shoulders. It was soothing to have the familiar instrument resting on her chest. She pushed the keys silently. Even without knowing how to play, she liked to feel the smooth buttons under her fingertips.

Charlotte's limbs trembled with fatigue. She was exhausted. She remembered Tatty telling her that if she could not sleep, she should close her eyes and think pleasant thoughts. She put away the accordion and rested her head on the pillow. She thought of the rumbling wheels of their caravan, the clowns singing Gypsy songs, and the clicking sound Monkey made when he chewed.

Charlotte's eyes grew heavier and heavier. Finally, she found herself alone in the middle of a desert outside an ancient temple carved into striated rock. The enormous sun filled the sky. It mirrored the red-orange landscape below. She ascended the sandy steps and passed through the open doors. Inside a vast hall, there were a hundred women assembled. Their faces were crisscrossed with paint, and their bare feet hovered above the ground.

They were Swifters. She was in the Lost Desert.

The Protectors floated to the middle of the room and held their hands over a crackling pit of fire. It smelled like burning spices and frankincense. Shadows flickered across the striped walls.

The three Swifters spoke in unison. "Don't you know you're one of us?"

Charlotte gulped. "What do you mean?"

The door slammed shut. A gust of wind spun through the hall. It wrapped itself around Charlotte's waist like a coil. She struggled to break free as it dragged her toward the three women. They spoke one after the other in shrill, crackling voices:

"Your father's veins flow with Swifter blood."

"From his mother and her mother before her."

"You are a Swifter through and through."

Charlotte shook her head, yelling, "I'm not a Swifter! I'm not a Swifter!"

The three women crouched over the fire, burbling and gurgling. The flames resembled people dancing in an ancient bacchanal.

"Soon, the truth will be revealed."

"Soon, you will stand among us."

"Soon, your power will surpass all!"

"Please, let me go," begged Charlotte. "I need to get back to my sister. To Sonja."

One of the Protectors rose higher than the rest. "She's not like you. Her blood comes from her mother."

"How's that possible? We're identical twins."

The other two Protectors floated up to join their sister. In unison they roared: "Not in blood! Not in blood! Not in blood!"

Charlotte was sweating. She could hardly breathe. The wind pulled her closer to the fire pit. The chant of the surrounding Swifters grew louder.

"Stop! Please! I'll burn!" screamed Charlotte. Everything went dark.

She opened her eyes and found herself in a room decorated with animal heads.

"A little bird told me you might pay a visit," a voice hissed. The sentence slithered into Charlotte's ear like a snake.

A woman wearing white gloves bedecked with diamonds sat in a cloud of smoke. Charlotte could not make out her face, but she knew it was the Contessa. She trembled all over and looked up and down the room for a way out.

"There's only one exit," sneered the Contessa. Her white glove pointed to an open window. Charlotte felt a pair of hands yank her off the floor. She whipped her head around, and to her surprise, it was Edgar. "Enjoy the ride!" he said, before pushing her out the window.

"Wait! Edgar!" She dropped, whooshing through the smog. "I want to help! I swear!" Faces whizzed past her as she fell: Tatty and Uncle Tell and Bea; Arthur and Alexandria and Staghart; Wolf Boy and Moritz and Ansel. "Help me!" she cried. The ground was coming up fast.

Someone else was falling, too. Charlotte reached out to catch her. She had to catch her. She had to catch her sister before they both hit the earth.

A siren rang.

Charlotte woke up in a sweat.

Chapter Thirty-Five

The Rescue Begins

A CRY LIKE A FOGHORN SHOOK THE CARAVAN. SONJA opened her eyes, anxious. Today was the day they were going to save Tatty. Charlotte's side of the bed was empty. Sonja yanked back the covers and jumped to her feet. Her sister was at the window. Her back was turned toward her. Sonja slunk up beside Charlotte without saying a word. She did not know how things stood between them after what had happened the previous night.

The sun was rising, and a pink mist hung over the meadow. A crowd of Tiffins was gathering outside. They whispered and chattered.

Sonja leaned out the window. "What's going on?" she asked an old Tiffin with knotted horns.

"Visitors," he rasped. "Come to take the Mother of All Geese and Fowl to the Crooked Peaks. The Foreteller's already gone."

Sonja slumped back in. "Uncle Tell left without saying goodbye."

"I know." Charlotte shuffled through a small pile of clothing. "We'd better get dressed before Alexandria barges in here."

Sonja wriggled out of her pajamas and into the dress she had worn the night before. Her arms and legs were covered with bumps and bruises from fighting Charlotte. She watched her sister put on a checked yellow dress, brush her hair, and place the crown on her head. The flowers had wilted, and their glow was gone.

Sonja gritted her teeth in an attempt to hold back from saying anything mean, but it did not work. "That looks ridiculous," she blurted.

Charlotte smiled. "Thank you."

A picture flashed into Sonja's mind: Wolf Boy holding her tight in the Ancient Gardens.

She blushed. She rummaged through the drawers in Mr. Fortune Teller's desk and pulled out a pair of scissors.

"What are you doing?" Charlotte asked.

Sonja grabbed a hunk of her hair and snipped it in half.

"Don't!" pleaded Charlotte.

"Why not? I've always wanted short hair. Besides, we've looked identical our whole lives. Isn't it time we became individuals? That's what you've always wanted."

Sonja clipped away at her hair. From time to time, she glanced at her sister. Charlotte looked horrified. For some reason, it made Sonja happy. After five minutes straight, Sonja clamped the scissors down onto the desktop. Strands and strings of hair lay scattered all around her feet.

"How do I look?" Sonja's hair was as short as a boy's. It was uneven in every direction and stuck out all over the place.

Charlotte swallowed. "Terrible."

Sonja shrugged. "Well, I never wanted to look good anyway." She hung her pennywhistle around her neck. It clinked against the locket. It was Charlotte's turn to wear it, but Sonja was not going to mention it.

"What's going to happen?" Charlotte asked. "In the City of Steel and Smoke."

"There'll be a battle, I suppose. Alexandria will probably hide us somewhere safe until it's over, when Tatty is freed."

Charlotte sighed. "Something tells me it's not going to be that easy." She buttoned up her jacket. "We'd better go. Edgar's probably waiting for me."

Sonja bristled. "Well, we can't keep the little prince of the Golden Underground waiting, now, can we?"

Charlotte's eyes turned steely. She slung the accordion over her shoulder and walked out the door. The sound of laughter drifted into the caravan. More and more Tiffins had gathered outside.

Sonja groaned. She wished she could just hold her tongue. She looked around the room. It was peaceful.

"I wonder if I'll ever see you again," she muttered into the empty room.

Sonja glimpsed the broken marionette propped up on the table. It made her sad to think of it alone in the caravan. She slipped on one of Mr. Fortune Teller's suit jackets and stuffed the marionette inside the front pocket. This way, they could keep each other company.

Sonja walked into a sea of Tiffins.

Two giant birds were perched on the long limb of a blossoming tree. They rocked back and forth. Their brown wings were wrapped around them like ragged cloaks. Feathers stuck out around their heads like crowns, and their broad, calloused beaks dominated their faces.

"Gobos," said a Tiffin woman with rosy cheeks. "Ancient birds. Fierce as fire."

Sonja remembered them from Tatty's thighs. They stared out with beady little eyes from their perches on the tops of two rocky peaks. The tattoos of the Gobos were almost as scary as the ones of the boars of the Golden Underground. In person, there was something gentle about the ancient birds.

Alexandria and Hester walked arm in arm through the crowd. Dottie hovered over them.

Sonja watched as Hester fastened her cane to her belt and strapped her shell over her shoulder. "I hate saying goodbye, so I won't."

Hester whistled. One of the giant birds jumped into the air. The Tiffins stepped back as its massive wings swooped, and its black talons spread open. It clasped the old woman's shoulders and lifted her up into the air. The second bird took off after them, and together they disappeared into the horizon with Hester dangling in the air.

Alexandria turned to Sonja. "What happened to your hair?"

"I thought it would be easier to tell us apart."

"But I had just figured it out," said Alexandria, disappointed. "Where's Charlotte?"

Dottie landed on Alexandria's shoulder. "I saw her by the carriage."

"Come on, then," said Alexandria. "Our ride's ready."

They walked to the middle of the meadow. A group of Tiffins was waiting next to a roofless, wooden carriage. Some of them were attaching themselves to the front of it with leather harnesses. Alexandria walked over to speak to them.

Sonja could not see Charlotte anywhere. Had she run off with Edgar?

She touched the marionette in her pocket and whispered, "At least I have you."

"Talking to yourself?" interrupted a voice. Wolf Boy approached with Moritz.

Sonja fidgeted with the ends of her jacket. Why did she feel so nervous?

"It's the first sign of insanity, you know," Moritz teased.

Wolf Boy made a face. "What'd you do to your hair?"

"This? Nothing. Just a new style." Sonja ruffled it up a bit.

Wolf Boy looked confused, then slightly hurt. She understood why: he had told her to grow her hair long. He walked off sulkily.

"I kind of like it," Moritz said. "And the jacket. Makes you seem . . . different."

"That's what I was hoping for."

Charlotte came running toward them. "I can't find Edgar anywhere!"

"I guess you don't know," Moritz said hesitantly. "He left in the middle of the night."

"He's—he's gone?" stammered Charlotte.

"I'm afraid so," confirmed Alexandria. She sat in a seat at the front of the carriage. The Changelings slid in beside her. "We looked everywhere for him."

"He was probably scared," grunted Wolf Boy. "He did kind of seem like the lily-livered type."

"All that matters is that the Golden Knot is safe," interrupted Alexandria. "He completed his duty by bringing it here."

Charlotte stood helplessly muttering, "But—I—he—"

For a moment, the news was like sweet music to Sonja's ears, but seeing her sister so lost and confused immediately dampened her joy. "Come on, Charlotte," she said, taking her hand.

Charlotte shrugged Sonja away. "This is your fault!" she burst out. "You always do this to me!"

"I didn't do anything," Sonja said, confused.

"I only stayed because of you. He wanted me to go with him."

"Go with him where?"

"I don't know!" Charlotte started crying. "Somewhere!"

"You two!" yelled Alexandria. "Get in or we're leaving without you!"

Charlotte stomped into the carriage and sat in the backseat. Sonja slid in beside her.

"I'm Max," announced one of the harnessed Tiffins. He had a square jaw and a dimple in his chin. He gestured to the others. "That's Axl, Pip, Bo, and Gull." They each waved as their name was called out.

"Strap yourselves in," Max advised as he faced forward. "Takeoff can get a little bumpy."

Sonja fumbled with a seat belt made of rope. "I have a bad feeling about this."

Charlotte glared at her. "Don't talk to me. Don't touch me. From now on you're not my sister!"

The Tiffins flapped their wings vigorously and rose into the air. The carriage flew up with a hard jolt. Sonja gritted her teeth and grabbed Charlotte. "Please, Charlotte! I'm scared."

"I told you to stay away from me!" barked Charlotte. She pushed Sonja off and slid to the opposite end of the bench.

Sonja bit her lip. She shoved her hand into her pocket and held on to the little marionette. She pressed her eyes shut and muttered a prayer.

The rest of the Tiffins whooshed into the air behind the carriage, waving and shouting. It ascended into a layer of clouds, bouncing in the turbulence, jostling from side to side in the shadowy mist. Soon, the air cooled, and the carriage popped up out of the clouds and into the sunlight. The ride became smooth and quiet. Dottie flew beside the Tiffins, directing the way.

Sonja's eyes snapped open. She glanced over the side of the carriage. The gray landscape rolled by below. "I can't see the Land Where the Plants Reign," she said in a shaky voice. She was terrified, but not as terrified as she would have expected. Maybe everything she had been through the past few days—was making her braver?

"The Edens disguise themselves," explained Alexandria, "even from above. There's a Pathway into them through the clouds. It's practically impossible to find, except for experts like Dottie."

"What's the plan when we reach the City of Steel and Smoke?" asked Wolf Boy.

"We'll land in the Outskirts and wait until evening, then walk from there. I know a secret way into the city. If Tatty's there, she'll be at the Contessa's tower. Once we locate her, Dottie will send word to the Protectors to come."

The nose of a large silver balloon burst through the clouds. It was a zeppelin filled with passengers. They pressed their surprised faces against the windows and pointed at the Tiffins as they flew past. Black smoke trailed across the sky behind them.

Charlotte was crouched over her accordion, rocking back and forth. Sonja started to say something but stopped herself. Instead, she turned away and stared at a girl licking an ice cream cone in one of the zeppelin's windows. Her parents sat beside her, reading the newspaper. The girl did not know how lucky she was, thought Sonja. She was probably going on vacation. Sonja waved to her. The girl stopped licking her ice cream and waved back.

In the distance, a city spread out as far as the eye could see. Million-Mile-High buildings stood in wide rows, poking up through a thick white haze. A faint hum filled the air. "Is that it?" Sonja asked.

"That's it," murmured Alexandria. She gazed into the horizon. "I haven't been back since my grandmother died. We lived in the old Garden Quarter. The last beautiful place left in the city. The Contessa eventually destroyed it. Along with everything else."

Thick smog rolled over the carriage. All at once, they were inside a cloud and could not see more than five feet in front of them. They coughed. The carriage rattled.

One of the Tiffins let out a shrill shriek. "Something bit me!" he shouted. Blood dripped from his toes.

They slowed down and treaded water in the milky sky. The carriage hovered in midair.

"I can't see a thing," said Max as he waved away the smog.

"We should press on," urged Alexandria.

Something banged into the carriage from underneath. The twins screamed.

"What was that?" yelped Wolf Boy. Moritz looked around uneasily.

"Dottie, check below," ordered Alexandria.

Dottie flew under the carriage. A second later, she burst out, cawing. "A—a—"

White feathers exploded from beneath the carriage and shot up into the air.

"A swan!" cried Sonja, terrified. She knew how vicious and bloodthirsty these birds were—she had seen them tear apart their caravan.

The swan circled above, its outstretched wings shadowing the carriage.

"Go, go, go!" Alexandria yelled.

The Tiffins dove. The swan torpedoed after them headfirst and slammed into the carriage with a smash. It lunged at the Tiffins over and over, jabbing its beak at their faces.

Max caught the creature by its neck and squeezed. One of its eyes popped out of its socket and hung from an electric wire. When Max let go, the swan spiraled toward the earth, its wings fluttering aimlessly in the wind.

"That's no ordinary swan," he said breathlessly. "Where did it come from?"

"It's one of the Contessa's," said Alexandria. "Manufactured. It must have spotted us flying over the city." Alexandria gestured to the ground. "We should hide until nightfall."

They began to descend into the Outskirts.

Sonja looked warily over the edge of the carriage. There was a sudden rippling movement within a patch of clouds ahead. "Something moved up there!" she shouted, pointing.

A hundred orange beaks and black faces emerged at once out of the clouds. The vast flock of white swans flew toward them in rows of ten abreast. They were perfectly synchronized. Their powerful wings slapped the air and filled the sky with a sound like a single, thunderous heartbeat.

Kats von Stralen *was* building the Contessa an army, just like Alexandria had said. Sonja tore off her seat belt and hid under the seats. Charlotte scrambled in after her. She trembled all over. "The Contessa visited my dreams last night!" she sputtered. "She knows we're coming!" Sonja threw her arms around her sister. Charlotte had shouted at her, pushed her away, rejected her in every way, but now they might die at any moment. Sonja had no choice: she forgave her.

Alexandria yelled to Dottie: "Fly to the Crooked Peaks! Tell Hester we need help!" Without losing another moment, the parrot shot straight down and disappeared into the smog.

The first row of swans were closing in fast, just a few feet away. They stuck out their long, muscular necks, narrowed their beady eyes, and hissed.

Alexandria whipped out a leather pouch and shook ten small metal stars into the palm of her hand. She threw them up in the air. They mingled, whirling above her head. She made a fist and flicked her hand open with a snap. The stars hurtled toward the flock and slammed like bullets into their targets. Bits and pieces of wire mesh scattered. Swans dropped like bombs. The rest of the flock scrambled out of formation in a panic as they watched their comrades fall one after the other.

The stars boomeranged back to Alexandria's hand. "That should slow them down."

"Incoming!" warned one of the Tiffins.

Another flock of swans rocketed up from below. They wore black leather hoods with crests of feathers over their heads and steel claws strapped to their feet. Sonja could see them through the gaps in the wooden planks. They were bigger and scarier.

"Hold on to your seats!" cautioned Max. The Tiffins flew straight toward the hooded swans. Just before they met head-on, they shot upward and made an arc through the sky. The swans were quick. They swooped in a circle, spun around, and landed smack in front of the Tiffins. They squawked a wild war cry. Small, ragged teeth stuck out of their gums. The Tiffins brandished their long knives, terrified.

The hooded swans swept over them like a tidal wave, and they were soon buried in a cloud of white feathers.

"The Tiffins!" yelled Wolf Boy. "They're going to get killed!"

Alexandria flung her stars into the frenzied mob, but the swans dodged and bobbed around them. One swan caught a star in the air with its beak and snapped it in two. Alexandria watched, ashen.

The Tiffins swung their knives left and right, stabbing and jabbing. Each time a swan fell, a new one flew in. They were overwhelmed. Wings smacked their faces. Beaks nipped their flesh. The knives fell from their hands.

All of a sudden, the carriage went into a steep dive.

The twins screamed as they flew out from under the seat. The Changelings caught them, and the carriage dropped a thousand feet like a stone. Sonja closed her eyes. If they died, she would never see Tatty again; she would never know her real parents; she would never make up with her sister; she would never get her Talent back; she would never *be* somebody. She thought of the last line of the last letter she had written to Kanazi Kooks:

If I don't succeed, I'll die.

Well, it looked like she was right.

Ten feet above the ground, the carriage jerked to a stop. It floated in midair. The Tiffins hung dangling from their harnesses. Sonja looked around in a daze, shocked. Alexandria's eyes were pressed shut in concentration. She had saved them. Sonja heard shouting and howling below. She looked over the edge of the carriage and saw a troop of Enforcers pointing Gatsploders up at them.

"Land or we'll shoot!" announced a voice into a loudspeaker.

"It's too heavy for me to lift up!" Alexandria said, struggling. "We've got to lose the Tiffins."

Wolf Boy grabbed a knife off the floor, lunged forward, and began to saw at the leather straps.

"They might still be alive!" cried Sonja.

Moritz shook his head. "I'm afraid not."

Sonja looked away as the Tiffins dropped to the ground like ragged dolls.

Alexandria clenched her teeth, and the carriage surged back up into the air. The Enforcers fired at them from the ground, but they were already too far in the clouds.

A deafening cry filled the sky. Sonja looked up to see the hooded swans tearing toward them. "Here they come again!" she screamed.

"We're ready!" yelled Wolf Boy. He turned into a wolf and drew his claws. Alexandria shoved a knife into Sonja's hand. "Get under the seats so I'll have one less thing to worry about! I can barely keep this thing up in the air as it is!"

The twins huddled under the back row.

"Incoming!" shouted Wolf Boy as a swan hurtled toward the carriage.

"I've got him!" exclaimed Moritz. He knocked into Alexandria as he leapt up and lassoed the swan with a seat belt. Sonja saw Alexandria stumble and hit her head on the edge of the carriage. She dropped to the floor, out cold.

Again, the carriage began to plummet, but this time, thirty swans swooped down and caught the harnesses in their beaks.

"Alexandria!" Moritz yelled, crouching over her unconscious body. "Can you hear me?"

All at once, the rest of the flock bombarded the carriage. They thumped into the boys and flattened them to the floor. One swan darted its neck underneath the seats. Its little eyes narrowed and its razor-sharp beak snapped at Charlotte and Sonja. The twins screamed, and Sonja lunged at it with the knife. The swan clamped its teeth onto the blade and threw it across the carriage.

"Pick on somebody your own size," Sonja heard a voice growl. Wolf Boy had fought his way out of the writhing heap, and dove on top of the swan. The swan chomped his ear, crunching off a bite. Wolf Boy yelped.

Without thinking twice, Sonja crawled across the floor and retrieved the knife. She thrust the quivering blade into the swan's back. The swan spun around and squawked furiously. Wolf Boy bit its neck, and the swan's eyes went blank.

They heard a shout behind them and turned. The swans were dragging Moritz overboard. Wolf Boy leapt toward him, but he was too late.

"Wolf Boy!" Moritz cried, falling away. His arms flailed as he stared up at his friend.

"Moritz!" Tears rolled down Wolf Boy's wolf cheek as he watched Moritz disappear into the smog.

Sonja looked around at the empty seats. Alexandria was gone. A lump formed in her throat. She gasped for air. She felt both suddenly heartbroken and puzzled. The pain of it seemed to hit her as hard as losing Tatty.

> *Beneath the waves she, silent, slips.*
> *A secret power in her fingertips.*

Charlotte jumped up and hung over the side of the carriage, searching the clouds. Her wreath of flowers fell off her head and dropped out of sight. "My crown!" she wailed.

"Your crown?" spat Wolf Boy. "What about Moritz? What about Alexandria? She's a Protector! What will happen to the Seven Edens now that she's gone?"

Charlotte started to cry.

"Moritz only had one life left." Wolf Boy sank to the ground, his tail limp. "He's gone. Gone!" Sonja dropped to her knees beside Wolf Boy. She buried her face in her hands. She had gotten used to Alexandria. She had even started liking her. Now she had been taken away from them like so many others.

The swans flew to the front of the carriage and circled it in the opposite direction. They were flying toward the City of Steel and Smoke.

"They're bringing us to *her*. To the Contessa!" Charlotte shook as she spoke.

Sonja looked up. She said quietly, "That's where Tatty is. We hope."

They flew over the spikes and tangled barbed wire on top of the high, metal walls of the City of Steel and Smoke. A deeper smog hung thick in the air. The streets were nearly dead silent. Even the trains that sped in and out and around the Million-Mile-High buildings made barely a murmur. Sleek, silver Flyers circled the buildings with the faintest propeller whir. Ribbons of coal smoke spiraled from their exhaust pipes. Enforcers in the cockpits shone searchlights out onto rooftops.

The swans pulled them toward the tallest building. There was a large black swan on its facade under the words UNITE THE CITIES spelled out in tall, steel letters. The carriage clunked down and landed on top of it.

Sonja watched the swans soar back up into the air. Their wings stirred the polluted sky. They disappeared into an archway on the other side of the roof. She huddled with Charlotte under the seats. Her sister held on to her accordion like a life preserver.

At the center of the roof, a red light popped on, blinking. An electronic beeping pulsed loudly. A motor whirred and clanked as a wide, steel panel in the floor slid open, and the three survivors watched in silence as an elevator platform slowly rose up from below.

CHAPTER THIRTY-SIX

The City of Steel and Smoke

"HOW-DI-DO, DUCKLIN'S," DRAWLED A BOY WITH A crooked smile. "We's a-meet again." He stuffed a wad of black tobacco into his mouth and chewed.

Charlotte squinted in the light. She recognized the boy from the night Tatty was kidnapped. It was Georgie. He had ginger hair, ginger eyelashes, and a round, chubby ginger face dotted with freckles. Georgie spat black spit onto the floor and wiped his mouth with the back of his hand. "Raise 'em up, boys!" Arrows pointed down at the twins, and grinning faces stared. Two hyenas gnashed their teeth.

"Where's our mother?" yelled Sonja. "Where's Tatty?"

Georgie grinned. "She's fars fars away. Brothers von Stralen hids her wheres she'll never be founds!"

Charlotte felt Sonja sink down beside her. It was all over. They had lost everybody and everything.

"Dids you ducklin's know that beasts are forbidden in this here city?" Georgie gestured to Wolf Boy. "Hidin' or protectin' such an-i-mals is punishable by death." He drew out a club from under his belt. "What's says you, ducklin's? Thinks the wolfie wants to play?"

Wolf Boy rose up slowly, growling. He leapt out of the carriage. All the Scrummagers at once began to swing their clubs and kick and punch. The hyenas snapped and chomped. A club with a nail on the end whacked into Wolf Boy's side. He yelped and crumbled to the ground. "Gets you up, beast!" Georgie thundered as the others continued to thwack and pound away at Wolf Boy like an angry mob.

"Stop!" Sonja screamed through sobs. "You're going to kill him!" She remembered that like Moritz, Wolf Boy only had one life left.

Charlotte covered her face with her hands. Tears flooded into her palms. If Edgar were here, he would save them. Charlotte felt a jolt of pain in her stomach. She doubled over and groaned.

"Cry, cry, lil' ducklin's," Georgie feigned a sad voice, "but it ain't a-gonna do your wolfie no good."

Wolf Boy rolled over, bleeding, onto his side. A boy with pimples and buckteeth crouched over him. His hair was cut short and stood up on end. It was Georgie's accomplice, Dirgert. "Thinks he's dead?"

Georgie nudged Wolf Boy with his boot. "Nah. He's breathin'."

"Somethin's happenin' to 'im," observed a third Scrummager.

The Scrummagers stared dumbly as Wolf Boy's body cringed and shuddered. His hair retracted, his snout receded, and in a moment he was human again.

"He's—he's a boy," stammered Dirgert. "Likes us."

"I's knows 'im!" cried out Georgie. "He's a Rain City Scrummager. Always thoughts hes was better thans the rest of us. Wolf Boy's 'is name." Georgie chuckled. "Nows I knows why!" He pointed at two boys, one with a flat nose and the other with drooping eyelids. "Bennie, Dickie Larue, gets the lil' ducklin's. We's a-gonna haves us some fun."

The two boys seized the twins and dragged them out of the carriage, kicking and screaming.

"Mine's got somes kinda time bombs stuck to her." Dickie Larue trembled as he dropped Charlotte on the floor. Her accordion was strapped over her shoulders.

"It's no time bombs, fool! It's a music-makin' machine." Georgie spat the last of his black tobacco onto the ground and grabbed a walkie-talkie hanging from his belt. "Georgie, here," he spoke into it. "Sends two Lifters. We's gots gifts for Mother."

A boy's voice crackled back, "Comin's rights up!"

Two trapdoors lit up on opposite sides of the floor. An alarm began to beep a pulse as the doors slid open. Two steel platforms rose up into place.

Georgie stepped onto one, with Bennie and Dickie Larue dragging the twins after them. Dirgert stepped onto the other, pulling Wolf Boy behind him, followed by all the rest of the Scrummagers. The hyenas sniffed Wolf Boy up and down, slobbering into his wounds.

"I's proposin' a-chall-enge!" announced Georgie. "Whos ever gets to the theaters first wins a double portion of goat's stew!"

Georgie pressed a button. "Ready!" The two platforms descended into two steel boxes. The walls were lined with levers, switches, and buttons. "Steady!" Georgie flipped a switch. The trapdoors slid closed and began to purr. "Go!"

The Lifter glided sideways, rumbling through the building, as glowing words flashed by: PROPAGANDA ROOM, ENFORCERS RECRUITING, FILES DEPARTMENT, OFFICES OF ANIMAL AFFAIRS.

The girls stood huddled together in a corner with their heads hanging. Charlotte prayed for Edgar to come back. She pressed her puffy red eyes shut and mumbled, "Please, find us. We need your help."

Georgie's Lifter stopped suddenly. THEATER flickered in front of them. The ceiling cranked open, and the platform rose up into an alcove at the rear of a large, bright auditorium. The entire room was paneled with steel. A recorded concerto played over blasting speakers. Vents blew in cold, perfumed air. A small audience of fifty people sat with their back to them, facing an empty marble stage. A banner above it said, WELCOME, FRIENDS OF THE UNITE THE CITIES FOUNDATION.

Stony Enforcers on either side of the proscenium held back growling white hyenas. A row of metal cages stood beside them with gorillas, orangutans, and chimpanzees inside. Some had been beaten and lay on the floor, tired and weak. Others shook the bars furiously and howled.

"Goods evenin', my allurin' ladies and spruced gentlemen," Georgie boomed. "Us adopted boys brings you traitorous engagers for your enjoyments!" He prodded the twins with his club. "Nows smiles, ducklin's." Charlotte glimpsed through cloudy eyes Richers on either side of them as they walked up the center aisle. The women were draped in feathers and furs and wore dead birds in their hats. The men, masked and bloated, sat beside them in black, starched uniforms laden with medals.

They sipped on bubbly, silver drinks in crystal tubes.

Charlotte grabbed a fat woman's arm and pleaded, "She'll kill us! She'll kill us!"

The woman swatted Charlotte's hand with an embroidered fan. "Away with you, little pest!"

Some of the Richers tittered. Others whispered to one another excitedly.

"Where's you been, Georgie?" a voice echoed from offstage. The other boys walked out into the spotlight. "We's been twiddlin' our thumbs a-waitin' for you."

Georgie dumped Wolf Boy on the ground. His face darkened, and he glared at Dirgert.

Dirgert grinned. "I's guessin' that means we gets double rations of goat stew this here evenin'!"

"Shuts your gobs, or I's be shuttin' it for you." Georgie stormed up the steps onto the stage. Dickie Larue and Bennie followed, dragging the twins behind them.

"Yous can't backs out now, Georgie. We's a-beat you faired and squared."

Georgie gripped his club. "Ifs you mutters another word about it, I's be clobberin' you."

"I's dares you." Dirgert pulled out his own club.

A door slammed in the shadows. High heels clacked across the marble floor. A puff of smoke spiraled in from the wings. "Now, now, boys," said a crisp, clear voice sharp enough to cut glass—and, probably, bronze, brass, and iron, too. "There's no need to threaten each other."

Charlotte could not bring herself to look up. She was too scared.

CHAPTER THIRTY-SEVEN

Contessa von Stralen

FIRST TO EMERGE FROM THE SHADOWS WAS HER CIGARETTE, bright white at the end of a long, slender holder. The Contessa slithered out after it, six feet tall, and in black from head to toe. Her hair was snipped short, jet-black, and slicked straight back. Square-cut diamonds covered her arms, wrists, and fingers like armor. A white-gold choker was clipped tight around her swan-white neck.

The Contessa swiveled and stared at the twins. Black makeup circled her cold gray eyes. She looked like a hungry tigress stalking her prey. Sonja felt her throat tighten. She gasped for air. Her twitching fingers tapped restlessly against her legs.

The audience burst into a round of applause. Some stood up and yelled, "Bravo, bravo!"

"Bow's in fronts of Mother!" Georgie shouted, pushing the twins to the floor. Their knees slammed against the marble tiles.

The Contessa snapped her fingers. A little box lowered from the ceiling at the end of a long wire. She flicked a switch on it, and the music stopped. She faced the Richers. "Friends of the Unite the Cities Foundation, I welcome you to our annual meeting. You were listening to what used to be the Sacred Heart Youth Orchestra. Those children now work in one of my factories attaching tails to hyenas. You, my dear comrades, are drinking a little taste of what was once their Talents."

The audience oohed and aahed as they sniffed their glasses.

"I've invited you here this evening because you've all contributed greatly to our ever-growing, ever-strengthening establishment. Our achievements have been remarkable. We've nearly rid the earth of beasts and forced accelerated growth in our cities." The Contessa flicked the cigarette out of her holder. It spun to the floor, and she stubbed it out with the tip of an alligator high heel.

"A year ago, I promised you a fighting army, each with a drop of my own blood to make them *really* vicious." She winked. "Well, comrades, I have kept my promise. We shall soon have a battalion large enough to squash any rebellion. We will finally get what we've always wanted! What we've always dreamed about! A world made of one puffing, vibrating city!"

Sonja stared blankly as the audience burst into another round of applause. The prophecy Uncle Tell had told them was coming true. The Contessa and her foundation *were* trying to cover the world in steel. They worked toward a day when the cities would grow large enough for their borders to touch. Eventually, the world would become a single, united entity. Under *her* control.

The Contessa smiled benevolently and motioned for silence. "There is someone I'd like you to meet. An individual who's made it all possible." She gestured with her hand. "Join me, darling."

A youthful man in the first row stood. He was wearing a rooster's-head mask with a high red comb. He ascended onto the stage, took the Contessa's hand, and kissed the only skin showing between diamonds. "I see you're wearing my gifts, Ignatia. You're dazzling."

The Contessa's cheeks flushed through layers of white foundation.

Sonja recognized the boy's voice. "It can't be," she murmured.

The young man pulled off the rooster's head and shook out his blond hair.

"Edgar!" Charlotte's face lit up. "You came! You heard me!" She flung off her accordion and leapt to her feet.

Georgie caught her. She bit one of his thick, freckled hands. "Ow!" he squealed, letting her go. Charlotte ran to Edgar and threw her arms around him.

Edgar stood stiffly. "I told you it was all going to end if you didn't come with me," he said quietly.

"End? I don't understand. You're here to save us, aren't you?" Charlotte pressed her face against his chest. "I'm sorry. I made a mistake. I should have gone with you. I will now. I promise."

"It's too late, Charlotte," snapped Edgar.

Charlotte straightened. She blinked. "I thought you loved me."

Edgar's face softened for an instant, then hardened again just as quickly. "No."

Sonja saw the Contessa lunge toward her sister like a giant spider. "Watch out!" she yelled. Charlotte was thrown across the

313

stage and landed on the floor beside Sonja. Sonja pulled her up. Charlotte looked at her blankly.

"Edgar's not feeling well," she said, dazed.

"Can't you control the prisoners?" hollered the Contessa. Georgie grabbed the twins and barked orders to the two boys standing next to him. They disappeared offstage and returned dragging a large, steel cage. Georgie shoved Charlotte and Sonja inside.

Something stirred behind them. Sonja turned around, startled. She stammered, "M-M-Monkey?"

Monkey, huddled and shivering in a corner, looked up at them. His eyes nearly popped out of his head. He leapt into Sonja's arms, barking excitedly.

"Oh, Monkey!" Sonja said, kissing him. "It's really you!" She froze, horrified. She said softly, "What did they do?"

Monkey touched his ear, now a tangle of scabs. He trembled.

"Some of my handiwork," a voice purred from above them followed by a puff of smoke. Sonja looked up. The Contessa stood over the cage. Her cheekbones were chiseled like two sharp rocks, and fine scars ran curved around her ears. Sonja had heard about face-lifts, but the Contessa's face was so taut, she thought it might crack like plaster.

"You two remind me of someone I used to know." The Contessa's pungent perfume mixed with her minty, stale breath made Sonja feel sick. She shrank to the floor, pulling Charlotte with her. Monkey cowered between them. "I didn't care for her much either."

Edgar joined the Contessa. He stared down at the prisoners through the bars. Charlotte straightened. "You might find this interesting," he said, withdrawing something from inside his coat pocket. He let it drop, catching it by the end of its chain. It dangled in the air.

Sonja gasped. "The Golden Knot! But you gave it to the Tiffins."

"That was a phony." Edgar beamed with pride. "This one's real." His eyes glazed over like two frozen lakes. He rubbed the pendant's smooth gold surface between his fingers. "The Protectors never respected the Longwalkers. Well, now they will."

"This is a joke, isn't it, Edgar?" Charlotte said softly. She stuck her fingers between the bars. "In a minute, you're going to break us out of here, aren't you?"

Sonja grabbed Charlotte. "Don't you get it? He's *bad*! Edgar's a traitor!" There was no question. He had told the Contessa they were coming. That was why the swans were waiting for them. Thanks to Edgar, Alexandria and Moritz were dead, and the Contessa had an Amulet. Soon, the Seven Edens would be destroyed. Edgar was to blame for everything. Sonja's eyes narrowed. She had always known she was right to hate him.

Edgar shrugged. "Traitor? I'm a Longwalker. I was never one of you. That's *your* mistake."

"Don't you care about the Albans?" Sonja returned, fuming. "The Golden Underground will be destroyed."

"They never helped my people. They let them die. I have a new family now."

Edgar handed the Contessa the Golden Knot. She cupped it in her hands. Its glow flickered in her eyes. Her scarlet lips spread into a tight smile. She turned to the audience. "This little trinket will lead us to the Seven Edens, to the source of the magic! Our armies will grow faster. Our dreams will be realized sooner." Her eyes widened. "If magic can bring life to the dead, it must be able to bring immortality to the living. With more coins from you, and more determination from us, we can test this theory." Her voice brewed into a dark rumble. "If we succeed, not only will we control the world, but we'll rule it forever!"

The room erupted. Men and women jumped to their feet, chanting, "Ignatia! Ignatia!"

In the middle of the mayhem, a man in a bright pink velvet suit leapt onto a chair. He had spiky hair and large, black-framed round glasses.

Sonja squinted. Could it be? She covered her mouth with her hand.

It was her idol, Kanazi Kooks.

The audience went wild.

A piccolo slipped out of his sleeve. He pursed his thin lips against the mouthpiece. A shrill, airy, metallic sound fluttered out of the instrument. He wiggled and wriggled his thin, wiry body like a snake.

Sonja pressed her face to the bars and watched, hypnotized. She had heard him on the radio, but he was even better live. The funny thing was that his music sounded almost exactly like her own.

Kanazi Kooks jumped to the floor and marched up the aisle. His head jiggled up and down. His elbows knitted back and forth. He leapt onto the stage, blew the final notes, and bowed deeply.

For a second, Sonja forgot where she was. She burst into cheers, yelling and clapping. Kanazi Kooks turned to face her. He blinked.

Sonja always thought that Kanazi Kooks would one day help them. She picked up her courage and yelled, "It's us! From the auditions! Charlotte and Sonja Tatters!"

Kanazi Kooks twirled the piccolo like a miniature baton and slipped it back up his sleeve. "Ah, yes. The twin musicians. Delightful. You know, I was once an Outskirts boy."

"I know! I've read all about you. You're my inspiration."

Kanazi Kooks saluted her with a flourish of his hand.

Sonja gripped the bars and cried, "You've got to help us, Kanazi!" She pointed at the Contessa. "She'll kill us!"

The Contessa raised a pencil-thin eyebrow. "I most certainly will."

Kanazi Kooks hesitated. "I would like to be of service, but unfortunately, I can't. It would be a case of conflicting interests." He took off his glasses and tucked them into his jacket pocket. He pulled out a comb and smoothed back his black hair flat. He changed into someone else right before her eyes. "You see, that woman is my mother."

Sonja's jaw dropped. It was Kats von Stralen. "Where's—where's the *real* Kanazi Kooks?" she shouted.

Kats von Stralen smiled deliriously. "Right here! Right in front of you! I *invented* Kanazi Kooks!"

Sonja slowly got the idea. She buried her head in her hands. Kanazi Kooks was nothing but an illusion. She was as big a fool as her sister.

"Stop clowning around, Kats!" snapped the Contessa. "Tell me where you've hidden that tattooed freak."

Kats von Stralen kissed the Contessa's white cheek. "Nice to see you too, Mother."

The Contessa frowned a creaseless frown. "Where *is* she?"

"On my boat. Chestnut Sabine's watching her. I got your message. I'm here to collect the Amulet."

Sonja hesitated. What boat? Where was there even an ocean or a sea? This world was dry.

Kats von Stralen reached for the Golden Knot, but Edgar snatched it first.

"It's mine until I get what you promised," interjected Edgar.

"Of course, darling." The Contessa kissed a blotch of thick, red lipstick onto Edgar's mouth. "You'll have your Jagged Rock as soon as we finish with this little trifle." She turned to Kats von Stralen. "Now be a good boy and take Edgar with you."

Wolf Boy jumped to his feet with a gasp. He threw Dirgert on the floor and looked around wildly. "Nobody's going anywhere!"

"Wolf Boy!" howled Sonja. She shook the bars of the cage. "Get us out of here!"

The Contessa put a fresh cigarette between her lips. The tip crackled. "Who's that?"

"He's a wolfie, Mother," Dirgert faltered. "Well, he's a boy thats was a wolfie that's now a boy."

"You really are an idiot, aren't you, Dirgert?" Smoke puffed through the gaps of her bleached teeth. "How about we make a deal, wolf? You transform into an animal, and I won't kill you."

"How about you let the girls go and I won't kill *you*?" Wolf Boy snatched up Dirgert's club from the floor and brandished it.

"Oh, come now," crooned the Contessa. "I'm sure our guests would be thrilled to see a metamorphosis."

The men and women chanted, "Wolf! Wolf!"

"Sorry. I've got stage fright." Wolf Boy charged into the throng of Scrummagers. He slapped the club across a row of knees. Three boys toppled over, groaning. Dickie Larue and Bennie surrounded him. Wolf Boy ducked and dodged left and right, then leapt up and smacked them in their faces. They hopped up and down, cursing and yelling. Georgie stood alone, cowering. Sonja watched in admiration. She had to admit: Wolf Boy had a wonderful wild animal spirit. She hoped one day he would teach her to have a little of her own.

"You'd better move, Georgie," warned Wolf Boy. "I always was stronger than you back in Rain City."

Georgie shook his head. "I's won't!" He held up his baton, trembling.

Wolf Boy was about to charge when there was a loud crack and a thwack against his back. His body buckled. His limbs hung limp. Sonja watched in horror as Wolf Boy collapsed to the floor with a thump.

The Contessa stood with a smoking Gatsploder. "Goodbye, wolf."

"And good riddance," said Edgar, flicking back his hair.

"Mother!" moaned Kats von Stralen. "You never let me have any fun. I wanted to see him change into a wolf."

Sonja screamed, "He only had one life left!" She pounded and kicked the walls of the cage. Wolf Boy was dead. The terrible words ran through her mind over and over.

The Contessa barked, "Shut her up, Georgie! Before I feed your dinner to the hyenas."

Georgie stuck his club through the bars and jabbed Sonja in the stomach. "Be quiet, ducklin', or we'lls be clobberin' you senseless!"

Sonja's cheeks were burning. Her body shook all over. Wolf Boy was dead.

She grabbed the club with both hands and shoved it into Georgie's belly. He gulped and fell onto the floor. The other boys whooped with laughter.

"Beatens by a lil' ducklin'!" hooted Dirgert.

The Contessa pushed the Scrummagers aside. She aimed her weapon at the twins. "You girls are trying my patience."

Monkey hid under Charlotte's jacket. Charlotte grabbed Sonja's arm and whispered, "Stop."

Sonja was not listening. A powerful rage was running through her blood like poison. She despised the Contessa and Kats von Stralen *and* Kanazi Kooks. They had taken everything and everybody from her. Her ears rang. Her head throbbed. Her fingers twitched wildly.

Sonja snatched up her pennywhistle and blasted into the little instrument with all her might. Out of the skinny, little tin sliver exploded a spectacular screech.

The room grew quiet. Everybody stared at the little girl inside the cage with the pennywhistle sticking out of her mouth. The Contessa stood still, her eyes wide. "I beg your pardon?"

Electricity surged into Sonja's heart, her brain, her lungs, her fingers, and her lips. It was as if each organ or limb had been woken up after a long, deep sleep. She blew into the mouthpiece of the pennywhistle with confident breath. Her fingers tip-tapped speedily up and down the instrument. Sonja could not believe her ears. She was playing music! Real music!

Suddenly, the entire cage lifted six inches into the air and floated.

Edgar gasped. The Contessa's mouth fell open. Kats von Stralen stared.

Sonja looked down past her feet, through the hovering metal lattice floor of the cage, as she played. Her Talent was back. So was the magic. And finally, her twitch was gone.

Charlotte gripped the bars of the cage and shouted to her sister, "The Protectors were right! It's still in us!"

Sonja's cheeks rose and fell with every breath. Her elbows flailed and bounced. She imagined the cage breaking, and soon, the bars began to bend and twist. She pressed her eyes shut and concentrated. A trickle of blood ran down her nose, and with one final blow, the cage slammed back down to the floor and burst apart. Bits and pieces of metal flew across the stage.

The audience sat flabbergasted.

Sonja leapt to her feet with wide, glittering eyes. Not only had her Talent returned, but she could now control it. Sonja kicked away the rubble and wiped the blood off her nose with the back of her sleeve. She glowered at the Contessa and said, "You're an old, ugly witch!"

The veins bulged from the Contessa's temples. "I'm not old!" She cocked her Gatsploder. "I'm not *old*!" she thundered.

The Scrummagers circled the twins, brandishing clubs and pointing arrows. They started closing in.

"You really think you're going to waltz right out of here? Alive?"

wheezed the Contessa. "Oh, no. I'm going to kill you first. Then you can waltz wherever you want."

A voice boomed from the other end of the room: "I don't think so, Ignatia." Sonja's heart fluttered. She turned, beaming.

Alexandria sat defiantly on Moritz's back. Her hair cascaded to the floor.

Chapter Thirty-Eight

A Resurrection

The Enforcers yelled, "Attack!" and a pack of hyenas bounded, snarling, toward Alexandria and Moritz. Charlotte peered out from behind Sonja, her head spinning. Was it really them? How were they alive? She did not trust her judgment anymore. She could not after what had happened with Edgar.

Alexandria pointed to a chandelier dangling from the ceiling and swished her hands in the air. There was a loud crack. A chain snapped. The chandelier dropped to the floor with a crash, pinning the hyenas under a tangle of metal, crystals, and wire. They whimpered and squirmed, trapped.

Moritz swerved around the chandelier and galloped straight toward the stage. Georgie kicked the boy holding back two more hyenas. "Lets 'em go, fool!" he ordered. The boy released the creatures, and they smacked their rubbery lips and charged through the audience. The Richers shouted and screamed, scrambling out of the way.

Alexandria flicked one hand and then the other. Chairs lifted off the floor and floated ten feet in the air.

A woman in a pink fur coat screamed from a hovering seat. A man with a vulture mask rasped, "Get me down from here!"

"Your wish is my command!" returned Alexandria. She snapped her fingers, and the chairs and the Richers came crashing to the floor. They landed on top of the two hyenas, flattening them with a crunch.

"How thrilling!" squealed Kats von Stralen. He took a snort from his snuffbox.

"Don't just stand there!" the Contessa screamed at the Enforcers. "Shoot them!"

Charlotte glimpsed Edgar cowering behind the Contessa. Sonja had been right. He was a criminal. He was also a coward. Edgar had chosen the easy way out of his troubles. She promised herself that she would never do the same, no matter what happened.

Alexandria and Moritz ducked and dove as bullets flew from every direction. A bullet whistled through the air and sank into Moritz's thigh. He stumbled to the floor, taking Alexandria down with him. Charlotte watched anxiously as Alexandria slipped the Great Tiffin's vial of clear liquid out of her sleeve and splashed a drop onto Moritz's leg. The blood dried up and the hole healed instantly.

Moritz jumped back onto his hooves, but the Enforcers had surrounded them, pointing weapons. "Surrender! Or we'll shoot!" ordered the leader.

With one quick sweep of Alexandria's hands, the cages on either side of the proscenium burst open. One after the other, gorillas, orangutans, and chimpanzees burst out, jumping and screeching. The largest gorilla pounded his chest and roared.

The Enforcers scattered, firing haphazardly as the wild animals charged.

The Contessa screeched, "Send reinforcements! Secure the area!"

Alexandria strode through the mayhem and climbed the steps to the stage. She stood face-to-face with the Contessa and said fiercely, "I'm taking the girls."

Charlotte stared at Alexandria. It was strange to admit, but she had never been happier to see anyone in her life.

"Why do you want them, Alex?" said the Contessa, genuinely curious. "Is there something you haven't told me?"

Alexandria gritted her teeth and squeezed her fists. The pistol jerked out of the Contessa's hand and flew into her own. She cocked it.

The Contessa jumped back, startled. She took a deep breath and stared at Alexandria. "There's no point, Alex. You've already lost. We have an Amulet. Soon, I'll know the way into the Seven Edens."

"I don't believe you."

"It's true!" Charlotte burst out. She pointed at Edgar. He looked away sheepishly. "He's a traitor. He gave the Tiffins a fake Golden Knot."

Alexandria's eyes darkened. She stared at Edgar. "I always knew there was something wrong with you. Even when you were a little boy."

Edgar hesitated. He looked like he was about to run when Kats von Stralen popped up next to Alexandria. "A little present," he said, beaming. "My own invention. I used it to subdue our more aggressive creations. Blocks magic temporarily."

A hypodermic syringe stuck out of Alexandria's arm. She yanked out the needle and flicked it away. She waved one hand, and then the other. Nothing happened.

"It works!" Kats von Stralen clapped enthusiastically. "You're my first human guinea pig!"

Alexandria grimaced and pointed the Gatsploder at the Contessa.

Kats von Stralen pulled out another. He pointed it at Alexandria and grinned. "Just like old times. Right, Alex?"

The Contessa opened her cigarette case and offered one to Alexandria. "They always made you feel better when you were little."

Alexandria squinted, furious. "I quit."

The Contessa put a cigarette to her lips. A ribbon of smoke spooled out of her mouth. "I never wanted a girl. When you were a month old, I put you in an orphanage. It was your grandmother who brought you home again."

Charlotte looked back and forth between the two women in disbelief. Was it possible that the Contessa was Alexandria's mother?

"And then she leaves her fortune to a sniveling brat like you? I couldn't allow it. Look what Kats and I accomplished. We've built an empire."

"You twisted his heart." Alexandria wiped her eyes. "You made him into a monster."

Kats von Stralen feigned shock. "A monster?" He laughed. "I'm afraid not, sis. Wasn't it *you* who abandoned *me*?"

"I was coming back for you, Kats!" cried Alexandria. "*She* never showed you my letters."

Kats von Stralen grunted. "I find that very difficult to believe."

"In the end, Kats chose *me*." The Contessa smiled vacantly. "Men always do. Even your pathetic husband. He squealed about the Key and the Amulets in exchange for a few little scientific trinkets and some . . . promises, shall we say?"

Charlotte gasped. Arthur was the informant.

Alexandria shook her head. "He didn't. He wouldn't."

"Oh, he did. He also told me another secret, Alex." The Contessa glanced at the twins. "I didn't quite follow him at the time, but now I see, he was talking about *these* two little darlings."

"Don't, Mother!"

Charlotte watched, confused. What did Arthur know? What had he told the Contessa?

The Contessa looked surprised. She snorted out a laugh. "They don't know, do they? Wow! You can't do *anything* right." She gave Georgie a look. He lunged forward and grabbed the pistol in Alexandria's hand. He twisted her fingers. They cracked, and Alexandria screamed. As they tangled with each other, the Contessa flicked away her cigarette and whipped out a long, slender stiletto from her garter. She pounced on Sonja and held the knife to her throat.

"Sonja!" yelped Charlotte. She had to do something. Maybe her Talent had returned, too. She snatched up her accordion and threw the straps over her shoulders. She pulled open the bellows . . . but nothing happened. Just squeals and whines and whimpers.

Only her sister's Talent had come back.

"Run, Kats!" commanded the Contessa. "I want the Pathways into the Seven Edens!"

Kats von Stralen yanked Edgar off the stage, and they raced through the mayhem. They ran to a Lifter and disappeared into the floor.

Sonja tried to reach for her pennywhistle, but the Contessa pressed the blade into her skin.

Charlotte held in her breath and pressed her eyes shut. Please, she begged the sky and the earth and all the creatures that inhabited it, do not let her sister die. She needed years to make up to Sonja for how she had treated her.

The Contessa held tight. "They're freaks like you, aren't they? I guess it's genetic. Your grandmother had powers, too."

Charlotte straightened. What did she mean by genetic? How were they related to Alexandria?

Alexandria shoved Georgie, smashing him into one of the broken cages. She turned to the Contessa. "Let her go or, I promise you, without fail, you're going to die."

"I told you to never keep anything from me, Alex." The Contessa held on to Sonja as she took a step toward the backstage door. "I always find out in the end."

A flash of black fur flew across the stage. Everyone turned to look. Suddenly, the Contessa and Sonja were lying flat on their backs on the floor as the stiletto scuttled away into the shadows. Green eyes stared down at them.

"Wolf Boy!" Sonja breathed.

Wolf Boy growled and plunged his teeth deep into the Contessa's neck. Sonja leapt to her feet and ran to Charlotte. The Contessa gasped and gurgled as Wolf Boy's jaws closed on her windpipe. Alexandria looked away. The Contessa kicked frantically. One of her high heels flew off her foot and shot into the air.

"The wolfie's killin' our mother!" squealed Georgie.

The Scrummagers charged.

"Look out, Wolf Boy!" warned Sonja. "Behind you!"

Wolf Boy let go of the Contessa and wheeled on his attackers. He slipped between Dirgert's legs and dashed across the stage as more Enforcers stormed toward them through the auditorium.

Alexandria yelled to the twins, "Let's go!" Charlotte held her sister's hand and they sprinted across the room. Wolf Boy ran alongside them. They reached Moritz. He huffed, spraying Wolf Boy in a mist of snot.

"Glad to see you, too, old friend." Wolf Boy grinned, wiping his face.

"I thought a Changeling only had two lives!" Sonja shouted.

"It's a long story," Wolf Boy mumbled. "I'll tell you some other time."

Alexandria jumped on Moritz's back and pulled the twins up behind her. "I looked everywhere in the building. Tatty's not here."

"Kats von Stralen said she's on his boat!" burst out Charlotte.

Alexandria's eyes widened. "Hurry, Moritz! Before we lose them!"

Moritz raced through pandemonium. Enforcers fired at them as they jumped over a dead gorilla and swerved among the injured people and the ruins of the barricade. The twins crouched as bullets crisscrossed over their heads. An Enforcer leapt onto Moritz's rear, trying to grab at Sonja. She screamed. Charlotte tore off her accordion and slammed it over his head. He dropped away along with the broken, smashed instrument. At least it had come to some use in the end, Charlotte thought sadly.

Moritz bashed open a steel door. Alexandria yelled, "Wolf Boy, tell the animals to follow us!"

Wolf Boy howled. The gorillas, orangutans, and chimpanzees scampered after them into a narrow stairwell.

"This way!" Alexandria cried, already two flights up. The twins clung to her. Charlotte pressed her head against her back. There was a faint smell of salt on Alexandria's clothes. She could hear a murmur in her chest after every heartbeat. Something about it all seemed familiar.

They galloped up five more stories, burst through another heavy door, and hurried into a vast gallery filled with stuffed and mounted animals displayed in rows of large glass cases. There were windows on every side of the room from floor to ceiling. The silhouettes of tall buildings showed faintly through the smog. Blinking lights flashed from rooftops like twinkling stars.

The apes spilled in behind them. Alexandria slammed the door shut and bolted it. For a moment, everyone fell silent. They stared at the vast collection of taxidermied animals. A tear rolled down Charlotte's cheek. The world was so cruel sometimes. She looked at Alexandria. She was staring out the window at a black dot in the horizon heading east.

"I know exactly where he's going," Alexandria murmured.

Charlotte was taken aback. She had never really looked at Alexandria properly. In a flash, everything was familiar: her hair, her eyes, her skin. She understood what the Contessa meant. She understood what the secret was. Charlotte wanted to scream—and she was about to—but then she said to herself, I'll scream later.

If we get out alive.

Chapter Thirty-Nine

The Colossal Birds

THE BOLTED DOOR BEGAN TO SHAKE. SPARKS CRACKLED off its surface. The hinges glowed orange. The door frame snapped apart with a bang and flew open. Georgie jolted into the gallery holding a blowtorch. The rest of the Scrummagers flooded in after him with a troop of Enforcers. Flashlights shone across the rows of display cases.

The twins peeked out from behind a taxidermied bear. Sonja was not scared. She had her Talent back—and her sister, Alexandria, Moritz. Even Wolf Boy. She looked at him, crouched under a stuffed roaring lion next to Moritz. They had both transformed back into boys.

He was kind of okay. He *had* saved her from the Contessa, after all.

"Hellos again, ducklin's!" yelled a voice. It was Georgie. "I's a-promisin' Mother to pulls out your hearts and feed 'em to the hyenas! Especiallys you, Wolf Boy!"

Alexandria gave a signal at the window.

Sonja gasped as a flock of fifty Gobos burst out of the smog and crashed through the glass. They opened their hooked beaks and let out deafening caws. A whirl of feathers and shards sprayed everywhere. Enforcers fired wildly. Arrows flew. The birds swooped onto the Contessa's minions like a dark, ancient storm.

The twins and the Changelings leapt from their hiding places and joined Alexandria. "The Gobos caught us before we hit the ground," she explained. "Dottie had led them from the Crooked Peaks just in time."

Moritz showed the marks on his shoulders. "Stuck their talons right into me." He grinned. "I didn't care. They saved me from the graveyard."

"Comes on, troops!" wailed Georgie. "Fires 'em!"

No bullets were shot. No arrows flew. Half the Enforcers were lying motionless on the ground, and the rest had scattered. The other boys were cowering in corners and trembling behind glass cases. Georgie turned to run, but a Gobo plucked him back by his shirt.

"Gets off me!" he wailed, batting his hands frantically. Sonja could not help but smile. Georgie deserved a little of his own medicine.

"What about you, Wolf Boy?" asked Sonja. "Aren't you going to tell us how you're still alive?"

Wolf Boy fidgeted with his cape.

"The truth is," he said reluctantly, "I never died before. That was a lie. Moritz knew. He let me pretend I had lost a life like he had so I would seem—so people would think—so everyone would believe I was—tough."

Moritz put his arm around Wolf Boy's shoulder. "You're as tough as anybody I've ever met."

"That's all well and good," Sonja huffed, "but it would have been nice not to make us all think you were dead."

Wolf Boy looked up at her with a smile. "You got your Talent back, didn't you?"

A propeller rattled and whined as it approached. A rickety Flyer hurtled through broken glass. The words *Maintenance Vehicle* were spelled across its side. Hester sat in the pilot's seat, smiling broadly as the aircraft skidded the slick floor to a stop. She popped her head out. A black crow was perched on her shoulder. "Need a ride?"

Dottie hovered next to her. "She shouldn't be driving this thing! She's nearly crashed a hundred times!"

Hester put the shell into her ear. "What did the bird say?"

Alexandria climbed up front with her. The children piled into the back beside a firebox and a heap of coal. "Kats von Stralen's going to the Dried-Up Sea," said Alexandria. "We have to inform the other Protectors. He's got an Amulet."

Hester cawed. The crow took off like a black veil in a gust of wind and disappeared into the smog.

The Gobos abandoned the writhing and moaning boys piled across the floor and began to fly around the room picking up gorillas, orangutans, and chimpanzees.

"Helps me!" Georgie screamed, hanging from a window ledge.

Maybe it was because he was an orphan and had never been lucky enough to find someone like Tatty? Maybe it was because she understood suffering a little more after everything she had been through? For whatever reason, Sonja forgave poor Georgie for every terrible thing he had ever done.

The Changelings shoveled coal into the firebox, igniting the waning fire. The pistons pumped back and forth, popping and wheezing. The motor rumbled to life. The propeller groaned and kicked into a fast spin. Hester pushed back a lever and turned the wheel. The aircraft swerved out of the building, swung around, and lurched forward through the air. The Gobos flew alongside it with their animal cargo dangling in the air beneath their feet.

A fleet of Flyers swooped down from above and hovered in front of them.

With a swift, sharp chop, Alexandria sliced her hand through the air. Nothing happened. Her magic was still blocked. This was her chance, thought Sonja. She jumped to her feet and pressed the pennywhistle to her lips. A single, powerful, piercing note shot into the sky like a scream.

The row of spinning propellers snapped off, and the aircrafts dropped out of the sky.

"Yahoo!" howled Moritz.

She looked at her friends' surprised faces and grinned. She had gotten pretty good.

"I wouldn't celebrate just yet!" yelled Charlotte. She pointed. A skinny black wind-up missile was spiraling up at them through the smog. Its winding key unraveled furiously.

"It's coming fast!" shouted Alexandria.

Sonja took a deep breath and threw all her powers at the angry object. The missile jolted to a complete stop. Watch this, she thought, and blew another string of notes. Screws sprang, popping sideways out of the rocket. The metal casing began to fall apart. The entire weapon disassembled right in front of their eyes, dropping away toward the ground in a hundred pieces.

"Incredible," murmured Wolf Boy. "You really are a musician."

Alexandria stared into the emptiness, shocked.

Hester nodded. "Your powers are strong for your age."

"More on the way!" warned Moritz.

"You got them?" Alexandria asked.

Sonja nodded with a smile. She destroyed one missile after the next, until there were no more. Exhausted, Sonja let her arms fall to her sides.

"That's it for now." Alexandria paused, thoughtful. "Until we get to the Dried-Up Sea."

Sonja collapsed into her seat. Charlotte laid her head on her shoulder. Sonja knew that even though her sister was happy for her, she was worried about where her own Talent was.

Moritz opened the lid of an old tin box he found under his seat. "Cracker?" he said, offering Sonja one.

She took it and bit into the gray square. "A little stale," she said, chewing, "but good." She watched Wolf Boy wolf down three crackers at the same time. His neck was painted with blood. "I think you're still hurt," she said, her voice faltering.

Wolf Boy pulled down his fur cape and turned. His entire back was wet and red.

"The bullet's still in you," cautioned Alexandria. She leaned between the seats and spilled a drop of the clear liquid from her little vial onto his wound. The tail of the little corkscrew peeked up backward and poked out through the skin.

"What is it?" asked Sonja.

"The Great Tiffin's saliva," said Alexandria. "It's a panacea."

Sonja looked horrified as Alexandria poured another splash.

The bullet was tugged one inch farther and fell out. Sonja took it between her fingers. The Contessa's insignia was stamped into its shaft. She looked up at Alexandria. "She's your mother?"

"Yes," Alexandria replied softly.

"Is that why the Swifters don't like you?"

Alexandria nodded. "I'm not only the Contessa's daughter, the Seven Edens' biggest threat in centuries, but the reason she knows about them." She shook her head sadly. "My letters to Kats. She never gave them to him."

"What about Arthur?" Sonja asked. "Did he really tell them about Tatty and the Amulets?"

"I'm afraid so," sighed Alexandria. "He's blinded by his work. One day, when he realizes what he's done, he'll regret it all."

Charlotte burst out all of a sudden: "Isn't that perfect? We have a snitch for a father, and a mother who abandoned us. Exactly what I was hoping my parents would be." Monkey stuck his head out of her jacket and blinked.

Alexandria looked at Charlotte uneasily.

"Charlotte?" Sonja said hesitantly. "What are you talking about?" Her sister had been acting funny ever since they had found out Edgar was a traitor.

"You were there! Didn't you hear the Contessa?"

"I wasn't listening. She had a knife to my throat."

Charlotte grabbed Alexandria's arm. "Is it true? Tell us!"

Alexandria searched her pockets and pulled out a cigarette.

"You said you quit," said Charlotte, trembling.

Alexandria frowned, but instead of putting the cigarette to her mouth, she crumpled it up and flicked it into the air.

337

"Well?" pressed Charlotte.

Alexandria looked at the floor, then at her hands, then at the twins. Her eyes were brimming with tears. "I'm your mother. Arthur's your father."

Sonja stared, speechless. How was it possible? They had known Alexandria and Arthur their whole lives, and never once had she thought they were her parents. They hardly visited the twins, and when they did, they were not the least bit affectionate. To tell the truth, when you got right down to it, Alexandria and Arthur had never seemed to care much about them.

"That means Kats von Stralen's our uncle," continued Charlotte, "and the dear, delightful Contessa is our grandmother!"

Sonja looked at Alexandria. There were so many questions she wanted answered. Had they ever loved them? Had they regretted leaving them? There was one question more pressing than the rest: "Why did you give us up?" Sonja asked quietly.

Alexandria buried her face in her hands. "To save your lives." Her voice was faint and weak. "The Protectors told me that the Contessa would kill you if she knew about you. I had no other choice. Hieronymus suggested Tatty."

"*She's* our mother!" Charlotte's face was almost white. She shook all over. "She's our *real* mother! Not you."

The aircraft lurched and jolted. Everyone looked out at once. The propeller was sputtering and slowing. The Changelings threw three shovelsful of coal into the firebox. The propeller spun back to speed, and the aircraft stabilized.

Arthur and Alexandria were not the parents Sonja had pictured. She had dreamed of other parents; different parents altogether.

Parents who would not have left them no matter what the danger was. Sonja unclasped the locket from around her neck and handed it to Alexandria. "I guess this is yours."

Alexandria hesitated.

"We don't need it anymore."

Alexandria took the locket and turned around in her seat. She stared straight ahead. Tears ran down her cheeks as she pushed the locket between her thumb and forefinger.

"You should get some sleep now," Hester urged the children. "It's a long way to the Dried-Up Sea."

The Changelings lay across the floor. Charlotte and Sonja slid down next to each other on the seats. Monkey snuggled in between them and immediately fell asleep. His heavy breathing reminded Sonja of home.

"They all lied," Charlotte whispered through muffled tears. "Edgar, Alexandria, Uncle Tell, Tatty. I don't know who to believe in anymore."

"How about *us*?" Sonja said softly. "Let's just believe in *us*."

Charlotte wiped her eyes. "I'm sorry I deserted you for Edgar."

Sonja smiled. "Lucky for me he turned out to be a traitor."

Charlotte laughed. She thought for a moment and then said, "Do you think I'll get my Talent back?"

"It will come to you. Like it did to me. You'll see."

"What if it doesn't? What if I remain as I am, and you go on without me?"

"Me go on without you?" Sonja raised her eyebrows. "There isn't a me without you."

Charlotte took her hand into hers and squeezed it.

"Maybe she really *was* trying to protect us," said Sonja.

Charlotte shrugged. "I guess. It doesn't mean we have to love her or anything, just because she gave birth to us."

"No, perhaps not."

"It does explain where our magic is from." Charlotte paused. "You remember the nightmare I had about the Contessa?" Sonja nodded. "That same night I dreamed about the Lost Desert and the Swifters. They told me I was a Swifter from my father's blood— and that you were different. You had your mother's blood."

"That would make me a Pearl Catcher." Sonja touched her hair. It had grown a whole inch since she had cut it, and that had been only a day ago.

"It's all dreams and make-believe, you know—nothing real," said Charlotte. "The truth is, I just want to find Tatty and go back to how our lives used to be and forget everything that's happened."

"Me, too," agreed Sonja, although she knew it was impossible.

Her sister was quiet now. Sonja looked at her. She was asleep. If Charlotte really turned out to be a Swifter, and Sonja really turned out to be a Pearl Catcher, then they were not identical. They were not twins. Charlotte had been fighting her whole life to be different from Sonja.

They were not even the same species.

Wolf Boy sat up and whispered in her ear, "You awake?"

Sonja shrugged him away. "No."

"I wanted to say that I'd be happy if I had a mother. Any mother."

Sonja turned over and frowned. "You don't understand." She could feel Wolf Boy's breath on her cheeks. He did smell like an animal, she thought, but in kind of a nice way.

"I think I do. I'm a real orphan. I know what *that* feels like." He cleared his throat. "I had an idea. When I was coming to my second life. You think a lot in limbo, you know." He paused. "You like me." Wolf Boy paused for another second and then wrinkled his forehead. "Am I right?"

Sonja stared. She swallowed. She turned back over in one blunt flip and pretended to go to sleep, but her eyes were wide and her body was rigid. Was Wolf Boy right? Did she like him?

"Good night, Sonja," Wolf Boy said, lying down. "Try not to dream about me."

Hester steered the aircraft around Million-Mile-High buildings, past a speeding train, and through a cluster of smokestacks. Alexandria slouched down in her chair. Hester patted her hand. "Don't worry, my child," she said. "They just need a little time."

Sonja stared at Alexandria's shaking back. She was crying. Sonja wanted to reach out to her. She wanted to take back the locket and all the things she had said. Something stopped her: an angry feeling inside. She pulled out the marionette and smoothed out her yarn hair. Maybe she did understand why Alexandria had given them up—but it still hurt her with a deep, sharp pain.

CHAPTER FORTY

The Dried-Up Sea

THE RISING SUN CRAWLED OVER THE HORIZON. Alexandria had not slept a wink. The locket hung from her neck. Over and over again, in her head, she had gone through the events of the night Mr. Fortune Teller had come to take the twins.

They were three months old. She had cut a piece of her hair and pressed it into a locket. She had wrapped them warmly in her woolen shawl. Her tears had wet their faces as she had kissed them each for the last time. Alexandria's heart ached thinking about it. Every day of her life had been haunted by that night.

Alexandria had always wanted children, not only to erase the scars her mother had left, but to help populate the world with strong and courageous souls. She had loved the twins when they were only a couple of cells forming embryos. She had loved them when they kicked four tiny feet against her belly. She had loved them when they were born, each a miniature replica of herself. She had loved them so deeply, she had never recovered from their departure.

They were thought to be the identical sisters from the prophecy who would one day have the power against the living and defeat those who tried to conquer the Seven Edens. That was why the Protectors could not risk the Contessa finding them. At first, they wanted to keep them hidden within the Seven Edens, but then they decided it was essential for the girls to understand the outside world, the world their enemies would come from. The Protectors had chosen Tatty and Mr. Fortune Teller as their guardians and the circus as their home.

Oh, Arthur, thought Alexandria. We shouldn't have given them up! It killed you, too. Once the twins were taken away, Arthur hardly spoke. He lost himself in his work. Alexandria pressed her face against the window. Clouds zipped past. Didn't they understand how much she had suffered? She had lived without her babies, her little girls, and now these two crucial young women.

Charlotte and Sonja sat up and stared sleepily into the distance. Monkey was still snoring, eyes closed. Wisps of white brushed the pale, blue sky. A flat city sprawled below. Wolf Boy and Moritz squeezed beside them.

"Ah, you children are awake," said Hester. Alexandria did not turn around. She was too scared to face the twins. "We're close," continued the old woman. "Just passing over Sandy Shores."

The aircraft descended toward the abandoned beach town. Idle trams rusted on their rails. Ramshackle scaffolding stood around half-built buildings. Broken bicycles were strewn across the cracked asphalt roads. A swing dangled, swaying, in a desolate playground.

Off the coast, beyond the city, there was—nothing.

"The Dried-Up Sea," explained Hester. "When the water disappeared, everyone picked up and left."

Alexandria remembered coming to Sandy Shores with her grandmother as a little girl, years before the water evaporated. She and Kats would play on the beach all day long. It was full of other children building sand castles, collecting shells, swimming, and playing. Now it was a rocky, craggy wasteland, littered with ruins of broken deck chairs, umbrellas, and acres of bone-dry garbage. A pier stretched out into the bleak horizon. At its end was a collapsed and deserted amusement park.

Alexandria understood why Kats had come back. Their summer vacations were the happiest memories of their childhood. Most of their other memories were of being terrorized by their mother. Alexandria had always protected Kats. At school, he was despised by other children and teachers alike for being a timid, clumsy, untalented boy who spent most of his time in the laboratory with test tubes and chemicals. He had never forgiven Alexandria for abandoning him. It was like she had left a shell-less turtle on a shore of hungry seagulls.

If I had taken him with me, she thought, none of this would have happened. She had gotten it wrong—just like everything else she did.

The Flyer stalled. The motor coughed to a stop.

"More coal, boys!" rasped Hester.

Moritz shook his head. "There's none left."

Hester blinked her one good eye. "I guess we're going to have to land." She yanked on a lever. The nose of the aircraft tilted down. They dropped into a rumbling dive.

"This isn't landing!" yelled Alexandria, gripping her seat. "This is crashing!"

The aircraft smashed into the ground, whooshed across the sand, and collided with a massive whale skeleton baking in the sun.

Dottie darted down after them. "Everyone all right?"

"Of course we're all right," Hester grumbled. She slid her thin arm out from underneath Alexandria. Broken feathers from her cloak lay scattered over the children. Wolf Boy and Moritz jumped out and helped the others onto the ground.

The air was dry and buzzing with gnats. Scorched coral and brittle fish bones mixed in the sand. The smells of the sea were putrid.

Alexandria dusted off her coat. "We'll walk from here."

The old woman cawed to the birds circling above them with frightened apes in their claws. One without a passenger swooped down and picked her up. Dottie flew after them, shouting, "I'll lead the way!"

The children followed close behind Alexandria. The sand was hot and scratchy under their feet. Crabs, cockroaches, and centipedes crawled among dried-up shrimp tails and powdery, broken shells. Hairless rats nibbled at empty turtle shells.

The silhouettes of a fleet of beached ships shimmered in the distance. The masts and stacks looked like a city skyline.

This is the place, thought Alexandria. She flicked her hood up over her head. "Be ready," she cautioned. "We're in dangerous territory now."

Hundreds of abandoned vessels dotted the landscape. Paint flaked off their hulls, and rust spread over them like a disease. The wind blew through hatches and portholes, creaking and howling. Massive engines had been dragged out into the sand and disassembled by roving Scrummagers.

The biggest of all the ships was jet-black and five hundred feet tall. The word *Starling* was printed on its hull in yellow paint.

Alexandria froze. It was the name of a rowboat their grandmother had given them as children. Kats had always told her that one day he would take her away, anywhere she wanted in the world. "Oh, Kats," she whispered, "how did we come to this?"

"Looks like he wants to be found," remarked Wolf Boy.

Alexandria whistled up to Dottie and pointed to a smaller boat listing in the sand below. "We'll take cover over there!"

CHAPTER FORTY-ONE

The Armies

CHARLOTTE WATCHED AS A GOBO DELIVERED HESTER behind the boat. She tapped her cloak with her cane, and a swarm of gnats buzzed dizzily out of the feathers. The rest of the birds began to land around her, and the apes scrambled away into the shadows among the scrap.

Charlotte turned to the looming black ship. She stood silent and frozen. Somewhere inside there was Tatty—and Kats von Stralen.

Dottie swooped down and landed on Alexandria's shoulder. "There's a hole at the base of the prow," reported Dottie. "Might be big enough for the children to fit through."

What did she mean by the children? Charlotte did not want to go anywhere near that boat.

A heavy shadow blanketed over them. She looked up. Charlotte stared in shock as a thousand swans converged in wide rows across the sun toward them from the vanished ocean. The hooded swans flapped grimly at the head of the battalion. They led the rest of the swans down onto the decks of the Starling. As they landed, they untwisted their wiry necks and screeched furiously into the sky. Flyers whizzed down behind them, propellers churning. Below, a cloud of dust approached like a storm. It was a fleet of armored vans roaring in formation. They squealed around the black hull and skidded to a stop.

Charlotte was terrified. She shuddered at the thought of being pecked to death by a flock of swans or shot in the heart by an Enforcer.

A solitary rider thundered down from the abandoned beach and raced toward them. His frizzy salt-and-pepper hair danced crazily. A cane was slung across his back with a bayonet at its end.

"Uncle Tell!" Sonja called out. "Over here!"

Charlotte panicked. Why was he alone? Where were the others?

The old man reached them, out of breath. His face was red and sunburned, and he was drenched in sweat. "I couldn't get the Gillypurs to fight!" he sputtered, sliding off the animal's back. "They just wouldn't come! Only Rhubarb here!"

A barking voice threatened over a loudspeaker, "Weapons to the ready!"

Enforcers strapped to the wings of the Flyers wound the keys of the first round of missiles. Bullets loaded and clicked into Gatsploders. The van doors slid open, and growling hyenas scampered out, pulling Enforcers after them by their straining leashes.

Charlotte clung to Mr. Fortune Teller. "There are too many of them!" she moaned. "We don't stand a chance!" Something flashed in her mind—something that might help. "Edgar hid the Albans' armor," she suddenly blurted. "It's in a secret chamber inside Jagged Rock."

A trumpet sounded in the distance. They looked to the horizon. A hundred winged men came whooshing down from the clouds with slingshots in their hands.

"The Tiffins," Alexandria breathed, relieved. "Finally, they've arrived."

"There's more!" shouted Wolf Boy, pointing.

A hundred women with long flowing hair came charging up behind them on horseback along with a herd of galloping animals led by Staghart. The Pearl Catchers and the Changelings had arrived.

"Your tribes are here," chuckled Hester. "Right on time."

Alexandria turned to Dottie. "Show the children how to get into the ship, and then go straight to the Golden Underground. Tell Ansel about the armor. There might still be time for the Albans to help us!"

Charlotte looked back and forth between Alexandria and Mr. Fortune Teller, her eyes darting anxiously. "You can't be serious."

"Hieronymus and I have to fight with the others," explained Alexandria.

"It's just like you!" Charlotte burst out. "First you abandon us! Now you send us to be killed! You're a great mother."

Sonja stared at the ground, silent. Her lips trembled.

Mr. Fortune Teller squinted, confused.

"They know," Alexandria said in a voice barely audible. "I told them."

The old man swallowed. "I see they're taking it well."

He put his hands on the twins' shoulders. "You see our numbers out here. If Alexandria and I don't stay and fight, the Contessa will win. We wouldn't send you children alone if we didn't believe you had the strength to find Tatty and the Golden Knot and return them to safety."

"What if we can't do it?" cried Sonja. "What if we get killed?"

"You're going to have to take that chance for love." Alexandria's voice broke. "It's what I should've done for the two of you. It's what I should've done for Kats. I should've risked everything so we could be together. I didn't know it then, but I know it now." She put a lightning bug cocoon into Sonja's pocket and fastened the locket around Charlotte's neck. "Remember: my brother hates to be wrong. He'd rather be dead than wrong. Use it against him." She took one last look at each girl and turned away. Her face was streaked with tears. "Now get going before it's too late."

"Uncle Tell!" sobbed Charlotte. She felt like she was being thrown to the lions. Without her Talent, she was helpless.

"Go on," the old man ordered sternly. "No time to waste."

Wolf Boy and Moritz crooked out their elbows and offered them to the twins. "Let's go find Tatty," Wolf Boy said gently. Sonja took his arm, determined. Charlotte watched her helplessly. Somehow, they had changed places: now Sonja was courageous, and Charlotte was scared. Charlotte clung to Moritz, trembling.

"Don't worry, Charlotte," he whispered, patting her hand. "We'll make it. Somehow."

"Let's go!" Dottie squawked, flying off.

The children ran after her, slipping behind a row of small wooden boats. The Starling loomed, massive, growing above them as they approached it. Tall masts reached up from the deck and stabbed the sky. Charlotte wondered if they would ever get out of there alive. Dottie hovered over a rusty, jagged hole punched through the black hull near the ground. It was the size of a cast-iron skillet. "Here!"

Wolf Boy and Moritz kicked at the edges of the puncture, widening it a few inches. Moritz tried to squeeze inside headfirst, cramming his shoulders—but he was stuck.

"You're too big, old horse," said Wolf Boy.

Moritz wiggled and squirmed and groaned.

A bright flash burst in the sky, and the land shook with a powerful boom. Dirt and dust were showered everywhere.

Charlotte grabbed on to Sonja. This was what war was like. It shook her to the depths of her bones.

"Hurry, Moritz!" Dottie shrieked. "It's started! You have to go back!"

Bullets whizzed and zipped. Voices screamed. Animals howled.

Wolf Boy put his hand on Moritz's shoulder. "The others need you."

Moritz yanked himself out of the hole and stared at Wolf Boy, helpless.

Monkey peered out of Charlotte's jacket. "Oh, no," she cried. "I for-got Monkey!"

"I'll hide him somewhere safe," promised Moritz. He pulled out the trembling animal and placed him on his shoulder. He bit his lip. "I'm sorry I'm not littler." He turned and dashed off, retracing their steps. Dottie flew in the opposite direction on her way to the Golden Underground, dodging bullets and swerving explosions.

"Are the others going to be okay?" Sonja said anxiously.

"That depends on us." Wolf Boy turned into a wolf and slipped nimbly through the hole. Sonja followed. Charlotte took a deep breath and crawled in after her.

> *Dear Jack Cross,*
>   *I lost my head for a while. I might not make it out*
> *of this ship alive. (It's a long story.) Either way, I hope*
> *you'll remember me.*
>
>   *Love, Charlotte*

CHAPTER FORTY-TWO

The Starling

IT WAS PITCH-BLACK INSIDE THE SHIP'S HOLD. THICK droplets tapped on the tops of their heads in the dark. Sonja felt in her pocket for the lightning bug. She pulled it out and peeled off its cocoon. It shimmied loose and whizzed around them. It made her think of Alexandria. It reminded her: be brave.

"No!" gasped Wolf Boy. He flicked his tail. "We'll be seen!"

Sonja caught the insect and closed it in her hands. She opened her fingers a little to make a dim lantern.

In the half-light, the room was deep and wide, crammed with rusty pipes, pumps, and furnaces. The children ducked under a jumble of wires and filed along a wall of levers and gauges. They climbed a steel staircase to a balcony. A ladder at the far end stretched up to a hatch in the ceiling.

Sonja handed Charlotte the lightning bug and blew into her pennywhistle softly, playing a very quiet tune. The hatch's lock wheel began to slowly creak, twisting clockwise as they watched. It sprang open. Wolf Boy poked his snout up into the next floor.

A long-toothed rat stared at him with its mouth open, briefly stunned, then dashed away. Brittle feet scurried all around him in the blackness, then fell quiet.

"All clear," said Wolf Boy, and hopped up onto the floor. The twins followed.

The lightning bug flew out of Charlotte's hands. It lit up stacks of canned meat, peas, and sardines. Sonja picked up a can and shuddered. There was a cartoon on the label of a white Persian cat holding a fish skeleton in its mouth: Chestnut Sabine.

Footsteps clunked above. A trapdoor slammed open, and a hot light blasted into the storeroom. Wolf Boy and the girls ducked behind stacked crates. The boxes smelled like mold and damp. Sonja's heart raced as boots clomped down the stairs.

"The lightning bug," she whispered. Wolf Boy leapt out, caught the glowing insect on his tongue, and looped it into his mouth. He scrambled back on tiptoe just as two teenage boys reached the floor. They wore gray smocks with red numbers printed on their chests. One hummed a dreary tune like a funeral march. The other stared ahead blankly. They each picked up an armload of cans, turned on their heels, and stomped back up the stairs. The trapdoor shut, and the light was out.

The lightning bug squeezed out between Wolf Boy's front teeth, staggered onto his nose, and buzzed away, shaking its wings.

Charlotte caught it in her hands.

"More adopted Scrummagers," Sonja said miserably.

They crept up the stairs and cautiously peeked out the trapdoor. They watched the Scrummagers disappear around a corner.

"Let's see where they're going," said Wolf Boy.

The twins followed Wolf Boy down the dark corridor. They passed along a row of open doors that each looked into an identical bedroom: stark and gray, with a triple bunk bed in the corner and pale patches where Sonja imagined postcards and pictures had once hung. Specks of daylight glowed through scratches in the blackened portholes.

Sonja shuddered. There was something truly miserable about these rooms.

The Scrummagers spiraled up a clanking metal staircase. Wolf Boy led the twins silently after them. They reached the top and froze. A toilet flushed. A light went out. A door opened, and a teenaged girl with yellow curls walked out and stared at them. She wore the same gray smock as the boys. Hers said 33. She blinked her yellow eyelashes, turned, and started to walk away.

She looked more like one of the factory children than a Scrummager, thought Sonja. She hurried after the girl and grabbed her arm. "Wait a minute," she said. "We're looking for our mother. A woman with red hair and tattoos. Have you seen her?"

The girl fixed her gaze on Sonja. Her eyes were vacant. She did not say a word.

Sonja slowly released her, puzzled. The girl rubbed her arm and quietly made her way up a narrow staircase. Sonja turned to the others. "What's wrong with her?"

"I don't know," said Wolf Boy, "but she's seen us now. We'd better find Tatty before the whole ship's alerted."

They followed the girl up the stairs, past a kitchen with pots bubbling and rattling on a stovetop, and into a dark room cluttered with tables and stools. Fly strips dangled from the ceiling. The faint smell of fish hung in the air. They watched the girl slip between a pair of swinging doors, which flapped behind her.

Sonja pressed one open an inch and peered in.

On the other side was a vaulted room with shelves mounted on every wall from floor to ceiling lined with thousands of little glass balls. A silvery substance sparkled inside them. They were the same balls they had seen dangling from Chestnut Sabine's collar.

"The stolen Talents!" gasped Charlotte. "Perhaps one is mine, and Jack Cross' and Emily's and Gustave's are here!"

More teenagers in gray smocks stood on ladders shelving and labeling the glass balls. Another group surrounded a boy with glasses who was crouched over a table skimming the silvery substance from a boiling pot and spooning it into a larger bowl. Sonja watched as he poured the precipitate—a bubbling gold liquid at the bottom of the pot—into a jar. One of his helpers sealed the cap and packed the jar into a box with a label: *For Factory Use Only.*

"They're separating the Talents from the magic," muttered Sonja. They were using the magic to make the white creatures. What were they doing with the Talents? Something brushed against her calf. She looked down at her feet. Chestnut Sabine stared up at her with a prickly grin.

In the same instant, the cat slashed a sudden claw straight into one of Sonja's legs, and Sonja pounded a penalty kick straight into Chestnut Sabine's rib cage. Blood seeped through Sonja's tights as the angry cat somersaulted through the air—but landed on all fours, hissing.

Sonja felt a strong, sharp jab in her arm. A light switched on, and everyone whisked around to see Edgar with a Gatsploder in one hand and a stainless-steel hypodermic syringe in the other. A drop of blood bubbled on the tip of the needle. "Surprise, surprise," he said with a smirk. Chestnut Sabine snarled. "The kitty cat found you."

Charlotte hid behind Sonja. Sonja knew her sister was too scared to face him. Well, she was not. Her eyes were angry slits. "Did you give him the Amulet, traitor?"

"Of course I did," he said smugly. "Once we've defeated your ragtag troop, we're off on a whirlwind tour of the Seven Edens. Just me and Ignatia and Kats."

"You make me sick," spat Sonja.

Wolf Boy growled in agreement. He hunched his shoulders, ready to lunge.

"Now, now, Wolfie, this time you *really* only have one life left." Edgar trained his weapon on Wolf Boy's skull. "Don't waste it."

Sonja blew into her pennywhistle—but nothing happened.

"Magic-blocking serum. It's flowing through your bloodstream as we speak." He gestured with his weapon. "Now walk. There's something you won't want to miss."

Edgar led them through the swinging doors into the room of Talents. One of the teenagers looked up. His expression was exactly as blank as the girl from the corridor.

"Help us!" begged Sonja. "Please!"

The boy looked away again, and the rest of the teenagers continued to work. They were not Scrummagers. Sonja remembered what Gustave had said at the factory: the longer the children go without their Talents, the more they lose of themselves. These teenagers were the result of years of living without their Talents. They were like the walking dead.

Edgar kicked open a metal door with the initials K.K. engraved into it. They crossed into a black room. The lightning bug slipped out of Charlotte's hand and circled above them. There was a glowing figure in the center of the dark. They walked closer.

Sonja stared. Her voice creaked in disbelief, "Tatty?"

Tatty stood naked with her arms stretched straight out from her sides. Her eyes were pressed shut, and the Golden Knot hung around her neck. Her tattoos were swirling wildly all across her skin and shining out onto the walls like a carousel: Changelings raced between trees, Albans swam underwater, and Tiffins flew up into a blue sky.

"The tattoos!" Charlotte cried. "They're changing!"

A glowing map materialized across Tatty's body: Block City, the sewage pipe, the Forlorn Forest. Rain City, the canals, the Golden Underground. The paths into the Seven Edens were being revealed.

"We have to stop it!" yelled Sonja. She bolted toward Tatty— then halted with a jolt. The entire floor appeared to ripple in the darkness. The lightning bug zipped past them, low, and illuminated a hundred angry cats with backs arched and tails in the air. They surrounded Wolf Boy and the twins.

Footsteps clacked out of the shadows at the edge of the room. "Not particularly faithful creatures, felines," Kats von Stralen said, emerging into view. Beneath his hat, his black hair was slicked straight back, his eyes were bloodshot, and his skin was pale and damp. He reached up into the air and clapped his hands just as the lightning bug buzzed over his head. The little light went out. "But they know where their bread is buttered, I suppose."

Sonja stared at him. He was their uncle by blood. He even resembled them. How could they come from such a monstrous family?

Kats von Stralen pulled out a parchment from inside his jacket and began to unroll it. "You're too late, of course. I already have the map into the Seven Edens." He stroked Tatty's cheek. "We had fun, but it must come to an end. Just like it did with your bearded friend. I sold her to a sideshow."

Poor Bea, thought Sonja.

Tatty's eyes remained closed. Kats von Stralen jerked the Golden Knot off her neck with a snap. The tattoos stopped moving at once. The glow from Tatty's skin slowly dimmed away. The room went dark, and Tatty collapsed to the floor.

Chapter Forty-Three

Charlotte's Concerto

A HUNDRED LIGHTBULBS FLICKERED OVERHEAD ON A spectacular chandelier, and the room lit up. A black velvet curtain was drawn across a wall of windows. Charlotte saw a piano in the corner. She felt as though she had not seen one in years. Other instruments were strewn on gilded furniture. There were portraits of the Contessa: on a divan with swans, in military garb with a pack of hyenas, on a throne with a map of the world under her black stilettos.

The boys from the storeroom were spooning sardines into ceramic bowls, dozens of them, in neat rows. Behind each bowl was a fresh, clean linen cat bed.

Kats von Stralen sank into a couch and crossed his legs. Red silk socks peeked out from under his trouser cuffs. He took out a snuffbox and snorted black powder into his nostrils. He snapped his fingers. All the cats at once bounced toward him, away from Wolf Boy and the twins, stepping on top of one another as they slithered up onto the cushions.

Kats von Stralen stroked Chestnut Sabine's downy neck. She purred. "Don't worry, my darling," he crooned. "You know I love you most of all."

This was their chance, thought Charlotte. She pulled Sonja's arm, and they sprinted to Tatty, dropping to the ground beside her.

"Tatty! Can you hear me?" Charlotte picked up a robe off the floor and pulled it around Tatty's shoulders.

Tatty squinted open her puffy eyes. "Is it you?"

Sonja said urgently, "It's us, Tatty! It's us!"

Tatty sat up and pulled the robe tight. Her makeup was smudged, and bruises colored her cheeks. Chestnut Sabine's scratches were now scabs, thin stripes. "I must look a mess," she said in a hoarse voice. She ran her fingers through her matted hair.

"We're here to rescue you," Charlotte whispered.

"Oh, girls!" Tatty grabbed them. "I knew you'd come for me. I just knew." She started to cry. The twins melted into her arms. Charlotte sniffed the faintest scent of vanilla perfume on her neck. For a moment, she forgot where they were. All that mattered was that they were back with Tatty.

Kats von Stralen cleared his throat.

"I wanted to break the good news to Tabitha." He swung the Golden Knot like a pendulum. "While you were dozing, my tattooed darling, you graciously shared the paths into the Seven Edens with me."

"Oh, no," Tatty muttered, shaking her head. Charlotte and

Sonja held on to her. When Tatty had been chosen by the Great Tiffin to become the Key, she had sworn to protect the map even if it meant taking her own life. She had failed.

"We've got an army outside, von Stralen," Wolf Boy said calmly, inching forward. "You're going to lose this war."

"How extraordinary!" Kats von Stralen put his hands on his hips. "You really *can* change into a wolf. A talking one, too!"

"Sure he talks," grunted Edgar, "but that doesn't mean we have to listen to him. Just give him a bone and let him chew on it in the corner."

Charlotte turned away. Edgar made her skin crawl. How could she have ever thought she loved him?

Wolf Boy lunged into the air and landed on top of Edgar like a bag of cement. Edgar thudded to the ground, flat on his back. His pistol scuttled away across the floor. Wolf Boy growled through his teeth, "You're right. That's enough talk."

Edgar whisked his dagger up to Wolf Boy's neck. He inched the tip through thick, matted fur. A drop of blood ran down the blade. Edgar smiled a sick smile and croaked, "Those were your last words, Wolf Boy."

"Drop it, or you're going to get a bullet through your head." Edgar and Wolf Boy looked to Sonja. She was standing with her legs planted and both hands gripping the Gatsploder pointed at Edgar's face. Edgar slowly released his knife. Wolf Boy flicked it away with his snout. Tatty snatched it up.

Charlotte could not believe her eyes. Sonja had become fearless. Charlotte slumped over. She was sure to be left behind.

Sonja turned to Kats von Stralen. "Hand over the map."

Chestnut Sabine and the rest of the cats sprang to their feet, hissing.

"It's not loaded," said Kats von Stralen.

Charlotte saw Sonja's eyes flicker down to the weapon, then back to Kats von Stralen.

"Go ahead. Try it."

Sonja's fingers trembled on the trigger.

Kats von Stralen smirked. "Don't you even have the guts to—?"

The weapon clicked. Sonja tried again five times fast—*click, click, click, click, click.* She threw the pistol at Kats von Stralen, who ducked it nimbly and watched it bounce off the wall.

"Temper, temper!" he said with a quick, surprised laugh.

Edgar grabbed Wolf Boy, distracted, by the ears and jerked him aside. Wolf Boy yelped. Edgar scrambled to his feet and dashed across the room. Wolf Boy recovered, then sprang forward and hunted him. Edgar backed carefully toward the wall of curtains.

"This is it, Edgar," Wolf Boy snarled, slinking.

Edgar stumbled. "Kats! Do something!"

Kats von Stralen shrugged. "I think I'll let him finish the job." He stroked Chestnut Sabine.

"F-f-finish the job?" stuttered Edgar. "We had a deal!"

"You had a deal with Mother. You buttered her up. You gave her diamonds. You tried to replace me."

"I didn't! I wasn't! I swear!" Edgar cried. Sweat dripped off the tip of his nose.

"There's only room for one son—and that's me."

"Charlotte!" wailed Edgar, waving his hands in front of him as Wolf Boy inched closer. "He's going to kill me!"

Charlotte buried her face in Tatty's chest. She could not listen to him cry. He had been her first kiss—but this was war. There was nothing to be done. "I'm sorry," she said under her breath.

Wolf Boy flew into Edgar like a lion. They slammed through the curtains. Glass shattered like an explosion, and they disappeared.

A roaring battle burst into the room: crashing, smashing, screaming, howling, and rattling bullet-fire.

"Edgar!" Charlotte leapt to her feet and ran to the curtains. She pulled at the tangled fabric.

Sonja squeezed in next to her, searching. "Wolf Boy! Where are you?"

Tatty hurried over to them and put her arms around the anxious twins.

Kats von Stralen brushed Chestnut Sabine off his lap and stood up. The entire company of cats trailed behind him as he drew open the expansive curtains and revealed a long curving wall of windows. The battlefield spread out before them in one wide vista. "Isn't it glorious?" he beamed, eyes wide. "The wonderful world of carnage."

Crashed Flyers dotted the landscape, blazing in red flames. Enforcers and hyenas swept across the dunes like dark shadows, killing everything in their path. Black smoke puffed into the sky where swans tore at Gobos with beaks and talons. Tiffins plummeted, their colored wings streaking and iridescent like falling rainbows.

The Protectors were overwhelmed and outnumbered.

"Uncle Tell!" Charlotte screamed, pounding on the window. "Alexandria!" She turned to Kats von Stralen. "Don't you care about your sister? She's going to die!"

"Sister?" guffawed Kats von Stralen. "Alex abandoned me years ago. I only have Mother now." He looked into his snuffbox. It was empty. He chucked it over his shoulder, pulled out a glass vial chock-full of black powder, and took a snort in each nostril.

The Contessa's voice screeched through a loudspeaker. "No prisoners! No survivors! Wipe them out!"

"I'm this close to finding the secret to immortality." Kats von Stralen brought his forefinger an inch from his thumb. "I hope that will stop Mother from nagging me. I've already built her an army—and created the perfect workforce!"

A teenager brushed past him, mopping the floor. Kats von Stralen yanked him back and threw his arm around his shoulder. "Take Number Two, for example." The boy stared vacantly. "He was one of the first. We took his Talent six years ago. Now he's just a shell of a human being. He's *ours*. Mother's very, very pleased."

"Is that what's going to happen to me?" cried Charlotte in a panic. "What about the children in the factories?"

"Oh, it happens every time, eventually. Every child. If you take away their Talent, they lose their hopes, their dreams, their future." His mouth curled into a smile. "Ingenious, isn't it?"

Kats von Stralen shoved the boy away and pulled out a deck

of cards from his jacket pocket. "Mother thinks Talents are just a by-product of extracting the magic. She wants to sell them. As a special drink, if you can believe it." He shuffled the cards and tossed them in the air. "I know they're worth more than that." The cards formed a perfect arc over his head and landed in his other hand. "I'm still developing the use of magic on humans. But Talents—it's very simple. If you inject a Talent directly into your heart, it becomes your own."

He flung the cards back and forth over his head. "This one's from a little boy from Block City's outskirts. Willy Blitzen. A minor Talent, but good for parties."

Charlotte stared, dumbfounded. Kats von Stralen was using all the stolen Talents himself.

"Frankly, I've got more Talents than anybody who ever lived. At school they said I wouldn't amount to much. I think they underestimated me." Kats von Stralen gestured to the paintings of the Contessa. "Some of my work," he boasted. "Thank you, Vivienne Hinkerstein, a Rain City cobbler's daughter."

Kats von Stralen picked up a violin and plunged into a quick, fiery rhapsody. He played impeccably, hopping across the floor, swinging from side to side. "This one came from a boy in one of the Schools for the Gifted," he shouted over the music. "Young Mr. Jack Cross!"

The name catapulted into Charlotte's ear and shot through her heart. His Talent was inside Kats von Stralen. How on earth was she going to get it out?

Kats von Stralen flung the violin onto the couch and darted

over to the grand piano. He rolled it into the middle of the room. "Now for the finale!" He winked at Charlotte. "A Talent you might recognize." He sat down, opened the keyboard lid, and began to play. His fingers sparkled across the black and white keys. He laughed broadly. "Tickling the ivories!"

Charlotte listened in disbelief. The rhythms, the colors, the nuance: it was her *voice*. "That's my Talent," she muttered.

"Now that I have so many Talents," Kats von Stralen said, continuing to play, "I'm planning to sell the leftovers. The problem is, I can't have children stealing them back."

He slammed the piano lid shut. He picked up a flute off an armchair and stuck it out at Sonja. "Kanazi Kooks was already good—but after I injected *your* Talent, Sonja, he was astounding. I was the toast of all the cities. I quote the *Daily Swan*: 'Last night, the great Kanazi Kooks became *the Greatest Kanazi Kooks*!'"

Kats von Stralen flung the flute straight down at the floor, where it landed with a smack. It bounced, flipped, then rolled away. "How am I going to face my public now? Your Talent died in me when it returned to you. I want it back."

He withdrew a pocket-sized Gatsploder from up his sleeve. "Number One, Number Five, and Number Six! On the double."

Tatty clutched the twins and brandished Edgar's dagger. Three teenaged boys marched toward them. Tatty lunged. "Stay back!" she cried.

Kats von Stralen pointed the Gatsploder at Sonja's chest. "I'll shoot her straight through the heart."

"She's only a child!"

"Think I care?"

Tatty closed her eyes. She dropped the dagger to the floor. Kats von Stralen gripped Sonja's arm in his fist like a vise. The three boys dragged Tatty and Charlotte to a set of shackles on the wall.

"Tatty!" Sonja yelled, struggling. "Charlotte!"

Charlotte locked eyes with one of the boys as he buckled a clasp around her wrist. Her voice rasped: "Help us."

Something flickered in the boy's face. His hands froze in the air for an instant. "Get back to work!" ordered Kats von Stralen. The boy continued what he was doing.

Two teenaged girls rolled a gleaming, metallic hospital gurney into the room.

"Your coach has arrived, mademoiselle." Kats von Stralen slammed Sonja bodily flat down onto the bed, and the girls strapped her in. "This procedure may have a few complications," he cooed in her ear. "You've already had your Talent taken once. The second time? Hard to say. Could be fatal."

"Why are you doing this?" cried Sonja. "Don't you know you're our uncle?"

Kats von Stralen dabbed his forehead with a handkerchief and licked his dry, cracked lips. "Uncle?"

"Alexandria's our mother."

Tatty stared, astonished. "You know?"

Charlotte nodded. "We know."

Tatty's voice trembled. "I've dreaded this moment for years. I've always been afraid I'd lose you."

"It doesn't change a thing, Tatty dearest," Charlotte whispered gently. "Not a thing."

Kats von Stralen stroked Sonja's cheek. "You look so much like her," he said softly. "Alex, I mean. When we were children. She took care of me, you know. She protected me from Mother." He paused, then laughed. "She was always fighting in the schoolyard for me, too. Most days, her face was covered in marks and bruises." A tear inched down his cheek. "Then our grandmother died and left her that dratted pearl. She ran away and never came back. Mother said if I cried another tear for Alexandria, she would slice it off my cheek." He gestured to the scar running down his face. "She did." His eyes darkened. His jaw clenched. He snapped his fingers. "Who needs family, anyhow?"

One after the other, the company of cats leapt onto the gurney, crowding like a swarm. Their eyes were slits, their fur stood on end like electricity, and their breath stank of sardines.

"Get off me!" Sonja screamed, writhing and jerking and yanking at the straps.

Chestnut Sabine gingerly tiptoed up Sonja's legs and onto her chest. "Time to get better acquainted," Kats von Stralen said as he twisted Sonja's head and pressed the side of her face hard into the steel with both hands and the full weight of his body.

Chestnut Sabine cocked her head and savored the moment. The horrible, miserable, vain, spoiled, evil, rotten, unfortunately very intelligent little cat thought, this time she would swallow the Talent whole so it would never return. She flicked back her whiskers and lowered her tongue into Sonja's ear.

Charlotte pressed her eyes shut. She had to save her sister. She had to save her *right now*. Come on, come on, she said to herself. She racked her brain.

The locket around her neck popped open.

Charlotte looked down.

The glass cracked, and the lock of Alexandria's hair sprang out and spiraled, braiding itself around the locket.

Charlotte turned to Tatty, puzzled. Tatty stared with eyes wide open. "It's Alexandria. She's trying to tell you something."

The words flashed through Charlotte's mind: *My brother hates to be wrong.* Charlotte took a deep breath. It was now or never.

"Funny!" Charlotte blurted. Her voice rang out, echoing strangely across the room. Everyone, even the cats, turned to look at her, startled. Chestnut Sabine stared with her tongue sticking out. "Funny, I mean, how you took my Talent for playing the piano, but I can still play."

Kats von Stralen frowned. "No, you can't."

"No? Oh, well." Charlotte shrugged.

Kats von Stralen said calmly, "I just played the entire first movement of the 'Cat Eyes' Sonata in B-minor. Perfectly! *I've* got your Talent."

"I wouldn't say perfectly."

"What?" Kats von Stralen let go of Sonja's head.

"I said, 'I wouldn't say perfectly.' That wasn't *my* Talent. Must be somebody else's. More of an amateur, if you know what I mean." Kats von Stralen did not move a muscle. Charlotte cleared her throat. "Maybe it's only a matter of opinion, but I have a hunch

I could play circles around you with both hands tied behind my back."

Kats von Stralen straightened sharply. He stormed across the room. Chestnut Sabine jumped down and hurried after him. Kats von Stralen's shadow swept up Charlotte's body as he approached and stood in front of her. He brought his face to hers. "We'll see about that," he whispered. His breath smelled like icy spearmint. "But if you're lying?" Their eyes locked. Charlotte swallowed hard. "Who knows what I'll do?"

Kats von Stralen unlatched Charlotte's manacles. Tatty smiled encouragingly with tears running down her cheeks. "You'll be fine, dearie, just fine."

"Well, what are you waiting for?" barked Kats von Stralen. "You've got a masterpiece to perform!" He poked his bony finger into Charlotte's back, and they walked slowly toward the piano with the cats scampering after them, meowing.

Sonja started to speak as they passed, but Kats von Stralen snapped his fingers. "No time for goodbyes!"

Charlotte began to sweat as they reached the piano. She could hear her heart beating loudly in her ears. Kats von Stralen pressed her down by both shoulders onto the bench. He opened the cover of a little wooden metronome and set it ticking.

"You may begin," he said coolly.

Charlotte stared down at the keys. Her feet barely touched the tops of the pedals. The bench was cold and hard. She had learned to play the piano before she had learned to walk—but the instrument had never felt less familiar to her than it did at this moment.

Dear Jack Cross,

I owe you an apology. I don't think I'll be able to fulfill my promise.

Sorry, Charlotte

The Contessa's voice thundered again over the loudspeaker outside. There were more screams and explosions. Uncle Tell and Moritz and Alexandria were out there fighting, thought Charlotte. Alexandria had her faults, but she certainly had courage. Charlotte touched the silky braid around her neck. Alexandria was her mother. Courage must run in her blood.

Kats von Stralen sniffed his last pinch of black powder and draped himself across the couch. Chestnut Sabine curled in a ball beside him. "Well?" he barked at Charlotte. "We don't have all day!"

Alexandria had told her to risk everything for love. This was her chance. Not only for Sonja and Tatty and Alexandria and Uncle Tell, but for *everybody*. She made a fist. She stuck out one finger. She banged it down on F-sharp above middle C. The note echoed bluntly.

Kats von Stralen looked curious. "Well, that was odd."

The battle continued to roar outside.

Charlotte could not let them win. She *would not* let them win. She gritted her teeth. She slammed three fingers down at once—a strange, dissonant chord.

Kats von Stralen stared blankly. "Can she play at *all*?"

The Contessa's world would be a terrible one: full of factories and pollution and greed and cruelty and desperation. There would be no laughter, no dreams, no art, no music, no stories. Most importantly, there would be no love. Charlotte's cheeks were hot. She hurled both of her hands into the keyboard, fingers splayed. What came out was certainly an angry noise—but not music.

"Useless!" thundered Kats von Stralen. He withdrew a long, serrated blade from underneath the couch and leapt to his feet. "Get her out of here!"

The three teenaged boys closed in around the piano. Tears of desperation streamed down Charlotte's face.

Sonja screamed, "Your Talent! It's in you, Charlotte! I can feel it!"

Charlotte looked to her sister. There was fire in their eyes. She stomped her foot down on the sustain pedal. She backhanded the metronome onto the floor. She lifted her arms high up into the air like a mad sorcerer—

—and Kats von Stralen's face went whiter than white.

Every section of the orchestra seemed to sing in unison from this single instrument. The boys stood, frozen, and watched Charlotte's body bounce back and forth as she conjured a tempest.

This was not only music, but a symphony.

Kats von Stralen's nose twitched. He sneezed. The knife slipped from his fingers and jabbed with a twang into the floor. His legs felt like rubber. His head began to ache. He mopped the sweat off his face with a handkerchief and limped toward Charlotte—then crumpled to his knees. With every note, a new chill rippled down his spine.

"Number One!" he howled. "Shoot her!"

Number One did not move.

"Do as I say!" demanded Kats von Stralen. "Or I'll—or I'll—" Another bolt of pain struck his chest. He clasped his hands over his ears, but the music throbbed through his fingers. "I'll do anything!" he pleaded with the teenager. "I'll give you back your Talent!"

A soft "No" came from the boy's lips.

Kats von Stralen grabbed Chestnut Sabine by the scruff of the neck and roared, "Stop her! She's killing your master!" He threw her, scuttling, across the floor.

Chestnut Sabine looked to the other cats. Her eyes were fierce. She screeched and hissed and spat—and all her brothers and sisters followed, racing behind her as she dashed toward the piano.

"Watch out, Charlotte!" Tatty warned. "They're coming!"

Charlotte wheeled, twisting around to look, but her dancing fingers did not leave the keyboard. The cats leapt through the air, long claws like needles poking out of their paws, spiky teeth bared—but in midair, right before they reached Charlotte's neck, a powerful thrust blasted them, spiraling in every direction. They somersaulted, spinning around and around the room like a tornado. Finally, they tumbled across the floor, dazed and groaning. Chestnut Sabine lay on her back with her feet in the air, mouth open, eyes closed.

"What have you done to my darlings?" wailed Kats von Stralen.

Charlotte stood up—but the music continued without her. Her feet hovered off the floor.

"Like a Swifter!" cried Sonja.

Charlotte floated toward Kats von Stralen. Her eyes were glazed over, and her hair whipped across her face. Voices whispered inside her—voices of other women. They were coming.

"You think you're scaring me? Mother will be here any second now!"

Charlotte pointed. A wind snaked around Kats von Stralen's body, and his jacket began to unbutton itself.

"No! I won't let you!" he sobbed. Kats von Stralen crossed his arms over his chest and clutched himself. The wind slipped inside his jacket and yanked the parchment out of his pocket. He tried to grab it, but it shot into the air.

"You've got it, Charlotte!" rejoiced Sonja. "You've got the map!"

The roll of parchment rocketed across the room, unraveling until it stretched out fifty feet. The paths to the Seven Edens were a winding thread of black ink through the middle of the intricate web of images and text across the extended band of paper. The wind sliced through it lengthwise, straight down the center, dissecting it into halves, then thirds, then fifths. It ripped and chopped and tore and shredded the paper into thousands of tiny bits that danced in the air like snow.

"My map!" Kats von Stralen grabbed at the darting fragments. "My map!"

The wind burst out the doors and swept into the room full of Talents. The glass balls shimmered, clinking. They shook and cracked. They smashed and crashed and exploded. The teenagers raced away in all directions, covering their heads as glass showered over them. The wind whipped up a stormy cloud of silver dust and gold mist and rushed back in. It swirled and glittered, filling the air with twinkling specks.

Kats von Stralen lay on his back. "It's beautiful," he muttered, stretching out his arms. Silver and gold specks trickled through his fingers. "Like the stars we saw every night from the beach." Tears ran down his face. "Alex, remember our vacations with Nana? I wish it was then, not now." He cringed with pain. "I wish it was then, not now." He rocked from side to side. "Alex!" he screamed. "Why didn't you come back for me?" The pain grew stronger as his chest pumped harder. Suddenly, thick streams of silver dust whooshed out of his ears. He gasped one last breath—and was silent. The stolen Talents had been ripped from his heart, and his heart had ceased to beat.

The music ended. The wind stopped. The locket snapped in two. Charlotte dropped to the floor gently.

Chestnut Sabine, half dead, mewled quietly.

The other cats limped, bruised and wet. They gathered to sadly poke and lick at Kats von Stralen. Their leader was no more.

Chapter Forty-Four

The End and the Beginning

A HAND SWUNG UP ONTO THE WINDOWSILL BETWEEN shards of shattered glass. Wolf Boy poked his head up. His face was dirty, and his fingernails were caked in blood. He squinted through the glittery haze. The shivering teenagers watched him from the corners. Sonja wriggled on the gurney. Tatty hung from the wall. Charlotte lay in a heap on the floor in front of him. He scrambled up into the room. He picked up the two halves of a broken locket and knelt beside Charlotte. He held his hand close to her mouth. Her warm breath tickled his fingers. He let out a deep sigh of relief.

They were alive.

A few feet away, Kats von Stralen was not. His eyes were peeled open, and his lips were parted. A yellow crust had formed around the edges of his mouth. Chestnut Sabine crouched on his chest with her ears pricked up. She snarled as Wolf Boy approached. He grabbed her by the scruff of the neck and stared into her eyes.

"You're just a cat," he said, and threw her across the floor. She limped away through the open door, snarling and hissing.

Wolf Boy stared down at Kats von Stralen. No wounds, no marks. What had killed him? Bits of paper like confetti dusted his body. Wolf Boy picked one up and studied it.

"The map," he muttered under his breath.

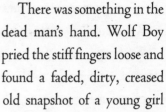

There was something in the dead man's hand. Wolf Boy pried the stiff fingers loose and found a faded, dirty, creased old snapshot of a young girl with long mahogany hair wearing a sailor dress. Alexandria had looked so much like Charlotte and Sonja. Wolf Boy searched Kats von Stralen's jacket.

He pulled out the Golden Knot.

He put it in his fur cloak along with the photograph, walked over to Sonja, and gently nudged her shoulder. She squinted open one eye and then the other. Her face brightened. She tried to sit up with a jolt, but the restraints pinned her down.

"I missed all the fun," teased Wolf Boy.

Sonja suddenly looked around in a panic. "Where's Charlotte? Where's Tatty?"

"They're fine. Kats von Stralen's dead."

Wolf Boy stared at Sonja. Her eyes looked like a doll's. Big and brown. He liked her dark, messy hair, even cut short.

"Why are you looking at me like that?"

"You smell like honeysuckle."

"Really?" Sonja sniffed her shoulders.

There was so much about Sonja that annoyed him, but none of it seemed to matter. Wolf Boy leaned over her and kissed her lips. They were soft and small and trembled under his.

"Untie me," she whispered.

Wolf Boy unbuckled her ankles and unlatched her wrists. She slapped him hard across the face.

He touched his stinging cheek. "What was that for?"

"Don't do that again!"

Wolf Boy turned away and walked off. "I won't. Ever!" he yelled. That was it. That was the last straw. He would not try to be friends with her again. He tossed the broken locket away.

"Wait!" Sonja said. She jumped down, picked up the two halves, and hurried after him. Maybe she had been too hasty. Wolf Boy unhooked Tatty from the wall, and she fell down into his arms. "Hang on to me," he told her.

"What are you, a Changeling?" Tatty asked sluggishly.

Wolf Boy smiled. "Sure am."

"Good choice, Sonja."

"But—I—he's—" she stammered. "Oh, never mind!"

Charlotte opened her eyes. "Sonja? Tatty?" she called out. The others joined her from across the room. She saw Kats von Stralen lying motionless. "Is he dead?" she murmured.

Wolf Boy nodded.

"I think it was me. I killed him."

"It was the only way, dearie," Tatty said, pushing back Charlotte's hair from her face.

Sonja handed her one of the broken pieces of the locket. Charlotte clasped it in her hand as she looked up at the glittering cloud growing above them. She smiled. "The Talents and the magic. They're free."

Wolf Boy pointed. "Look! Something's happening to them."

The gold and silver dust was mixing and swirling into perfect, tiny orbs—each no bigger than a pea—some gold, some silver, some halfway between. The orbs began to move, whizzing and whooshing, diving and climbing. One zoomed around Tatty and the children, then hurtled straight at teenager Number One. He turned and ran, but the orb overtook him, circled around his head, and squeezed with a thump right up his left nostril. The teenager stopped in his tracks. He jerked from side to side as the bundle of energy bumped up and down inside him.

One by one, the little orbs popped into the other teenagers' noses. They jumped and writhed and wriggled on the floor—and finally, the room went quiet.

Everyone could see it at once. Something was different. All of the teenagers' eyes had come back to life. Their Talents had returned.

"Where are we?" asked a girl, looking down at her smock.

"I thought I was having a nightmare," a boy with dimples said, "but I think I've been here the whole time."

Number One approached the twins.

"I'm Nathaniel," he said. "Are you rescuing me?"

"I'm Eloise!"

"I'm Augusta!"

"I'm Bartholomew!"

381

Tatty, Wolf Boy, and the twins enthusiastically shook hand after hand.

All at once, the multitude of orbs smashed out through the wall of windows, into the falling night, and over the Ship Graveyard. They cast a glow on the dusk-lit embers below.

The piles of dead were everywhere. Flyers and swans circled in the smoky sky. Enforcers and white beasts prowled the scorched landscape. The Protectors' troops had retreated out of sight.

"We've got to do something!" Wolf Boy climbed out the window and started down a rope ladder.

Tatty and the twins called after him.

"Wait for us!" Sonja yelled.

The wind rustled Wolf Boy's hair as he descended the twisting rungs. "No! Stay here! You have to protect the Key!"

They watched as he quickly reached the bottom and jumped to the sand. He was alone among enemies on the chaotic battlefield. He turned one way and then another. A hyena crept slowly toward him. He stood frozen.

"What's he doing?" cried Sonja.

Wolf Boy looked up at them and smiled a strange, wild smile. He pointed to the shore.

A thousand giant beasts were pouring down into the Ship Graveyard. The riders gleamed—golden.

"The Albans!" exclaimed Charlotte. "They found their armor!"

The leader lifted a spear. Drums pounded. The boars charged into the fray while Enforcers fired their pistols and missiles flew in every direction. Sonja watched as the hyena gnashed at Wolf

Boy with his bloody teeth—but in an instant, Wolf Boy clutched it by the neck and pinned it fast to the ground. He was strong, she thought, even in human form. Sonja felt her heart skip a beat. What was that?

The Protectors' troops streamed out of the hulls of the surrounding ships and joined the Albans.

"More coming!" Tatty exclaimed, pointing.

An army of female foot soldiers emerged from the smoke at a steady walk, in perfect unison. Their faces were slashed and crisscrossed with black symbols, and red paint coated their hands. Glass globes hovered over their palms as they chanted.

"The Swifters," Charlotte murmured under her breath. She remembered hearing their voices in her head. They had told her they were coming.

The globes lit up with a powerful white light. The Swifters drew strands of lightning out of the clouds like swords and threw the bolts zigzagging back up into the sky. Flyers exploded. Metal and fire showered to the ground.

One small black Flyer zipped in and out among the others. A dozen swans flew alongside it. The Contessa's voice reverberated out of its loudspeaker: "Launch all missiles, you idiots! Hit them with everything!"

The rest of the Flyers attacked again, firing bullets and shooting missiles, as the Swifters catapulted another round of bolts into the air. The ground boomed with every impact, and the sky was filled again with fireworks.

"Retreat!" a man's voice yelled from one of the surviving aircrafts.

"Retreat!" he repeated, but there was no one to answer him. The others were gone already. He followed the last of them full speed into the distance.

Only the small black Flyer and its escorts remained, circling above.

"Mongrels!" roared the Contessa. "Pigs! Brutes! Beasts!"

A panel slid open between the teeth of a swan's face painted on the aircraft's nose. A twelve-barreled Gatsploder locked into place and started shooting, rapid-fire. The deluge of corkscrew bullets ripped into the Tiffins and Gobos. They tried flying away as one after another fell to the ground. The Swifters' chant grew louder. They threw more and more lightning at the small black Flyer, but the swans swept in front of the bolts and shielded their master. Their feathers turned black and burned to ash, but the wounded birds flew on.

The small black Flyer swooped down and fired on the Swifters. Their chants turned to screams as they scattered. The Contessa's voice shrieked over the loudspeaker: "How do you like that, you freaks?"

A platoon of Enforcers ambushed the remaining Pearl Catchers. They shot one in the back. They stabbed one in the eye. A hyena leapt on another and grabbed her by the neck. Alexandria emerged from the chaos and kicked the creature in the head with the heel of her boot. It was dead before it hit the ground.

"Alexandria!" Sonja screamed. Charlotte watched over Sonja's shoulder, eyes wide.

Clusters of dynamite dropped out of the small black Flyer and rained down on the struggling Pearl Catchers. They burst on the ground into balls of fire. Alexandria disappeared in the smoke.

Sonja picked up the brass flute and thrust her arms through the broken window frames. The edges of the shattered glass scratched her skin with bloody slivers. "It's not over yet," she muttered. She held her breath and closed her eyes. She squeezed her lips and pressed them against the cold mouthpiece. A piercing note sliced through the sky and cut into the small black Flyer. The doors exploded off the sides of the aircraft. The Contessa, in the pilot's seat, looked out, confused. She pulled back on the yoke, climbed rapidly, and circled.

"Help me!" Sonja yelled sternly.

Charlotte was already at the piano. She whacked her hands down onto the keys, and her own furious music accompanied her sister's. The ground shook. The wind blew. Charlotte's fingers skipped and skittered while Sonja's fluttered like a bird's wings—and the twelve-barreled Gatsploder on the small black Flyer jammed with a crack and a jolt and burst into flames.

An Enforcer copilot sprayed the fire with an extinguisher as the Contessa angrily steered them through the buffeting winds. The charred swans were tossed in the tempest, and black-and-white feathers spun like caps on a stormy sea.

Sonja's eyes flashed open. She looked to Charlotte across the room. Suddenly, they could hear each other's voices in their heads:

Is that you, Sonja?

Yes. It's me.

It finally happened.

Alexandria was right.

You sound funny in my head.

So do you.

Well, shall we end this?

Most definitely.

A long, rusted cannon as thick as a tree trunk extended twenty feet into the air from the prow of the ship above them. It was covered with cobwebs and barely attached by a pair of creaky lug nuts. It looked like it might fall off at any moment.

They both stared at it and played like mad.

It groaned.

It growled.

It squealed and squeaked.

It began to shake as the gears inside fought, grinding and turning, and the barrel pitched upward into the sky.

Sonja ran out of breath with a gasp. The flute dropped from her hands.

Charlotte's muscles seized up. Her fingers left the keys and froze in space.

The battlefield went silent.

A thick steel pin went *click* inside the antique weapon, and it fired. With a deep, reverberating boom, a cannonball shot out, arced through the air, and perforated the small black Flyer dead-on.

It exploded into a thousand pieces that each disintegrated into a thousand more until there was nothing left but dust. One swan, flapping in the pandemonium, found itself alive and alone. The last of the Enforcers stared up into the empty sky. They sprinted back into their vans and skidded away. The remaining white animals raced after them. The lone swan hovered, puzzled.

Finally, it turned around and flew off in the opposite direction.

Now it's over, Sonja said in Charlotte's head.

Charlotte nodded as the two girls stood side by side, looking down at the destroyed landscape. The Protectors' troops of every variety—the Tiffins and the Swifters, the Albans and the Changelings, the Pearl Catchers and even the boars—all stared up at the two young girls above them.

A joyous cheer erupted. They all began to yell and dance and cling to one another in sheer jubilation. Charlotte and Sonja fell into each other's arms, exhausted. Tatty embraced them both. "The

Protectors always told me what you would be capable of one day. I always believed them—but I'm still astonished." She wiped away a tear. "I'm so proud of you two." Charlotte and Sonja gave her little kisses all over her face and neck. She laughed heartily. They could not be happier to have their Tatty back.

"Come on!" Wolf Boy shouted up to them.

They hurried down the rope ladder. Flyers were still ablaze, and smoke hung heavy. Shoes and weapons were strewn all over the place. Tiffins and Pearl Catchers and Changelings were scurrying to and fro, bringing water and healing ointments to the injured.

"Hello," uttered a small voice. Ansel stood behind them, covered head to toe in gold armor. He held a boar by its reins. It wore a charm of herbs around its neck. "Thank you for the message. We found the armor at Jagged Rock."

"Your brother," Wolf Boy's voice faltered. "He died. I'm sorry."

Ansel lowered his eyes. "One of the Alban guards confessed that it wasn't a boar who killed my father. It was Edgar. Even so, I don't know why, but I mourn his loss."

"Me too," Charlotte said sadly.

Wolf Boy gave Ansel the Golden Knot. "This is yours."

The Alban clasped it in his hands. It glowed through the spaces between his pale, slender fingers. "Somehow," he said, "I thought it might be mine."

Hooves padded through the sand. A flash of salt-and-pepper hair caught the twins' eye.

"Uncle Tell!" they cried in unison.

Mr. Fortune Teller waved his cane. He slid off Rhubarb's back. The girls hugged him so hard, they nearly knocked him over.

He chuckled. "Don't forget, I'm an old man!"

"Not that old," Tatty said, approaching.

Mr. Fortune Teller stretched out his hand toward her. His eyes glistened like two white marbles. "I see you found our Tatty," he said in a whisper.

"Oh, Hieronymus!" Tatty cried. He pulled her to him and they held each other with the twins smashed like a sandwich between them. Rhubarb whinnied and licked their heads with his thick tongue.

Wolf Boy cleared his throat. "Hello, Hieronymus."

The old man quickly straightened. "Wolf Boy," he said, shaking his hand. "Good to see you, my boy."

Two Pearl Catchers shuffled by, murmuring to each other in hushed voices.

"Where is she?" Sonja said loudly. The Pearl Catchers turned. "Where's Alexandria?"

"A Protector has died," one of them said. "We must help with the pyre."

Charlotte looked at Sonja. *It's her. It's Alexandria.*

In shock, the twins followed the Pearl Catchers into the crowd forming up ahead. Tiffins, Changelings, and Albans gathered around the dead body. The girls pushed through, hearts pounding. They wished they had told Alexandria they forgave her. They wished they had told her they were happy she was their mother.

Charlotte and Sonja saw two long feet splayed out on the ground.

It was Staghart.

A green leaf covered each of his eyes. His hair had been pressed back from his forehead. There were sixteen bullets in his chest.

Alexandria, kneeling beside him, began to pull them out carefully while the others watched with tears in their eyes. Hester crouched next to them with handfuls of sand in her fists. She said quietly, "Sorry, my dear. Sorry, I never got to say goodbye."

The Changelings wept. The Great Tiffin stood over them, mouthing a silent prayer.

Wolf Boy jolted past the twins. "Staghart!" he cried. He dropped to the ground, horrified. He buried his face in his hands. "He knew he was going to die," he said. His voice cracked. "He knew." Sonja wanted to comfort him, but instead she stood frozen. She was not sure what to say. Moritz appeared behind Wolf Boy and put his arm around him. Monkey jumped from Moritz's shoulder onto Charlotte's. He hopped from her to Sonja and back again.

Alexandria turned to the twins. Her face was caked with dirt, and one eye was black and bloody. She smiled sadly. "Give me a hand, will you?" she said. Charlotte and Sonja pulled her up. She wrapped her lanky arms around them. For the first time, she held them tightly, and they squeezed her back.

"We did it," Sonja murmured.

Alexandria nodded. "I knew you would."

Dottie hovered down from above them. "I didn't!" she said. "Scrawny girls like you? I can't believe it. Frankly, I'm impressed."

Charlotte grinned. "Thanks, Dottie."

Mr. Fortune Teller and Tatty joined the crowd. Monkey jumped onto Tatty's shoulder, barking. Tatty brushed her fingers over his missing ear.

"When we get home," she whispered, "I'm going to make you as many pancakes as you like."

"Tabitha," said the Great Tiffin. "I delight in seeing you." He kissed her hand, setting her tattoos in motion. Images of all the creatures around them came to life and danced across her skin. Everyone gasped, dazzled by the images. Some murmured, "The Key."

"I failed you," Tatty said softly. She looked up at the winged Protector. "They would have had the map if it wasn't for the girls."

"You brought them up, didn't you?" he said, smiling. "I think you succeeded marvelously."

The Great Tiffin placed a hand on each of the twins' shoulders. He smelled of honey, and his slender fingers ended in long, iridescent nails.

"You have fulfilled the prophecy. You have saved the Key. You have defended the Seven Edens." The Great Tiffin's violet eyes twinkled like little jewels. In a squeaky voice, he said, "We thank you humbly!"

Everyone cheered and clapped and yelled. Two larger Tiffins lifted Charlotte and Sonja onto their shoulders and bobbed them up and down through the crowd.

Alexandria and Tatty looked at each other timidly.

"Hello, Tatty," said Alexandria.

Tatty smiled. "Hello, Alexandria."

Alexandria said softly, "Kats von Stralen?"

Tatty paused. "Dead."

A murmur swept the crowd as the Three Swifters moved to the center of the group. One pointed at Charlotte: "She tore his heart apart! She has the power against the living!"

The Tiffins brought the twins to the ground gently.

Alexandria looked at Charlotte. "Is it true?"

Charlotte swallowed and whispered, "Yes."

"This is for you." Wolf Boy gave Alexandria the photograph he had found in Kats von Stralen's hand.

Alexandria's face went stony. Without a word, she turned and walked away. Dottie looked to the others, then flew after her. Charlotte and Sonja started to follow them, but Mr. Fortune Teller held the girls back. "Let her have a moment. Good or bad, he was her brother."

The middle Swifter raised her pale, thin eyebrows and stared hotly at Charlotte. "*She* drew us here! She's got Swifter blood in her!"

Charlotte looked around wildly. "No, I don't!" Of course, she already knew deep inside: the Swifter was certainly right.

The Three Swifters hovered closer to Charlotte. They reached for her with painted red hands. "She must come to the Lost Desert!" they said in unison. "She must live with the Swifters!"

That unknown something inside Charlotte urged her to go, but she quelled the impulse again and clung to her sister, wide eyed. Something else inside her was stronger. "I won't," she murmured. "I won't."

The Great Tiffin stepped in front of Charlotte and ruffled out his wings, hiding her. "She's made her choice," he said to the Swifters.

The women's eyes lit up like six small flames. They parted their thin lips and spoke one after the other:

"She will come."

"Sooner than she thinks."

"We will be waiting."

A hundred other Swifters floated up into the air out of the mass of creatures. The three women lifted off to join them, and together, they flew away into the night.

The Great Tiffin turned to Mr. Fortune Teller. "Dawn approaches. We must start the pyre and say our goodbyes to Staghart."

The old man nodded. "We'll find Alexandria. Come, girls. Come, Tatty."

Sonja glimpsed Cornelia crying on Wolf Boy's shoulder. Her cheeks burned. Her pulse quickened. Who did this girl think she was, slobbering all over Wolf Boy? The truth be told, Sonja *did* like Wolf Boy. She not only liked him—she sort of, maybe, possibly, slightly, somewhat . . . loved him. Sonja strode quickly through the crowd and stopped in front of him, face-to-face. "I wanted to kiss you back," she said quickly.

Wolf Boy stared, confused. Cornelia frowned.

"In the ship. I'm sorry. I was scared." Sonja stood up on her toes and pressed her lips to his. She felt like a box of fireworks had just exploded inside her. Moritz covered a giggle with his hand.

She looked at Cornelia with an eyebrow raised. "Oh, and by the way, I'm not human. I'm a Pearl Catcher."

Wolf Boy watched her in a trance as Sonja joined Tatty, Mr. Fortune Teller, and Charlotte.

"What are the three of you gawking at?" Sonja said, irritated.

They walked out of the crowd. An enormous swirl of gold dust was spiraling up from the legion of dead white animals. It mixed with the cloud of orbs and drifted toward Sandy Shores.

"The Talents. They're going back to the children," said the old man happily.

Charlotte smiled.

Dear Jack Cross—

She paused. Never mind. One day, she would tell him in person.

Alexandria and two Pearl Catchers had carried Kats von Stralen's body to the bottom of the hull. She sat over him, hunched, with Dottie perched on her shoulder. His cats had flooded out of the boat and were scattered across the desolate sea, wandering aimlessly.

As they approached, Alexandria looked up. Her cheeks were powdered white with dried-up tears. "It's for the best," she said. "He was a good kid, but he grew up into something else."

Kats von Stralen looked like a young boy in the dimming light. Alexandria touched his cheek. "I'm sorry," she said to her dead brother. "I should have come back for you." She put her hand-kerchief over his face and crossed his arms against his chest. She turned to Charlotte. "You had no choice, Charlotte."

"You didn't, either."

Sonja pulled the marionette from her pocket and placed it next to Kats von Stralen. "So he won't be alone."

Alexandria stood up. She took Sonja by one hand and Charlotte by the other. Tatty hooked her arm through Mr. Fortune Teller's.

The five of them returned together to the pyre to say goodbye to Staghart. Dottie flew beside them, and Monkey scurried among the wreckage looking for something to eat. The rising moon peeked over the horizon.

Charlotte and Sonja looked at each other as they walked with the adults. Everything they had lost, they had recovered—and more.

Charlotte?

Yes, Sonja.

Happy?

Very. You?

Sonja nodded. *Think they know we're speaking to each other?*

Charlotte glanced at Tatty, then at Alexandria. *I don't think so. This is going to be useful, isn't it?*

Especially with two mothers.

Tomorrow, they would go home. Wherever that was meant to be. The one thing they knew for certain: they would be together.

Rain City (Reprise)

IT TOOK THREE HOURS FOR THE FIRST CLUSTER OF ORBS to reach Rain City.

The tiny spheres descended, glowing through the drizzle, falling toward a haggard crowd waiting in a long line, toward a team of yelling Enforcers and barking hyenas, toward hooded faces riding pedal-cars. Everyone's eyes looked up, puzzled, and reflected the dots of dancing light.

The orbs swirled down around the tallest of the Million-Mile-High buildings. They whizzed down single file along a skinny steel track. They darted down under an iron gate, circled a squat, brick factory, and sparkled past a bronze swan with outspread wings. One after another, they squeezed through a keyhole in rapid succession, then zoomed up a staircase and down a corridor. They spilled into a cavernous black room and filled it with light.

The orbs hummed and hovered, roaming below the ceiling above a thousand rows of stiff cots, a thousand sleeping children, a thousand nightmares-in-progress.

Jack Cross' eyes opened. One of the orbs slowly approached him. He sat up. He stared at it, hypnotized, and said out loud, "Are you looking for me?"

With a sudden dip and a whoosh, the orb zipped up Jack Cross' nose. He grabbed his throat. The orb shot down his windpipe and plunged deep into his heart. His eyes jolted wide, and his mouth snapped open in a soundless scream. A surge of electricity blasted through him to the ends of his fingers and toes.

Out of the corners of his eyes, he could see the glowing balls hovering, closing in all around the room. One for every startled child. Each returning to where it belonged.

Jack Cross whipped off the thin bedcovers and jumped to the floor, bare feet thumping down on cold concrete. He searched noisily under his cot and pulled out a violin case. His breath quickened. He snapped open the lid and blew a layer of dust off the instrument. He grabbed it by the neck and slapped it onto his shoulder. His chin snapped down on the chin rest, and he swung the bow into the air. He held it, stiff and still, just above the strings.

Then he took a deep breath and twiddled his fingers to warm them up.

Suddenly, the room exploded all at once: picture painting, poetry reciting, dancing, running, singing, leaping. Music! Each of these children had a name, a history, and a Talent.

As he played—and he played wonderfully—Jack Cross looked down at the musical note hanging from his pajama top. He thought about Charlotte, the brown-haired girl from the circus, who had promised to get back his Talent. He had been hearing her voice in his head ever since she disappeared. One day, he would find her. One day, he would thank her. He might even write her a song.

ACKNOWLEDGMENTS

Special thanks: to Wes. To two witches, Taryn and Hanan, for your endless support. To the true Staghart, Fouad. To my first twin, Tarek. To the real twins, Kim and Amy (and their mother, Susan). To Jake. To Jonathan. To my cousin, Sara. To my oldest friends, Roo, Danny, and Jono. To the big girls: Emily, Mavette, Bernie, and Jen. To the little girls: Whistler, Ruby, Rose, Mei, Coco, Bella, Violet, Clementine, and Imogene.

To my editor, Jennifer Besser; my agents, Amanda Urban and Jennifer Joel; and our designer, Marikka Tamura. Also, to Cecilia Yung and Kate Meltzer.

TEEN AND YA FICTION
FROM PUSHKIN PRESS

THE RED ABBEY CHRONICLES

MARESI

NAONDEL

Maria Turtschaninoff

Translated by Annie Prime

'Combines a flavour of *The Handmaid's Tale* with bursts of
excitement reminiscent of Harry Potter's magic duels'

Observer

THE BEGINNING WOODS

Malcolm McNeill

'I loved every word and was envious of quite a few…
A modern classic – rich, funny and terrifying'

Eoin Colfer

THE RECKLESS SERIES

I. THE PETRIFIED FLESH
2. LIVING SHADOWS
3. THE GOLDEN YARN

Cornelia Funke

'A wonderful storyteller'

Sunday Times

was at the school, the day she'd picked up Chris and informed them that they were moving to Texas.

Those same parishioners remembered Chris's grandmother as extremely odd, refusing to believe her only child had gotten pregnant out of wedlock and claiming that Chris's had been an immaculate conception. When others refused to believe her, she'd left the church.

No wonder Chris had turned out the way he had, Mira thought. Knowing what his grandmother had done, then fed a daily diet of madness.

The forensic anthropologist determined that the grandmother had been dead for quite some time and had classified her death as a homicide as well – the woman's hyoid bone had been crushed, the probable manner of death strangulation.

What had happened? Mira wondered. Had Chris just snapped one day and killed her? Then, unable to deal with that reality, brought her back to 'life'?

Back to life, she thought. To the world of the living. Leaving behind the demons of the past, letting go.

Mira supposed she should find it strange that she was recalling such events now, at the marriage of two people who had become her friends. But she didn't. If not for those events, she wouldn't be here now. Not physically. And not emotionally. She could have ended up like Karin Bayle, so unable to let go of the past that she had thrown her future away.

Her future. Connor. She curled her fingers tighter around his, happier, more at peace than she'd ever thought she would be again.

The newlyweds started down the aisle, heading toward the open church doors and the beautiful day – and future – beyond.

Holding tightly to Connor's hand, Mira followed them.